The Sin Factor

Sandy Loyd

Published by Sandy Loyd
Copyright © 2012 Sandy Loyd
Editing: Pam Berehulke at Bulletproof Editing
Cover design: Kelli Ann Morgan at Inspire Creative Designs
ISBN: 978-1-941267-12-7

For more information on the author and her works, please see www.SandyLoyd.com

This book is also available in electronic form from some online retailers.

Dedication

As with all my stories, <u>The Sin Factor</u> is dedicated to my husband. Without him behind me I wouldn't have written so much.

I also want to dedicate this story to all the men and women who serve in the United States Armed Forces, protecting our country. May God bless you and keep you safe. Thanks for all you do.

Chapter 1

Tree branches swayed, bending to the will of a brisk breeze. Dusk prevailed—that moment in time when it was neither dark nor light.

Avery Montgomery slowly turned to peer at the surrounding landscape, scrutinizing the trees and brush to her left and directly behind her where the gravesites ended. In front of her and still visible in the twilight row after row of pearly headstones fanned out in precise lines.

Shivering, she rubbed her arms.

She waited.

As if her thoughts had ordered the air to still, the leaves stopped their movement. For endless minutes all was calm, until a prickly sensation at the back of her neck indicated his presence, a feeling she'd had before.

Every nerve ending in her body stood at alert. Still waiting. For what, she had no idea.

She closed her eyes and chastised herself. After all, she stood in a cemetery—Arlington, at that. She took a deep breath. The smell of fresh-cut grass eased the eeriness of standing so close to the remains of dead soldiers.

Yet, the feeling of being watched didn't dissipate. Did he realize she sensed him watching? Why assume it was a he? She pretended not to notice. If she pretended hard enough, then *he* wasn't real. Pretending had become a huge part of her life in recent years. She had no reason to doubt her pretense wouldn't work. It had all those other nights she'd stood staring at the graves of two men who'd died almost two months ago.

Avery's focus returned to the headstones. She concentrated on the chiseled words.

Major Michael Andrew Montgomery.

Major Marshall Compton Crandall.

One had been her husband for most of her adult life and the

other had been his best friend. Both died serving their country, a sacrifice honored with an Arlington burial.

She glanced toward the heavens. If only she could go back in time and undo her past. Unfortunately, it was written, never to be undone, and she would have to live with the consequences.

"You look so sad."

She pivoted and leaned toward the voice. The soft sound penetrated her ears and reached into her soul, as if directed solely, intimately to her. Squinting, she could only see shadows of trees in the now moonlit darkness.

Ignore it. It isn't real.

Avery shrugged it off and sighed. She was obviously hallucinating. She stood alone in the middle of a cemetery, and cemeteries were notorious for evoking weird feelings.

"I guess I am sad," she whispered, going against her mind's reasoning because she felt compelled to answer. Oh dear God. She was going crazy. Why did she have this overwhelming need to hear his voice again? Avery's narrowed gaze searched the darkened brush once more. She spent a moment listening. When no other noise sounded, she turned back to the two graves.

In seconds, tears emerged, and it dawned on her that she *was* sad...grief-stricken...for what would never be...for what her transgressions had manifested.

"I'm so sorry, Mike. I never meant to make such a mess of things." More tears trickled. Her husband had gone to his grave with no other word than the confusing letter he'd sent right before he died. She'd never know if he'd forgiven her or not.

Stop it. It's too late for forgiveness.

She wiped away her tears.

A ping sounded a few feet away. In the next instant, a force hit her from behind, throwing her off balance. Her legs buckled from the weight. Too stunned to do anything but put out her hands to soften the fall, she hit the ground with a hard thud.

"*Oomph,*" she cried out none too gracefully as the air escaped her chest. She slowly gained her wits and tried to move, but couldn't. Something...or someone...hampered her. A man. He rolled with her, using the headstones as a shield. A chunk of earth bounced off the ground only inches away and she identified the ping.

"My God! Those are bullets." Arms flailing, she struggled to get up.

"Stay down," he said, his voice low but urgent.

She couldn't do much else with the man sprawled on top of her. She recognized her figment's voice. A living, breathing human voice.

"This is Arlington," she whispered, fighting to rein in her out-of-control imagining of a gun-toting terrorist hiding in the bushes taking potshots. "Why is someone shooting?"

~

Jeffrey Sinclair caught the panic in her voice. "I don't know why, but I intend to find out." He shifted and covered her more protectively. Through layers of clothes, he felt her heartbeat race. Or was it his?

He managed to yank his radio out of his pocket and hit the button just as another bullet ricocheted off a headstone to his left. "Three shots fired." With his lips next to her ear, he kept his voice low. "As far as I can tell, from northwest of my position."

"On it," came the reply.

Silence prevailed. In those quiet seconds, the alert edge left his body in an exhale, but she remained as immobile as stone.

"You're safe," he assured her in a soothing tone. "I won't let anything happen to you." Sin wasn't the protecting type, but as the promise escaped his lips, he realized he meant every word.

She nodded and seemed to relax a bit. Her lemony scent blended with the dampened earth and invaded his nostrils. An inconvenient blast of awareness shot through him. As the danger diminished with each passing minute, leftover adrenaline had his heartbeat quickening, pumping more alertness through every vein and artery. He felt trapped in some kind of suspended time warp, intensifying the craziness of lying prone over some stranger. Well, not exactly a stranger. He knew enough, and though he couldn't deny an attraction to her, he damn sure hadn't expected Avery Montgomery to affect him like this.

Hold it together, Sin.

Remember why you're on top of her in the first place. Someone shot at her. Unfortunately, his mental commands couldn't extinguish her warmth radiating beneath him. The hard contours of his body dug into her softness, adding to his awareness…and his discomfort. He closed his eyes, willing Des to hurry, and forced himself to relax. To keep breathing.

Five…ten…twenty seconds ticked by and still nothing happened.

Finally, he lifted off her enough to let her roll onto her back but he wouldn't relinquish his protective posture. Damn. Not his smartest move because now she lay underneath him face up. Darkness obscured her full features, but he didn't need to see her to know she was gorgeous.

The rapid thumping of his heart continued to override the silence. With her head inches from his, the soft air of her even breathing caressed his neck. His blood pounded faster.

Don't think about it. Think about the situation. Where in the hell is Des?

Finally, the radio came alive again. "All clear. Whoever was shooting is long gone. I'll scout around a little more, see what I can find."

"Thanks, but be careful. It ruins my night when someone uses me for target practice," he answered.

Sin pushed up onto his forearms and looked down to see Avery suck in air and open her eyes. At the same time, the full moon came out of hiding and a bit of light reflected off her face, highlighting a frightened brown gaze. He began to pull away, but the glimpse of sadness he also saw stopped him cold. For long seconds their stares locked. Peering into such vivid, expressive eyes was the wrong thing to do, but he couldn't look away.

Her turbulent gaze spoke volumes, created a bond of sorts. A *mental connection*, for lack of a better term, that was damned unwelcome and tossed his thoughts into chaos. Questions that had rested on the tip of his tongue scattered to the far reaches of his mind.

Whoever said the eyes were the windows to the soul had it right. He didn't know her—they'd never met—but it was as if he'd known her forever. How stupid was that? Or maybe surreal. This entire scene had a dream-like quality to it.

Of its own accord, his gaze dropped inches lower, to her mouth. An incredibly beautiful mouth. He certainly wasn't considering doing something so stupid like kissing that mouth, was he? Yeah, because even as his brain shouted no, his body had other ideas. At that point, stupid just didn't seem to matter.

In slow motion, he lowered his head, giving her plenty of time to turn away.

Avery didn't move, yet that expressive gaze seemed to beg him for something, which spurred him to continue. She still didn't pull away even when his mouth hovered over hers before grazing back and forth. The not quite kisses sent searing flashes of heat straight through him. When her lips connected with his, he wrapped his arms around her in an effort to bring her closer. Never had a kiss seemed so elemental…like breathing. Like being in heaven.

"I don't see any shell casings. I'm betting the bullets came from a high-powered rifle," his radio squawked. "So, I'll try to find the bullets."

Instantly, he broke the kiss and felt a twinge of regret.

Whether it was for the interruption or his impulsive act, he wasn't certain.

~

As the voice seeped into Avery's thoughts, reality hit. Her entire body stiffened. Panic re-entered her consciousness, along with total embarrassment, as the reason she lay underneath a stranger in a cemetery in the first place returned. Someone had shot at her. She had to get out of here. Get home and make sure her son was okay.

"Sin?" the same voice asked. "You there?"

He lifted off her and said into his radio, "I'm here," then rolled away to say more.

Sin? Was that his name? How fitting. He truly was some specter sent from hell to torment her. She wasn't someone who rolled around in graveyards with strange men after being shot at. She was a grieving widow. A mother, for heaven's sake. Didn't she have enough to feel guilty over?

"Are you okay?"

She glanced up at the sound and caught him eyeing her with concern etched into his expression. *Are you okay? Question of the year.* No, she was not okay. She'd never be okay. To prove it, she'd just spent the last few minutes in mindless absurdity, wishing the kiss with a complete stranger could go on forever. She nodded and worked at pretending she wasn't staring into the most incredible gaze, one that saw more than she cared to expose.

Avery rubbed her temples. Who the hell was he? Whoever he was, he'd probably saved her life. Risking another glance, she took a deep breath. Even in the shadows, she noted an arresting presence. His face wasn't pretty. Too many angles and hard edges…adding to his undeniable maleness. And he had a power about him that held her in its force, which only increased her internal turbulence. No wonder she'd felt protected underneath him and totally safe, which made no sense at all.

In the blink of an eye, her fear returned full force. She was totally aware of her vulnerability. His size, dwarfing her five feet nine inches, suddenly made her feel defenseless.

"You sure?" He waited a moment, watching her closely. When she didn't offer a reply, he stood, bent to help her, and flashed a quick, lopsided grin. "Sorry about that kiss. I got carried away."

Avery took his offered hand and allowed him to pull her up. "I...um...no problem." What else could she say? She'd gotten carried away too? He probably thought kissing men she'd never met in cemeteries after being shot at was her norm.

Someone shot at her.

"I need to go." She yanked her hand out of his grasp. *Home.* Everything would be okay if she could just make it home and check on Andy. That thought became a driving force.

"Hold on." He reached for his wallet, retrieved a business card, and held it out. "My name's Jeffrey Sinclair."

Avery stopped her retreat long enough to take the card.

So his name was Sinclair, not Sin. The fact didn't ease her conscience any after what she'd just done. Sin or no Sin, she'd made a complete fool of herself. She had to get out of here.

Despite a million questions peppering her brain just then, she turned and darted out of instinct, disturbed by the kiss as much as what preceded it.

Never in a billion years would she consider herself someone who'd meet an unknown man's mouth so crazily. Not when, according to Mike, she was frigid and never got emotional. But here she was an emotional mess and the thought only swamped her with more emotion.

She veered in the direction of her parked car as more humiliation rose up over her reaction to a complete stranger. His presence had made her feel cherished. That alone seemed totally illogical, but when he'd bent to kiss her, she hadn't been able to turn away. In those few seconds she'd felt more alive than she had in fifteen years. Mike's kisses had never generated such a response.

"Wait. I'd like to talk to you. Make sure you're safe."

That same gripping, almost disturbing voice carried on the wind. She fought to ignore the urgent tone, but somehow the quality reached past the physical, just as his concerned stare had done, touching something deep inside of her she didn't want touched.

"No…" she said over her shoulder. "I'm fine. Really. I appreciate your help, but I've got to get home." By the time she made it to her car she was running. She slowed her steps and looked back. He'd made no attempt to follow, thank God, just stood and watched her in the moonlit shadows. With her focus still on him, she hit the keyless entry. Lights flashed and the locks snapped up. She scrambled inside.

In seconds, Avery had her seat belt fastened and the car started. She worked to keep her foot steady as she put the car in gear and sped off.

Maybe running away denoted cowardice, but cowardice was the least of her troubles.

~

"What happened? Why is she leaving?"

Jeffrey Sinclair ignored the questions, still keeping a protective watch as her car's taillights flashed brighter when she slowed to turn left onto the main road leading out of the cemetery.

"Sin?" Desmond Phillips strode up to him. "Why didn't you stop her?"

He turned to his business partner and grunted. "She's not going anywhere."

"But it's obvious at this point she's part of it. She's been here every night we've staked out the gravesite. This would've been the perfect opportunity to discover what she knows."

"It can wait. What I want to know is…why would someone try and kill her?"

"Diversionary tactic," Des spit out. "Had to be. A high-powered rifle with a silencer? He was probably using a scope. Had a clean shot and missed. On purpose. To draw us out. Which in my book indicates some kind of involvement."

"Maybe." Sin's gaze moved to the now empty street. He clenched a fist, hating that he had no answers. Why had he spoken to her? Even more disturbing, why had he kissed her…her, of all women?

He snorted. Hell, he knew why. He hadn't been able to stop,

that's why. Now, more than ever, she intrigued him. Each and every evening she'd made her nightly visits, he'd stationed himself just feet away. Watching…waiting…wanting.

"Shit," he whispered, then shook his head. Why deny his attraction? She was one gorgeous woman with curves in all the right places. He'd dealt with attraction before and never lost his head. Not like tonight, when she'd seemed so forlorn, peering at him with those haunting eyes, begging him to give in to the need.

Sin's fingernails dug deeper into his palms to the point of pain. He needed to find out if a connection existed between his company's stolen technology and the two dead Army officers. He couldn't let attractive females sidetrack him. As Des said, the lady now appeared to be involved. But to what extent?

"It's a waste of time to keep watching tonight. Nothing's going to happen now."

Des' voice yanked him back to the the reason they were lurking in a cemetery—the anonymous tip concerning the thefts from Sinclair Phillips & Coleman Electronics. "I agree." He nodded. "Whoever we were waiting for most likely got scared off with all the commotion."

"Had to be a setup." Des flashed a light onto the grass surrounding the headstones. The light caught something shiny. He stopped, then crouched and dug at the ground with his pocketknife.

"But why?" Sin drew a hand through his hair before resting it on the back of his neck. He began rubbing, trying to massage the kinks out. "What the hell have we stumbled into? Nothing makes sense. It's as if someone's playing a sick game. With our company. With our livelihood." The last phase of testing SPC's prototypes had been right on schedule until they'd gone missing. Now they had to deal with two more thefts.

"According to Colonel Williams' report, neither Major Crandall nor Major Montgomery fit the traitor profiles, and there's nothing to show their involvement." He watched Des extract a bullet from a nearby tree. Yet Montgomery had been in charge of testing the powerful light-driven tracking, listening, and recording devices. The dead major was the last known person to have them in his possession. In an attempt to learn all he could about him…and about *her*, Sin had memorized the pertinent details.

The stunning brunette's life read like a storybook romance on paper until Montgomery's death. Her deceased husband had been an all-American—athletic, good-looking, gifted—the poster boy for his college fraternity. The high school sweethearts had lived in the D.C. area, attending local Alexandria schools until college. He'd been two years ahead of her, graduating *summa cum laude* from Georgetown University before entering the Army.

"The colonel's right. Major Montgomery served ten years with a spotless record and several medals." Sin exhaled a resigned sigh. "He's a fricking war hero, not your usual scumbag who's sold his country's latest technology to the highest bidder."

Crandall's file read similarly. Despite the glowing words, Sin wasn't about to remove either officer from his short list of suspects. Military Intelligence had cleared them of all wrongdoing, but he and his partners couldn't afford to overlook any possibility. Too much was at stake.

"Maybe Montgomery needed the money."

"Money wasn't an issue." Sin met Des' gaze. "He came from old money, had access to a hefty trust fund. In fact, according to the file, several generations of Montgomerys earned money through interest, not hard work, and they all had one thing in common. They believed in giving back to society through public service, which plays into the war hero scenario."

He didn't want to think he harbored a prejudice toward dead heroes, but if Sin were totally honest, he'd have to admit to one. He'd always held such men in contempt, those born with not only the silver spoon but also the whole meal.

"Crandall didn't have Montgomery's megabucks, but their backgrounds are parallel." Sin scrubbed a hand over his face. How could they be anything but heroes with that upbringing? Poster boys like Montgomery always had it easy, had their way paved, so much so they never had to truly fight for anything, always got their pick of everything just because of who they were…the best jobs with the best salaries attracting the best mates. The gutter Sin had climbed out of was totally at the other end of the spectrum. Unlike Montgomery or Crandall, he'd had to fight for everything.

Still, he dealt in logic and probabilities. Logically, the probabilities pointed to their innocence. As the colonel had stated during their last meeting, they had nil to go on as far as motive for tying either man to any treasonous treachery.

"The wife's involved. I know it. She's been here every night we have." Des pocketed the bullets and was now shining the light in the distance. "That means something."

"Coincidence. She *is* Montgomery's widow, after all."

"Too much coincidence for my liking. Who visits a gravesite so often these days?" Des' voice held disbelief. "And for so long?"

"A grieving widow whose husband recently died?"

"Maybe." Des nodded, still searching. "Or maybe she's in on it and the husband wasn't?"

Sin's gaze followed the beam of light hitting row after row of white stones. "She's definitely someone to question, but you can't really think she's involved in passing stolen technology?"

"I'm suspicious of everyone until I understand their motives," Des said. "If she were the target tonight, she'd be dead. And since she was alive enough to run away, my gut tells me she's part of the ploy to draw us out."

"You're too cynical. I'd think you'd be less biased, given your previous occupation," Sin teased. Such scorn resulted from Des' colossal mistake—marrying the wrong woman. Sin understood because he hadn't made the best of choices in a wife and had his own form of cynicism in dealing with the opposite sex. Still, he tried to be objective about it.

"Cynical or not, she's someone I want to interrogate." Des flicked off the light, but not before Sin caught the annoyance on his face.

Yep, Des' expression and tone indicated he'd already tried and convicted the lady. Sin wasn't inclined to condemn her so hastily. She just didn't seem like the traitor type. Having never finished her degree, she'd dropped out to marry Montgomery ten years ago and had a baby some seven months after the wedding.

Okay, so they had to get married, Sin thought. But that was kids being too hot and heavy and not using birth control. As far as he was concerned, being stupid and horny rarely led to selling out your country for monetary gain. He could even see how it might have happened, given Avery was a woman a man could lose his sanity over enough to forget the condom.

Lucky bastard...then again, maybe not so lucky as the guy's ashes are buried only two feet away and she's still vibrantly alive. If she were his, he wouldn't want to be separated from her for an instant.

"There has to be something," he whispered, not liking the ditch his thoughts had plowed into. "Some link with her dead husband to all of this."

"The wife *is* the connection, I'm telling you." Des pointed his flashlight at him as if making a point. "Wives, especially wives who've been married for so long, generally know not only where the bodies are buried, but how many and how deep."

Sin didn't reply. Right now the widow was the only solid lead they had.

"What about Williams? Maybe the military's made progress."

Sin frowned. "I doubt it." Colonel Williams was the Army official in charge of procuring and, in his mind, the person who supposedly got things done. Yet their Army liaison seemed useless in this situation. "He's not concerned with the theft, thanks to the fail-safe." If the prototypes landed in the wrong hands, they'd shut down without the proper sequence of numbers, and then self-destruct in fifteen hundred hours. Roughly seven days from now unless reactivated. "I rushed through the process and finalized our contract with the Army without thoroughly weighing the consequences. I certainly didn't think anyone would steal our product before it'd been fully tested." Sin sighed. "I thought the military would provide an element of security."

"It's understandable." Des clapped him on the back and grinned. "If you can't trust your government, who can you trust?"

"That's no excuse." Sin clenched his jaw. "Not for us. Not for me. Fulfilling this contract is too essential to our success." If the components weren't found in time, Williams would declare the project a failure. SPC Electronics, would be out millions, a loss they couldn't afford right now. Due to a provision in the contract stating SPC would be paid only upon confirmation of the technology working, there wasn't a damned thing Sin could do to stop the verdict.

"It's obvious the colonel has little interest in helping us." Sin shook his head in frustration. "He doesn't give a shit about whether or not we go under. His main concerns are saving face and not having to deal with military bureaucracy." With only a week left, the clock was ticking.

"I've still got a few friends on the force who owe me some favors." Des started walking toward the road. "I'll see if they can analyze these bullets." He patted his pocket. "Maybe we'll learn something useful."

Sin nodded and silently fell into step. At least Williams had provided him with a special sticker, the same one surviving spouses and family members received to enter the national cemetery after hours. "Maybe we should reconsider hiring a PI."

"We don't need outsiders." Des exhaled heavily. "They hold too many risks."

Sin nodded. Trust was the biggest issue, that and finding an investigator with the clearances necessary to deal with such sensitive information

"You're right, of course," Sin finally said, as they reached his car. When Des sent him a questioning look, he added, "We should talk to Mrs. Montgomery, and the sooner the better. Let's go back to the office to see if Eric's still there." Eric Coleman was their third partner.

He hit the keyless entry. Both opened their doors and slid inside simultaneously.

Sin wasn't looking forward to questioning the lady, given his earlier reaction. Maybe Des could do it without him. The minute the thought was out, he discarded it.

An ex-homicide detective, Des could spot inconsistencies and lies within seconds of talking to a person, a handy skill to possess due to the sensitive nature of their business. He was also a real pro at solving puzzles, but his friend wasn't what Sin would call a people person. With his square, muscular physique, he'd make a perfect bouncer in one of D.C.'s hottest nightclubs. And despite his stern, military-like bearing and short, dirty-blond buzz cut, both throwbacks from an early Marine Corps experience, the ladies must like him as he never lacked female company.

Sin watched Des snap his seat belt into place. Smiling, he started the engine and pulled onto the road. As he drove, his grin spread. He stifled a chuckle. Since Sin had already irritated the female in question with his actions, he couldn't risk poking the stick of Des' contemptuous personality at her and inflaming her further. SPC's chief of security might attract women like pollen-loaded daisies attracted bees, but his demeanor toward them was spiked with vinegar, not honey.

Questioning Mrs. Montgomery required teamwork, and they

made a great team…sort of like good cop/bad cop when they interviewed prospective employees and clients.

Sin's breath came out in a long sigh. Unfortunately, he'd have to play his good cop part if he wanted to gain any useful information.

The memory of having her soft body under his flashed and he shifted uncomfortably on the leather seat.

"Damn," he said under his breath, punching the accelerator. No matter how hard he tried, the image wouldn't shake free. He didn't need any more complications.

And Avery Montgomery might prove to be a huge one.

~

Once Avery was miles down the road, well away from *him*, the incident replayed in her mind. *Incident?* She snorted, unable to describe what happened so simply.

An out-of-control kiss, maybe, but definitely not a mere incident. Guilt immersed her, filling her with more self-loathing. How could she have acted like a complete idiot…a lovesick fool without any restraint? She was a grieving widow, not some sex-starved hussy.

If that were true, then why did some part of her wonder what would have happened if they hadn't been interrupted? No. She hadn't liked kissing him. Fear, grief, and remorse had hit her all at once, creating her erratic behavior. Even so, she had to admit that Mike's kisses had never affected her like that.

At a red light, she closed her eyes for a brief second. Without the man's influence, she could finally think clearer. Someone had shot at her. Her earlier fear returned full force. Ice water ran through her veins replacing some of the other emotions. She stared in the rearview mirror searching for unseen threats and making note of those behind her.

When the light changed, her foot pushed the gas pedal. Hard. The car shot forward and sped up quickly. Her eyes kept checking the rearview mirror as she drove. One car in particular caught and held her attention. Her heartbeat increased.

Avery breathed out a relieved sigh the moment the car turned off, blocks from her house.

She pressed the garage door opener so that it was fully open when she pulled into her driveway at the rear of her Georgetown house. She didn't wait to hit the button to lower the door. As it closed, she put the car in park, turned off the engine, and stared at the wall in front of her.

Maybe she should have gone to the police. No. Arlington was military jurisdiction and she'd rather avoid anything to do with the military, especially Colonel Williams. She didn't fully trust him. Yet, what about the guy she'd kissed? Who was he?

Her hand went to her pocket, where she'd stashed his business card. She pulled it out and read: *Jeffrey Sinclair—CEO of SPC Electronics*. He said he wanted to talk to her. What was he doing at the gravesite, and not just tonight? She had no doubt he'd been there on those other nights she'd visited. And her biggest concern…who was shooting and why? Was she the target or was *he?*

Had to be him. And I got caught in some kind of crossfire.

Movement at the door separating the kitchen and the garage drew Avery's attention and Terry poked her head out after opening it.

Her sister watched for several minutes before she stepped forward and smiled. "Everything okay?" she asked, opening the car door when Avery made no attempt to move.

Avery couldn't help but notice how close the question was to what *he* had asked. As far as she was concerned, the answer hadn't changed. She wondered if she'd ever be *okay* again. She sighed, tucked the card away, intending to research the company later, and climbed out of the car.

"Sure." She returned the smile. Except it felt forced. Without meeting Terry's curious gaze, she grabbed her purse and headed inside. She needed to think…analyze her behavior…before she told anyone about the events of the past hour, and that included her sister.

The minute Avery got through the door, her son rushed her, extracting a more natural grin. It was hard not to smile when Andy was around.

"Hey, kiddo!" She ruffled his hair before wrapping her arms around him as he hugged her waist. She walked further into the kitchen without breaking contact. "You have school in the morning. Shouldn't you be in bed?"

"I was too scared to go to bed alone. Aunt Terry said I could wait up for you."

Avery hugged her son more fiercely. "Sorry I wasn't here,

honey."

"That's okay. But I'll be able to sleep if you tuck me in."

Andy didn't wait for an answer, instead went skipping off toward his room with absolute conviction she would follow. Avery did, relieved he was so resilient, and wishing she could steal some of his resiliency. If only her mind worked like a child's, then she could forget the past and bounce back, ready to tackle the next phase of her life. Like a mantle, the shadow of her deeds fell on her shoulders again, weighing her down like the heaviest stones.

When she entered her son's room, Avery found him under the blanket, holding up a book and watching her with hopeful expectation. She grinned and strode toward him, unable to deny his unspoken request. Manipulated or not, she was a sucker for Andy's sweet expression.

She slid in next to him, got comfortable, and pulled him closer. With him curled beside her, she opened the book and began reading. Ten minutes later, she unwound herself from his slumbering form, careful not to wake him.

Avery stood and stared at her son's features, so much like Mike's. Raw pain gripped her, held her in its clutches, and ripped her heart in two. Andy was the spitting image of her husband at the same age. She had the many pictures in albums to prove it. Was this her punishment...to be haunted by her actions every time she looked at her son...never to forget?

Why had she sent that letter? Why hadn't she spoken up when she'd had the chance? Now it was too late. Would Andy forgive her if he knew? Avery sighed and tugged the blanket around him, more as a protective gesture than to keep him warm in the late May evening. She brushed a lock of dark hair off his forehead and smiled, still staring but no longer seeing her son's face.

Of course he'd never learn of it. She'd gone to great lengths to make sure. That last letter to Mike was now safely locked away from prying eyes, as was his answer. For some perverse reason, she'd saved both and kept going back to them night after night, as if she needed the reminder to never make the same mistake again. Sometimes she wished the military hadn't been so efficient in sending Mike's belongings back to her.

Her hand went to the heart-shaped locket she wore around her neck. Fingering the sweet gift Mike had sent her, she realized the memento was another reminder. Would she ever be able to take it off and move forward?

A tear broke loose, then trekked down her face. Where had her marriage gone wrong? Why hadn't she been able to love her husband enough for a lifetime? Now that her life was so jaggedly torn apart with his death, why did she wish she could undo what she'd done? *Because your letter most likely caused his death.*

Avery retreated from her son's room.

In the kitchen, Terry stood at the stove and lifted the whistling teakettle. The piercing sound died instantly. No one spoke.

She approached the counter noting two inviting cups and tea bags. "Just what I need."

"You looked a little frazzled." Terry spent a moment pouring hot water over the bags. Once done, she set the teakettle down before handing her the cup. "Figured you could use my calming remedy before I take off."

Avery's lips curled at the edges, forming the genuine smile that wouldn't come earlier. Terry's answer to every problem lay in a cup of tea—that and the accompanying conversation.

"Thanks," she murmured, lifting the cup to her lips. She leaned against the counter .Breathing in the aroma of the hot liquid, her smile increased. There might actually be some validity to the thinking, since she *was* feeling better.

"You shouldn't be skulking in cemeteries so close to dark. They aren't safe."

Avery almost choked on her tea. "I was visiting my dead husband's grave, not skulking. Besides, Arlington's an exception." No need to reveal how dangerous her visit had actually been.

The night's events had proven Arlington National Cemetery wasn't the safest place on earth, in fact had become a place to avoid, for now. Being shot at was enough to scare anyone senseless. She was safe and sound in her own kitchen. The danger had long passed. Now that the threat seemed far away, almost a distant memory, the idea somehow paled to the thought of being yanked to the ground by a stranger and then kissing him in a wild moment. A flush of heat streaked up her face. She quickly brought the tea closer to her mouth to camouflage her reaction. She and Terry shared secrets. Her sister even knew of Avery's request for a divorce from her husband, something no one else knew except her lawyer. She couldn't share this. Not yet.

If Terry caught wind of anything happening tonight, Avery would have to relay all the specifics…and quite frankly, she wasn't exactly sure what those specifics entailed. She certainly wouldn't be able to articulate so much as an inkling of what she'd been thinking. All she'd do is upset her sister. She had no idea why someone shot at her or even if she was the target.

Had to be him. As for the other? It was anyone's guess why an unknown man had drawn such a strong response, especially when her husband, whom she'd idolized as a teen and felt the luckiest person in the world to marry, never had. It had to be some kind of awkward response to her situation. Guilt and grief mixed with fear, resulting in an emotional overload.

"You look like you're feeling better. Your color's back." Terry shook her head and tsk-tsked like the older sister she was. "I just wish something more than a cemetery visit had caused it."

Avery's laugh, an indisputable burst of humor absent since before Mike's deployment to Afghanistan four months ago, felt natural. She took another long sip of tea. Then she exhaled, holding on to her smile. Maybe she was analyzing this from the wrong angle. Maybe the emotional overload from her near-death experience had been a good thing because suddenly she felt less encumbered. Freer. Something *had* happened tonight outside of the craziness of stray bullets and kissing strangers. Something inside her had changed, making her think of life beyond guilt.

She sighed. If only that were possible. She had no idea what the future held. All she knew was at that moment she felt…alive.

~

He'd begun tailing Avery Montgomery's car on her way out of the cemetery, following her until a few blocks from her house where he'd turned off and had circled back. He now sat half a block away, watching the house through binoculars.

All was calm. Upstairs, a few lights burned, revealing several open windows. He did a visual of the dark yard and noted a couple of tall trees. One might provide the means to get inside. Due to the earlier incident at the cemetery, tonight wasn't the time to try. She'd be wary and on her guard. He was thankful she hadn't called military police. That would have caused major headaches for all involved.

He rolled his eyes, wondering how this fucking operation had derailed so far off its original track. He didn't like putting innocent civilians at risk but the risk was necessary in this instance, according to his superiors. He started the car and pulled away from the curb.

He'd return at dawn and wait for an opportunity to search her house.

Chapter 2

Neither Sin nor Des had spoken during the short drive to SPC Electronics.

"Nothing makes sense." Sin punched in the security code to the four-story building. The windowless first and second floors held laboratories and the most advanced clean rooms for production. The rough neighborhood wasn't a concern. Not much could penetrate the thick stone walls and steel doors. With the added security systems in place, the location was actually a benefit; unobtrusive on the outside, drawing little attention to what took place on the inside.

The heavy door slammed shut behind Des. "No, it doesn't."

"Why the tip about a transfer of stolen property taking place and then the shit going on tonight?" The anonymous caller a week earlier had known about stolen SPC property, even alluded to other goods being traded. A leak existed somewhere. Corporate espionage forced him and his partners to take the call seriously and act on it.

Des shrugged and offered a puzzled frown. "A frickin' nightmare."

"Maybe a theft was inevitable. We've been lucky in the past."

"Not luck. Security's always been one of our strengths. We've never had any problems before dealing with the government."

Sin nodded. Recruiting Des had been one of his best moves, sheer genius, so he couldn't dispute his boasting. Nor could he dispute his last comment. Up until eight weeks ago, theft was never a buzzword. Since then, two other products had turned up missing, which in turn led to an overall wariness of the military. Logic told him there was a connection.

Their footsteps echoed in the empty hallway. Security lights lit their way to the lobby and daytime entrance.

"Maybe the colonel's right and terrorism's involved." His statement didn't sound convincing, mainly because Sin wasn't convinced.

Des snorted. "Too easy an answer, if you ask me. Terrorism

seems to be the catchall these days, the reason for everything wrong with the world."

Sin nodded. Williams firmly believed in his theory, but greed got his vote. Very few even knew of the existence of his microscopic computer that picked up power from the sun and used satellites for transmissions and receptions. Fewer still knew how it operated.

They met the guard on duty near the elevator, who stood at their approach. "I see you two are burning the midnight oil."

"Hi, Jimmy." Smiling distractedly, Sin pushed the call button. "How're you tonight?"

"I can't complain. Everything's quiet."

"Good." The elevator doors opened. He and Des entered and took a silent ride to the top floor. Both stepped into an elegant reception area. Plenty of glass and granite were visible in the shadows cast from the light at the far end of the floor.

Sin hit the switch. More light infused the spacious room, creating a striking effect. Hardwood floors and dark wood furnishings and moldings offset the rich earth-tone colors covering the sofa cushions. He liked luxury and had determined to do a proper job when he'd renovated the ninety-year-old warehouse. The same burst of pride he always felt when he happened to take note of what he'd built shot through him and boosted his resolve of uncovering the shit causing havoc within these walls.

He and Des continued past their dark offices toward the obviously occupied one.

Eric Coleman had just hung up the phone when they entered his airy space. He looked up and smiled. "Damn, Sin, were your ears burning? Colonel Williams is on the warpath, doing his war dance. You're definitely on his shit list. I had to do some fancy talking to calm him down. I really wish you wouldn't rile the customers." He indicated for them to sit in the two plush, upholstered chairs in front of his mahogany desk. Darkness peered in between the three-inch wooden slats covering the wall-to-wall windows facing the street below. "The man says to check your voice mail. He's been calling your cell for hours."

"Just what I need to make my night a total bust, the colonel on my back." Sin lifted his cell phone out of his pocket.

"I take it things didn't go as planned at the graveyard?" Eric leaned forward.

Sin pressed the On button. "You don't want to know." Within seconds, the device rang, indicating messages. He connected to voice mail and sighed the moment an automated voice told him there were six in all. He held up a finger to silence his partners. "Let me see what he wants, then I'll fill you in."

As Williams' yelling burst into his ears with the first message, his mind wandered to earlier. At the cemetery, he'd shut off his phone. Didn't need a blaring ringtone to notify *her* that he was so close. He rolled his eyes. After tonight, his stupidity had already given him away. Then fate intervened in the form of muffled gunshots, totally blowing his cover.

Sin listened to the repeated message…five times…wondering if he'd have made himself known without someone shooting at her. "Shit," he said under his breath and punched the right button when the computerized voice asked if he'd like to return the call. Definitely food for thought, yet by the same token, not something he wanted to think about. A curt "Yes," interrupted his thoughts and brought his focus back to his bigger problem.

"Colonel Williams?" He didn't wait for substantiation, just continued with, "This is Jeffrey Sinclair returning your call."

"About goddamn time you called me back."

"I've been a little busy trying to find my missing technology."

"My sources tell me you were at the cemetery. Were you watching the woman again?" When Sin didn't reply, he added, "Leave the widow alone."

Sin stiffened at the strong rebuke and remained silent.

"You're wasting your time at Arlington. If I had known she was your primary target, I'd have never given you access."

"We were at the cemetery on a tip and she just happened to be there, which indicates some kind of involvement." Sin stopped short of telling him about the shooting. Obviously, his sources weren't watching that closely.

"And I told you the major's wife is a dead end. Montgomery wasn't involved."

"We each have our opinion." Sin fought to keep annoyance out of his voice.

"Mine is based on fact and a thorough investigation. Montgomery's record is spotless."

"Then where are my prototypes?" Sin paced, raking a hand

21

through his hair.

"Not in Arlington, I can assure you. We're concentrating our efforts where the theft took place. If you want results, I suggest you do the same."

"McNeil's still in Kandahar checking out your theory, working with your operatives." A loose interpretation. Not one of those *operatives* understood the word cooperate was a derivative, nor did anyone seem to know what cooperate meant as far as he was concerned.

"Focus your efforts in Afghanistan. Not on dead war heroes, or their wives," Williams practically growled, then cut the connection.

Sin wiped his face in frustration. "Damn it all." He hit the Off button. Why was dealing with the United States government so difficult? They were the worst customers. If only millions of dollars weren't involved, he could walk away. The guy knew much more than he shared, gave them just enough information pointing in certain directions. Of course, the colonel couldn't divulge military secrets and Sin wasn't concerned with them. His main concern was locating his stolen property.

Was it by design his tech guru Scotty McNeil couldn't uncover anything useful in Afghanistan? Was the United States military, represented by Colonel Williams, prevaricating? After weeks of getting nowhere with the man, the idea solidified in his mind. He and Williams didn't seem to be in the same room. Hell, he wondered if they were even in the same house.

Sin rubbed the bridge of his nose, easing the headache he felt coming on.

"So what'd Williams want?" Eric asked. "Is the bastard causing you more trouble?"

Nodding, he stuck his phone in his pocket.

"I told you how to handle him. Just get Des to meet him in a dark alley and realign his thinking."

Coleman's teasing extracted an urge to smile. Giving in, he chuckled, which felt good and eased the tension in his shoulders. "The guy could run for office, he's so full of it."

"Quit worrying about him or I'll have Des go behind your back. What you don't know won't hurt you."

"I'm game. Never a dull moment." Des poured himself a cup of coffee from the pot Eric always had brewing. "Sure beats those long, boring hours in Homicide."

Sin rolled his eyes, knowing full well they were only half joking. In the good old days, his two friends preferred using a dark alley to settle conflicts. In fact, all three of them knew how to fight dirty, a necessary skill when growing up in one of the roughest neighborhoods in the country. Eric with his glib tongue, Des with his brawn, and him in charge, leading them into all kinds of shit. How they ever ended up as fine, upstanding men of the community was a testament to their character, not their upbringing.

"Aside from beating up assholes, is there anything else you need me to do tonight?" Des took a sip of his coffee.

"No." Sin grunted. "I should talk to Scotty before we do anything, and despite the colonel's objections, I plan on a face-to-face meeting with the widow to discover what she knows." He rose. "I'll call Mrs. Montgomery in the morning and set up an appointment."

"Want some company?"

At Eric's slanted eyebrows, Sin chuckled, shaking his head. "No. I'm taking Des with me. He knows the criminal mind and I want his opinion of her responses."

"Damn." Eric grinned, then kicked his feet up on the desk and crossed them. "She's a looker. I wouldn't mind peeking inside her brain, not to mention at other endowments."

"Des and I can handle her." Sin snorted. "Alone." Eric Coleman's expertise was sales and he was a damned good salesman. He was also a ladies' man, the complete opposite of Desmond Phillips who disdained the fairer sex and never actively sought any woman out. "We don't need you and your smooth tongue complicating issues. Remember, she's an unknown element, and as such, she's off limits as a potential bed partner."

"Just my luck. Des gets all the fun and I'm stuck here, talking to dull customers."

"Which is your specialty," Sin shot back. "I prefer to solve problems, not create them."

He glanced at Des. "Keep the morning open."

Des nodded. "I'll drop off the bullets I found at the graveyard first thing. I should be free after eight thirty."

"I'll try to set something up for then." He started for the door, adding over his shoulder to include Eric, "I'll let you both know what I hear from McNeil."

Now, if he could remember to follow his own advice about dealing with the sexy woman when the time came, life would be grand.

Chapter 3

"Finish your breakfast," Avery said to a dawdling Andy. "The bus should be here soon."

The warm light of the sun's rays seeped into the kitchen, heralding another gorgeous day.

The previous night she'd researched SPC Electronics and its CEO after Terry had left, finally deciding the incident at the cemetery had been directed at Mr. Sinclair. The idea made much more sense and eased the worst of her fears.

Sleep had still been elusive, despite her buoyant mood before going to bed. In the darkened room, with nothing to distract her thoughts, the never-ending DVD of the night's events played over and over in her mind. Up before dawn, she'd fussed about, cleaning and straightening. If she stayed busy enough, she could keep from thinking about her empty life or her mucked-up attempt to change things.

The phone rang. "You've got five minutes." Avery glared at her son to get him moving before lifting the receiver.

"Mrs. Montgomery?"

She recognized the strong male voice. Instantly, the events of the night before resurfaced in vivid images. "Yes, this is Mrs. Montgomery," she said, more caustically than intended.

"This is Jeff Sinclair. We met last night. At the cemetery, remember? I'd like to talk to you about what happened."

Of course she remembered. She certainly didn't want to rehash her craziness. Nor did she want to get anywhere near the guy if someone had shot at him. "Look, Mr. Sinclair," she said in her firmest voice. "I don't think we have anything to talk about. Good-bye."

"Wait, don't hang up. Someone shot at you. I'm concerned for your safety. I believe it's tied in with your deceased husband, Major Michael Montgomery."

Avery caught the frantic tone and hesitated, wishing she'd never gone to the cemetery last night. Her heart rate eventually slowed to a fast trot and she could finally speak without giving any of her inner turmoil away. "I appreciate your concern. There's no reason why anyone would shoot at me, especially none that tie to Mike. I'm fine, Mr. Sinclair." He was simply mistaken. With sunlight now hitting her back, her fears from being shot at had totally faded. She *was* fine. She had no intention of a repeat meeting or returning to Arlington any time soon, so she would remain fine. Avery smiled into the phone. "Don't worry over my safety. In fact, you should worry more about your own. You're the most likely target. Not me."

When he didn't answer right away, she prodded, "Mr. Sinclair? Are you there?"

He cleared his throat. "Yes…I'm still here."

Again he fell silent. She held on tightly to her last bit of fortitude and tapped her foot, waiting for him to say something, anything at all. When silence prevailed for another ten seconds, she huffed, "You have my full attention. I'd like to know what you have to say that relates to my dead husband." As she spoke, she realized she'd been unsuccessful in keeping annoyance out of her voice. She inhaled a deep breath, steadying herself. No sense being rude.

"I'd rather not say over the phone," Mr. Sinclair said.

"Then I guess we have nothing further to discuss."

"My company manufactures products," he hurriedly explained before she could disconnect. "Specifically for the military, and your deceased husband, Major Montgomery, was working on one before he died. I was hoping you could answer some questions. The product was stolen and I believe the shots fired last night are tied to their theft."

Her brow furrowed. "I'm not sure what you're getting at."

"I told you, I'm worried about your safety, which is why I'd like to meet with you."

Sighing, Avery reached for her most polite tone. "Look, Mr. Sinclair. My patience for intrigue is running low today. I can understand your fears, and I'm sorry to hear about your company's problems, but I don't think it's wise to meet. Plus, I don't appreciate your insinuations about my husband. He died a hero." She happened to look at the clock. It was time for her son to be heading out the door. "I'm sorry, but I can't help you." She replaced the receiver. She may be taking the coward's way out again, but she had enough to deal with without adding more guilt from her actions of the night before.

She turned to Andy. "Time's up. Get your lunch, and I'll take you to the bus stop."

Her neighbor from across the street had already arrived at the corner when she and Andy walked up.

"Good morning," Mary Miller said cheerfully. "Can you believe school is almost out?"

Avery nodded and placed her usual frozen smile on her face. Thank God for Mary, for the distraction of chatting each morning while waiting for the bus with their boys. "This year seemed to fly."

Mary returned the smile, then her grin widened when she glanced at Andy. "How 'bout you, tiger? Are you ready for your camping trip with the Boy Scouts this Saturday?"

Andy grumbled an acknowledgement, a much more vocal answer than his usual, before running off with Tommy, Mary's son and Andy's best friend.

Mary looked at her. "What about you? Are you ready for some quiet?"

"I won't know what I'll do with myself without Andy to fuss over."

In four days, Mary's husband was taking the boys on the yearly camping trip, which would leave the women alone to do whatever for a week. Before the events of last night had jerked her back to the living, Avery hadn't really thought about doing anything more than what had become routine in the aftermath of losing a spouse: clean and read and watch a little TV, just trying to get through the endless days and endless nights. She sensed her usual distractions wouldn't work. Too much energy flowed through her now, filling her with a need to do something different.

"Not me. I know exactly what to do." Mary laughed. "I've got my entire week planned, starting with having my hair done along with the works. You know…manicure, pedicure…I may even have a massage. Want to join me?"

As fun as it sounded, Avery shook her head. "I may go shopping." She sighed. How sad. Her life wasn't much different now than when Mike was alive. His one true love had been the military, which put her and Andy in second place. Over time, despite having what others considered a perfect life, she'd realized hers was only a façade. Her thirtieth birthday came and went nine months ago, opening her eyes to a few truths.

A decade had disappeared and all she had to show for it was Andy. She yearned to share her life with someone other than her son. Mike had never stayed around long enough to share anything. He'd signed up for every opportunity to advance his military career, which meant being deployed to hotbeds around the world for months on end. After years of experiencing his absence, empty years filled with utter loneliness, Avery not only didn't know her husband anymore, she no longer knew herself.

She glanced at Andy, playing kick ball with Tommy. A real grin took over her face, reached all the way to her toes, and felt good. She was so tired of feeling guilty and sad, especially since her near miss last night reminded her how alive she was. In order to give her son what he needed, she needed to figure out how to live again without negative emotions. "I haven't been to Nordstrom in ages." Her smile died. "Since before Mike's death."

"When are you going?" Mary asked.

"Probably Saturday afternoon." Shopping seemed like a good start.

"Want a little company? I should be done by two, three at the latest. Maybe we can grab some dinner to celebrate. Start the week out right."

"Let me think about it." Avery hesitated, then added more honestly, "I'm not sure if I'm fit company yet."

Mary gripped her hand and squeezed. "Okay, I understand."

"I don't know what I'd do without my family and friends." Avery sensed from the compassion in her eyes that Mary did understand. "Tell Steve that I really appreciate his taking Andy under his wing like he has." Something she was very thankful for.

Terry, her only sibling, had never married and their father was dead. Mike's father had died a few years later. Both grandmothers adored their grandson. He certainly didn't lack for warmth or caring, and Andy loved all the women in his life. Yet, now with Mike's death, her son had no male influence other than her friend's husband.

Great! More reason to feel guilty.

The genuineness of her expression faded. Her fake smile returned, the same one she'd come to rely on so much in recent months, as well as past years. She was used to putting on a friendly face so the world couldn't see her misery. She pretended not to notice the loneliness. Or the guilt. At some point, pretense had to work. She couldn't be an effective parent and hold on to the bleak emotions forever.

The bus turned onto their street, interrupting her depressing thoughts.

"Bye, Mom," Andy shouted, waving as he stepped onto the platform.

"Bye, sweetie. I'll see you after school. Have a good day." She waved back, wiggling her fingers, but her son had already pushed his way onto the bus, ignoring her words and gesture.

Avery sighed as the bus chugged out of sight. "Well, guess I should get busy. I have a lot to do today," she said in her most cheerful, phony voice, heeding an impulse to get away. It was a blatant lie. She had nothing to do. Nothing to prevent her mind from rehashing everything.

"I'll see you later. Call me if you need anything and I meant it about Saturday." When Avery was about to shake her head, Mary grinned and held up a hand. "Think on it. Don't say no yet. I'd love to have dinner with you, no matter your mood. We can try the new Italian place I spotted not too far from the Capitol." Her friend never gave her a chance to answer yes or no, just crossed the street and walked away at a brisk pace.

Avery watched her, unable to stop another genuine smile from overcoming the fake. She turned, about to head up her walkway, when the sight of a man coming from the other direction halted her in midstride. Her grin died. In seconds flat her heart rate increased, pounding out of control like some Indian drummer beating a frenzied war dance totally preparing for battle. Her face flushed with heat as she recognized *him*. What the hell was he doing here? Outside her house?

In broad daylight, without the shadows hiding his full features, he was devastating to look at. Her memory hadn't done him justice. The man could model for Michelangelo's David, he was so perfect. She was used to perfect men. Mike had been perfect. Or so she'd thought. Perfection on the outside generally hid imperfections on the inside.

Avery resumed walking, hurrying to get away. But all too soon he was right behind her, gripping her elbow. "Please, Mrs. Montgomery, we have to talk."

"I believe stalking is a crime," she hissed, whirling around with her chin held high.

His nearness overwhelmed her. He towered over her, his well-built, muscular frame much larger than she remembered. Though tall herself, she felt diminutive, almost dainty, next to him and the unusual feeling threw her off balance. Of course, the whole persona of the man threw her off balance.

The business casual look he presented suited him. The hunter green sport shirt outlined a beautiful upper body and emphasized strong forearms as well as offsetting a dark complexion. Her gaze followed the shirt's path to his face, its color highlighting expressive eyes, making them appear like emerald shards glinting in the sun. That was only the top half. The lower half was just as unsettling. His tan slacks appeared to be created for someone with his sleek, catlike grace and muscles.

She fought to ignore his energy…that same vital force she'd encountered the night before.

But just like then, her efforts were wasted, throwing her way off balance as the air around her became charged. The atmosphere crackled with power emanating directly from him.

"I'm investigating SPC's theft, not stalking." He crossed his arms. His serious green gaze, as arresting as it had been last night, caught hers and held on tight.

Avery stiffened, struggling to maintain her dignity. "Why are you outside my house?"

His face remained placid as he completely disregarded her glare. "I told you on the phone, I have some questions I'd like to ask."

"And I told you, I'm busy." She kept her head up, refusing to let him bother her, wishing more than anything he'd simply disappear. Retreat was her only option.

"You're not concerned someone shot at you?"

"No. They were shooting at you, not me. You should stay out of cemeteries." She turned to go, purposely putting one step in front of the other in an effort to regain some balance. "Now if you'll excuse me."

"No, I won't excuse you. And even if I didn't disagree, you know damn well we need to talk."

Avery's shoulders lifted in an unconcerned shrug. "After last night, I doubt we have anything to discuss."

"Given that kiss, honey, I'd say we have quite a bit to discuss."

"How dare you!" She stopped dead in her tracks and pivoted, unable to believe he'd actually bring it up. And he'd called her honey, like she was some bimbo. Her hands clenched. She could feel her fingernails digging into her palms because she held her fists too tightly closed. Uncurling her fingers, she glowered at him.

"Oh, please." He snorted, ignoring her best efforts at presenting an outraged stance. "I do dare, because as I recall, I gave you plenty of time to back away." His gaze raked up and down her body and an insolent grin spread across his face. "I only reacted to some weird connection. Same as you did." He put up a hand when she was about to shake her head. "Don't try and deny it. I was there, remember?"

Avery's hand fisted again, even as the heat of embarrassment rushed up her face. She wanted to smack that smug expression off his face. The urge to throw his words back at him was overpowering, but she couldn't. They both knew he spoke the truth, so why bother pretending otherwise. Still, she wasn't about to back down.

"I was scared and not myself." She threw out her most disdainful look. "A gentleman would've known that and not taken advantage of the situation."

"I never claimed to be a *gentleman*," he said, making eye contact.

His smile grew lazy...almost...well, sexy was a good way to describe it.

Then his gaze took another trip down her body. Avery closed her eyes and swallowed hard. Goose bumps formed, sending chills along their wake, which coincided with the heat flooding through her system that had nothing to do with embarrassment.

Why is this happening? She definitely shouldn't be having such thoughts, nor should she find him attractive, but on some weird level an attraction existed.

She opened her eyes and their stares locked again. Every cell in her body responded to the message his lingering gaze sent, flashing brighter than a neon sign. Though she tried, there was no way she could stay angry. Not when he viewed her through those jade eyes. Eyes that said too much and reminded her of her stupidity, even as a trickle of that same connection he'd just mentioned flooded her with warmth.

Avery finally forced herself to look away and not react any more than she already had. What was it about this man, this total stranger that caused her to indulge in such craziness around him? Had to be a sign of grief or guilt overload.

"And as I recall, I apologized for my actions. In my book, a lady always accepts an apology."

His words yanked her focus back to his face...to his beseeching, expressive eyes. Wrong thing to do. "Well...um...I...um..." She quickly glanced down and concentrated on her hands, where her attention stayed. Just her luck, her mind *would* quit functioning at the most inopportune time. She cleared her throat, still stalling, unable to prod her thoughts to flow.

"Come on. Like I said earlier, all I want to do is ask a few questions," he prompted, after a bit of silence between them. He paused a beat, then said, "How about if I promise not to touch you again," drawing her attention. He lifted his hands in a gesture of surrender, sporting a lop-sided grin. "And to show you how sincere I am, I'll make sure my partner's present."

"You brought your partner?" When he nodded, Avery looked around. "Where is he?" She risked another glance at his intriguing features.

"We're meeting in a Starbucks, two blocks over." He flashed another mouthful of straight, white teeth. "I'll even spring for a cup of coffee."

Avery eyed him carefully, wondering if she'd lost all of her common sense at actually considering his request. The guy's incredible smile reached his eyes and added to what she'd already determined—Jeff Sinclair was an attractive male. Nor could she dispute another possibility. What if her assumptions were wrong? It might be better if they did talk, if only to hear his take on the shots fired, and having someone else present might ease some of her embarrassment over her crazy behavior from the night before.

"Questions?" she said warily, still watching him. "That's all?" She'd ask a few of her own.

His thousand-watt grin didn't diminish one bit as he nodded.

Oh heavens! Those searing green eyes crinkled at the edges and would have to draw her gaze again. She shouldn't be agreeing to remaining anywhere near the man. For some reason he affected her. She'd die before she'd let him know how much. She sucked in a deep breath, reaching for courage.

"I need to get my purse and lock up. I'll meet you there," she said, once her resolve stiffened and she felt in control enough to talk without squeaking.

"That's okay, I'll wait. Like I said, it's only a couple of blocks, so we can walk."

Avery nodded, realizing she had no choice as he didn't appear to give up easily. "I'll be right back, Mr. Sinclair."

"Call me Sin." He presented that same smile and held her gaze, almost daring her to use his nickname.

"You just wait out here, *Mr. Sinclair*," she said, not succumbing to his baiting. "I'll hurry."

She turned and headed up the path at a fast gait, thankful he hadn't followed. She needed space. Her steps sped up the closer to the house she got.

On her way inside, a few thoughts struck. Maybe her grief was abating. Maybe that's why she responded so strongly to him. Maybe it meant she was overcoming her loss, as well as her guilt. Or maybe this was all part of her punishment.

She did grieve over losing Mike, but right now she mourned more for her husband's loss of life and son's loss of a father rather than her own loss. Guilt over not wanting to be married to Mike still lurked. She regretted not having the guts to say something before he went back to Afghanistan for his third tour four months ago. The moment Mike had returned from his last duty away, Avery had known she couldn't spend the rest of her life with him.

Their dream of living happily-ever-after had died long ago. She wasn't certain it'd ever been her dream. Yet, he'd seemed happy and content. He'd given up so much in his absence. She hadn't had the heart to tell him she wanted out. In hindsight, she saw her actions as cowardly, and like a true coward, she wondered if she'd ever stop running.

~

Sin watched Avery Montgomery move up the path like she was escaping some madman. "Way to go, Sinclair," he said under his breath. "Just goad her into not talking, why don't you." Raking a hand through his hair, he blew out a frustrated breath. "Damn." Maybe he *was* a madman. He certainly didn't feel too sane right then.

What the hell had possessed him to provoke her like that? *I get within two feet of the lady and I act like some jungle-living, chest-beating moron overdosing on testosterone.* He needed to stay focused and not get sidetracked by the likes of *her.*

He sighed and rubbed his face in an effort to clear his brain of her, but his mind paid no attention, working in double time instead.

Good God, she was more stunning without darkness muting her features. He'd always seen her at dusk. And her pictures hadn't captured her true essence.

Sure, she's pretty…okay, beautiful…and don't forget the great body with the sexy curves.

Stop it! Don't even think about those long, endless legs perfect for wrapping around a man or those lips he knew from experience were perfect for kissing or that shimmering hair or those beguiling brown eyes.

"Shit," he muttered. He was an absolute madman to be entertaining thoughts about any of those things. He'd come across plenty of beauties over the last few years and had never allowed any of them to affect him. So why did Avery Montgomery affect him now?

Her front door opened, pulling him out of his disturbing thoughts, thank God. But the moment he glanced up and saw her breeze onto the porch, his concern deepened. She was one gorgeous woman, and ignoring the attraction he felt for her might prove a tad difficult.

"I'm ready, Mr. Sinclair."

"Sin."

She ignored him and started off down the street.

He sighed and followed, knowing damn well he shouldn't push her but unable to stop the impulsive need to do so. Yep, he was acting like an absolute madman. He probably should have let Des and Eric handle questioning her.

"Look, Mr. Sinclair—"

"Sin," he said, interrupting her after they'd been walking a long block without speaking. He flashed a quick grin. "Remember?"

"I prefer formality, Mr. Sinclair."

"Okay." Her *Mr. Sinclair,* emphasized with such inflection, said it all. She wasn't about to use his nickname. Not in this lifetime. "I guess that means I'm stuck calling you Mrs. Montgomery."

"Yes. Despite what happened last night we know nothing about each other. I think it's best to keep it that way."

His grin expanded. "I know enough."

Avery's body tensed and her facial muscles stiffened, becoming a thin façade they were stretched so tightly.

"Sorry," he murmured, relenting. After all, he'd given his word. If she wanted formal, he'd do formal. "I got carried away again." He wiped all amusement off his face and reached for sincerity. Once he could, he met her gaze with a solemn expression. "I'll try to refrain from now on."

"Thank you," she replied, her tone as rigid as her straight back.

Picking up her chilly vibes, he wondered why her sudden cold shoulder bothered him when he'd determined not to let her affect him. He sighed, praying formality would work to keep those enthralling brown eyes so full of something he couldn't quite grasp from drawing him in deeper. Matters between them would definitely play out easier if they were surrounded with a wall of formality. Still, the thought of how long it would take to tear the wall down flitted through his brain.

While walking, he cast a sideways glance, studying her unobtrusively. Sunlight stroked her long, glossy hair, highlighting all the colors of brown, from light to dark. He never knew brown could be so beautiful…so rich…so lustrous a color. His hand curled into a fist. He stilled an urge to run his fingers through such richness, wondering if it was as soft as it appeared.

They came to the end of the block, halted their progress, and waited for the light to change. Relief washed over him when he saw Des enter the coffee shop on the other side of the street.

Sin had no business entertaining any fantasies about Avery Montgomery. Sexy woman or not, she was a means to an end, and had information SPC needed. Once he obtained that information, they could each go back to their lives and pretend they'd never kissed.

He mentally snorted. Yeah, right. If that was so, then why was the idea so unappealing? Even worse, why did the image of what came after kissing keep him awake most of last night?

Damn. He didn't need more complications. His out-of-control thoughts alone told him she was turning out to be a big one. Thankfully, the light changed.

"There's my partner now." Sin grabbed her hand and pulled her along with him, his pace increasing the closer they got to the Starbucks. The sooner they had their talk, the sooner he could get away from her so his wacko thoughts could even out.

Sin held the door for her, then entered.

Des had just finished paying for his coffee and was heading toward them.

"Thought we'd sit outside and enjoy the nice morning." His partner indicated the wrought iron tables through the glass.

Nodding, Sin led Avery back outside to an empty table. She sat as Des walked up and pulled out a chair.

"Desmond Phillips, meet Mrs. Montgomery. Mrs. Montgomery, Mr. Phillips," he said, emphasizing the formal social titles. While they shook hands, Sin added, "What can I get you?"

She told him and he strode inside and up to the counter. "You can do this," he whispered.

"Excuse me, sir? I didn't catch your order."

Sin sighed, flashing the sales clerk behind the register a quick grin before he ordered.

"Here you go, ma'am," he said minutes later, handing Avery a large cup of coffee. He sat across from her and focused on his drink. Lord knew he should keep from looking at her as much as he could.

"Mrs. Montgomery was telling me about her son. He sounds like quite a kid." Des waited until he glanced up before adding, "Andy's nine and is going to Boy Scout camp in a few days."

"Ah. I didn't know." Sin nodded, made eye contact with him, and noted the goofy grin covering his partner's face. His gaze narrowed, shifted from Des to the lady, then returned to Des. What had he missed while he was buying coffee? The guy smiled at few people and never at women, yet here he was practically throwing her a party.

"I'm sorry. I was talking your ear off. It's just that if anyone asks about my son, I can't seem to help myself." Avery took a sip of coffee, then sent Des a warm smile, ignoring Sin as if he hadn't joined them. "Mr. Sinclair said you had some questions about my husband in regard to your company."

"Why were you at the cemetery last night?" Sin blurted out, interrupting what Des was about to say. Even he couldn't miss the accusation in his voice, but he couldn't stop his annoyance from slipping into the words. The way she'd said Mr. Sinclair, like the name was something distasteful she'd dragged out of the trash and held away from her nose. He didn't like being ignored and he wasn't a piece of trash. "Your husband was testing our technology and now that he's dead, it's missing," he added, his tone even more accusatory.

"What?" Sparks practically flew from her eyes as her spine stiffened into its earlier board-like position. "I beg your pardon?"

"Ignore him." Des sent him a fuming glare. "He's being an ass. He's worried, with good reason. As SPC's owners, we're very concerned about what happened on the night your husband died, the same night our product went missing."

"You mentioned something earlier, but I can assure you, if something went missing Mike had nothing to do with it," she said through clenched teeth and a frozen smile. She raised her chin a notch, adding to her combative expression. "He played by the rules and gave his life for his country, and I refuse to listen to any innuendos about his honor."

"You misunderstood. My partner can sometimes be a little abrupt when our business is in peril." Des flashed him a warning look before turning back to Avery, offering an encouraging, apologetic grin. "He didn't mean to suggest anything of the sort, did you, Sin?"

"Of course not," Sin said, backing down. Finger-pointing and insinuation wouldn't get him his answers. Still, something wasn't right. How the hell had their roles reversed in less than five minutes? The words were so similar to something he would say when they interviewed others.

"This is a new side to you, Des. When did you become a knight in shining armor?"

"Don't be rude," his partner chided. "I'm sure Mrs. Montgomery has every intention of helping us, don't you, ma'am."

"Yes, of course I want to help any way I can. It's why I'm here. But I won't tolerate accusations. Mike's work was his life and I refuse to let anyone smear his name."

"No one is making accusations or smearing names. Right, Sin?"

"Right," Sin murmured, staring in stunned fascination as Des' lips curled into another smile and he patted her hand like he might a small child's he was trying to comfort. "I'm sorry if I gave you the wrong impression."

"See? No problems." Des skewered him with another pointed stare telling him to behave.

Sin only rolled his eyes when Des met Avery's gaze and his tone turned more soothing. "We were hoping you could answer some questions."

Her facial features relaxed into a genuine smile and a hint of color brushed over her cheeks.

"I'm not sure how much help I can be," she gushed, hanging onto Des' every word, lapping up his attention like a hungry kitten drinking cream.

"Let us be the judge of that."

"Wait a minute." Sin laughed. "Now I know I've stepped into the *Twilight Zone*. Did I miss something?"

"How could you miss anything, you've been right here the whole time."

"Because you're smiling and being nice…to a woman, no less."

Des scowled. "You want to know what your problem is, Sin?"

Sin's eyebrows rose. Definitely a new side to his friend. The lady must be affecting him too.

"Not really, but I can see by your expression you're dying to enlighten me." For some reason, Des' attitude annoyed him, so the words came out more sharply than he'd intended.

"You're too cynical. Sometimes you've just got to go with your instincts."

"Really?" Damn, he was in big trouble if Des was defending her and rebuking him for his behavior, hurling his own words back at him. "I think we're veering off course. We're not here to discuss my personality flaws. We're here to ask questions. Of the lady. Remember?"

"I agree. And I'd like to know what's going on." Avery's voice drew his attention. She glanced at Des, bestowing another small smile. "Mr. Sinclair said something about missing technology my husband was testing. From his earlier words, I gather he thinks it's tied to the shots fired last night, but I don't see how. Before I answer anything else, I'd like to know why you were watching me."

"We weren't watching you at the cemetery." Des looked at Sin, then cleared his throat. "Well, we were. But not you, per se. We were led to that spot after acting on a couple of anonymous tips." Des hesitated, then briefly explained their problem, ending with,

"We're not sure how this affects you…or your husband, but we can't rule it out just yet, especially since someone decided to open fire."

Avery grazed her bottom lip in between her teeth, eyeing Des thoughtfully. "I know nothing about Mike's work," she finally said, sighing and shaking her head. "My husband was always discreet."

"He didn't write to you about his life in Afghanistan? About his co-workers or any problems?" Des prodded.

"Some, but he'd never mention problems or co-workers." Her smile became brittle, making her face look as though it would crack into a million pieces if someone touched her skin. Her gaze moved to her coffee and she kept it there while she added, "His work was classified." Her fingers were busy rolling and unrolling a napkin. "I felt lucky to know where he was stationed and to receive what little information I did. I certainly never expected to learn more." She glanced back at Des and shrugged. "I'm really sorry. I wish I knew more so I could help you find what you're looking for."

"Don't be silly. Any information, no matter how trivial, is a big help. Just knowing your husband kept the classified parts of his job secret tells us something."

Ready to burst at the seams, Sin listened patiently as Des went all mushy over Avery in attempts to mollify her, no matter that the miniscule amount of information she provided did little to help their cause. After twenty minutes of him and Des plying question after question even as she threw out many of her own, with no better answers than *I don't know's* on both sides, Sin heaved a frustrated sigh. They were getting nowhere fast.

What's more, her vulnerability emerged several times during the short interview. In his opinion, she'd been telling the truth. Des' mannerisms shouted that he thought so too. By this point, Sin didn't know what to think.

During a lull in the conversation, Avery stood. "I'll be right back." She turned and headed inside after asking the busboy for directions to the ladies' room.

Sin watched her retreat, waiting until she was out of earshot before glancing at Des. "Well?" His gaze narrowed as he observed his friend's facial features. "You've obviously changed your opinion about the widow. Last night you had her tried and convicted, and now you're singing her praises. What's happened to change your mind?"

"I can't change my mind?" Des asked hypothetically.

"A complete one-eighty?" Sin raised his eyebrows, then snorted. "No. Not you."

"She's different than I thought." His shoulders rose in a nonchalant shrug. "Softer. There's a sincerity about her, a warmth I hadn't expected. Comes out in her gaze…in her smile." Des stared in the direction of the ladies' room. He shook his head, grinning like an idiot. "I'm surprised to hear myself say this, but I like her."

"Hello. Earth to Des." Sin snapped his fingers in front of Des' face. "Stay focused. What about our problem? The reason we're here questioning her, remember? What's your initial take on that?"

"I had her talking until you sat down. *You* clearly make her nervous. If you said boo, she'd probably jump ten feet. I also thought it interesting to note that when she spoke of her husband, she wouldn't meet our eyes. Plus, she kept glancing at the paper napkin she rolled and unrolled. Indicates nerves. She's definitely edgy. Maybe it's you. Or maybe it's something else entirely."

Sin laughed. Nervousness and edginess were the least of his worries. If Des only knew what had gone through his mind while observing Avery answer their questions, his partner would damn well wonder about his reasoning skills. He certainly did.

He wanted to find her guilty, especially after Des started his Prince Charming routine. In those long minutes of watching her, he comprehended fully how much she affected him. She *was* nervous, so maybe he affected her, as well. He'd like to think she felt the same strum of attraction zinging through him every time their eyes met, an attraction that had seemed to grow the longer they were in the same room together, a mushrooming cloud he couldn't contain.

Damn. He scrubbed his face with a hand. He had to stop thinking such crazy thoughts.

Business, Sin. Focus on business.

"Or maybe she's fooled us both and it's deceit, rather than nerves," he added in an effort to put up a shield, to further remind himself she was someone he should avoid. "Did you ever consider that?"

"Could be. She *is* holding something back." Des smiled, the mischievous glint in his eyes saying everything. "I notice you've also suddenly acquired a nervous reaction." His nod indicated the table.

"The lady doesn't make *you* nervous, does she?"

"Shit," Sin whispered, stilling his hand's tapping. He grabbed his coffee, took a long drink, and then to stop his feet from taking up where his fingers left off, he planted them firmly on the ground. "No," he said in his firmest tone, reaching for convincing. "She doesn't make me nervous."

"Of course not." Des chuckled, clearly not buying his denial.

"It's only pent-up energy," Sin insisted, his glare daring him to disagree.

They eyed each other cautiously before Des flashed a quick grin. "Pent-up energy? Nice try, but I don't think so." He chuckled again and shook his head. "Here's how I view the situation." He stretched out, leaned back, and took a sip of coffee. Then he caught Sin's gaze again, holding on to it as he spoke. "Since there's obviously vibes going back and forth between you two, I think you should play chummy with the widow. Take her out to dinner. Wine and dine her. Get close to her so she'll trust you, then maybe we'll learn what she's holding back. While you're doing that, I'll break into her house. Go through her things."

"Whoa, hold on a minute." Sin put up two hands, motioning. "Time out."

"What? You don't want to take her out?"

"No, I don't want to go out with her," he snapped.

"Okay. Not a problem, 'cause I really like the lady. If she makes you too nervous, then I'd be happy to spend a few hours in her company wining and dining. Of course that means you'll have to break into her house. Still remember how to pick a lock?"

"Yeah, I still remember how, but I'm not going to break into her house. You're not going out with her, either. Is that clear?" Sin's voice raised enough on the last two sentences to draw a couple of curious stares.

"Clear as glass…and like I said…" Des' grin spread, showing all his teeth. Paying no attention to the small audience, he added, "Vibes don't lie."

"Okay, okay. So I'm attracted to her," Sin admitted under his breath, once the onlookers went back to their coffee, hating his friend's accurate perception. Des knew him too well.

He pulled a hand through his hair, letting it land on the back of his neck and rubbed out the kinks. This wasn't going the way he wanted. He should be running in the opposite direction, not considering Des' suggestion. He couldn't deny his idea held merit. He wasn't quite sure which he found more appealing…learning what she was holding back, or the thought of being around her.

Sighing, he met Des' gaze and demanded, "Answer me this. How in the hell do you expect me to get her to go out with me when, in your words, she's nervous around me and is ready to jump ten feet if I say boo? I mean, we don't have a lot of time, and though I'm no slouch with women, let's face it. I'm not in Eric's league, either. It's going to take some doing for me to soothe her fears."

He didn't add that his actions the night before bore the major brunt of his dilemma.

"Hmmm, you're right." Des' focus moved to the table. "Even Eric's charm probably won't calm her in time. Let me think on it." He stroked his chin. Finally, he looked up and nodded to the coffee shop's entrance. "Here she comes now. I've thought of a solution, but I don't have time to explain it, so for God's sake, just go along with me."

Sin moved his head up and down slowly, wishing they had more time to sort this out and that Des didn't look so satisfied. He had a sneaking suspicion he wouldn't like his plan. He was pretty sure that spending more time with Avery Montgomery would only complicate matters further, especially after spending the last half hour with her. On the other hand, no way in hell he was going to allow either partner any time alone with her.

Chapter 4

"You know, Mrs. Montgomery. We've been talking." Des waited until she sat and he had her full attention to continue. "We're worried for your safety. We think you should let one of us be with you at all times for the next few days."

"You're not serious?" Avery's gaze moved first to Des, then to Sin and back to Des. "Thanks for your concern, but I'm perfectly safe."

Sin kept all emotion off his face as a trickle of unease crawled up his spine. A date in a crowded restaurant he could handle. However, the hours he'd have to spend alone with her, if Des persuaded her to go along with his plan, was another matter entirely.

"You're not as safe as you think," Des said. "Something's not right and until we figure it out, you're in danger."

"I disagree. This is Georgetown." Avery waved his comment off in an obvious effort to convince them, though a bit of light died from her eyes and her smile diminished somewhat.
"Plus, I don't plan on making any more evening visits to the cemetery."

"You really should reconsider," Des said. "I'm a trained detective. Sin and Eric, our other partner, know how to take care of themselves if there's any trouble."

"I don't think that's necessary as I doubt there'll be any trouble. I appreciate your concern." She glanced at her watch and jumped up suddenly. "Oh, look at the time. I really need to go. I've got a busy day scheduled. Thanks for coffee."

Des' hand on her arm stopped her as she turned to leave. She looked at him, her brows arching in a silent question.

"You need to take this threat seriously. We do." He eyed her intently, his expression as severe as his tone. "Someone shot at you and if Sin hadn't been there last night, you might not be sitting here today."

Another glimmer of fear leapt into Avery's eyes and they grew the size of quarters as she sank back into her chair. Then her brow furrowed. "You really think I'm in danger?"

"You tell me. The whole incident last night could be something else entirely. Or the same someone who shot at you most likely presumes you know more than you do about your husband's secrets. We believe there's a connection. What if the next shots hit you? Or your son? Are you willing to risk it? Risk your son getting injured or worse?"

Sneaky bastard, Sin thought, watching Avery's reaction. Des, a master manipulator, was using what instinct told him of the woman to nail her agreement.

"You're wrong." She swallowed hard, absorbing his meaning. "The fired shots have to do with you and your company's thefts, not me." Her back straightened. Despite her bravado, her complexion paled, making those brown eyes appear a deeper, darker color, almost black. "They have to. Nothing else makes sense."

Maybe too sneaky. "Des, you're scaring her." Despite his reservations, Sin rather liked the feisty woman who told him she preferred formality, much better than the frightened one Des' comments brought out. "It could be unrelated or a random act," he said, in an effort to ease her worst fears.

"You obviously don't think so." She eyed him with the precision of a bridge inspector looking for structural flaws. "Do you?"

"No. I'm with Des. I'm not a big believer in coincidences. I believe in being cautious."

"Cautious? You guys are complete strangers." Her chin inched up.

"Yeah, but having someone around would be safer. For you and your son," Sin added sincerely. Des made too much sense. She was in danger and she needed to take the shooting seriously. "It wouldn't be for long, only until we learn if there's a connection or until the fail-safe is activated. By then, it shouldn't matter because the prototypes will be useless."

"No. You're asking too much. If you think I'll jeopardize my son's safety by allowing anyone into my home, including you two, you're nuts." Avery glanced at her hand, focusing on her fingernails, totally lost in thought. "This whole thing has nothing to do with me," she said a moment later. "I'm sure of it."

"What if you're wrong? Face it, Mrs. Montgomery. You *are* right in the middle of this. That first bullet was aimed at you, not Sin,"

Des said, increasing his pressure. "We *are not* the threat. We're only offering our services because we're worried about you. And your son."

Avery's focus went to Des, then to Sin and back to Des. "Maybe I should go to the police?"

"Did you report the incident?" Des' eyebrows lifted an inch.

She shook her head.

"Reporting it might not be a bad idea. But you should do it soon and be warned. Since you didn't do it last night, they probably won't take the incident seriously and even if they did, the police don't have the manpower to give you the security we think you need, given the boldness in the act. And as to any reporting? You'll have to do it without us. We're hesitant to divulge why we were at the cemetery in the first place. Not when national security is at risk. Your husband was working on top-secret prototypes that were stolen." That much was true, Sin thought, wondering where Des was going with his line of bullshit. "We shouldn't even be discussing our product with you, but we know you wouldn't want your husband's name dragged through the mud with false rumors and innuendo."

Avery's gaze narrowed. "I don't follow you."

"I'm only looking at worse case, if details of the stolen goods ever got out to the press and the press investigated." Des snorted. "In my opinion, they're always on the prowl for scapegoats and might rush to judgment before checking facts, especially if it involves dead heroes selling secrets to the enemy. Makes good headlines and sells newspapers."

"But that would be a lie." Outrage flew across her features. "Mike was a Montgomery. His record was impeccable, just like his father's and grandfather's."

"All the more reason to discredit him. The higher up they are, the better people enjoy watching them fall. No one cares if the truth gets distorted in the process."

"Mike's work was important to him." She pounded the table so hard the silverware danced, and her expression hardened. "He died a hero, protecting his country. It's the only thing I can hang on to for my son. I won't let the reasons for his death be impugned."

"No one wants that," Sin murmured, remembering how earlier she'd defended her husband's deeds. "Des is a natural pessimist at heart and tends to overstate the problem."

Sin knew all about defenders of heroes. Diane had been one. His smile died as the memory of his deceased wife resurfaced. He rarely thought about her, so the sudden burst of pain stabbing at his heart, a direct result of Diane's treachery, took him by surprise. He thought he'd long overcome feeling such pain. Apparently, he'd been living under a delusion all these years.

While Des and Avery Montgomery discussed how they could mitigate problems when she filed a police report, more images of the past filled Sin's thoughts. Diane, the biggest mistake of his life, had up and left him for her hero, a man Sin had known nothing about. The guy had originally deserted Diane and then had returned to steal her away. Neither had given any thought to the fact that Diane was carrying Sin's son. In their hurry to escape during a dark, rainy night, Diane's hero died in a very unheroic fashion when a red-light runner had changed the course of everyone's history, broadsiding their car.

In one split second, Sin's life had ended. No, that wasn't true. It'd ended when he realized the depth of Diane's treachery. His unborn child's life being snuffed out without a chance to live because his mother died on impact while running away from him only compounded his horror over the accident.

He thought he'd had a connection with Diane. Too late he'd discovered how totally, undeniably, unequivocally...how utterly wrong he'd been.

Now, after an unforgettable kiss, his life seemed to be again spiraling around attraction. Too much like the one other time he'd felt the edge of attraction so acutely that all his common sense had flown out the window. The emotionally crippling head-on he'd suffered with Diane had almost destroyed his life. Desire had fueled their connection. He'd been no better than a stud...a fill-in...for the wealthy hero Diane had pined over. Sin had barely escaped the woman and her lies unscathed. He'd never go through that again. Hadn't his wife's secrets been enough to curb any kind of desire for someone like Avery Montgomery? A woman with secrets? One grieving for a wealthy hero, no less?

The similarities and truth of it all were too vivid in hindsight. A woman like Avery Montgomery would probably respond no differently than his dead wife. Even now, she was allowing nothing to tarnish her hero's image. In fact, he'd bet she'd do much more to keep that image alive, just as Diane had.

"Since we're all after the same ending, you might reconsider using us for protection," Sin said, determined to hold firm to his decision. "We can help each other. Our main goal is to find our product." Thank God, the earlier wall of formality that had somehow come down during the last twenty minutes snapped back into place. Formality now suited him just fine.

He only had to remember his purpose and keep any and all desires in check.

"I completely understand your goal." Avery rolled her eyes. "I've survived thus far without *protection*, so I think I'll decline your nice offer."

Sin shrugged. "Your prerogative." Plan *A* didn't seem to be working. They'd have to switch to plan *B* to learn the lady's secrets, only Des could wine and dine her while he searched her house. Yet, if that plan was so perfect, then why did the idea of Des taking her out suddenly annoy the hell out of him?

"You're darn right, it is my prerogative." She stood. Her smile didn't reach her eyes. "You have to be living on another planet to think I'd consider it in the first place."

"Your concern is justified. It was just an idea." Presenting white teeth, Des pulled a card out of his wallet and started writing on it. "How about this. Keep our card handy. It's got my cell number and Sin's, as well as our office number. If you need us, we're but a phone call away. In the meantime, I'll have an officer I know in the Georgetown district stop by and talk to you. The police might be helpful, even if it's just to drive by your house more often."

"Thanks." Avery pocketed the card and nodded. "I should get going. I have a busy day planned."

"I'll walk you home." Sin shoved away from the table and stood. He'd parked close to her house so it seemed stupid not to offer.

"You have our numbers," Des said at the point of separation. "Call if you change your mind." He waved and walked toward his car to drive back to SPC, leaving Sin and Avery in front of the coffee shop.

"Mr. Phillips seems nice." Avery pushed strands of brown hair behind her ears, then shaded her eyes with the same hand. "He obviously knows what he's doing. I like him."

Sin nodded, watching her watch his partner stride down the block as a surge of jealousy snuck up on him. He studied the lady, trying to figure out why she affected him so much. In those few seconds, he caught something in her stance, in the tilt of her head. Both definitely reminded him of Diane. His gaze narrowed and he noted more similarities. His slow, resigned sigh came out in one long breath. He damn well didn't need reminders of the worst time of his life, so he damn well had to keep his distance.

"Come on, let's go." He refused to be taken in by those beguiling eyes that yanked on his insides every time their gazes met. They started off in the direction of her house.

Sin didn't speak while walking. Every now and then, his gaze wandered over her and the same question kept gnawing at his soul. If Avery Montgomery felt the same attraction and acted on it, would she prefer her hero if he came back to life? It was such a stupid thought, and really had no bearing, but he couldn't dislodge it from his brain.

The sizzling attraction he'd felt with Diane had swayed him, but not her. Great sex hadn't been enough to hold his wife once her hero had reappeared. Nor had the fact that she and Sin had made a baby together. Was Avery like Diane? Was it his destiny to be attracted to those who would always see him as second best, behind wealthy heroes?

She's only a woman. A means to an end, nothing more. You can do this. He threw out a mental snort. If that were true, then why was he disappointed he wasn't going to play bodyguard?

"Damn," he muttered. Was he a glutton for punishment, just shoveling it in, not caring how much pain he might endure? He'd bet big money Avery Montgomery was cut from the same cloth as Diane, the colors and weave identical. It had to be the reason he felt such a strong attraction. He didn't doubt Avery held secrets, just like Diane had.

Even Des thought she was hiding something. He only had to remember that.

~

"You're awfully quiet. Is everything all right?" Avery observed Mr. Sinclair once they reached her front porch. The entire walk had been made without a word between them. For some reason, his silence bothered her and she had no idea why.

"Everything's fine." He gave a careless lift of his shoulders, not meeting her eyes, a sure sign everything *wasn't* fine. "Don't have anything to say, so why waste time. Small talk's not my thing."

"I see." He was definitely a peculiar man. Then, she shrugged. What difference did it make? She'd never see him again.

"Well." She stuck out her hand. "Thank you for everything."

He looked at her hand and a sardonic smile touched his face. "What's this, a dismissal?"

"I'm just trying to be polite, but I can see manners aren't your thing either."

His grin stretched. "You got it." He nodded to her front door. "But I'm not a total ass. I'll wait here until you're inside, safe and sound."

A burst of laughter rose up. "Thanks." Still smiling, Avery turned, rushed up the steps, and reached into her bag for her keys. She couldn't help liking both men. They seemed genuine. Something about them made her feel comfortable, despite the attraction she felt for Mr. Sinclair. Who knew what would happen if she was anyone other than who she was and not some guilt-driven lunatic? She stuck the key into the lock. The thought dissolved when she turned the key.

The dead bolt was already unlocked.

A streak of unease climbed up her spine.

She was sure she'd locked it. Or had she?

She glanced over her shoulder and her concern must have shown in her face because all humor left his expression.

"Is everything okay?"

"Sure. Just fine." She offered her perfected fake smile and nodded. "Thanks again."

"Remember, Mrs. Montgomery. Call us if you need us." He then sauntered toward the street and a parked car.

Avery hurriedly pushed her way inside and looked around. Sunlight illuminated the foyer and living room, the hardwood floors gleaming. The room was as neat and tidy as she'd left it with not an item out of place that she could see. As she slowly made her way through the house, everything appeared normal. She stepped into her bedroom and breathed a little easier after finding the room undisturbed, just like the others. In her home office, she flipped on her computer, hidden in an alcove. The monitor came alive. She rolled out the black leather desk chair, sat, and began tapping the keyboard to go online with intentions of a more detailed search of

SPC Electronics and its principal owners.

Two hours later, a good-looking, clean-cut man in a suit and tie stood in front of Avery after she opened the door in response to the bell. The thirties-something guy flashed a badge along with a disarming grin.

"Detective Frank Keyes, ma'am. Des Phillips asked me to stop by."

"Of course." She stood aside and held the door open. "Won't you please come in?"

"Thank you. Des mentioned something about an altercation last night at Arlington National Cemetery. Arlington's military property and out of county jurisdiction, but I'll be happy to file a report."

"I appreciate your time and any help you can offer." She took the card he held out and shut the door, noting a bulge under his jacket that could only be a gun and shivered. In less than twenty-four hours, guns and bullets seemed to permeate her life. Mike, who'd been a trained warrior, would have been very comfortable in this situation, but Avery didn't like the idea of being smack in the center of a mystery, not with her son so close.

Did Mike's death have something to do with what was going on?

Doubts now filled her, especially after her meeting this morning and her online sleuthing. The more she learned about SPC Electronics and its owners, the more she wondered.

She smiled at the officer and pushed her thoughts to the side. "So, how do you know Mr. Phillips?" she asked, leading him toward her sofa.

"He and I were rookies together. We even ended up being partners for a couple of years before I transferred. He quit the force soon after."

"Oh?" Avery didn't know any cops. Her sister had dated one, but she'd never met him. This detective came across as being quite competent, just as Mr. Sinclair and Mr. Phillips had.

"Yeah." He grinned. "I'm still a flatfoot and he's now head of security for a big company with a job title that sounds better than detective. Makes more money, that's for damn sure." He pulled a Blackberry out of his pocket, sat on the edge of her sofa, and glanced expectantly at her. "So, tell me what happened."

Twenty minutes later, both stood.

Detective Keyes shoved his device into his pocket. "Well, like I said earlier. A shooting at Arlington's not something I can follow up on, but I'll make sure an officer patrols the area more often. This'll go into a database, but too often stuff gets buried, so I recommend reporting the incident to someone in charge at the cemetery. If you have any trouble, my cell number's on my card."

She nodded her thanks and watched his retreating back, wondering if she should call Colonel Williams. He might have more manpower to protect her. The minute the thought was out, she dismissed it. She didn't like dealing with the man. Or the military. Not when their needs had always come first to Mike. Now that her husband had died, she'd rather avoid anything to do with either one.

Avery closed the door and threw the dead bolt.

Eyeing the lock, she rubbed her arms to ward off her unease. She glanced around her empty, lonely house. An intense rush of isolation hit her.

She paced, practically wearing a rut into her polished oak floor.

Face it, Av. Mike's gone and your stupidity can't be undone. Why make it worse with more self-loathing? Will that help Andy?

Of course it wouldn't. She'd spent so long pretending everything was fine. But the old tactic did no good now, she realized, as all four walls closed in, along with the feelings of hurt and sorrow. She could no longer stay inside this house, rehashing more guilt, more disappointment. Not over something she couldn't change.

Avery grabbed her purse, only this time she made a mental note of flipping the dead bolt into place on her way out. Since Andy wouldn't be home for hours, she'd force herself to enjoy the late May weather, if only to be a more effective mother when her son did come through that front door.

On the bottom porch step, she held her face toward the sun. Warmth spread, making her feel alive as she walked. Birds chirped and insects buzzed. The scent of lilacs and roses wafted past her nostrils. She glanced around and noted distinct colors in the green grass and trees that contrasted so sharply to the blue in the sky. Even the few fluffy clouds appeared as if they were outlined in white against such a vivid backdrop.

Noisy tourists lined the streets, laughing and snapping pictures.

Avery smiled. For the first time in two months, hope surged

inside of her. Made her think she could work past her guilt, at least for now. As she wound her way among strangers, it was impossible to hold on to the dark emotion on such a glorious day with so many happy people around.

With no purpose in mind, Avery continued walking the streets of Washington, D.C.

"Stand over there, Billy."

The shout interrupted her thoughts and she looked up. A mom was lining up her kids to take a picture using the Whitehouse as a background.

Avery glanced at her watch, shocked that it was time to turn around in order to meet Andy's bus. For over two hours she hadn't thought once about guilt or sadness.

The walk back was made in a similar frame of mind until she approached her block. A strange sensation tickled the back of her neck.

She halted and slowly pivoted.

An eerie silence pervaded the now empty street, giving her the heebie-jeebies.

"Stop it," she said under her breath. "There's no one behind me. There's no one watching me." After last night, her mind seemed to work in overdrive. The closer to her house she walked, the more her unease grew.

At the bus stop, the feeling dissipated when Mary strode up. Her fear, however, remained as the two women chatted.

Something was going on and that something had to do with her visit to the cemetery and those shots fired. Avery's intuition wouldn't let her think otherwise. She *was* smack in the middle of this, just as Mr. Phillips had suggested. His crazy offer popped into her thoughts, which suddenly seemed more reasonable now than earlier, especially with Andy and his safety added to the mix. Maybe they could help each other out.

Her mind waged a bitter battle as her son and Tommy blasted out of the bus minutes later.

Her reaction to Mr. Sinclair was the biggest hurdle that caused her to question her judgment. How could she even consider the idea of allowing perfect strangers to guard her home? Okay, not perfect strangers. Googling had given her plenty of background information. And Detective Keyes had spoken highly of all of SPC's owners, not just his ex-partner. She had to admit, she'd feel safer with men like Mr. Sinclair and Des Phillips around. Both seemed as if they could handle unknown threats.

But what if she were wrong and their presence affected Andy's safety? Would she be making a bigger mistake? What a dilemma. Maybe she could talk them into guarding outside.

Andy's chatter about his day interrupted her thoughts, and she glanced up to see Tommy and Mary waving their good-byes.

Avery and her son started for the house, with him still talking. The entire time they walked, her mental war continued raging.

Chapter 5

"Face it guys, the widow isn't cooperating and we can't do much about it." Sin paced in an effort to still pent-up energy, wishing he knew more. He glanced at Des, sitting behind his desk. Eric stood in the doorway. "Williams thinks I was chasing shadows at the cemetery, so I should follow his advice and check in with Scotty."

"Oh yeah." Eric stepped further into the room. "I meant to tell you the minute you came back from lunch. He called while you were out."

Sin focused on Eric with eyebrows raised. "Maybe he's learned something useful."

"Bingo. Tried your cell, but didn't leave a message. Figured you'd be back soon enough. Anyway, he hacked into a battalion computer and found some interesting shit."

Sin chuckled and rubbed his hands together. Scotty McNeil was a brilliant constant. If left to his own resources, he always came through doing what he did best, manipulate computer technology to his advantage. He grabbed a chair and sat. "Maybe now we're finally getting somewhere."

Eric nodded. "Wanted me to give you a heads-up. E-mailed you a message, since he couldn't get a hold of you. He was shutting off his cell phone to get a few hours of sleep."

Sin looked at his watch and sighed. "It's too late to call Afghanistan."

He tapped his foot impatiently, annoyed at the nine-hour time difference, then scooted his chair around and indicated with his hand for Des to move his monitor and keyboard closer. "Might as well check e-mail." He began typing as Des leaned closer and Eric moved to stand behind him.

"Looks like Scotty hit pay dirt." Sin whistled, after reading the gist of the file along with his partners. "Williams definitely held out on us."

"That bastard," Des said. "Why keep this information from us?"

Sin only shook his head and continued reading the more

inclusive accounting that focused on the investigation of one man. Private First Class Manuel Esperanza, one of the two soldiers who'd been injured while riding in the jeep the night Montgomery and Marshall died. He'd also been on CQ duty the week before in the battalion headquarters. Charge of Quarters duty gave him full access to the area.

"Still, it's only circumstantial," Sin murmured, voicing the thought. "The prototypes were locked in a safe when not in use, and Esperanza's injuries warranted medical attention just as Scotty's had."

"Then why is the PFC missing, presumed absent without leave?" Eric asked.

Des snorted. "Yeah, he's AWOL, so it's no coincidence they have no other major leads."

"Pity it takes hacking into our country's military secrets to finally have a solid direction in which to search." Sin couldn't muster any remorse for Williams and his operatives. They obviously didn't think much of him or his partners, totally underestimating them and their abilities. Everyone underestimated Scotty, saw only what Scotty wanted to show, which was why Sin had sent him to Afghanistan in the first place.

"The colonel must not realize who he's dealing with." Eric's tone held a bit of contempt.

Sin silently agreed. His team didn't always play by the rules if they could get away with it, especially when those rules impeded their progress. None of them had achieved this level of success by adhering to rules those in charge put into place. Rules created, in his opinion, to benefit the creators to keep others—like himself and his partners—from catching up with them. Sin had no qualms with using a stolen file if it produced results.

Scotty wouldn't leave any trace of his break-in. He'd sent his message using SPC's technology, one Scotty created, after which no sign of the message would exist once Sin deleted it on his end. He'd go a step further and wipe any evidence of his deletion from the hard drive as well as his phone.

Williams wasn't the only thorough man.

His attention went back to the file. His memorizing gaze skimmed the page. When done, Sin tapped his pen and let his thoughts flow. "Do you think Williams believes this Esperanza took the CD case, or at the very least knew who did?" he asked aloud when no one spoke for an extended moment. Esperanza's next of kin lived outside of Baltimore, south of the city.

"Gets my vote," Eric said. "Especially after reading Scotty's comments."

Typed in red at the bottom of the last page: *That's where he may be headed.* The sentence below it was underlined and bolded: *Esperanza's a lead. No one can get in and out of the two countries without some kind of assistance.*

"No wonder the colonel doesn't want us investigating if Esperanza's planning on being this close to D.C.," Des said. "What if he's in on the other thefts too?"

"Hmmm." Sin couldn't see a connection, but that didn't mean there wasn't one. He closed the file then did his deletes. While the computer churned, the ticking clock drew his gaze. "I need to talk to Scotty before forming a conclusion." He scooted his chair back into place and stretched out his long legs. His thoughts drifted to the woman who hadn't been far from his consciousness. "Mrs. Montgomery is the key to all of this. I just know it."

"Interesting." Eric's eyes got rounder.

"Yeah." Des gave a rundown of their breakfast. "We struck out. The lady doesn't trust us." A grin replaced his scowl and he nodded to Sin. "Especially him."

Eric gave a soft whistle. "Even more interesting." His expression turned speculative. "What about Williams? You're not going to tell him about Scotty's message or about the shots last night at the cemetery?"

Sin's head moved slowly from side to side. "Not on your life. Something's not right with him." The logical technician inside his brain told him this. His knack for computers, and all that chip technology offered, made him a wealthy man, but logic had always been his main tool, one he relied on now. His lack of experience in dealing with government contracts became too obvious, making him a tad nervous. "I don't trust the colonel, not enough to risk bankruptcy," he admitted. "I'm beginning to think we've made a huge mistake, venturing into this new project. No way I'll let that asshole stop us from saving our company."

No, Sin wasn't willing to roll over and play dead like some dog wanting a pat on the head. Not when he and his friends had spent years building a solid reputation and were finally ready to reap the rewards of all their hard work.

~

"Wait up, McNerd."

"Shit," Scotty McNeil muttered, halting just before entering the officer's mess hall. He looked back. Captain Marring waved and hurried in his direction.

"It's McNeil." He pushed his heavy-framed black glasses higher on his nose, having no choice but to wait. The moron had information about his departure.

Glancing around at the desolate landscape, he wiped at the sweat beading on his brow. His undershirt was already saturated with moisture. Hot. It was fricking hot and everything in this country was brown. Dirt and sand-colored mountains, with a few palm trees thrown in, were what you got in Afghanistan, once outside the cities. Here in the boonies it was like living in caves. How anyone could stay here so long to fight in such an ugly, desolate part of the world was a mystery to him.

If he never saw the desert again, it would be too soon. His focus moved to the dining room he was about to enter. Nor would he miss the drab brown space where he ate drab food...three times a day. How did they do it? The same shit...over and over? Their daily routine never changed. Why would anyone want to be an officer in today's US Army or Marines? In a reflexive move, he rubbed his upper arm, easing the ache from his minor injury.

It might have been fun to play Rambo in the beginning of this stint, but with the monotony added to the dangers, he realized the draw of playing spy wasn't enough to do it long term. He admired those who did it day in and day out, but some took themselves much too seriously, namely one, he amended when the GI Joe wannabe finally caught up.

"Colonel Anderson said you needed transportation at nineteen hundred."

Nineteen and subtract twelve. Okay, he was leaving at seven o'clock. Why couldn't he just say that? Just goes to show, once a frickin' jarhead, always a frickin' jarhead.

"I take it you're in charge of getting me to the airfield?" Scotty flashed a sardonic grin at Captain Kenneth Marring, "Kenny" to his fellow officers and friends. Using his first name was something he'd never agree to. He hated the Marine officer, and his hatred was deep-seated.

"Yeah, I'm on geek patrol, so I'll be driving. It's my job to make sure you get on the plane." Marring pushed ahead of him like it was his due. "Can't say I'll be sorry to see you go. In fact, I'll breathe easier since your stench will depart with you on the plane out of here."

Scotty ignored the insult and followed *Kenny,* who stood a good eight inches taller than his own five-foot-six-inch frame. The guy outweighed him by at least seventy-five pounds.

"You'll be happy to know I share your sentiments." The screen door slammed shut behind him. "But I beg to differ on the cause of the stench."

They headed in the direction of the food line.

Army cooks had been up well before dawn, preparing the same drab breakfast they made every morning. What he wouldn't give for a mimosa or eggs Benedict. Scotty grabbed a tray and silverware, eyeing Marring and noting his starched brown desert BDUs with creases in all the right places. There was something fricking unnatural about a soldier who didn't sweat, who appeared too fricking fresh on this fricking hot morning.

"I can't say I'm sorry to go." Scotty couldn't wait to get out of this hellhole and away from this jerk. He had no use for morons like the captain who thought their shit didn't stink because they could kill the enemy. He'd been dealing with his type since grade school when, as a scrawny kid, he'd received his first pair of glasses and earned the despised nickname *four eyes.* Muscle-bound jocks like Marring were all the same, all thought the world owed them because they were some kind of gifted gods. Though he was sure the *god* in front of him thought differently, he was the gifted one, but the guy was too stupid to appreciate it. To get even for all the *McNerd* and *four eyes* taunts, Scotty loved playing mental games with his adversaries. Marring was the perfect diversion because the man never even realized a game was in play half the time.

"Private First Class Manuel Esperanza. Tell me about him," Scotty said, unable to resist extending his game a bit longer and laughing inwardly at the spark of recognition in Marring's eyes before it disappeared. A quick second was all he'd needed to see he'd hit pay dirt. Of course, he knew he would. Marring was so predictable.

"Thanks, Gibbons." Scotty offered a friendly salute, took his usual plate of eggs over easy from the PFC, and added sausage and toast. Then he grabbed a cup of coffee before walking toward the table full of other officers, giving them a nod. Their conversations died instantly.

He pulled out a chair and sighed, so totally used to their behavior. He was the outsider, the liberal geek with the PhD from UC Berkley. They had nothing in common and if there was commonality in their backgrounds, Scotty kept the barriers up, unwilling to make a connection for personal reasons.

"Why'd you mention Esperanza?" Marring asked cautiously, sitting beside him.

Scotty grinned. Like stealing a baby's ball, he thought. "I hear he's vanished. Gone AWOL." His grin died and he looked around. "Though I can't see why anyone would be so stupid as to leave the protection of the American forces out here."

"Not AWOL. He's listed as missing."

"Oh? My sources must be wrong." Scotty's smile spread as Marring's back stiffened, telling him he'd hit another nerve and making him wonder if a person had to be military to wear that rod up his butt. "Still, where could he go? We're not exactly in friendly territory and even if we were, the desert's not my idea of heaven." He shook his head and ate a bite of food, chewing thoughtfully before adding, "I can't wait to get back to the States and see green…in the grass…in the leafy trees. D.C. should be green…I mean, it does rain there in the spring and cherry blossoms are a hell of a lot prettier than sandy, rocky dirt. Thank God I'm out of here. How about you guys? Anyone going home soon?" As intended, his comments threw the conversation in another direction—the amount of time left on their tours of duty.

"Your tour's almost up, isn't it, Kenny?" Henderson, another captain, asked.

"You got it. I'm a short-timer. Twelve days and counting. Then you'll have to get used to not seeing my ugly mug," Marring replied, before picking up his cup of coffee and taking a drink, seeming to forget all about the PFC. "I'm thinking of adding to my commitment."

"I got eighty-five days," said a first lieutenant at the end of the table.

Another shouted, "I have fifty-two."

Scotty noted they all made the countdown in days. For some reason, saying one hundred and eighty days must seem much shorter than saying six months. *Mind games.* Even these courageous gods of war played them to survive their surroundings.

"So you're going back to D.C.?" The question came from Major Bodin, one of the quieter officers. "Is that where you're from?" He rarely spoke, always showing interest when he did, and because of that Scotty felt more affinity with him than anyone else at the table.

"No." He offered a sincere smile. "I grew up in the Bay area. San Jose, about an hour south of San Francisco. I lived in Santa Clara before moving to D.C."

"That's a pretty area. It's green there too, as I recall."

"Yeah. Greener than here, that's for sure," Scotty agreed. Northern California had its own terrain, with varying verdant shades as the dominant colors. So he was used to green.

"Afghanistan's not so bad. It's just different."

"Different, meaning brown." Despite hating the ugly, barren color of this region and wanting only to step onto the plane this evening, one thing spoiled his return to the states. He still hadn't found the Xcom2s, which were his conception. The military had reported the ambush as incidental, a common occurrence having nothing to do with the disappearance, a reasonable assumption. Yet, Scotty had only one reason for leaving Kandahar behind empty-handed.

The prototypes' trail led to Baltimore and he intended to follow.

~

"This is Captain Marring," he said, leaning back when the call was answered. "Colonel Williams wanted an update on McNeil. He'll be on a transport leaving for Landstuhl at nineteen hundred hours and I'll personally escort him to his ride." A smile worked its way over his face. "He should be back in the States within forty-eight hours, depending on what's available in Germany."

"Anything else? Any sign of the missing prototypes?"

"No, sir." Marring's smile died as quickly as it formed. He sat up straight and cleared his throat. "We haven't confirmed any interest. Everything's quiet. It's almost as if they never existed."

"Look harder. They exist and someone has an interest. The

same someone stole them right out from under our noses. Colonel Williams won't let this rest until he discovers what happened to them."

"We are looking hard, just haven't had any luck, is all. But they'll surface. They always do." He was just about to hang up when he remembered McNeil's question in the mess hall. "This may or may not be important, but I thought it worth mentioning. McNeil brought up Esperanza."

"Hmmm." The line went quiet for a moment. "I wonder why he'd bring him up, unless he suspects something."

"Who knows with that nerd? He probably threw the name out, baiting me like he usually does, just to see what I'd do. Most likely he's been talking with the enlisted men, asking questions, and discovered he's missing. I'm surprised they'd speak so openly, but the information isn't classified and the little weasel is nosy as well as tenacious."

"Then, it's probably nothing. I'll relay your message that he's leaving. I'm sure Colonel Williams will be relieved."

"Makes two of us. I'll be glad when the asshole is out of here. He gives me the willies."

~

Colonel Williams hit the keyless lock on his car, then headed at a brisk pace in the direction of his office, intending to get a jump start on his busy day. His ringing cell phone stopped him in midstride. He pulled it out of his pocket and looked around as he hit the On button. "Yes."

"You asked me to give you an update from Afghanistan when it came through."

"Okay. I'm listening." He resumed walking. "Tell me what's happening with McNeil. I don't trust the bastard."

"He's leaving Kandahar, just as you wanted."

"Have you been monitoring his e-mails? His phone calls?"

"Of course. They're benign. Just the usual stuff."

"And he hasn't sent anything recently?" he asked, slowing as he came to the walkway leading into the building.

"No, none I'm aware of. Why?"

Williams ignored the question. "Did Marring say anything else?"

"What's going on that you're not telling me?"

"Nothing. I'm just being cautious." He sighed heavily and his gaze focused on several people making their way from the parking garage to the walkway. He turned away and lowered his voice. "Could McNeil use another means to get a message out?"

"Possible, but improbable. He doesn't have a lot of options given his location."

"That's not good enough. My source tells me he sent something to Sinclair last night. I need to know exactly what. So far he's acting as predicted, but I don't want any surprises. Do you understand?"

"Yes." The line went dead before crackling to life again a moment later. "This might have something to do with it. Marring stated that McNeil mentioned Esperanza. But like I said, there's nothing in his e-mails to SPC."

"And you didn't think this was important?" He swore under his breath. "What'd Marring do when he heard the name, and how the hell did McNeil make the connection?"

"He played it cool and didn't react, figuring it was a lucky guess."

"Lucky guess or not, I want McNeil watched more closely from now until the moment he steps on that transport. You got that? We can't afford to mess this up."

"Yeah, but I wouldn't worry about the guy. He'll be on a plane within hours, and according to Marring, he was obviously fishing. After all, Esperanza was present when the Xcom2s disappeared and now he's disappeared. McNeil's no dummy. Put two and two together, is all."

"I'll stop worrying when we find out exactly what happened the night Montgomery and Crandall died. Until then, I expect everyone to worry."

He closed the phone with the flick of his wrist. A moment later, he opened it and punched a preset number. "McNeil is leaving Afghanistan."

"You woke me out of a deep sleep to repeat something I reported to you?"

"I want to know about the message he sent last night and exactly what it said."

"Shit." Silence prevailed for extended seconds before he asked, "And how am I to get that information?"

Williams halted his steps again and glanced around. "I don't care how, just do it."

"Look, you told me my job entailed watching, listening, and reporting, which is what I've done. There's nothing in our agreement to include extracting information in such a manner."

"Then I'm changing our agreement."

"It'll cost you double."

"Fine. As long as you deliver, I'll pay," Williams replied in a low growl.

"It may take some time. In my opinion, the partners have closed ranks and are being extremely secretive now."

"I have faith in your abilities. It's why I hired you. Now I expect you to earn your money."

~

Jeremy Brubaker, AKA Jimmy Bond, turned off his cell phone and restrained the urge to hurl it across the room in a burst of temper after being awakened from a sound sleep. Working the graveyard shift sucked. How did people do it, night after night? He felt like a vampire and he'd only been on his current job for a few months.

"Dammit all," he muttered as he punched the pillow, lying back down and wrapping an arm around his head in an effort to get comfortable. Sleep would be impossible now. The colonel had hired him to infiltrate SPC Electronics and knew he'd pulled an all-nighter as SPC's guard. Hadn't they just talked not more than three hours ago? Maybe the man never slept—but not him. He functioned better with a solid night's—in his case—day's sleep.

He groaned. Couldn't Williams have waited a couple more hours before issuing his commands? This new ultimatum meant he'd have to be up earlier than normal for another all-nighter in order to do some digging.

He grinned, remembering his usual fifteen hundred a day had just doubled. He had no real complaints, especially since he could add the twelve bucks an hour he made from SPC as a bonus.

Hell, it sure beat sitting outside someone's townhouse at midnight, waiting to snap a picture of some asshole cheating spouse leaving some hot babe of a mistress to go home to dull wifey-pooh. Still, the assholes usually went home before one, so he could be in bed by two.

He closed his eyes, planning a way to satisfy Williams without getting caught. One thing he'd learned. SPC's partners were no pushovers. In fact, he felt a weird kinship with them. They were human, didn't put on airs of being better than everyone despite being successful business owners. Even called him by his first name. Most of the people he'd worked with over the past few years seldom remembered he even had a name, much less used it in such a personal manner.

When he'd first started this job, he didn't know what to think, had the lowest opinion of the three men, given the nature of his employer. They had to be doing something wrong for a US Army colonel to hire him to spy. Jeezus H. Christ. He *was* James Bond. He chuckled softly at the name he'd chosen for this gig. When his thoughts returned to SPC's principals, his smile died.

What the hell have I gotten myself into?

He fluffed the pillow and turned over. Best to try to get some sleep. He had a niggling feeling that tonight, he'd damn well find out.

Chapter 6

"So what now?" Sin asked Des the next morning.

His partner had just gotten off the phone with his detective friend. They hadn't heard from Avery Montgomery, nor had they heard another word about their stolen products.

Everything was quiet. Too quiet. Scotty was stuck at Landstuhl AFB awaiting transport to the U.S., and Des had no other leads.

"Frank said he put in a good word on our behalf to Mrs. Montgomery." Des sighed. "He also advised her to go through the military and report the incident. If she does, we're screwed."

"We're already screwed." Sin wiped his face in frustration. "She seemed to like you. Maybe you can get her to go out to dinner if you ask nicely once her kid is off at camp, and I'll give her house a quick once-over." He certainly didn't want to date her. Not when every time he got within ten feet of her, he acted like a sixth-grader with his first crush. Nor did he want Des to, but they had to do something. In five days and a few extra hours, SPC would come crashing down around him because the money to remain solvent would be gone forever.

Des' cell phone rang. He glanced down and smiled. "It's the widow."

Sin's eyebrows rose and he listened intently as Des spoke.

"Good morning, Mrs. Montgomery. I trust everything's okay?" His brow furrowed as she spoke. "Really?" He waited a few seconds, then nodded. "Sure. We can work something out. Why don't Sin and I stop by?" He checked his watch. "Say, in an hour?" Des pressed the Off button and looked up, grinning. "The lady's a little spooked and is asking if we'd be interested in guarding outside her house." He shrugged. "It's a start."

"A damn good start." Sin stood to leave. "Let me clear my schedule and talk to Eric about clearing his. Between the three of us, we can work out a guard duty schedule." He laughed. "Hell, maybe in a day or so, she'll let us inside. And if not? We'll just have to figure out a good time to break in and satisfy our curiosity."

~

"So we're agreed? You'll do it?"

Mrs. Montgomery's hopeful glance met Sin's and then moved to Des' face. Noting the relief in her voice, Sin tamped down a surge of jealousy when Des gripped her hand resting on the arm of her chair and squeezed reassuringly.

"Of course we'll do it." Des smiled. "Didn't we say we'd help?"

Over coffee in Avery Montgomery's living room, the three devised their plans. Sin would take the first watch, as Des called it, and would stay until Eric relieved him around four. Eric would stay until eight when Des took over. The partners would all take turns.

Somehow they'd agreed that Sin would spend the first night watching her house from his car. All Des' doing, a human steamroller leveling every one of his or Avery's objections. He never imagined his friend could be so charming and cajoling, so convincing and unwavering. Definitely a protective side Sin had never seen before as the green-eyed monster festered inside his gut. That Des cared enough to offer their services so freely shouldn't bother him. But it did.

The trio eventually drifted to Avery's front door. Sin remained on the porch with her while Des said his good-byes and jogged down the wooden steps in the direction of his SUV.

"Since small talk's not your thing, I won't say a word if you decide you'd like another cup of coffee," Avery said, drawing his attention. "It's the least I can do since you'll be spending hours in your car, guarding." Though a little early for lunch, she offered, "I can also make a sandwich."

"No thanks. I'm fine." He'd let Des or Eric do the wining and dining for information. As for him? He thought it best to avoid all chumminess. His nod indicated his car at the curb. "I'll be right over there." He turned to go.

"If you change your mind, let me know."

Something in her tone stopped him. On the last step, Sin glanced back. Her sad expression tugged at him. She seemed almost disappointed he was rushing away. He dragged a hand through his hair and rubbed his neck, sighing. Why was he letting those expressive brown eyes conveying so much anguish get to him? Unable to ignore that puppy-dog yearning, he nodded. "On second thought, I'd love a sandwich. And maybe another cup of coffee."

"Great."

Suddenly he felt as if he'd granted her some awesome gift. "Maybe we can eat outside and enjoy the day," he added, knowing he shouldn't. Hell, if it hadn't already been a beautiful, sunny day, the smile she threw his way would have changed the weather.

"How about the deck? It's right this way." She led him through the hallway.

While walking, Sin looked around, noting her taste and trying to get a feel for her from the surroundings. The interior was immaculate throughout. She obviously spent a lot of time cleaning and decorating. He liked the muted colors and traditional furniture. The older house was brick, prevalent in the neighborhood, but the kitchen had been updated with new appliances and countertops.

Now outside, he sat at the deck table. This time of the morning it was still shady, so he didn't put up the umbrella.

Within minutes, Mrs. Montgomery placed a steaming cup of coffee and a roast beef sandwich in front of him.

"Thanks," he murmured.

"I'll be right back with mine."

She hurried back into the house and soon sat across from him, the warm smile on her face still telling him this was more than just eating lunch. The sadness he saw lurking in her eyes brought out a sensitivity he hadn't known existed, and made him want to do something besides scarf down food to cheer her up. He polished off the first half of his sandwich, then began on the second, trying to think of how to start a coherent conversation. Nothing came to mind, so he remained silent.

When the food was gone and he was almost done drinking his coffee, he cleared his throat.

"Look, I've been thinking."

"Yes?" She looked up at him expectantly.

Sin swallowed hard at the warm smile she bestowed upon him, as if his thoughts really mattered. "Yeah. I'm really sorry about that kiss."

"You have no reason to be sorry. It was more my fault than yours." Her smile turned a bit sheepish. "I wasn't myself."

"Neither was I." His grin stretched at the apt excuse. Then, he sobered. "Not my finest moment, taking advantage of you like that. I really did get carried away."

She laughed. The sound of it wrapped around his insides and

squeezed. Damn, he wished he'd stayed away. He should get up now and go before he made a bigger fool of himself. Sitting across from her and pretending he didn't find her attractive was hard.

Following his mental urgings, he pushed away from the table and stood. "Well, thanks for the food and the company." He nodded. "I'll be out front if you need me."

"No problem. I appreciate your being here."

He felt the heat of her gaze on his back as he walked toward the fence gate. He heaved a sigh of relief when he unlatched the gate and closed it behind him.

All the way to his car he wondered why he didn't want to leave her.

~

Avery watched Mr. Sinclair's departure as a surge of disappointment over his apparent disinterest filled her. She snorted as self-derision seeped into her consciousness. Like he found her attractive and like she should even be thinking such thoughts.

Remember, Av, he's a stranger, here for one purpose only. To find his missing prototypes.

Surely she didn't care whether or not he stayed and kept her company. Was she that pathetic? She glanced at her empty house and felt a surge of loneliness she couldn't contain with pretense. She sighed and began clearing the lunch dishes. Cleaning the kitchen would occupy her thoughts for a while. Then she could read or watch TV, anything to keep from thinking of Mr. Sinclair sitting in a car in front of her house.

She rolled her eyes. She really was pathetic, either filled with guilt over her actions or filled with ideas of wanting more, never satisfied with what she had.

Don't think about it. Thankfully, she was able to push the thoughts aside and stayed busy with cleaning the kitchen.

"Come in," Avery said, answering the knock at the door hours later, glad that her torture had ended with this partner's arrival. "I assume you're Mr. Coleman?"

"Yeah. I thought I'd introduce myself. I'm taking over for Sin." He offered a boyish grin too engaging to ignore. The man actually had dimples. "And the name's Eric. Mind if I call you Avery?"

"No, you can't call her Avery," Mr. Sinclair said, drawing her attention behind Mr. Coleman. She hadn't realized he'd followed his partner up the porch stairs. A dark, almost menacing scowl covered his face. "She prefers Mrs. Montgomery." He crossed his arms, almost growling.

Mr. Coleman laughed. "I think I'll let the lady decide, if you don't mind."

"I do mind. Let's keep this professional." He nodded to her. "I just wanted to let you know I was taking off. I'll be back around midnight."

Avery returned the nod and smiled. "Thank you. I'll see you then."

"Well, he's not a in a very sociable mood." Mr. Coleman's gaze followed hers, as Mr. Sinclair strode in giant steps toward his car, almost running. "He must not have had his Wheaties this morning." He turned back to her. His smile, as well as his dimples, seemed to grow. "You're not really going to make me call you Mrs. Montgomery, are you?"

"I'm afraid so."

"Such an inhumane request. And from such a pretty woman, no less," he said with a tsk-tsk.

"I think it best. Especially for such a glib ladies' man." She grinned. "I fed Mr. Sinclair, and I have extra. Would you like a sandwich?"

"A sandwich sounds great, since I didn't get lunch."

"You can eat on the deck. It's through here, Mr. Coleman." She stepped aside, allowing him to enter.

"It's Eric."

"No. Mr. Sinclair was right. I prefer Mr. Coleman." *Definitely a ladies' man.* He was hard to say no to when he flashed those dimples. He darn well knew it too, she had no doubt.

"Why?" He waited, as she closed the door.

"What do you mean, why?" Avery stiffened slightly, eyeing him warily. "I need a reason?"

"No, but what's the big deal? We're both over twenty-one, and I'm thinking time will pass a little more pleasantly without all the Mr. and Mrs. stuff. Last time I called anyone Mrs., I was talking to my high school history teacher." He broke off and caught her gaze, his smile increasing a thousand watts in brilliance. "How 'bout it? Can I call you Avery? I like the name. Sounds much friendlier than Mrs. Montgomery."

"I wasn't aware of friendship being part of this." She fought the urge to return his smile. The guy was a charmer. Probably had all kinds of women eating out of his hand.

"One can never have enough friends, Avery."

She sighed, trying to act put upon when his expression told her he probably wouldn't back down on the formality. She should be annoyed, but she couldn't muster up the emotion.

"Friendship works." She headed for the back deck. "As long as you realize friendship is all we'll ever have."

He was clearly flirting with her, no doubt working to throw her off balance and unsettle her with his words. The owners of SPC were good at throwing her off balance, as she'd already discovered. So what if he was attractive...striking, even? Nothing in his features, in his demeanor, in the way he looked at her, disturbed her in the same way everything about Mr. Sinclair disturbed her. No, this good-looking partner didn't affect her at all, except to add color and excitement to her dull world.

What harm could come from a little flirting? It certainly seemed a better way to pass the time than feeling guilty and sad, wishing for things she shouldn't be wishing for.

"Ah, a challenge." The screen door slammed behind him. Eric strutted to the table, pulled out a deck chair and sat, then leaned back with one arm extending along the top of the cushion with such attitude, as if he belonged there. "I like that in a woman."

He stretched out both legs and crossed them.

"I'm sure you do." She laughed. Good grief! Most women would kill for those gorgeous eyes and long lashes, along with those eyebrows, which only acted as exclamation points, drawing attention to and highlighting their beauty. "Unfortunately, you're not my type."

So not her type. But he was unquestionably more approachable than Mr. Sinclair, with his easy charm and friendly smile.

He chuckled, then put his hand to his chest, pretending despair. "You wound me."

The picture of him grinning, his head topped with blacker than black hair, and those ebony eyes the color of dark roast coffee, almost as black as his jet black eyebrows now rising in such mock indignation, made it hard to take him seriously.

"Down, tiger, or I'll sic my son on you."

"That's right. I heard you have a son." Eric looked around the yard. "Where is he?"

"School, where most kids his age are this time of day. He'll be home in a half hour, when the bus drops him off. So, don't get too comfortable. Once he's here, things have a way of exploding."

Thoughts of Andy brought forth others she'd forgotten. Like Terry.

Heavens! How could she forget her sister? There was no way to hide Eric as Terry had planned to stop by on her way home from work, like she normally did. They'd always been close, always spent a lot of time together due to Mike's usual absences. Yet, since his death, Terry had been even more accessible, offering companionship and support.

What would she think of her guardians? Didn't take a rocket scientist to figure out Terry would tell her she'd lost her mind. Maybe she had. In her defense, the minute she'd made the decision to hire them, her earlier unease had abated, if not completely, then enough to allow her to breathe easier. Terry would just have to understand.

Avery scrutinized the obvious lady-killer lounging so casually across from her and another thought struck. What would happen when her sister met this hunk?

Terry viewed love as one big war game and men as an enemy to conquer, playing with the skill of a general. She took no prisoners, just left devastated male hearts in her path.

"I'll be right back with a sandwich," she said. "Might as well have a full stomach while you sit in your car, guarding." Heading inside, Avery stifled a laugh. What an interesting diversion it would be to see the man-eater versus the lady-killer in battle.

~

"Yoo-hoo! Av… Anyone home?" The voice came from the front of the house. "Where is everyone?"

"We're out here," Avery shouted, as Eric lunged for the football Tommy had tossed to him.

"My turn. My turn," Andy yelled.

Eric chuckled and waved. "Go long." Andy did, running to the corner of the yard. Eric threw it right to him. "Touchdown," Eric said, laughing. "You're going to be the next Jerry Rice with your speed and those magic fingers."

71

Andy scrunched up his nose. "Who's Jerry Rice?"

He tsk-tsked, shaking his head slowly. "In my opinion, he just happens to be one of the best receivers to come out of the NFL and you don't even recognize the name."

"What are you doing back here?" Terry came through the door and stopped dead in her tracks the instant she spied Eric.

Avery grinned, watching the assessing expression pass over her sister's features. Terry's gaze moved to hers, and her eyebrows arched with the obvious question. *Who's the hunk?*

"His name's Eric Coleman." Somehow, after Andy had charged through the door, he and Eric had connected. Despite her protests, Eric assured her his presence in the yard would go a long way to scaring off anyone lurking.

Andy certainly seemed to idolize him and enjoy the male influence.

"Eric Coleman? Hmm." Terry's attention slid back to him where it stayed for a while. Finally, she asked, "And why is he in my sister's backyard?"

"He's a friend and it's a long story." Noting the subtle change in her sister's interest after the friend comment, the word predatory flitted through Avery's brain. Oh yeah, the man-eater had just zeroed in on her next prey. She was positive Hall and Oates had Terry Howard in mind when they wrote their song. "I'm sure he's dying to meet you, too." She laughed. "Come on. I'll introduce you. He and Andy have become fast friends."

"Okay," Terry replied, her focus not wavering as she darted across the deck and down the stairs.

"Eric," Avery called. "There's someone I'd like you to meet."

He nodded, then threw the ball to Andy before sauntering in their direction. Slowing, his interested male gaze took an appreciative trip up and down Terry's body, clearly appreciating all her female assets.

"This is my sister, Terry Howard. Terry, this is Eric Coleman."

They shook hands, each eyeing the other with unconcealed speculation.

"Oh yeah," Avery murmured thoughtfully. They'd definitely provide a bit of entertainment. She grinned. Her sister ate tasty morsels like Eric Coleman for breakfast. Probably would consider Mr. Sinclair a late-night snack.

Her smile died.

For some reason, the thought of Terry doing anything with Mr. Sinclair chafed. He was hers. She'd make darn sure if anyone did anything with him, it would be her doing it.

Oh heavens, where had those thoughts come from? Embarrassment filled her, making her think she was slowly going insane. Mr. Sinclair and his friends were here for one reason and one reason only. To guard. They'd be gone in a few days and then she'd be back to her empty life.

Yet, Avery couldn't dismiss her son's laughter. She loved hearing the sound as he caught the football Tommy threw. He seldom laughed lately, which added to her original guilt. Now that she'd rejoined the living, she realized guilt had seemed to take on a life of its own, affecting both of them. For Andy's sake, she wanted more of his laughter in the house and that meant working past her guilt.

"Come on, Mr. Coleman. Go long," Andy yelled.

Eric glanced up, letting go of Terry's hand. "Duty calls. You ladies will have to wait your turn for my humble attention." Grinning, he ran a ways ahead and turned. "Okay, fire it in here, Jerry."

"The guy's a god. He's playing ball with your son, no less." Terry turned and locked gazes with her. "As I recall, Mike was never so attentive when he was home."

"Let's not discuss Mike's shortcomings, please. Not tonight."

"All right, if you don't want to talk about that, then tell me about Eric Coleman."

"Like I said, it's a long story. Come on and help with drinks and I'll fill you in."

"Lead on." Terry followed her into the kitchen.

"And that's it," Avery said, after giving a brief rundown of her experiences in the past forty-eight hours. "That's why he's here. He and his other two partners are taking shifts." She formed individual patties out of a pound of hamburger.

"Someone shot at you and you didn't tell me? And you think someone's been following you?"

When Avery nodded, Terry went over to the window and stared out at the three playing ball. "I don't like the idea of letting strangers into your house, Av. What do you know about them?"

"Quite a bit, actually. I did an online search and I know enough to feel comfortable. I told you, they're businessmen who have a vested interest in a product Mike was testing that's gone missing. No one knows what happened to it, and they believe someone thinks I do."

"You really think someone's following you?" When she nodded, Terry's expression turned skeptical. "What if they're doing it themselves, in order to scare you? Did you ever think of that?"

"It crossed my mind, but I don't think so."

"You don't?"

"No." Avery's chin went up. "I trust them. Besides, they're guarding outside."

"But why not go to the police?"

"I filed a report." Done with the patties, Avery washed her hands and replaced the meat with soft drinks from the refrigerator, pulling out several cans of soda as well as two juice boxes, and setting them on the counter. "But if I want more than beefed-up patrolling, that means going through the military."

"Okay. Then do it. Colonel Williams seems competent. Shouldn't you at least talk to him?"

"I'd rather not. For some reason I don't like him. Or trust him."

"And you trust that guy out there?" Terry's disbelieving nod indicated the yard.

"Yeah, I do. I trust them all. From the moment they started guarding this morning, I felt safer."

Her sister spent another long minute at the window before she shook her head and sighed. "And you say there are three partners? Are the other two as gorgeous as him? And exactly who did the saving? You never said."

"Well…" Avery cleared her throat, as the memory of *him* covering her infiltrated her brain. Heat infused her. Just the thought of kissing him had an embarrassed flush rising. She took a deep breath, shooting for an indifference she didn't feel. "Mr. Sinclair is the one who actually saved me, pushing me out of the way and to the ground."

"Mr. Sinclair?" Terry studied her face with the precision of one poring over a map looking for the best route, examining every possibility. "Why do I get the impression something's missing?"

"I told you what happened." Unable to hold up under such

scrutiny, Avery opened the cupboard and absorbed herself with its contents, so Terry wouldn't notice the bit of shame she couldn't keep out of her eyes. Terry knew her too well. "What could be missing?"

"Oh, I don't know. You tell me." She held up her hand, counting one finger at a time. "The man saves your life, then sends his partners to help protect you, and you say you trust him, yet you call him Mr. Sinclair. There has to be a reason you're distancing yourself."

"I thought it best to keep things from becoming too casual."

"Casual?" Terry nodded at the window. "Looks to me like casual is that man's middle name. You two certainly seemed on friendly enough terms, so why not with this Mr. Sinclair. If I didn't know any better, I'd say you have a crush on him." She stopped talking and glanced her way, a sudden knowing grin splitting her face in two. "That's it, isn't it? Oh my God! You like this guy. That's why you're so flustered." She clapped her hands and laughed, all but jumping up and down. "I never thought I'd see the day. Imagine! Someone other than Mr. Perfect attracting you. I was beginning to think you were a lost cause."

"I was a married woman. I would never cheat on my husband. You know that."

"Yes. I also know Mike had every opportunity to change and be the person you needed. I don't like bashing a man who can't defend himself, but face it, Av. You sacrificed yourself for nothing. He wasn't there for you." Terry's expression hardened. "You can't live the rest of your life feeling guilty for letting go of a dead relationship he never nurtured."

"I should've done more."

"What more could you have done? In my opinion, you gave him too much. From the very beginning, you idolized him. And for ten years, he lapped it up like it was his due."

"Our problems weren't entirely his fault. Distance and time took their toll."

"Plenty of marriages survive distance and time, but in order to do so, both parties need to work at it." Frowning, Terry met her gaze. "Can you honestly tell me Mike worked at it? Ever?"

"No." Avery shook her head, wishing the subject had never come up. Terry's words made her feel worse, like she'd been some sort of doormat. "But I never asked him to, either, so I'm just as responsible." Only she hadn't known how to change his attitude...how to make her feelings known, so she'd just accepted and pretended, easy to accomplish since he was rarely around. "He assumed everything was fine." Maybe on some weird level, she'd hoped her letter would have woken him up to her unhappiness. Maybe it had, but she'd never know for sure. "Besides, it doesn't matter now."

"You're right. But since we're talking so candidly, I have a question. What does *Mr. Sinclair* have that Marshall didn't have? He was one hunk who would've walked on hot coals for you, if you'd ever given him a chance." Terry sighed. "I could never figure out why you didn't give Mike the boot and grab on to him years ago."

Avery closed her eyes, reliving more guilt as the memory emerged of Mike's best friend who died alongside of him. Would she ever be free of the dark emotion?

Terry never understood her feelings, and probably never would. Marshall had been much more than a hunk. He'd become her true friend, someone to talk to. He'd seen the way Mike treated her, like she was some kind of ornament. A prize coveted that, once won, was put on the shelf, only taken down and shown off when it suited her husband, as Marshall had pointed out often enough the last few times she'd seen him.

Instinctively, she'd always known Marshall would have jumped in once she got the guts to tell Mike what was in her heart. Once she'd made the decision to leave her husband, she'd vowed never to give her heart to another man who was only around sporadically. Avery wanted more. Never again could she give everything to a charismatic man who cared too much about his work and not enough about his family.

Marshall had offered her no better an option than Mike had. Like Mike, he'd been married to his job. She'd liked him...even loved him in a brotherly way he'd have disdained, if he'd ever learned of her true feelings before he died. They'd never discussed them. She'd made it quite clear that such topics had been off limits. She'd taken her marriage vows seriously. She took sending her divorce papers just as seriously.

She didn't want to think about this. Not tonight.

"Let's not talk about Mike. Please?" Avery begged. "I don't

want to discuss Marshall either." Thinking about him made her feel guiltier, because in rejecting him, she'd known her worst fears had become reality. "Tonight, I just want to laugh with my son. Let go of the guilt enough to have fun with the man outside who'll never require anything more than flirtation."

If only she could rid herself of the guilt, life would be so much easier. She'd never wanted to hurt anyone. Not Mike. Not Marshall. But she had the e-mails and the letters to prove she'd inflicted pain on both men.

"I'm sorry, Av. I know I shouldn't preach." Terry gripped her hand and squeezed. "But I've bitten my tongue long enough. Some things just need to be said. You did what you had to do, so don't regret it. I know you don't believe this, but I seriously doubt your letter killed Mike. As hard as it is to accept, Mike just didn't give a shit about you or Andy enough to make me buy he'd let anything affect his mission. His actions over the years spoke too loudly."

Tears sprang to Avery's eyes as too many bad memories confirmed her sister's words. Still, she had his last letter. In it, he'd begged her to wait. So again, Terry didn't know the whole truth. "You don't understand," she whispered.

"Maybe not, but I hate seeing you torn up with guilt." Terry offered a sad smile. "Mike *did not* deserve you. He certainly never made you happy. I don't think I've seen you smile and laugh as carefree as you were outside in years. Nor do I think it's wrong to find someone else attractive after all you've been through. You deserve some happiness, Av. So does Andy." After giving her two cents, she turned and pushed through the kitchen door.

Avery wiped away her tears, then grabbed the tray of drinks and followed Terry outside, determined to think more positively, if only for her son's sake.

Eventually her sister left, and Andy got busy with a homework assignment for his last day at school. Eric went out to his car.

After grilling burgers, Avery took one out to him.

Mr. Phillips replaced Eric around eight and rather than come inside, he called to let her know he was in place and if she needed anything to let her know. Mr. Sinclair didn't call when he replaced Mr. Phillips at midnight. He simply sat in his car in front of her house.

Now at one forty-five, while perched on her bedroom window

seat, Avery watched him diligently eyeing her property. From this angle and bathed in pale moonlight, he appeared almost lonely.

She smiled, rejecting the idea. A guy like him wouldn't be lonely. Not like her.

Sighing, Avery wished she could ignore Terry's earlier words. Yet, her sister had voiced her concerns too many times in the last few years as well as months for Avery to dismiss them. She'd spent her twenties being a dutiful military wife and in doing so she'd given up expecting anything in return. Maybe Mike hadn't deserved her love and loyalty, but he didn't deserve to die in his prime fighting for his country either. Life seemed so unfair at times. Her son *had* deserved a full-time father just as she'd deserved a full-time husband.

Her hand went to her locket. She fingered the piece and stared out the window. A sad thought surfaced. Even if Mike had lived, she wondered if anything would have changed, despite his letter. She wanted to believe they would have, yet after Terry's honest appraisal, she knew better.

She stood as another truth hit. As crazy as it seemed, she felt safer knowing SPC's partners were watching, especially Mr. Sinclair. He appeared determined to protect her, but he didn't deserve to watch her house all night with his tall frame folded into an uncomfortable car. The least she could do was offer her sofa.

Avery slipped out the front door and headed down the porch steps. She halted on the walkway when she spied an empty car.

Listening, she pivoted. Where was he? Her heartbeat sped up. The fine hairs on the back of her neck rose. The same sensation she'd felt the day before swept over her.

Taking tentative steps, she slid into the shadows, then moved to the gate. She put her hand on the wood to open the latch just as it jerked out of her hand.

Her loud gasp broke into the quiet night and she flinched.

"What the—"

She looked up, frozen.

Angry green eyes stared directly into hers. "What're you doing out here?" Mr. Sinclair practically growled.

"You scared me." Avery placed her hand on her chest and took deep breaths, trying to still her heart's rapid beating.

"That doesn't answer my question."

"I came out to see if you wanted to come inside. The living room sofa's definitely more comfortable than a car." Noting the way he searched the terrain behind her, she asked, "What's wrong?" He now seemed more wary than angry.

"Nothing."

Ah, *nothing*. That explained *everything*. She smiled. Andy always used that explanation too, hoping to hide whatever it was that bothered him. The small connection gave her the courage to voice her thoughts. "It's not nothing, and you know it."

He eyed her for an intent moment. Then, he sighed and ran a hand through his hair. "I thought I saw something." His gaze roamed over her backyard, and he continued scrutinizing the dark shadows. Finally, he shrugged. "It was probably a cat or a raccoon." His attention returned to her. "You sure you don't mind if I sack out on your couch?" He rubbed his neck and stretched. "You're right about that damned car being uncomfortable."

"I wouldn't have offered if I minded." She offered another smile. "Come on. You look beat." Once inside, she glanced back at him. "I was going to have a snack. Chocolate chip cookies and milk always work to put me to sleep. Would you like to join me?"

"Sure. Why not." He shrugged and followed her to the kitchen.

"So you couldn't sleep?" He leaned against the counter as she pulled out the milk and grabbed the ziplock bag of cookies she'd baked earlier.

"No. I have too much on my mind to sleep tonight." He didn't need to know insomnia was a big part of her life. Avery unzipped the bag and set it in front of him, then opened the cupboard. While she finished pouring two glasses of milk, he reached for a cookie.

"Thanks." He took a bite and grinned. "I have a sweet tooth, so this hits the spot."

She returned his smile. "My remedy usually works." She offered a careless shrug. "Though I think the milk's better for sleeplessness than the chocolate." She bit off a chunk and chewed. After swallowing, she added, "But I have to admit, I love chocolate chip cookies. I'm lucky I'm not three hundred pounds considering my obsession for them."

He gave her a considering glance and if Avery didn't know better, she'd say there was a spark of attraction in those jade slits, sending a little thrill of excitement through her. She shook it off as he said, "Your secret's safe with me. I'll never tell that you're a closet cookie monster."

She laughed. "I can only return the favor." She motioned to lock her lips and tossed the key. "My lips are sealed. No one will learn of your sweet tooth from me."

"Pity," he murmured with his gaze zeroed in on her mouth. The spark was back, but only for a second before he lifted his glass of milk and sipped. After that he avoided looking at her, and she him, while they silently polished off their late-night snack and drank the rest of their milk.

"Bathroom's upstairs, second door on the right," she said later, after digging out a blanket and a pillow.

"Thanks." He accepted them and nodded. "I'll be gone around six when Des said he'd relieve me."

Avery left him to check on Andy, wondering what had drawn him out of his car earlier.

She slipped into bed, suddenly very glad of Mr. Sinclair's protective streak. As crazy as it seemed, his presence on her sofa gave her an added sense of security.

Chapter 7

"Is that your Mr. Sinclair?" Terry asked when the doorbell chimed the next evening.

"No," Avery stated firmly, rising. She and Terry were outside on the deck while Eric threw the football with Andy and Tommy again. Eric and her son had definitely formed a quick friendship. Avery shouldn't let him get too attached, but he'd be going to camp in a few days, and hopefully, by the time he got back she'd no longer need bodyguards.

"This guy is the former detective I told you about." She started for the screen door, wary of Terry's expression almost shouting that she was forming more questions about Jeffrey Sinclair. Why couldn't Terry just drop the subject?

Her sister jumped up and followed. "I'm not interested in former cops."

"Of course not." Avery noted the derision in her voice and smiled. Terry's one and only defeat in the game of love happened to belong at the hands of a detective. She rounded the hallway and headed for the front door. "I can't believe you hate all cops because of one lousy experience, though."

"I don't," Terry denied much too quickly. "I only want to know when *he's* taking a shift." Without falling for Avery's diversion, Terry's confident smile was back in place. "I'd like to meet this paragon."

Avery ignored her and opened the door. "You're prompt. Come on in."

"I try to be." Mr. Phillips grinned. "Where's Eric?"

"Out back. Two kids hijacked him again." Once he was inside, she nodded to her sister. "Desmond Phillips, meet Terry Howard."

His smile died and a different persona slid over his face.

"Ma'am," he murmured, offering a brief nod of acknowledgement, but his stiff movements and harsh expression held nothing of the charming man she remembered from the day before.

Her gaze flew to Terry. Lo and behold, Terry stood staring at the floor, just as stiff.

"Hello, Des," she said softly. "How nice to learn you're one of my sister's guardians. I didn't connect the name, otherwise I'd have warned her off more than I already did." After speaking, she did an about-face and stormed off.

Avery closed the door, having no idea of what had transpired in those few seconds. One thing she did pick up on—Terry had her own secrets.

"Sorry about her rudeness." Shrugging, she glanced at Mr. Phillips and granted her warmest smile. "Would you like a drink before you guard?"

"No, thank you." He shook his head. "I need to talk to Eric."

"Go on back."

"What was that all about?" Avery asked, coming up behind Terry once Mr. Phillips was out of sight.

"Nothing." She turned and left the room.

Avery sighed and went to get drinks, flinching when the upstairs bathroom door slammed shut, a good indication *nothing* wasn't quite the truth. She arranged an assortment on a tray, and pushed her way out the screen door to the backyard.

"Looks like everyone could benefit from a cold drink, especially you, Eric." Avery acknowledged both men who stood talking. She carried the tray full of drinks over to the table. "You're welcome to stay for dinner. You've certainly earned a meal. I'm grilling chicken. There's leftover potato salad that's usually pretty tasty on the second day."

"I'll take a juice box, Mrs. Montgomery, but I gotta get home." Tommy grabbed one and headed toward the back gate. "I'll see you tomorrow, Andy."

The kitchen screen door banged, drawing everyone's attention.

Terry proceeded to the grill, ignoring all stares and presented her back. She then placed the meat on the side, opened the lid, and turned on the gas.

"So, what's going on?" Eric asked Mr. Phillips a few minutes later, after receiving Avery's no in response to his query about whether she needed help with dinner.

"Nothing." Mr. Phillips' glare contradicted the one word.

Avery smiled. Apparently *nothing* was more commonly used than she'd thought.

"Don't give me that shit. Something's bugging you. You were yakking up a storm earlier in the office about how great the widow was and now you're standing around, scowling."

Pretending disinterest while she cooked, Avery tried not to eavesdrop, but her curiosity was too strong. She wanted to know what was up with Mr. Phillips too.

"In case you haven't noticed, I usually stand around and scowl."

"Too true." Eric chuckled, then sobered. "But answer me this. What's up with the sister?"

"What do you mean, what's up with the sister?" Mr. Phillips all but snarled.

"Des, you haven't taken your eyes off her." Eric grinned. "And I can't figure out why you're glaring. She's a looker."

"She's also a player."

"Even better in my mind." Eric's gaze sought Terry out. He watched her for several minutes, before saying, "I just want to make sure I don't step on any toes if I decide I want to spend a little time with her."

"You're asking me?" Mr. Phillips snorted. "You're a big boy, Eric. You don't need my permission for anything."

"Then why do I get the feeling that if I made a move toward her, you'd tear me apart?"

"I wouldn't waste the effort on someone like her."

"Yeah, right!" Eric grunted and lowered his voice. "I recognize the scent of male markings. It's the same territorial sign I got from Sin this morning, telling me he didn't like it when I flirted with Avery."

Avery was all ears once she heard her name, knowing she shouldn't, but unable to stop from listening now.

"You're delusional." Mr. Phillips offered a laugh that very plainly said he wasn't amused. "At least where the sister's concerned."

"Am I?" Eric asked, with eyebrows raised.

She mentally rolled her eyes. Eric was right. Mr. Phillips might as well shout his interest to the world, it was so evident. Definitely something had gone on between Terry and the former detective. The two men continued staring at each other while Avery kept her attention glued to them, too engrossed to turn away.

Eric shrugged. "Maybe I got the wrong message, then." Eric's gaze returned to the table Terry was in the process of setting now that dinner was almost ready. Avery averted her eyes, focusing on the chicken as he added, "So you don't mind if I hang around for a few hours?"

"Hell no! Why would I mind?" Mr. Phillips pulled a hand through his short hair, his fierce scowl turning fouler. "Stay or go. Makes no difference to me, since I'm here regardless until Sin relieves me. But you seem to have forgotten why we're here in the first place. Our purpose is not to make time with these women." He stalked down the deck stairs, heading for the gate, and added over his shoulder to Avery, "I'll be in my car if you need me."

~

"Do you mind if I use your bathroom?" Des asked, after Avery opened the door. "And thanks for dinner. That was nice of you." He held out the empty plate and stepped inside.

"You're welcome. And of course you can use my bathroom." She took the plate and pointed. "It's upstairs. Second door on the right."

"Thanks." He nodded and hit the stairs two at a time, intent on a walk-through to assess the top floor of the widow's house, mainly to search for her home computer. When tapped, computers provided all kinds of secrets. A quick check of the downstairs the day before had told him virtually nothing, except that what he'd wanted to scope out must be upstairs.

Des slowed, waiting until Avery was out of sight before he darted into what must be her bedroom, hoping for a chance to discover what the lady was holding back.

A smile snuck up on him as he walked further into the room and glanced around. Light spilled from the hallway, showcasing a spotless, inviting area, appearing like some magazine picture all done up in different shades of blue and lace.

A man could learn a lot about a woman just by examining her bedroom. This space suited Avery Montgomery, told him she was a romantic and very neat.

His focus went to a dark alcove, looking much like a small office with a desk.

He crept back to the door and listened.

Avery and Terry's chitchat floated up the stairs, along with

Eric's deep voice rising every now and then. Good. At least his flirting was good for something. He was keeping them occupied downstairs, which would allow Des a few minutes to snoop.

Now in the alcove, he grinned. She'd even left her computer on standby, making it easier to access. He spent a few minutes reading her documents file, before opening her recycle bin.

Eureka.

"Oh, Avery, I expected more from you. The least you could've done was empty the bin," he murmured, sticking the thumb drive he brought inside the slot and restoring her deleted files, then copying them, as well as a few other files, including deleted e-mails that drew his interest. The entire time the computer crunched, he listened for any out of ordinary activity from downstairs. When done, he deleted the files again and put the computer back on standby.

He also opened the desk drawers. A few letters were underneath some papers in the bottom one. After giving the drawers a more thorough once-over and seeing nothing else of interest, he quietly closed them.

He was just coming out of the room when he spotted Terry on the staircase.

"What are you doing?" she asked, her glower as accusing as her tone.

The smile he threw out didn't quite reach his eyes. "Isn't it obvious? I'm being nosy." He sidestepped past her. "I wanted to check out the top floor and ended in Avery's bedroom."

"Don't go getting any ideas about her. She's not one of your conquests."

"You're talking to the wrong man, honey. I don't do conquests. Too bad you can't make the same claim."

Terry stiffened. "Such a typical comment coming from you. Joan told me all about you."

"Which means, you've been talking to the wrong woman."

"I don't think so. You hung out with Rod. Guys like you stick together. You're no better than he was, according to your ex."

"You should get your facts straight before making damning accusations." Des stopped his descent and pivoted, capturing her attention and shooting back a glare of his own. "I'm certainly not going to defend myself to you denying that woman's lies."

"I don't know what your game is." She rushed down the stairs with all the finesse of a mother bear defending her cub, halting on the step above him. "But you leave my sister alone. You got that, Desmond Phillips?" She stabbed him in the chest with her finger.

He didn't appreciate her poking him or tossing out demands. If she'd been a man, he'd have ripped the finger out of its socket. But noticing her heightened color and puffed-out chest, accentuating full, rounded breasts that happened to be at his eye level, he realized no one would mistake her for a man, least of all him. Not Terry Howard. One hot, gorgeous woman who liked the fast lane. The complete opposite of Avery in every way and no different from Joan, his ex. Hot or not, he wasn't a total fool. She'd never have another opportunity to play her games with him. He'd never again let his attraction for her sway him, not after learning her true character.

"In case you haven't noticed, your sister is over twenty-one, and Avery doesn't strike me as someone needing your defense." He started back down the steps and added over his shoulder, not bothering to keep his withering tone in check, "You can take your warning, along with your superior attitude, back to Joan and both of you can go to hell."

~

Later that evening, Avery knocked on Des' car window. He glanced up as the glass partition rolled down.

She smiled. "Come on, Des, we need you." She used his given name, hoping to charm a smile out of him. A junkyard dog came to mind in describing his demeanor, as surly and as antagonistic as a man could be. "Please." Her grin stretched. "The game is much more fun with four players."

They'd finished the dishes an hour ago and had tried to entice him then, receiving nothing but his curt no. At this point, she was determined to draw him out of his funk, knowing full well Terry played a big part of that funk. Avery liked Des. The thought of him sulking alone in his car bothered her. Reminded her too much of herself. She wanted to see him smiling and laughing like earlier.

"Just one game, then you can come back outside until Mr. Sinclair arrives."

As far as she was concerned, all three made her feel safe. None of them should have to sit out here. She opened the car door, grabbed his hand, and yanked, refusing to take no for an answer.

"See?" Avery asked, thirty minutes later as all four sat at the table after playing a quick game. Andy had just gone to bed. "Isn't this better than being grumpy in your car?"

"Des can't help it." Eric threw his piece in the box. "Grumpy is his natural disposition since his divorce."

"No." Terry flicked an imaginary piece of lint off her shirt. "His divorce has only added to his personality, according to his ex."

Avery eyed her sister's face, searching for some clue as to Terry's unfriendly attitude before her attention returned to Des. The two obviously shared some history, but whatever that history was, Avery couldn't figure it out with merely a glance. Her sister wasn't one to show hostility toward any male, especially one as virile as the man sitting next to her. Though several inches shorter than Eric or Sin, Des' compact body didn't diminish his power or his attractiveness one bit. Funny, but his surly disposition seemed to make him more so.

Oh yeah. Her sister had her own secrets. Secrets she meant to unearth.

"I'll get it." Terry hopped up and started for the hallway at the sound of the bell.

Avery sighed and followed.

Terry opened the door. "I take it you're *Mr. Sinclair.*" Her gaze took a trip over his body. "It's about time you got here. I've been dying for a glimpse—couldn't leave until I got one."

"Terry!" Avery nudged her out of the way and opened the screen door wider. "Come in, Mr. Sinclair. Don't mind her, she's always tactless when she's had a few too many."

"Mrs. Montgomery," he acknowledged.

"I've only had one beer," Terry said with a throaty laugh. "So, you're babysitting my sister? How interesting."

Avery's smile froze on her face as a flicker of annoyance chafed her raw with the effectiveness of an emery board.

His lips curled into the start of a smile and his nod indicated Terry. "I take it she's family? She definitely resembles you." After stepping inside, he made eye contact with Terry and held out his hand. "Hi, I'm Sin."

"Sin? Great name. It suits you. I'm Terry." All but purring, she took his offered hand while continuing to assess him with female appreciation.

Avery clenched her jaw, ignoring the way his name rolled off Terry's tongue, like it was some kind of decadent candy her sister couldn't wait to taste. She met his gaze, still holding on to her frozen smile. "We're in the other room."

"I'm a little early. I trust everything's quiet."

"Very. Eric's still here. Right this way."

She herded them toward the dining room, working to forgive her sister for her natural boldness and vibrancy. Terry's moves were so subconscious, she probably didn't even realize she'd flirted outrageously.

~

As they entered the room, Sin surveyed the scene, noting Eric and Des putting away a game, both cracking jokes and laughing.

"Enjoying yourselves?" He quirked an eyebrow, holding on to his irritation by a thread. For some reason, seeing the two acting so jovially and having such a good time when he'd spent the past twelve hours obsessing annoyed the hell out of him.

Des' smile vanished and he straightened.

"Sin," Eric said cheerfully. "You should've been here."

"No, I shouldn't have. And neither should you." Sin caught the satisfied demeanor of a cat that got away with swallowing the canary. It might have worked for Eric, except for the yellow feather sticking out of his mouth. "So *why are* you still here, Eric, when I expressly told you the lady was off limits."

"Don't worry, he's not after her. He's hitting on the sister," Des said, moving away from the table. "Walk me to my car and I'll be happy to give you a rundown on the night."

"That would be nice." He smiled at Eric, but there was no humor in it. "Both of you. Outside. Now." He shot a quick glance in Avery's direction. "If you'll excuse us."

His narrowed gaze re-centered on Eric, and he couldn't stop his ire from spiking. "Seems my partners have forgotten their purpose for being here."

His disapproval hung in the air.

"Eric's done nothing wrong," Avery said. "It was my idea. I invited him." Her back stiffened as her expression hardened. "We did nothing more harmless than play a stupid board game and have a little fun. So don't go putting a damper on one of the nicest evenings I've had in a long time."

He eyed her for lengthy seconds. Jealousy started as a ripple of displeasure, quickly swelling to pure, molten waves of anger, and washed over him at her protective stance, so staunchly defending Eric. His fingers curled and uncurled before tightening into a fist. He released the fist, sucking in gulps of air and letting them out in long, slow breaths, working to compress the strong urge to pound his partner into the ground.

"It's not what you think." Des' voice, along with a hand on his shirt pulling him toward the door, yanked him out of his haze of fury and helped him regain his control.

"Come on, I'll fill you in."

Sin nodded, thankful for the diversion of putting one foot in front of the other. Made it easier to breathe, which made it easier to stifle the desire for spilling blood.

Man, he must be a freaking lunatic to be having such crazy thoughts about one of his partners. How could he have any ill feelings toward these men? Not Eric or Des. They were a team. Had been through the hell of childhood together, and their bond unbreakable.

Sin followed Des in the direction of his parked car and while walking, one thought consumed him. It would take more than a woman to destroy their connection. He only had to reinforce the memory on occasion.

Eric stormed out of the house and stalked up to him, his angry, hot eyes shouting he was ready for battle. "Are you on drugs or something?"

"No."

"Then why the fuss back there? I'm not into stepping on your turf, man. You know that. You've staked your claim very clearly."

Sin snorted. "There is no claim. I'm simply interested in the job we're supposed to be doing. The reason we're guarding the lady in the first place."

"Drop the affronted, injured party act." Eric scowled. "It's not working. I was under the impression our job was to get her to lower her guard and feel more comfortable around us. Your badass scene won't accomplish shit. Avery asked me to dinner and I had nothing better to do, so I figured why not. Before you go and get your underwear in a wedgie, you should know I also helped keep the women occupied while Des snooped." He put up a hand. "No, don't bother thanking me, but I do require an apology."

"Apologize, Sin, so I can report. Then we can leave and you can get back inside before Avery decides you're too much trouble to let spend the night."

Sin's glance went from Des' face to Eric's. Yep! The lady was turning him into an absolute madman. "I'm sorry I lost it back there. She reminds me of Diane." He raked a hand through his hair and blew out a lengthy, deliberate sigh, making eye contact with Eric. "It's not much of an excuse, except when I think about Diane and what I went through, I go a little crazy. I should know better than to take it out on you guys."

"Apology accepted." Eric nodded.

Des clapped him on the back. "No problem. We understand." He chuckled. "Excess baggage from life's worst experiences can make anyone crazy." He then whipped out a thumb drive and grinned, holding it up. "And like Eric said, his presence allowed me to snoop. Now, whether it's useful information or not, still remains to be seen. He's right about tonight. Having the two of us there this evening did put Avery at ease."

Sin nodded. "Anything else I should know about before I go back inside and grovel?"

"Not much." Des slowed as they neared his car. "From what I can figure after talking to Andy, the dad wasn't around much. He's been lapping up Eric's attention like a thirsty desert drifter after water. He's a great kid. I can see why Avery talks up a storm to anyone who shows an interest." He hit the keyless entry. The locks clicked open and the lights flashed on his sporty silver Lexus. He leaned against the car and met his gaze, searching. "Did you hear anything from Scotty?"

"Yeah, I talked to him." Sin sighed. "He should be back in D.C. sometime tomorrow. He's got an address in Baltimore, so on Saturday one of us can make a quick trip with him." His focus remained on Des. "Keep him in line so he doesn't go all gung ho."

"Shit," Des muttered. "I suppose that look means you want me to go along?"

"I know you hate such duty, but you work so well with him." Sin rested his hand on the back of his neck and rubbed, wishing none of them had to deal with these types of problems. Another day had gone by and they were no closer to finding his prototypes. If things kept going the same way, their company wouldn't survive or at best be severely crippled and take years to recover. "I need you on this, Des. A trip to see this Esperanza might actually produce something."

"You really think he's a lead?"

Sin nodded. "Scotty thinks so and I'm inclined to listen to his reasoning on this one."

"Yeah, the guy's a little weird but he has good instincts," Eric agreed.

"Then you go with him." Des snorted and indicated the house down the block. "Oh, that's right. You'd rather make time with the sister."

"I can follow McNeil, but Sin's right. You're the detective and you've got the experience of what to do when he finds the son of a bitch." Eric smiled, the famous Coleman dimples etching deep caverns into his face. "My specialty is making love, not war." Then, almost as an afterthought, he added, his grin expanding, "Besides, your presence only complicates our job. The sister doesn't like you, and since it appears she's a fixture, it's best if you're not around when she is."

"All right, guys. We're getting off focus again. We should all refrain from any extracurricular activities with either woman and keep to our mission," Sin interjected when Des looked ready to refute Eric's gibe with his fists. "Since both of you seem to be having trouble, it might be best if I stick with Avery for the time being."

"I can handle it and not let the sister bother me." Des stepped to the curb and grabbed the door handle. "You're going to need relief."

"Yeah. We'll play backup so you can stay focused, because it's obvious the lady bothers you." Eric moved to cross the street, heading for his parked Jeep Cherokee and said over his shoulder, "I'll stop at the office first thing in the morning to take care of any pressing business. I'll be by later to give you a break."

"Fine," Sin said, knowing neither man would let it drop. Besides, Des was right about relief. "Just don't forget what you're supposed to be doing. Both of you." He turned and started back, wishing the idea of spending the night in her house didn't sound so appealing. She'd offered her guest room this morning on his way out the door.

He would have to remember his own advice about focusing on the task.

Chapter 8

"You should be careful around Desmond Phillips." Terry handed Avery the game once they'd cleaned up the table after Mr. Sinclair had ushered his partners out of the house.

"Why? I like him." With box in hand, Avery strode to the hall closet to put it away.

"I don't trust him." Terry followed. "I caught him coming out of your bedroom."

"He used to be a detective, so he was probably scoping it out, giving it a once-over like he did downstairs." The thought of him in her bedroom didn't bother her. It wasn't a sexual thing, simply gave her an added feeling of security. "Did you ask him why he was in there?"

"Yes. Said he was being nosy and wanted to check things out."

Avery shrugged. "At least he's honest. Quit worrying. I'll be fine."

"You know nothing about him. About them."

"I know enough." She stared at the closed front door. Enough to realize she liked having them around, but not enough to think she'd ever understand any of them. They all seemed so different. Definitely a diversion in her dull life and worth a little effort in deflecting her sister's objections. She smiled and met Terry's gaze. "Don't worry, Ter. I'll be careful, but I'm going with my instincts on this with them. They make me laugh. I haven't laughed, really laughed, in such a long time. I'd forgotten what it feels like."

"Oh, Av." Terry rushed up and wrapped an arm around Avery's shoulder, giving her a reassuring squeeze. "I'm sorry. I'm being selfish with my pettiness."

"Your feelings are no more petty than mine." Avery leaned back, her gaze narrowing while she searched her sister's face. "But I'm curious. Why don't you like Des?"

"It's a long story." Terry broke away, offering a nonchalant shrug. Her focus landed on the floor. "He's a good friend of Rod's."

"Ah, I see." Avery chuckled softly. "So he's guilty, just by association?"

"No. There's more to it than that. We share a short history." She sported a sheepish grin. "Very short. After it ended, I met his ex-wife at a support group. Let's just say she offered lots of insight about him."

"So you're going off an ex's angry words in therapy?"

Terry's burst of laughter filled the room. "I guess if you put it like that, there is a slight possibility I could be wrong, but it doesn't mean I have to like him."

"No. But don't let not liking him ruin things with Eric."

Her sister's laughter erupted again. "Oh, Av. There's nothing to ruin. Eric's not long term." Terry grabbed her sweater on her way to the door. "I gotta go. Some of us still have to work in the morning. But I'll be back." Her eyebrows rose up and down when she enunciated the last sentence.

"See you tomorrow. Thanks." Avery closed the door behind her sister, her grin still in place. She watched through the glass as Terry passed Mr. Sinclair, mumbling something that sounded like good night. She waited until he made it up the porch stairs before opening the door for him.

"I take it all is well with your partners?" She closed and locked the door, then faced him. "I never meant to stir up trouble with my invitation."

"We worked it out," he muttered, not meeting her eyes. "I should check the doors and windows, if you'll point them out, then you can show me where I'll be."

"Sure." Okay, he was back to being Mr. Uncommunicative. "I like both your partners and felt comfortable with them in my house," she said, in an effort to ward off the deafening silence while he checked. "Surely you can understand how hard it is to have people around and not want to get to know them?"

He grunted, but no real word came out, something that had become the norm in those few minutes they walked around the house.

Avery sighed. Fine. He doesn't want to talk; he doesn't have to talk. She could do uncommunicative again.

"The guest room is right this way." She started up the stairs once the first floor was secure.

He mutely followed until the top step. "I should check the upstairs windows, just to be on the safe side."

"Okay." Again, he trailed behind her to Andy's room, neither speaking. "I usually leave a couple of windows open when the weather permits," she said when he turned to her, the silent question filling his eyes after checking Andy's bathroom window and seeing it wide open. "I like fresh air. It's too small for anyone to squeeze through and the window's not easily accessible from the outside."

He nodded, not even bothering to grunt, and wordlessly followed her to her bedroom.

Walking into the darkened room, she moved toward the lamp to turn it on. In the dim silence, she heard his even breathing...felt his presence a few feet away. Everything in her being responded to his nearness during those few seconds of semidarkness and shadows. The hair on the nape of her neck tingled, sending shivers in the form of goose bumps down her back. Her heartbeat quickened and her breath all but got caught in her throat. She had to force herself to keep walking once she'd flipped the switch and light infused the room.

While pretending indifference, Avery furtively watched his interested glance steal around the room, roaming over her private sanctuary with the precision of a hawk searching for prey from the air.

She pointed in the direction of the windows and lowered her eyes, not daring to meet his gaze for fear he'd see what lurked inside her soul. "Like I said, I like fresh air so I leave those windows open."

"They're too accessible." Mr. Sinclair closed and latched both. "Leave them closed for the time being."

The inspection continued until they stood outside the guest room.

Avery nodded at the closed door. "All clean and ready to go. Fresh towels and such in the bathroom, which is right through there." *Way to go, Avery, just babble like a complete idiot, why don't you.* Why wouldn't it be clean and ready to go? It didn't take a genius to see the obvious bathroom behind the open hall door, the same one he'd surveyed just moments ago. At this rate, she'd never experience another kiss, because he'd think she was a total fool. He didn't look like the type who kissed fools. Good grief! How could she be thinking of kissing him now? Of all times?

A quick glance told her he was paying her no mind, so in those few seconds she let her eyes feast on the gorgeous hunk. He looked tired, but still good enough to kiss. Heat infused her face. He chose that exact moment to look up. For long seconds, their eyes locked. Though more heat seeped into her cheeks, a sure sign of blushing, she couldn't look away.

Finally, he cleared his throat and his gaze lowered, ending the moment, much to her relief.

"Thanks. I'll see you in the morning." He reached for the doorknob, opened the door, and stepped inside. The door closed behind him with a final click.

She stared at the empty space, trying to figure out why she was wondering what he would think if she suddenly grew as courageous as Terry and followed him.

Avery groaned. What was wrong with her? It wasn't like her to think such things. She pushed away her crazy thoughts and started for her bedroom.

After showering, she pulled open a drawer and froze. Terry always teased her about her unusually neat drawers, but having such precise underwear placement made it easy to spot the fact that someone had rifled through her things. She glanced toward the now closed windows and shivered, even though a cool breeze no longer flowed into the room.

Terry's warning about Des being in her room resurfaced. Had he gone through her things? Did Mr. Sinclair and his partners have another purpose other than protecting her as they'd led her to believe? Had she made a mistake allowing them into her house? She prayed not, because she'd come to trust all three, especially Desmond Phillips.

More likely, someone had stolen into her house. A trickle of fear slid down her back.

Avery quickly donned her nightgown and locked her bedroom door before climbing into bed, very aware Mr. Sinclair slept only a few rooms away.

Lying in the dark, more unanswered questions filled her, the biggest focusing on why she was suddenly a target. Plus, she had a sneaking suspicion her protectors weren't telling her everything.

Tomorrow she meant to find out the complete answers to all her questions.

~

Sin paced long after closing the door behind him. He stilled the urge to run back out into the hallway and drag the sexy woman, who'd all but shouted her awareness from those beguiling, soul-searing brown eyes, into the room with him.

The entire time he'd searched the house with her next to him, he couldn't miss the pop and sizzle of attraction between them. The air had been so charged with electric current, he was surprised his hair hadn't stood on end.

Hell, he didn't have to be in Eric's league to recognize the signs of female interest. Avery Montgomery was as interested in him as a man as he was in her as a woman.

"Shit," he whispered, drawing a hand through his hair, working to contain his unbridled thoughts, which stemmed directly from his overactive libido. But there was more that pulled him than mere attraction. The emptiness in her eyes drew him in deeper. Made him think of hugging her or doing something just to see her smile.

Remember, she reminds you of Diane.

Sin hadn't thought about their similarities since yesterday morning. Funny how he had to remind himself of the fact now. Somehow, after spending the last few minutes in her company, his memory quit working altogether.

No, no, no, no. Forget the woman. She's a means to an end.

While he brushed his teeth, he wondered if that was true, then why was it so hard to shed the idea of finding out what she'd do if he'd joined her in the shower he'd heard running a few minutes earlier. He spit out the last of the toothpaste and examined his face in the mirror, looking for signs of dementia. He'd absolutely lost his sanity.

Sin and his partners were businessmen. None of them, except for Des, were cut out for this type of work. Yet, they were all acting like idiots. And Scotty was coming home, ready to play Jason Bourne with Des.

Nothing was going as planned. That right there told him he should just pack it in and forget about his stolen prototypes. Scotty would be home tomorrow, which meant they could work day and night on producing another set. It wouldn't take but three or four weeks and an extension on one of his company's major loans.

What if they produced another set and it disappeared, too?

The thought sobered him. He couldn't trust the military…not again…not with his company's livelihood at stake. He had little choice but to stay on his course.

Avery's secrets had to produce concrete results.

Sin climbed into bed with one thought. He was positive the woman down the hall was hiding something. Until he found out what, he and his partners would stick around.

In the meantime, what would it hurt to work a little harder on drawing out her smile?

Chapter 9

The man remained in the shadows, studying the Georgetown house.

The lights blinked out.

He watched for a while before reaching into his pocket and pulling out a cell phone. His chances of getting back into the house without drawing notice were nil, so he might as well call it a night. He opened the phone, pushed a preset button, and leaned against an ancient elm tree.

"Yes?"

"It's me. Esperanza," he said, his voice slightly above a whisper. He raked a hand through his short hair and his gaze returned to the dark second floor. Only moments ago, he'd been hiding in the tree when his way in had been locked tight. Now he stood a good fifty feet away.

"I've been waiting to hear from you. What have you got?"

"Nothing."

"What do you mean, nothing?" Williams asked, his tone rising. "I thought you found a way inside the widow's house? You've had plenty of time. Why haven't you checked it out?"

"I tried again tonight, but I was interrupted in the midst of searching her room. Not once, but twice. I barely escaped out the window both times." He pulled a CD case out of his pocket and knew if he opened it, he'd find more of the same and exactly what he and Captain Marring had found when they'd opened it eight weeks earlier...nothing.

"Shit." The man on the other end sighed audibly into his ear.

Esperanza understood his apparent frustration. He was just as frustrated. He tapped the empty case against his hand, thinking and refocusing on Avery Montgomery's bedroom window.

This new development with the widow wasn't anticipated. He was so close, yet so far from discovering what he'd travel thousands of miles to learn—where the prototypes that Major Montgomery and Major Crandall had been working on had ended up. Had either man somehow gotten them out of Afghanistan before the ambush? Were they responsible for selling America's secrets to her enemies? That was the only option left, in his opinion. No theft had occurred after the ambush, and no one else had access before the ambush.

"Can you get back in to resume searching?" Williams asked after a brief silence.

"No. She's had company all night. Sinclair's partners have since departed. He replaced the two less than a half hour ago. Then he closed my access and made sure it was locked. They handle themselves too well to take unnecessary risks. I don't dare make another attempt with him watching."

"You mean Sinclair is there, guarding her?" Williams' voice now held surprise.

"Yeah, he's here all right. Has been for two days. Looks like her bodyguard is determined to protect her, seeing as how he's spending the night in a spare room. I told you we should've handled Montgomery's widow in a different way once she left the cemetery the other night. Now they've joined forces."

"I only meant to scare her into staying away. I didn't realize the move would cause him and his partners to play heroes. According to their background checks, they tend to shy away from forming attachments with helpless women."

"Well, they're veering from past behavior to become the lady's shadow, which doesn't bode well for us," Esperanza said. "Of course, they do seem to have another agenda besides guarding. Phillips, the ex-detective who interrupted me the first time, even did his own searching, then got on the computer and copied some files."

"Hell yes, they have another agenda. They want what we want. Just what I need, a bunch of unknowns screwing up our plans. We've got to get them apart, otherwise, this whole operation could blow up in our faces. I thought the other night would've taken care of everything."

"I told you they were shrewd. You underestimated them."

"I can't believe they'd be so bold as to use the widow. Your shots should've been enough to warn them off as well as her."

"So much for best-laid plans. You'd better hope they don't report it. Otherwise they could make your life miserable."

"I'm well past miserable. I've studied their file at length. They're street punks who've made good. My mistake is miscalculating their tenacity in searching for their prototypes. Of course, I never suspected they would use a fail-safe either, which plays a big part of why they say they've never been content with my assurances. I need to figure out what they've learned and then neutralize them." Williams paused. "What else can you tell me? Do you have any idea if they've found anything?"

"I doubt it. I didn't come prepared to listen in on their evening. I couldn't make out much of their conversation when they came out of the house. I did, however, catch a few names. They were arguing about the woman." Another memory of their conversation filled his mind just then. "I also heard my name mentioned along with McNeil's. If they've become a bigger threat, why wasn't I informed?" Even though Esperanza was an alias, he didn't like knowing civilians had unearthed his involvement.

"It's not a problem. I've kept them busy with other distractions. As soon as I discover how much they know about Montgomery, I'll take care of them. You just take care of the lady. Do you understand?"

"I understand perfectly." Esperanza gripped the phone tightly, holding on to his building fury. "Why would they be mentioning my name?"

"It was in the report. McNeil knew you were present and then also learned you disappeared. It would surprise me if they hadn't mentioned your name."

"Vital information you withheld." According to Williams, desperate times called for desperate measures and the higher-ups had given their blessing. "If this goes south, don't expect me to fix your incompetence." Though Colonel Williams outranked him and was also in charge of this operation, the man didn't scare him. What they were doing wasn't exactly military protocol, and the colonel's ass was on the line, not his. Still, this could turn bad in a heartbeat and Esperanza wasn't about to risk his career.

"Don't worry." The colonel's voice drew his attention back to his problem at hand. "They have no way of uncovering the specifics."

"I hope not, because the variables would change."

"Nothing's changed."

"You'd better not be holding back other details," Esperanza threatened, his voice menacing. "I can't revise if I'm not informed of pertinent details. I don't work that way."

He ended the call and slunk into the shadows, heading toward his car.

Nothing about this assignment had gone as planned. He was surrounded by fuck-ups. And fuck-ups tended to leave dead bodies in their wake. Being held responsible for those dead bodies scared him more than the colonel's displeasure.

~

Des decided on a detour before heading home, intending to check out the office, to make sure things were still quiet. He could take a look at the files on the thumb drive at the same time.

As he drove, Sin's responses to Avery Montgomery infiltrated his thoughts. She definitely affected his friend. He could even understand his attraction. If not for Sin's obvious interest, he could see himself getting chummy with her. Over the course of their short acquaintance, especially after tonight, he'd completely revised his opinion of the lady. Though she might be hiding useful information, she couldn't hide her compassion. The memory of Terry Howard's accusing glare entered his brain and his grip on the steering wheel tightened.

Des wouldn't give credence to the thought that she affected him in any way. One night with Terry Howard, along with her actions afterward, had told him all he needed to know. She and Avery seemed as different as night and day. Worlds apart. Avery projected authenticity while her sister projected phoniness.

He parked.

In minutes, he let himself into the employee entrance after punching in the security code. He strode to the elevator expecting to see Jimmy pop around the corner at any moment. He glanced down the dark hallway and hit the Up button, wondering why the night watchman wasn't nearby.

He shrugged. Must be making his rounds.

The elevator doors opened and Des rode it to the fourth floor, then stepped off and strode toward his office. A quick beam of light coming from the middle office had him freezing with his hand on the overhead switches. His attention focused on the darkened hallway until he caught the flash of light again. Someone was in Sin's office.

"Damn," he whispered, reaching down and unsnapping the

holster at his ankle. He gripped the .22, wishing he still had his police-issue 9mm Glock. The small-caliber weapon wasn't nearly as effective in an unknown situation. It did offer protection for times like now when he had no choice but to investigate. SPC's secrets were being stolen right from under his nose, and as head of security, he wasn't too keen on the idea of it happening during his watch.

Holding the weapon with the barrel pointed up, Des snuck in the direction of the offices.

For countless moments, he stood motionless behind a wooden post near Sin's door, listening and watching the beam of light flicker every now and then. Based on the movements, whoever was in there had no idea he lurked on the other side of the door, waiting.

Suddenly the door handle turned and Des aimed, the gun at the ready with the safety off. A dark figure emerged from the office. He stealthily stepped away so as not to be seen when he recognized Jimmy and observed the night watchman going into Des' office. He waited several minutes to give him time to be off his guard before he opened the door and flipped the switch.

"What the hell...?" Hands shielded his eyes from the unexpected bright lights.

"My thoughts exactly." Des aimed for his heart.

"Oh, it's only you. Good evening, Mr. Phillips."

"Jimmy." He nodded and indicated his desk with the gun. "What're you doing in here?" Des flashed a semblance of a smile, but there was nothing friendly in his bearing.

"I thought I heard something so I came to check it out."

Des' gaze narrowed as he took in Jimmy's stance and attitude. His lips curled into a genuine grin. He had to give the guy credit. He had balls the size of melons to try and bullshit him in such a way. "Sit down." He pointed the pistol at a chair and stepped further into the room.

"I got rounds to do," Jimmy said, his manner not so confident now. "Since you're here, I'll get to them."

Using his foot, Des pulled the chair out, shoving it toward him, then said a bit louder, "Sit."

Jimmy complied, the entire time his focus stayed glued to his face, as if searching for some avenue of escape etched into his forehead.

Des' grin widened. He read too much of his inner thoughts in the large print expression, allowing him a glimmer of Jimmy's apprehension.

"Now that you're sitting, let's talk." He strolled behind his desk, plopped down in the seat, and leaned back. He lifted his legs onto the desk, the entire time keeping his attention and the weapon trained on Jimmy. Silently, they eyed each other. The seconds ticked by. Ten…twenty…thirty. Finally, a full minute had elapsed before Des added, "Maybe I should rephrase. I want *you* to talk. I'll listen and it'd better be good."

"I told you. I got off the elevator and heard a noise in Mr. Sinclair's office. I checked it out." Some of Jimmy's apprehension disappeared, replaced with his earlier cockiness. He sat back and stretched, crossing his legs in front of him. "That *is* my job, isn't it?"

"Yeah. I'll give you that. Checking out suspicious noises does come under your job description, but you should know I got off the elevator ten minutes ago, about nine more than required to check things out. So, try again."

Jimmy shifted in his seat. "I'm thorough."

"Thorough?" Des noted his satisfied smirk and bit his cheek in an effort to keep from laughing. "That's your best answer?"

Jimmy's head notched an inch higher, his chin jutting out, going for more attitude.

Des shook his head, tsk-tsking. Too bad he was in a hurry. Any other time, he'd enjoy spending a few minutes toying with the guy, as he liked nothing better than to verbally bat his suspects around like a cat with a small creature without the brains to realize its precarious position. Such amusing games kept him from dying of boredom when he'd been back on the force facing tedious open-and-shut cases. Though tempted, he couldn't play silly mind games now, not when too much shit was happening all around him. He needed to stay focused.

"Fine." Des reached into his pocket for his cell and flipped it open, keeping his weapon trained on the guard.

"Who are you calling?"

"D.C.'s finest." Yeah! Not so confident now, Des thought, watching doubt creep back into Jimmy's eyes. His smile lurked, tugging harder to break free. "I still have a few friends on the force who'd love to investigate an industrial espionage case and solve it, hoping for a leg up on making a promotion." After punching in a preset number, he put the phone to his ear, still aiming. "I don't know who you are, but I'm positive you're no night watchman." When an automated voice answered, Des waited for the message to play. "Hey, Rod, it's me, Des. I got an interesting lead for you. It's tied to the bullet and shell casings I asked you to examine. Can you give me a call back when you get this?" He glanced at Jimmy and his grin broke free. "Thanks," he murmured, before flipping the phone shut.

"You're off base, man."

"I doubt it." Des met his gaze. "Let's see. How long have you been a night watchman at SPC? I never made the connection before, but our first theft didn't occur until after you started working here." He paused. "I don't believe in coincidences any more than Mr. Sinclair does."

"Now you're so far off, you're in the next county."

"We'll soon find out, won't we?" He stuck the phone back into his pocket, still grinning. "I'm betting you didn't take the time to wipe your prints from Sin's office, figuring you were safe enough from scrutiny, but no matter if you did, 'cause I know you didn't in here, and those prints will tell me everything I need to know."

"I was just doing my job."

"Not any job for SPC. Not in Sin's office." Des shrugged. "I'm also betting there are more of your prints in other areas. Areas where your prints shouldn't be."

"You've made your point." Jimmy sighed heavily and wiped his face, eyeing Des carefully. Still, he didn't speak, just kept his gaze on Des' face, clearly weighing his options.

Pachelbel's "Canon in D" blared from Des' cell phone, pulling both men's attention.

Des reached into his pocket for the ringing phone, and chanced a brief glance at the caller ID. "Rod," he said. "Must be hungry. I didn't expect him to return my call so promptly," he said, about to open the device.

"Wait," Jimmy shouted.

Des halted, glancing at him with the question in his eyes.

He nodded. "I'll talk. I can't afford any more trouble with law enforcement. I could lose my license."

"Now we're finally getting somewhere." Des smiled and stuck the phone back in his pocket after putting the ringer on vibrate.

"Like I said, I'm listening and it had better be good."

Twenty minutes later, Des scanned Jimmy's—no, Jeremy's—face, absorbing the information and trying to make some sense out of what the PI had just revealed.

"So, let me get this straight. Williams hired you to keep an eye on us?" His attention remained focused on him, looking for confirmation. When Jeremy nodded, a sliver of dread washed over him. Shit. Not what he wanted to hear. The PI started with SPC a good two months before their prototypes were stolen. Maybe Sin had reason to be worried about the colonel. Something wasn't right. "What do you know about the other thefts?"

"Not much. I inspected the grounds and reported a few weak areas in your security. If it were up to me, I'd look at any new hires in your production department. It doesn't take an actuary to figure out the math. The incidents are connected."

"Why would a colonel in the United States Army contrive to steal our secrets?"

"Money? Power? Take your pick. Greed and the desire for more power are potent draws." He swiped a hand across his face and snorted. "Even I got caught up and let the thought of more money influence my judgment on this. I knew better, especially after working here for a few months. You guys seem like you're on the up-and-up."

Des nodded distractedly, his mind spinning. "What's he paying you?" he asked a moment later.

Jeremy Brubaker sighed, shaking his head. "Enough to make the risk I took worthwhile."

"How about you come to work for us? We could use a good security specialist."

"You're joking, right?" Jeremy laughed.

"I wasn't going for humor. I'm sure you realize this is not a laughing matter."

"Maybe not, but you should know I don't work cheap."

"We can afford you."

"You haven't even heard my price." Jeremy's attitude returned in full force, now fully present in both his cocky grin and confident voice. "What if it's too high?"

Des chuckled. He'd been wrong about the size of the guy's balls. They weren't mere cantaloupes; somehow in the course of a few minutes, they'd swollen to watermelons. He met Jeremy's gaze, still grinning. "I don't have to worry about meeting your price. You'll work for what I offer because of my compensation package."

"Compensation package?"

Not so cocksure all of a sudden. Des' grin reached each ear. "Yeah. I'm gonna keep from beating you to a pulp. And on the off chance that's not enough compensation, how's this? I'll even throw in keeping your little indiscretion tonight a secret and will refrain from turning you in and making your life pure shit. How's that for incentive?"

The cocky smile died instantly as Jeremy eyed Des, once more clearly weighing his options. Finally, a self-deprecating smile crossed his face and he sighed. "Works for me."

"Good. I'm glad you're seeing things my way. And to show you what a nice guy I can be, I'll even let you stay on the government's payroll, a solution benefiting both of us."

"I got no problem becoming a double agent." Jeremy chuckled and rubbed his hands together. "I rather like the idea of Jimmy Bond turning on MI6, especially when MI6 isn't on the up-and-up. But I've got to keep Williams happy with information. Got any suggestions?"

"Tomorrow I'll talk to Sin—" Des cleared his throat. "I mean, Mr. Sinclair, and we'll work out a plan for dealing with this. In the meantime, you just keep guarding, but do me a favor and stay out of our offices. Otherwise our next talk won't end so pleasantly." He met his gaze so the guy could see the sincerity of his words. "Don't cross me, or you'll find out firsthand how much I like beating the shit out of cocky PIs who need a good lesson. You'll have no idea of when or where that lesson will take place and no trace to me. Understand?"

Des choked down a chuckle at Jeremy's expression, saying it all. He'd gotten his message loud and clear. When he made no move to leave, Des waved his gun, holding on to his gut to help keep his laughter contained. "Go on, get out of here, get back to work."

"Yes, sir." He jumped up and headed for the door.

After re-holstering his weapon, Des spent an extended moment simply staring at the empty spot Jeremy had vacated, thinking. He rose, feeling the thumb drive in his pocket. He opened his desk drawer and stuck it inside. Then he closed and locked it, before following the same path Jeremy had taken. He'd dealt with enough for one night. He'd deal with Avery's secrets tomorrow.

Chapter 10

A strange foreboding filtered into Sin's consciousness, jerking him awake. He opened his eyes to see a boy staring at him from the foot of the bed.

"Are you Mr. Eric's friend?" the boy asked, eyeing him cautiously.

"Mr. Eric's friend?" Sin wiped the sleep from his face, figuring he must be Andy, Avery's nine-year-old. Cute kid, even if he had awakened him.

Sin sat up, grabbed the pillow, fluffed it up, and stuck it behind him. A quick glance at the clock on the nightstand told him it was six fifty-seven. Eric would relieve him sometime after nine. "Do you always spy on your mom's guests?"

A child's innocent, curious smile, completely without guile, took over the boy's face. "I'm not spying." He shrugged, then added, "I wanted to see what you looked like. Thought maybe you were a werewolf. But you're not."

Sin snorted and bit back a smile. "Why would you think I was a werewolf?"

"I heard Mr. Eric tell my mom to ignore you. He said you had a mean bark, but you weren't going to bite."

"He said that?" He'd have to have a word with Eric.

"Yeah. And when I told Tommy, he said werewolves don't exist. Tommy says you're probably an alien in disguise, coming from outer space to Earth to take us over. So I had to see for myself."

"Andy." The shout came from a distance, most likely downstairs. "You're not bothering Mr. Sinclair, are you?"

"No," Andy shouted back, his grin instantly turning from sweet to impish. He glanced over and said in a conspiratorial whisper, "I'm not supposed to be in here. But I had to find out. Now I can tell Tommy you're not from Mars, either."

"Yeah, I'm definitely not from Mars," Sin said, then added under his breath, "But sometimes I wonder where in the hell on

Earth I'm going."

Andy turned and scampered out of the room.

"And I don't bark," Sin yelled at his departing back. "Mr. Eric doesn't know what he's talking about."

He quickly showered, then followed the scent of strong coffee and the sound of humming, winding his way down the stairs to find the widow. He was eager to see her, eager to begin flirting.

"Good morning." Avery looked up when he entered the living room.

"Good morning." Her beautiful smile took him by surprise, tugged at his gut, and drew his gaze, which fastened on her lips. The memory of kissing those lips filled his mind. In a burst of awareness, blood rushed south, something that had become a common and unwanted occurrence during the past four days.

"It's nice to see you up and about, Mr. Sinclair. Did you sleep well?"

"Well enough." If he hadn't been looking at her lips, he'd have never realized she was talking to him. In an effort to throw her off balance as she'd just done to him, he snared her gaze, grinning wickedly. "Are you ever going to call me Sin?"

"Sin?" Her eyes widened, then narrowed as if she were trying to decipher his mood. "Are you feeling all right?"

"Yeah," he said cautiously. Like someone yanking a rug out from under him, the question threw him more off balance. "Why wouldn't I be feeling all right?"

"No reason." Avery went back to her straightening. "It's just that your sentences have more than one syllable this morning. I've gotten quite used to your grunts."

"What can I say?" Sin chuckled, noting the teasing quality in her voice, which only made him want to flirt with her and keep her smiling. "I'm in a talkative mood today."

"Be still my heart." She clutched her chest, patting her hand in an exaggerated manner. "You're actually carrying on a conversation."

"Yes, I am. You got a problem with that?" Yep! Apparently, Avery was doing some flirting of her own. His grin stretched. "And you haven't answered my question."

"What question?"

"About calling me Sin."

"You really expect me to call you Sin?"

Her incredulous tone made him realize how important this step had become. "Or Jeff. I don't see the big deal. You called Des and Eric by their first names. So why not me?" He shrugged, going for a nonchalance he suddenly didn't feel. "Besides, whenever I hear Mr. Sinclair, I always look around, expecting to see a much older man behind me."

"Now you're teasing." Avery laughed nervously and fluffed a pillow.

"Maybe." Sin waited until she glanced back at him to catch her gaze again. "I don't bark all the time." A hint of pink stole up her face and he couldn't take his eyes off her. She tended to blush easily around him. The idea of seeing how far down the blush went was more than a passing thought. He was in such humongous trouble…felt more than the stirrings of desire, and it had nothing to do with sex. He should quit flirting with her. She affected him…too much.

"I take it you've met Andy." Avery offered an apologetic smile, still blushing.

Her actions did nothing to cool the heat now pulsing through him, courtesy of his out of control imagination.

"I hope he didn't bother you."

"No. Des hit it right on. He's a great kid." Sin chuckled softly, knowing he shouldn't, but unable to keep from adding more fuel to the fire in his gut, he said, "And like Eric says, I never bite. Sometimes I'll even roll over and whine, wanting a rubdown."

Avery's nervous giggle clutched at his insides, gripping harder when another blush highlighted her cheeks, making him wonder about his sanity, given his reactions. Maybe he should keep the barriers of propriety up, and not tear them down.

Had the experience with Diane taught him nothing?

Okay, he preferred the lady in front of him off guard and relaxed, not stiff and frozen or sad and forlorn, but he could have accomplished that without winning any congeniality contests.

"So, how about it? Are you going to call me Sin?" he asked, totally ignoring his mental advice. He was dying to have her reciprocate—to tell him to call her Avery. Her first name was different and suited her. Last night, Des used the name like they were best friends. For some reason, of which jealousy most likely topped the list, he had to rate in front of his partners. He just had to.

"Sin?" Her smile grew, reaching her eyes, and at that moment he didn't care one bit about barriers or jealousy or even Diane. Sin loved seeing her genuine smile and realized he'd do or say anything to bring on another one.

"How did you get your nickname?"

"Isn't it obvious?" He returned her grin, pushing out the rest of his concern. He simply couldn't help smiling when she was around and he was tired of fighting his desire to do so. And why stop flirting when it worked so well at putting her at ease? Besides, flirting would help him achieve his new goal, which had altered so far from his original, and was now charging toward understanding her loneliness and working to ease it. Maybe by doing so, it would ease some of his own loneliness. "I lure unsuspecting women into sin."

"I believe it."

Avery's gaze stroked him, warming his insides, causing the fire to reignite. His smile turned speculative.

Damn!

Why did the sudden yearning to be temptation enough to lead *her* into sinning fill his soul, only to completely waylay him from any of his goals?

"Stop that." She relaxed her shoulders, still grinning. "You're distracting me. I'm beginning to wish I'd never asked about your nickname."

"Well, you did." Sin eyed her suggestively, without concealing the desire he felt from showing in his eyes. He was having fun flirting with her. What harm would come of it?

"Yes, I did." Ignoring his blatant, heated look, she giggled nervously and busied herself with another cushion, spending a long moment fluffing, before glancing his way again. "What would you like for breakfast?"

"You." More pink stole up her face. He liked knowing he could make her blush so easily. Liked knowing he was a bit of a temptation. After all, he needed to use every advantage…intended to do so.

Avery' laughter increased. "You're incorrigible." She headed for the kitchen and added along the way, "You'll have to settle for a cup of coffee with eggs and bacon."

"Spoilsport." He followed, chuckling, knowing he'd made progress because she hadn't called him Mr. Sinclair.

"You read my mind." He took the mug of coffee she offered when he entered the room.

"Would you like cream?" Her eyebrows slanted up.

"Black's fine." He held up the mug in a salute. "Thanks."

"So, you lure unsuspecting women into sin?" Avery threw the question out as she opened the fridge. "Is that really how you acquired the nickname?"

"What do you think?" He stood near the door and brought the cup to his lips, watching her move gracefully around the kitchen.

"I think you'd be good at luring, so my guess is it's a true statement."

She'd spoken in such a matter-of-fact way, he couldn't help but respond with a grin.

"You'd be right. I *am* good at luring. Want me to demonstrate?"

She laughed. "No conceit in your family." She pulled out a pan, spent a moment laying the bacon inside, and placed it over a burner after turning it on.

"Why deny it?" Sin's gaze zeroed in on her smiling mouth. "And you didn't answer my question."

Another hint of pink stole across her cheeks. Damn, if he didn't love her blushes. With her it was such a turn-on, made him wonder if she'd blush after they made love. *If* was now out of the running. Too many *when's* filled his mind. *When* would he be able to kiss those adorable lips again? *When* would he learn what happened after kissing? And most specifically... *When* would they make love? That last thought stopped him. He shrugged it off. It was an honest question.

"I think I'll pass on the demonstration." Her focus returned to the heating bacon on the stove.

"There you go being a spoilsport again." *Patience.* He had to remember she was a grieving widow and would most likely require much patience. And flirting.

"Sorry," Avery murmured, turning and opening a lower cabinet while she let the bacon cook. She lifted a bowl and set it on the counter, next to the eggs. After taking out four, she put the carton back in the refrigerator. She glanced at him expectantly before she returned to the now sizzling bacon. "You were telling me about your

113

name."

"Hmm…I guess I was." Sin sighed, pushing out his errant thoughts, going for something less distracting. "It's an old neighborhood nickname I picked up a long time ago." His grin spread as one of his better memories from his past pushed forth. "What can I say? I was gifted with leadership early on."

Avery laughed, muttering something about conceit again, and he chuckled.

"It's true," he said, still grinning, defending his claim. "I happened to run the kids in the neighborhood whose mothers called me spawn of the devil and chastised me at every opportunity for leading their babies into sin. Those same guys—all sinners before I ever made an appearance, by the way—thought it cool to think I led them to the dark side, so they started calling me Sin. The nickname stuck. I was twelve at the time. I really thought I was a badass back then. So did everyone else."

"Ah! I see. So, at the ripe old age of twelve, you ran with a bunch of badasses?"

"Yeah. I come from a rough area, full of rough kids." Sin's smile died. "Not your typical suburban cul-de-sac, that's for sure. And at fourteen, right before my fifteenth birthday, a couple of D.C. cops yanked our bad asses into an alley."

"Really?" Avery looked up from her cooking, eyeing him intently. "I don't see you being a bad enough kid for cops to yank on." She went back to her bacon, meticulously flipping the pieces. "What'd you do?"

He shrugged. "I can't remember. Probably stole a carton of cigarettes or fifth of vodka or something. We hadn't gotten into hard drugs, thank God, just hard liquor and cigarettes. It's a miracle none of us are hooked on tobacco or alcohol today given our youthful indiscretions. Anyway, rather than book us, like Des, Eric, and I thought would happen, they dragged us to a park instead. Challenged us to a game of football, saying if they lost, they'd leave us alone for the summer. If they won, they owned our bad asses for that same summer."

"Wow! You guys go that far back?" When he nodded, she smiled. "So what happened?"

"Despite being the baddest asses alive at the time, we not only lost, we got hammered."

"No! Not badasses like yourselves?" She placed crisp brown strips on paper towels before pouring out the grease.

"Yep. Turns out, there's a lot of skill involved in the game…much more than brawn. All three of us had gone through growth spurts and had gained muscle that spring. Damn, we thought we were so tough and mighty. Thought we couldn't lose, since it was three to two and we'd played street football together for years." He sighed and shook his head, meeting her amused gaze. "They suckered us, lured us in like professional hustlers, and we swallowed the bait whole. The three of us spent the summer busting our bad asses, working them off, and not liking it much. Pride wouldn't let any of us back out of our word."

"That's a good story." Avery took an egg, cracked it, and emptied the contents into the bowl she'd taken out, then repeated the process. "I don't have any good stories from my childhood. Mine was pretty boring."

Sin grunted a reply, suddenly wondering why he'd divulged so much information, especially about something he rarely discussed with anyone, much less a woman. His childhood memories were better off left buried.

She studied him for a long moment before going back to cracking eggs. She grabbed a whisk and began beating. "But somehow I'm thinking your childhood wasn't all good, and you're leaving out much of the *bad* stuff."

"Maybe." He shrugged, feeling a little self-conscious all of a sudden. "None of us had storybook beginnings. We didn't do Little League."

"Then, I'm glad you had mentors."

The warmth of Avery's smile reached her eyes, making him yearn for any childhood to speak of other than his own.

"You're lucky they intervened."

"You have no idea." Nodding, Sin looked away. "They were some good guys," he said of the two men who'd saved him and his friends from a future destined for failure. "Who taught us about life, made us realize where ours was headed if we didn't change our ways. They also taught us the real game of football and introduced us to more cops. Having so many cops riding your ass made it more difficult to stay bad." He rubbed the back of his neck, studying the oak planks in the floor before meeting her sympathetic gaze again.

"The three of us were lucky. We all survived our ugly beginnings."

Avery absorbed his admission, seeming to understand his reluctance to expand on what he'd already divulged.

He'd certainly revealed enough...maybe too much. He wasn't inclined to lengthen the conversation due to the subject matter, but he wasn't uncomfortable. Quite the opposite, in fact.

Neither spoke. Sin lounged against the counter with both arms and legs crossed, letting his eyes have their fill while she finished cooking breakfast, just as he had the other night after she'd offered him cookies. He loved watching her elegant, easy movements. The silence added to the intimacy between them. He could stand here all day content to do nothing but gaze at her.

~

"Here, Sin, grab these." Avery handed him two plates full of food, wondering at how easily she'd made the transition from Mr. Sinclair to Sin. Though totally out of her element, she couldn't stop the tingle of excitement racing along her spine, giving her a sense of adventure. He'd actually flirted with her. She'd never dealt with men like him before, had only dated one man, Mike, in high school and college before marrying. Now she understood her sister a little better. She felt bold, almost daring, and very much alive...such a contrast from her usual pretenses and guilt.

"You remember where the dining room is, right through that doorway." Sin nodded and started for the closed swinging door, as Avery picked up another tray and followed. He placed the plates on the table, and looked up.

"Sit wherever," she said, answering the obvious question in the rise of his brows. "Andy and I don't stand on ceremony in this house."

"Okay. Since you have no set rules, you can sit next to me." He moved the plates so they sat side by side, before pulling out a chair for her.

The implied politeness of his gesture tugged on her heartstrings. She eyed him thoughtfully, really looking at him, and saw only sincerity in his vivid green eyes that, along with his earlier honesty about his youth, made him that much more attractive. The genuine smile now sliding over his face put her more at ease, despite the internal havoc on her senses his nearness created. She liked him and liked the fact that, as good-looking as he was, he was also nice and considerate, not to mention human.

Avery's glance moved to his hands as she sat. Such lovely hands. Strong, capable hands. She'd bet her life's savings those hands would do much to make sure any woman he made love to enjoyed the act.

Good grief! Where had that thought come from? While Sin helped scoot her chair in, more heat flared. She patted her face and glanced away so he wouldn't notice. Why oh why was she so easily embarrassed around him, and thinking such crazy thoughts, acting like some lovesick adolescent with her first crush? He most likely viewed her stammering and silly awkwardness as moronic, no doubt used to savvy, experienced women like Terry.

The ringing phone interrupted her thoughts. Avery offered an apologetic smile and stood to answer, thankful for the excuse of having something else to focus on other than his hands or her ineptness or her crazy thoughts. She had enough guilt on her plate, thank you very much.

"Hi, Terry," she said, after checking the caller ID. "What's up?"

"Nothing. I just wanted to make sure you made it through the night without mishap."

"Why wouldn't I?" Avery sighed, giving a backward glance before moving through the swinging door and lowering her voice. "I'm perfectly safe in my own house. Sin is here only as a precaution."

"Calling him Sin now, are we? Did something happen after I left?"

"Nothing happened," she denied. "We checked the house, including all the windows. Then he went to his room and I to mine. Alone." As she ended her sentence, the memory of an unknown intruder rifling through her underwear drawer entered her thoughts.

Her smiled died.

Avery stiffened and her focus centered on the swinging door. The idea of someone in her house, going through her things, didn't sit well any better this morning than it had last evening.

"I'm busy and since you've gotten your report, I'm cutting this short."

"Wait!" Terry protested as she was about to hang up. "Want to do lunch?"

"I could be persuaded." Lunch with Terry sounded like fun,

something that had gone missing for too long from her life, she suddenly realized. Andy could play with Tommy at his house. "Where?"

Terry suggested a restaurant they both loved and Avery agreed to a time. "I need to make sure it's okay with Mary first. If there's a problem I'll give you a call, otherwise, I'll see you then. Good-bye, sister dear." She hung up before Terry could ask any more questions about her evening. With every intention of learning exactly what Des had done in her room last night, she pushed through the dining room door. Slowing her progression, she wondered how best to approach the subject.

"Terry and I are meeting for lunch today while Andy plays with Tommy, so Eric can leave early and Des can arrive late."

"No problem. You're the boss." Sin stood to help her with her chair again.

Avery nodded distractedly, still thinking. Finally, she took a deep breath, opting for the direct route. "Terry also told me she saw Des coming out of my room last night."

"She did?" Surprise spilled out of Sin's green eyes when he met her gaze.

"Yes, she did." Her focus remained on him as she lifted her napkin off the seat. "But I'm betting you already knew he'd been in there." She sat back down, holding his gaze. Finally, her attention turned to her plate. She toyed with her food, then glanced back at him before clearing her throat and striving for nonchalance. "Would he go through my dresser drawers?"

Sin was just about to take a bite of food. Instead, his hand dropped to the table and his food-filled fork rested on the plate. His eyes narrowed and he warily studied her face.

"Someone went through your dresser drawers?" he asked, almost as nonchalantly, except Avery saw something flicker in those jade pools of liquid intensity before his eyelids lowered.

Oh yeah, he definitely knew Des had been in her room, given his body language. His actions did nothing to soothe her fears, in fact did much to set off tiny alarm bells that wouldn't stop ringing.

"I'm sure of it," she murmured, as apprehension filled her and all kinds of disturbing possibilities flashed inside her brain. Were they doing more than protecting? Like searching? And if so, why were they searching?

She looked at her food so he wouldn't see any of the doubt that surely shone in her eyes. Maybe Terry was right. She knew next to nothing about these men and here she'd allowed them access to her home.

Well, two could play at the game of digging for more information. Avery planned to do some snooping of her own and use the colonel to achieve her objective. After all, the man had offered his services if she needed anything. She could extend her lunch to include a visit with him.

"I doubt Des would search your dresser drawers," Sin said a moment later, drawing her out of her thoughts. She looked up, meeting his earnest expression. "It wasn't in his job description, but just to be on the safe side, I'll ask him."

Avery nodded, somewhat appeased with his response, but still wondering. If not Des, then who went through her things?

Total silence surrounded them, both absorbed in eating until Sin asked, "Why do you think someone went through your belongings?"

"What difference does it make?" She groaned inwardly. Just her luck, he'd ask. If he learned about her excessive neatness, he might think she was weird.

He shrugged. "I'm merely trying to determine the risk."

"I like order," she admitted, jutting out her chin after enduring long moments of his openly inquisitive gaze saying he wasn't about to drop the subject.

"Order?"

Avery sighed. "Terry accuses me of being a bit anal about my clothes' placement. She's always threatening to sneak into my closets to rearrange everything, so I'll lighten up." Her smile turned self-deprecating. "But I doubt she went through my underwear drawer last night simply to make a point."

"I see." Sin nodded.

"What do you see?" She watched his expression slam shut and lock tighter than any door with full weather stripping and dead bolts. Nothing would get past that look, not air, not anyone without a key. All of a sudden, more misgivings over her bodyguards invaded her brain, paralyzing her for an instant. What *did* she really know about him? Next to nothing.

"I need to look into it. I'll ask Des and get back to you."

Nodding and peering at his locked features, another thought

struck. She was unsure, if given the key, whether she'd want to unlock the Pandora's box of possible complications. She had this niggling feeling that once opened, her life would be forever altered.

~

"Mom…Mom…you gotta come and see this. We found a huge frog." Andy's shout, some twenty minutes later, came from the rear of the house.

"Oh joy." Avery frowned. "My favorite thing. Frogs."

Perched on the sofa, ready to make a few calls while waiting for Eric, Sin halted in the middle of rifling through his briefcase.

"Mom?" Andy yelled, running into the room with the force of charging wildebeests evading a predator.

"Does he always move at warp speed?" Sin glanced at Avery, amusement forming in his eyes, and grinned.

"Pretty much." She nodded. "Either that or his other speed, which is off. He only has those two. Fast forward and off." Her smile softened when her gaze landed on her son. No one within a mile could miss the motherly love and pride radiating from her expression. "Where did you find frogs, Andy?"

Avery had a very expressive face, using all of her facial muscles to indicate pleasure or disapproval. The brief thought of how it would feel to have her view him in such a way flitted in and around Sin's brain just then. He sighed, averting his eyes. His gaze moved to the end table, zeroing in on a picture. He recognized Avery and Andy, although the photo was probably five years old. He also recognized her dead husband from pictures in the file the colonel had given him. The three were a good-looking family, making him feel as if he was an interloper, treading somewhere he shouldn't. He shook the thought and caught the rest of the conversation between mother and son.

"Out back." Andy grabbed Avery's hand, pulling her. "Come and see. You too, Mr. Eric's friend."

"His name is Mr. Sinclair." Amusement lit her face like the burst of a new day hitting the morning horizon.

"Tommy and I wanted to see if Mr. Eric's friend, I mean Mr. Sinclair, plays football." He stopped his tugging and looked expectantly at Sin.

"I'm sure Mr. Sinclair is too busy to look at frogs or play football. He has a company to run."

"I'd love to." Sin rose, stuffing the papers back into his briefcase.

"You sure you don't mind?" Avery's expression changed to one of concern. "You don't have to, you know. They can survive until Eric gets here."

"Work can wait a while." He wasn't getting much done anyway with Avery hovering nearby, disturbing his concentration with her incessant cleaning. "I have an appreciation for frogs and have thrown plenty of passes in my day."

Andy beamed. "Mr. Eric says I'm the next Jerry Rice."

"Really?" Sin chuckled at the boy's puffed-out chest.

"Yeah, he's only the best receiver to ever come out of the NFL, in case you don't know."

"Then, what are we waiting for? I'm sure I'm in for a treat."

"Great!" Andy skipped, talking nonstop as Sin followed. "This summer's turning out to be awesome. Ya know, tomorrow we're going to Boy Scout camp. I'm gonna sleep in a tent. We have to pitch our own," he said solemnly. "We'll be out in the wild. I think there's bears…and mountain lions too. But I'm not scared."

The screen door slammed shut behind him as Sin sauntered out to the backyard, listening to Andy's litany of what would be happening during the week. He grinned and couldn't help thinking Des was right about the kid. He was a charmer.

"My dad's dead, you know?"

Andy's comment came after they'd thrown a few passes and were now just lounging on the grass waiting for Tommy to return from his house. A telephone call had pulled Avery inside, and she hadn't come back out.

Sin wasn't quite sure how to respond, given the subject matter. Finally, he nodded, striving for sincerity. "I'm sorry to hear about that. It's tough to lose a father. I know firsthand how hard it is."

"You lost your dad?"

"Yeah, I did. Only I was a lot younger than you, so I don't remember him." Except his dad hadn't died, had just up and disappeared one day. Maybe it would have been better if he had died. Maybe he could stop blaming himself for the loss, or maybe he'd be able to accept it much easier if that had been the case. "Must be tough, losing him now?" he asked, not wanting to think about his missing father. As far as Sin was concerned, the man was as good as dead.

"It's okay. I just pretend he's gone away like he usually did. I always wanted him to play catch with me, but he never had time." Andy broke off, picking strands of grass. "He was a hero, you know."

Sin nodded gravely. "Your mom told me."

"Is that what you did? Pretend?"

"Huh?" he asked, not quite sure he'd heard him correctly.

"When your dad died."

"Yeah, I guess," he said in a low voice.

As it was, his dad had left him and his mother when he'd been a baby. He never knew why, just knew his mom had never gotten over her loss. Sin wasn't about to let a man who didn't want to stick around affect his life any more than he already had. That was the reason he never sought him out even after his mother died of an overdose of sleeping pills.

He'd been seventeen at the time, but he couldn't hate his mother for leaving him…in fact understood her. She hadn't been a strong woman, health-wise or mentally. Having Maxwell Sinclair walk out of their lives destroyed hers.

In a way, he'd felt her same loss even though he'd pretended not to—just like Andy was doing now, Sin suddenly realized. As he'd matured, he'd realized another fact. In dying, she'd given him the means to be somebody, which is why he could never hate his mom for causing him more pain. Her life insurance policy, taken out two years and a day from the time of her overdose, provided enough money for college at one of the most expensive schools in the country.

Funny, Sin would much rather have his mother alive than the proceeds from her horrible death. He was a fatalist and determined to use what her death had given him. It was as if by succeeding, he could find some measure of reasoning for it. But truthfully, nothing would ever make up for the loss of her. Nothing.

"Pretending isn't hard." Andy met Sin's gaze and his chin jutted out as his tears threatened. "You wanna know what's hard?"

"What?" Sin looked away, his throat tightening from choking back his own tears. He knew all about pretending, and he didn't like peering into this child's face. It was too much like looking into a mirror.

"When I sometimes wake up and know it's not really pretend, when I know my dad's never gonna come home. It hurts, but I can't cry 'cause that would make my mom cry. I have to take care of her."

Sin cleared his throat and nodded. "I understand." He grabbed the ball and prepared to throw. "Go long," he said, hoping to get him off the subject. He didn't want to share any of the sorrow deep in his gut with a nine-year-old boy who was the son of a dead hero. They shared no common thread other than not having a father around.

The kid was such a natural athlete, his talent most likely inherited. For the brief moment Andy dove for the ball, the thought of his own unborn child and the question of what he'd be like had he lived entered Sin's mind. He usually avoided such thoughts, but watching Andy's childlike fervor made him wonder. He pushed back the pain, realizing he'd kill to have the chance to throw a football with the kid his unborn child would have become if he'd lived. What's more, if he had a son like Andy, he'd never ignore him. He'd definitely play ball with him, that's for damn sure.

A yell from the gate distracted Sin from his unwanted thoughts. Tommy charged into the yard. Andy threw him a pass, laughing and yelling, completely engrossed in his pretenses once more.

Sin enjoyed tossing the ball with the boys, and did his best to run them ragged. As the three of them sat a while later, taking another break, Andy looked up at him, a serious expression on his face. "Do you think Mr. Des likes my mom?"

"Yeah. I'm sure of it." Sin glanced at his watch, praying he wouldn't get into his dead dad discussion again. Anything but that. Eric would be relieving him any moment. He sighed. "I like her." He noted Andy's determined expression. The kid wasn't about to drop the subject. "She's a nice lady. Why?"

Andy tilted his head to the side, his face crinkled in thought. "She needs someone to watch after her when I go to camp. I thought he'd be a good choice. I like Mr. Eric too, but Mr. Des used to be a detective."

Sin's gaze narrowed, searching Andy's face. What was he trying to do? Set his mom up with his partners? Oh, hell no. Avery was his and neither Des nor Eric would encroach on his claim. Eric had been right last night. He had staked one. Somehow he had to get Avery's son to see it too.

"What about me? I just told you I like your mom."

"I dunno." The boy's appraising gaze swept Sin's face. "You bark."

Sin grinned and shook his head, holding on to his chuckle. "Nah, they were just messing with you. I don't bark. But I can pass."

"Yeah. You can." Andy nodded, eyeing him a long moment as if still unsure.

"So, how about it? I'll keep an eye on your mom. Of course my partners will help, which I'm sure you'll approve, since you like them, too. But I promise to take special care of her."

"You will?"

"Sure. See? A very simple solution. If I take special care of her you won't have to worry."

Chapter 11

Sin walked into his office a half hour after Eric relieved him, fully intending to discover if Des had searched Avery's dresser drawers.

"Got a sec?" Des knocked on his door minutes later and strolled into the room.

"Sure." Sin nodded and indicated the upholstered chair in front of his desk. "As a matter of fact, I was on my way to your office."

"Oh?" Des sat. "You got problems, too?"

"Just a couple of questions, but they can wait." He eyed him. "You first, you obviously have news."

Des threw a couple of files on the desk. "Read those."

Sin picked one up and thumbed through it. "What're these?"

"Employee records of our two latest hires on the production line. I got 'em from personnel."

"I can see that. What's up with them?"

"Jeremy Brubaker."

"You'll have to be more specific." Sin's brow furrowed. "I'm not familiar with the name."

"That's because you know him as Jimmy Bond, our night watchman." Des smiled and leaned back, stretching. "The man isn't what he seems. Neither are those two individuals. I ran their social security numbers and found out some interesting shit."

Sin nodded and waited for him to continue. When he didn't, he urged, "I must be missing something, so connect the dots for me."

"The records are manufactured. There's no DMV record, and all the other records, like bank and credit card, go back only six months. The social security numbers and addresses are fake. Jimmy's in cahoots with Williams." Des snorted. "They all are...came here to spy on us. Apparently you were on to something with the good colonel and had a damned good reason to question his motives."

"Okay." He frowned. "Go on, I'm listening. Don't stop now that you've caught my interest."

Des spent a few minutes detailing the night watchman's activities, along with their conversation after discovering the man in

Sin's office. Des had gotten in early for the express purpose of doing more digging. "So, what do you think?"

"You're asking me?" Sin shrugged, his frown deepening. Everything was unraveling and the first thread broke the day he signed the contract with the military for his technology and set out to test the devices. "You're the detective. You tell me."

"The only way I see it making any sense is if the colonel is part of what's been going on."

"That's a scary suggestion, but downright terrifying if it's true."

"Yeah, I just don't get why. If he's part of the thefts, he's gotta know the product will be useless in another week. Even worse, how do we go about proving he's involved?" Des sighed. "Definitely puts us in a precarious position, especially since our production line has been compromised."

"Have you talked to those two?" Sin nodded at the files.

"No. What I have done is readjust the security cameras to pick up their every movement and I have someone watching the monitors full-time. They won't be able to as much as pee without me knowing it."

"What about Jimmy?"

"Jeremy," Des corrected.

"Jeremy, then. What do we do about him?"

"We think of some information for him to feed the colonel, so he won't suspect him. Williams wants to know about your message the other night from McNeil."

Sin grunted, then eyed Des carefully. "Do you think you can trust using him like that?"

"It's a toss-up. I'll keep an eye on him. But I'm not too worried. Given his reaction to my compensation package, I doubt he's in any big hurry to rat us out. I got the impression he doesn't trust Williams any more than we do. I'm milking the fact and told him we'd come up with something for him to report." Des chuckled softly. "It never hurts to give him extra incentives. I have enough on him and my promises of bodily injury strengthened my stand. I made certain he knew they weren't empty threats." His smile died. He was silent, his intent gaze penetrating. "So, what's on your mind?" He hesitated. "Why were you on your way to my office?" he asked, corralling Sin's thoughts back to his concerns about someone going through Avery's personal belongings.

Were the two connected?

"When you searched Avery's house, exactly how thorough were you?"

"I gave a cursory inspection." Des shrugged. "Anything more than a quick once-over would've raised concerns." A sheepish smile slid over his face. "The lady's already nervous. I certainly wasn't about to make her more so with overdoing my nosiness so soon."

"You didn't go through her dresser?" Sin's gaze narrowed.

"No. Why are you concerned with Avery's drawers, anyway?"

"She mentioned noticing someone had gone through them. She also knew you'd been in her room. Said Terry caught you." He grinned. "You must be losing your touch to let Avery's sister catch you in the act."

Des snorted and sat up straight. "She didn't catch me."

"Oh?" Sin's eyebrows rose, holding on to his gaze.

"Okay, she saw me coming out of Avery's room," Des admitted, sighing and raking a hand through his short hair. "It's no big deal. Terry had no idea of what I'd been doing and my answer mollified her, I'm sure of it. But I never went through any dresser drawers. I did go through her computer and desk, though. Copied a few files I haven't had time to review yet. I got a little sidetracked with all the other stuff."

The melodious canon blared from Des' pocket. He pulled out his cell and checked the display before holding up a hand, stopping Sin as he was about to speak. "Hold that thought. I want to take this. It may be important."

Sin nodded, consumed with questions as his mind spun.

"Hey, Rod. Thanks for calling back." Des listened for a few seconds and a grin spread across his face. "Yeah, I got your message. I tried your cell this morning and didn't leave a message, figured I'd hear from you soon enough."

Sin realized while watching Des talk that he'd been praying his partner was somehow responsible, and after learning this wasn't the case his concern grew. Had someone else been in Avery's house? And was that same someone connected with the colonel?

A sliver of alarm ran through him.

"Okay, I'm listening…" Des broke off, shifting out of the chair to pace, but Sin paid him no mind, his thoughts on Avery. Was she in danger? If so, it meant she was definitely a connection and someone to keep a better watch over.

Or maybe there was another reason for the connection. Doubts surfaced.

Damn. He didn't want her to be involved, yet too many coincidences gnawed at his gut raising other questions. *Could Williams be guilty of industrial espionage? Is Avery part of this along with the colonel?* The idea made him cringe, but he couldn't ignore any possibility, especially since he'd been warned off at the cemetery and Williams had known about his visit.

Or is Avery the colonel's innocent pawn?

That thought sent sheer terror running through Sin's veins. He'd promised her son he'd take special care of her and it seemed their presence hadn't stopped an intruder.

"You're sure?" Concern in Des' voice drew Sin's attention. He'd stopped his pacing. Sin saw him nod, then saw his expression harden.

"I really appreciate your help on this. I owe you one." Des paused, ready to hang up. "Oh, that?" He shook his head and continued pacing, until he halted, ready to sit. "Nothing. I was messing with a guy, trying to get him to talk. He did. Since I still need him, I'd rather not tell you what he did just yet." He was quiet for a moment, listening. "Yeah, you're my ace in the hole." He chuckled and sank into the chair. "I'll catch you later and fill you in."

Des flipped the phone shut and stuffed it into his pocket.

Sin's eyebrows shot up. "What was that all about?"

"That was Rod. You know? My contact on the force?" Sin nodded and Des added, "Seems our bullet was shot from an M14, a military-issue rifle replaced years ago with the M16. Nowadays, the M14 is mostly used as a ceremonial weapon—like Arlington's burials. It's best known for its accuracy, also used in some variant by military sharpshooters, according to Rod."

"Hmmm. This just keeps getting worse. Why would a sharpshooter take a few shots at us? Is the other night, along with the thefts, tied to Williams?" Sin sat back, rubbing his forehead with his thumb and forefinger, absorbing the news. "It's so unbelievable, it works. My gut tells me the man's involved."

"Yeah, my thoughts exactly. He has to be. Too much points to him."

"But why? The other products don't have military uses, and as you pointed out, the one that does will be useless in another week."

"Damn good question. The answer's most likely greed, as our PI says. This whole thing just keeps getting curiouser and curiouser."

"Why search through Avery's drawers?" Sin voiced the question, thinking out loud.

"You're sure someone did?"

He nodded. "She thought so. She seemed pretty upset, and my actions did nothing to set her mind at ease." Sin sighed, wiped his face, and glanced back at the files on his desk. "I'm not cut out for this shit. I hate knowing people have hidden motives and I hate spying."

Des stretched and crossed his legs again, offering a placating smile. "Don't look at it as spying, we're protecting."

"Yeah, but are we protecting the wrong person? Do you think she's involved with the colonel?"

"No. I'd bet my life on it, but she's a link...a connection." Des' complete faith took away the brunt of his mistrust. "The link's her dead husband. He was the last known person to have the Xcom2s in his possession," Des said, alleviating the rest. "What if he was in on it with the colonel? Maybe Montgomery double-crossed him, and the colonel thinks Avery knows something."

"I wish we could forget about the Xcom2s altogether." Doing so might keep Avery safer. "If we weren't so dependent on the money their sale would generate, we could." But the minute his words were out, Sin knew running away wasn't the answer to their problems. Somehow, he and his partners had become enmeshed too deeply, and if anything, their course was set.

"You're not going to let some namby-pamby colonel get away with this, are you?"

"We may not have a lot of choice in the matter. Still, we got a bigger problem. How do you prove a man sworn to defend his country is dishonest?" He shook his head and rubbed his neck. "We're screwed."

"No! We've still got one lead...Esperanza. Call Eric. Make sure he watches Avery like a hawk."

"Eric's not a spy either, Des." He stood up and strode to the windows, searching the parking lot, wondering how this whole mess had spiraled out of control. "We're not prepared to take on the United States military. My God, that's like ants fighting giant spiders who have unlimited amounts of venom and webbing. We'd be eaten alive."

Des chuckled at Sin's colorful analogy. "Maybe, but we can't let it go without at least giving it our best effort. Besides, we're only taking on one dishonest colonel who probably has no clue we know so much. And don't forget Avery. There's a reason the colonel's interested in her. Until we can figure out why, we need to step up our protection."

Sin nodded, concurring with Des. SPC had nothing to lose at this point; neither did he. He picked up the phone and dialed. While waiting for Eric to answer, he mentally began restructuring the company's finances. Just in case.

~

"Want more coffee?"

Eric looked up from the open file on his laptop to see Avery holding a pot. "No, I'm fine."

"Well, I'd like a cup." She smiled.

As she turned and headed for the dining room, his thoughts shifted to Sin's warning. Five minutes hadn't elapsed since his call. All morning, Eric had tried to work while Avery straightened around him, though he hadn't thought there really was much to straighten.

Several times during the past hour, he'd glance up only to find her looking over his shoulder. Most likely she was just being nosy, but what if it was more than that? He'd surreptitiously kept her in his scope, pretending interest in his computer screen while she'd busied herself with what looked to be more obsessive cleaning.

At the swinging door, Avery glanced back. "I'll be a minute. I need to make a few calls."

Eric's gaze narrowed. Something in her manner drew his attention. She'd paused long enough to retrieve a card off the sofa table by the door, one he and Des had already checked out. It held Colonel Williams' name and number.

He froze, listening. When he thought she murmured Williams' name, he set his laptop aside and stole close enough to the one-inch crack in the swinging door where he could see and hear everything.

Incredible! She's making plans to meet the guy.

She hung up and Eric hurried back to the sofa. By the time Avery strolled into the room, he was engrossed in typing again. He hit the Save button and looked up. "You know. On second thought, a cup of coffee sounds like a good idea." He started to rise.

Avery waved him back down. "I'll get it."

Eric smiled. "Thanks."

When she was out of earshot, he grabbed his cell phone.

"Sin? It's me, Eric." His eyes stayed on the door as he whispered, "I think we got problems. Avery just made an appointment to see Williams."

"You're sure?" Sin shot back, his tone disbelieving.

"Yeah." Eric viewed the now empty doorway Avery had just vacated. His breath came out in one long exhale. "They're meeting after lunch at a running trail near the river close to the Pentagon."

"Shit." Sin sighed. A moment later, he said, "I'm picking up Scotty in an hour. Can you follow her without being seen, just in case she's not in league with the colonel? I'll make sure Des is waiting at the meeting place."

"I can try." Eric wiped his face and took another deep breath, shaking his head in a self-deprecating manner. "You know I stink at this kind of shit."

"You'll do fine. Stay with her. Don't let her out of your sight."

"I'll do what I can. I gotta go." Eric hung up when he heard Avery's voice.

"I'll be leaving in an hour to have lunch with Terry." Avery pushed through the door carrying a tray.

"Okay." He nodded and took the cup she offered. "Sure you don't want some company?"

"Not this time, though I'm sure Terry would love it." She sat across from him and smiled, keeping her eyes fastened on her coffee. She took a sip. "I have an errand to do afterward. Something I need to do on my own. I'm not sure how long I'll be gone. I'll lock up, then call your office when I'm done, so I won't tie up your afternoon. How's that?"

"Fine." He shrugged. "Des'll be here later when you get back."

"Thanks. I'm glad you're all so accommodating," she murmured behind her coffee.

"No problem." Eric prayed the lady wasn't involved. He liked her. She seemed too nice to be in league with Williams.

~

Colonel Williams hung up the phone and allowed himself a self-satisfied smile. He picked up the receiver and dialed.

Esperanza answered on the second ring. "Yeah."

"Where are you?"

"The Baltimore–Washington Parkway, heading back into D.C.. After an unproductive ten hours' waiting, I might add. No one seems to be interested in Esperanza's house."

"Well, this might make you happier." Williams nodded, fully understanding his impatience. Esperanza had driven back to the home they'd created for their purposes the night before. "She's meeting me, which will give you a perfect opportunity to go through her house." Williams didn't have to say who "she" was. Both knew perfectly well they were discussing the widow.

"When?"

"We're meeting at two."

"What about her bodyguards?"

"She's taken care of them. According to her, they'll be outside, watching the house. I'm sure you'll have no trouble slipping past unseen."

"I'll be there." Williams heard Esperanza swear under his breath. "But I've got a few details to attend to first. Thank God you gave me plenty of warning. Traffic's a bitch."

"Just use your time wisely. We may not gain another opportunity this good."

Esperanza grunted, before the line went dead.

Williams cut the connection, then punched in another number, and brought the receiver to his ear.

"DeSalvo."

"Are you tracking him?" he asked, not wasting time on pleasantries.

"Will you relax? This is routine," DeSalvo replied, obviously aware of whom he was talking to.

"No, I won't relax. Just answer the goddamn question."

"Yeah. I'm tracking him. I'll let you know when we have something. Are you satisfied?"

"Good," he said, cutting the call.

~

"Now that we have drinks, tell me about this Sin." Terry took a sip of wine before flipping open her menu. "I think he likes you." She paused, studying her sister before adding, "So, what're you going to do about it?"

"Terry!" Avery hid her embarrassment behind the menu. Leave it to Terry to say something so outrageous. Having selected the seafood linguine, she closed it and folded her hands together on top. "I don't plan on doing anything."

"Why? He seems nice. You said you checked him out."

"You know why." Avery took a sip of her drink, then shook her head. "Mike was killed only two months ago."

"What? You have to wait a year before you can go out with anyone?" Terry hesitated a heartbeat, then added, "Come on, Avery. You're still among the living."

"He was my husband. The least I can do is mourn him."

"Mourn him? For how long? When do you get to live a little and have some fun?"

"That's all life is to you, isn't it?" Avery tensed, her anger rising. "A fun game?"

"No. Not a game." Terry lowered her menu and peered over it, her expression grim. "But I definitely think a life without fun isn't worth living. I haven't seen any in yours for *too damn long.*"

"How can I think of fun when I sent my husband a Dear John letter?" Avery snapped. Then she inhaled a long breath and exhaled on a sigh. Terry was only trying to help. "I should've had the guts to say something to his face."

"Then, let's talk about why you didn't."

"I'd rather not." She'd never seemed to find the perfect time to broach the subject with Mike, so she'd procrastinated until it was too late and he'd shipped out again. Avery brought the glass to her lips, wishing Terry would just drop her line of questioning. She was tired of remembering her foolhardiness and lack of courage.

"Why are you so insistent on protecting his image when he was a total jerk? A jerk who didn't want to talk or share your life because his was all that mattered?"

"What do you want me to say?" Avery set down her menu and tried to keep her voice low, but the effort cost her. "Yes, he was arrogant. Yes, he was self-absorbed and selfish. He had to be that way to do his job. A necessary job that needed doing, I might add."

"What about you and Andy? What about what you two needed?" Terry reached across the table, covering her hand and squeezed. "He's gone, Avery. You didn't kill him. Snipers did. Quit feeling guilty because you're still alive. Join the rest of us and have a little fun."

Avery remained silent, wondering why she'd found it so damned hard to demand what she'd needed during her marriage. Yet, reviewing those years of acceptance in hindsight only made her appear more cowardly.

Terry leaned back, still holding her gaze. "This Sin seems nice and available. At the very least, consider the opportunity. A babysitter like him doesn't just happen along every day. He's simply divine."

No, thought Avery. *He's more than divine.* All three of her sitters were. She nodded, as the last hour spent with Eric yakking about Sin as if he'd parted the Red Sea flashed through her mind. It was almost comical and any other time she'd have laughed at the irony. Right now, she was torn.

According to Eric, the sun clearly rose and set on Jeffrey Sinclair, and such a testimonial made her realize she might have made a teensy-weensy error in calling Colonel Williams. She was nervous about her upcoming meeting. Somehow, she felt like she was betraying them. How stupid was that?

Eric's story of how they'd met as kids and later come to be partners had fascinated her and only added to Sin's appeal. Plus, the fact she found him extremely attractive didn't hurt.

Oh Lord, this whole situation was enough to drive her to drinking. Here Terry was encouraging her to be more than friends, and in going behind Sin's back with the colonel, she may be throwing away that chance. Even then, there was more to it than seizing an opportunity.

"Just think about what I said," Terry urged, interrupting her musings.

"Sure, but you don't know the whole story." Avery gulped a healthy swig of wine and sighed. "Mike and I didn't have the best sex life." She shrugged, looking away. That was putting it mildly. The horrible memory of the last time she and Mike had sex flitted through her mind. He hadn't even taken the time to hold her, getting angry with her because she wasn't responding like some wind-up doll. Though she'd shared most of her marital problems with Terry, this had been private. Suddenly she was uncomfortable with the idea of admitting her total ineptness in the bedroom. "I'm not like you, Terry. I wouldn't know what to do, even if I decided to consider the opportunity, as you put it."

Terry's wineglass halted an inch from her lips and her curious gaze sought Avery's. "Oh my God. You're serious, aren't you?" she asked after regaining her composure.

Avery nodded, studying her glass intently, fingering the stem. Sex with Mike had been tolerable, but never truly pleasurable…or as pleasurable as she'd been led to believe it should have been from all those magazine articles and self-help books she'd read in the last ten years.

She'd tried to spice things up with candles, sex toys, lotion…you name it, she'd tried it, but it never seemed to do much good, at least not for her. After a while, she gave up and just figured there was something wrong with her. That that part of her anatomy didn't work.

Frigid was the term Mike had used too many times during those months he'd been home.

"I'm no good at sex." She cleared her throat. "Mike had his faults, but so do I. According to him, I lacked passion. I wasn't the only one to come out of our marriage wanting more." She frowned. "I'm sure I disappointed him as much as he disappointed me."

"Oh, Av," Terry said, searching her face. "That's so sad." She waited until Avery risked eye contact, then she tendered a soft smile. "What about now? Are you attracted to Sin?"

A flush of heat rose up her face. "Yes," Avery stated honestly. Why deny it.

Terry's smile stayed in place. "Sexual attraction's a wonderful thing. There's no replacement for pheromones. Just relax. It'll come naturally."

"Okay." Avery brought her glass to her lips. *How in the hell have we even gotten on this subject?* After taking a healthy sip, she sighed. "Relaxation isn't exactly the feeling I get when I'm around him. The air kind of becomes charged," she admitted. "Definitely not conducive to relaxation."

"You go, girl!" Terry set her glass down and clapped her hands. A gurgle of laughter escaped her throat.

"I'm baring my soul and you're laughing? This is serious. I'm not as fast as you are."

"Oh God, Avery. That's so nineties. Women have come a long way in twenty years. We take the reins and decide what we want."

She sighed. "Of course there are those men out there who are threatened by women who know their own mind."

Avery didn't laugh. "In case you haven't figured out, the last time I went to bed with a new man was in the nineties and look what happened. I ended up pregnant. It's not like I've had more than one lover." So much for the reliability of the pill, as she'd been one of the *point zero one percent*. Still, she never regretted her decision to quit school, marry, and carry Andy to full term. She'd loved Mike with all her heart, though her first initiation to sex wasn't one of her fondest memories. Would sex with anyone, even Sin, be any different?

"I have no clue what my mind wants." *Or even if I can consider it.* She wasn't Terry. She was a grieving, guilt-ridden, lonely widow. Not exactly someone who should be thinking about sex.

"Oh? I'll bet when you drop the guilt, you'll have a very good idea of what your mind wants, and my guess is he'll pick up on exactly how you feel. Men always have their radar zoned in."

"Maybe," she conceded as the thought of his flirting this morning went through her mind.

"Maybe? Come on. Fess up." Terry's raised eyebrows extracted Avery's urge to chuckle.

"Okay. He's interested." She grinned. "More than interested." Her chin went up and she insisted, "But I'm not sure I can handle conking him on the head and dragging him to bed."

"Trust me, when the moment's right, you won't have to go to such lengths." Terry laughed. "An intimate dinner for two with just the right lighting and music, along with a couple of glasses of wine, can work wonders." She shrugged, still grinning. "After that, you just let nature take its course. Sin doesn't appear to be a man who misses opportunities."

She placed her hand over Avery's and squeezed. "Trust him to pick up on your cues, and more importantly, trust your instinct for when the time is right. Just remember. You deserve happiness, Avery. If it comes your way, don't be afraid to grab on to it with both hands. If nothing else, use Mike's death as a reminder of how short life can be."

Avery nodded, seeing the waitress bearing down on their table to take their order.

The two finished lunch, and after walking Terry back to her

office building, Avery hurried to her car. She zipped across the bridge and found a parking spot in the empty lot runners primarily used, with just enough time to make her meeting with Colonel Williams.

Most lunchtime runners were back to work by two and didn't come out until the workday ended after four, so the path was deserted as she walked to the agreed-upon destination.

She rounded the bend and the colonel stood fifty feet ahead. Her pace increased until she was close enough to take his offered hand.

"Colonel Williams." She nodded. "Thanks for meeting me."

"Not a problem. My office isn't far and I always enjoy getting out if I have the chance." He turned and began walking. "So, tell me. Why the call insisting on this meeting?"

"I have some questions about my husband's death." Falling into step next to him, Avery kept his pace. "I thought maybe you could clear them up."

"I'll try. My knowledge is limited to what I read in reports, though. I wasn't present when Major Montgomery died."

"I understand." She cleared her throat, remaining silent for a moment, thinking of the best way to introduce her concerns. "Actually, my questions pertain more to two men I met when I was at the cemetery several nights ago. Mr. Sinclair and Mr. Phillips." She stopped and met his curious gaze. "Are you familiar with them?"

"I am."

"Then you know my husband was testing their product? And Mike was the last known person to have the prototypes in his possession. What can you tell me about that?"

"Mrs. Montgomery." Colonel Williams' smile was warm and friendly. "I don't know why they are bothering you or what they've told you about the incident, but the last known person to have them in his possession is the thief, himself. So far, no one knows who that is."

"I see." She glanced down and stared at the ground, unable to meet his concerned gaze. "They think I'm in danger."

He chuckled. "They're overreacting."

"I'm not so sure. Someone shot at me the other night. Mr. Phillips and Mr. Sinclair think it's connected to Mike and the missing product."

"I'm aware of their position. We've had numerous discussions about it over the past few weeks. They're frustrated and desperate. I wouldn't put it past either to initiate the attack to gain your trust, since they're also under the mistaken belief of your husband's involvement. Both Major Montgomery and Major Crandall have been cleared of any wrongdoing."

"Why would they want to gain my trust?" Avery didn't want to consider the possibility, yet someone had gone through her things. Was Colonel Williams right about the cemetery? Had Des been the one firing, with Sin pretending to protect her? Was it all a ploy? Perhaps that's what Eric had been doing, trying to snow her with his praise of Sin.

"Who knows what's going through their minds. I certainly don't understand their thought processes. Could be, they suspect you. Maybe they're under the mistaken assumption you *are* involved."

"Why would they think that? I didn't even know my husband worked on their project."

"The prototypes are small—the size of a pinhead—and can be easily hidden. Maybe they think Mike sent them to you before he died."

"No. He would never do such a thing. Not Mike. He'd never jeopardize his work."

"Of course not. I don't believe that scenario any more than you do. But they might. It's a possibility you have to consider." Colonel Williams was silent for a moment, studying her face intently before asking, "Do they have reason to be suspicious? Did Mike send you anything before he died?"

Avery shook her head. "He kept in touch by e-mails mostly." She stopped short of saying she was the one who wrote most of the letters. He already knew about her letters, since he'd returned them to her. The colonel didn't have to know Mike was a lousy communicator who rarely wrote anything but a few lines in the short e-mails she received now and then. Except for the last letter and many e-mails, which came within days of his death, and the reason for those was to try and dissuade her from going ahead with the divorce. Her private concerns with Mike weren't any more the military's business than Des' or Sin's.

"Your husband and Crandall died at the hands of terrorists who ambushed their jeep." His sad smile re-formed. "We're quite sure terrorists are behind the theft and those terrorists are not lurking in graveyards, shooting at innocent women."

Yeah, she thought. And if Mike and Marshall had been paying better attention, maybe the ambush could've been avoided.

Avery nodded, praying the guilt she felt didn't show in her expression. Her letter demanding a divorce most likely led to their deaths, despite Terry's opinion to the contrary. One of Mike's pet peeves as a commanding officer had been the Dear John letters his men received. So many came at times when the men needed no distractions, especially distractions from loved ones at home. Mike had always lamented that the battlefield was the worst possible place for those kinds of distractions. Life in combat was already precarious and dangerous, and a man couldn't concentrate on staying alive or on keeping his buddies alive if he was worried about the home front.

Avery's letter had most likely kept both men from doing their jobs...of staying alive. She should have had the guts to tell Mike to his face and given him the time in between deployments to come to terms with a divorce, rather than distract him with news out of the blue like she had.

"Let me give you some advice." Colonel Williams' gruff voice pulled Avery out of her guilty thoughts. "If anyone presents a danger, it comes from SPC's owners. By keeping in close contact with them, you're placing yourself in more danger. Ask yourself about their motives. Did you ever wonder why they were at the cemetery in the first place?"

Avery sighed. "I see your point."

"If you'd like, I can furnish detailed dossiers I have on the three men. I made copies. It's against policy, but they aren't classified. They're full of background information you might find interesting. After all, it's only fair. They received a detailed dossier on you."

"What?" She felt as though he'd slapped her. Sin and his partners had received a detailed dossier on her? "I don't understand." She tried to keep surprise out of her voice as well as the hurt out of her eyes. He didn't need to know how much his revelation hurt.

"All part of routine investigations and information-gathering, I assure you. Since your husband was involved with testing their product, they were privy to your history. Would you like the copies I made?"

"Yes, I would." Avery nodded slowly, absorbing the news stoically as betrayal penetrated her being. How could they? These men she'd come to trust had known all about her. They'd invaded her space, fitting in so well. Was that planned?

They made her feel safe, even played ball with her son, most likely using him after learning Andy was her Achilles' heel. She fought back tears. Was she caught up in some twisted game they were playing? Were they responsible for the shots in the cemetery, as the colonel had implied?

And what of Sin?

How much did he actually know about her? Did he understand her loneliness?

Were he and his partners acting on the knowledge to gain her trust?

Oh Lord, she just didn't have any answers. She should definitely rethink her position on using them as bodyguards. She prayed she was wrong about them, and because she didn't want to believe they'd set her up, she'd first read the information before making any hasty assumptions. After all, seeking information had been part of her mission this afternoon, even if that information wasn't the best of news.

Colonel Williams looked at his watch and sighed heavily. "Well, I've got to get back. I have a pressing meeting in twenty minutes." He held out his hand, indicating for her to go ahead of him, and smiled. "Shall we?"

"Of course." She offered a wan smile and started on the path, working to keep her thoughts of Sin's possible betrayal off her face. Right now she didn't know whom to trust, but she certainly didn't trust Colonel Williams, and she didn't dare give him any signs of how disturbing she found his news. "I appreciate your time."

Neither spoke on the trail as they wound their way toward the parking lot. When they got to his car, he retrieved three brown files, the papers fastened inside at the top on each side with two-pronged metal clips.

Avery took the files and shook Colonel Williams' hand. "Good-bye and thank you." She climbed inside her car and tossed them on the passenger seat. She sat motionless, thinking about the files sitting so benignly next to her and wishing she wasn't so afraid to open them, petrified she'd learn they'd conned her. Eventually, the colonel drove away.

She took a deep breath to still her racing heart and sent up a silent prayer. *Please Lord, don't let them be deceiving me.* Her focus landed on the files, and unable to contain her curiosity any longer, she reached for the top one, bearing the name on the tab in capital letters—JEFFREY ROBERT SINCLAIR. Avery was dying to know about Sin's background. Dying to learn more about him.

According to the colonel, he'd read all about her. "Turnabout is only fair play," she mumbled, opening it. In seconds, the words engrossed her.

Avery finally flipped the file closed and sighed. Sin's early life was featured in comprehensive detail. Somehow, it was hard to picture him as the angry young man the file depicted—one of a thirteen-year-old hitting the juvenile court system. The case had been dismissed for lack of evidence, and the word EXPUNGED was stamped in bold letters across the page, which probably meant no one else had such access, but there was no denying his actions had been documented.

She flipped through both Des' and Eric's files quickly, seeing similar paperwork, but not quite as damning. All of a sudden, she felt like an intruder—spying, reading information she shouldn't be privy to. It was like reading a diary, or having an unfair advantage over three individuals she really liked.

Why had the colonel given these to her? To dissuade her from hanging out with them? Was he the game-player? Maybe. Fortunately, Williams didn't know her very well. The information only made her all the more curious and interested in Sin. He had to be an exceptional human being to have endured such a past and become the man she was beginning to know.

She turned the key and backed out of the space with only one thought on her mind. After her lunch with Terry and her meeting with Williams, and despite the guilt she carried or how crazy it seemed, now, more than ever, she wondered what Sin would be like as a lover.

Chapter 12

Des looked up and flicked the switch to open the car window in response to Avery's taps. Once it rolled down, she said, "I'm back."

"That you are, lovely lady. That you are." He grinned, unable to hide his chipper demeanor. Avery wasn't in league with the colonel after all. "Did you have fun at lunch?"

"Yes, as a matter of fact, I did." She returned his grin. "How about you? Did you have time for lunch?"

"I grabbed something on the way," he said, climbing out. "I could get used to someone worrying about me. Of course, then I'd have to deal with Sin. Not a pleasant thought."

"You're teasing." Avery choked on what sounded like a forced laugh.

"Unfortunately, I'm not, but I have eyes." He slammed the door, hit the remote lock, and looked away, sighing. "I'm not into coming in second place either, nor am I into hurting a good friend."

She appeared flustered, without a clue as how to respond to his comment. He probably should have kept his mouth shut. The silence was deafening as they strode up the walkway side by side.

Des waited patiently while she unlocked the front door.

"And since you did ask, I was wondering if there's any of that cherry pie left from last night," he finally said, interrupting the quiet and trying to ease the tension his stupid remarks caused. "It'd sure hit the spot about now."

"There's plenty left and you're welcome to it." Avery laughed, seeming quite happy to have the conversation on something other than what it had been on only a moment ago. "I might even be persuaded to have a piece with you." She turned the knob, breezed through the door, and stopped short.

"Oh my God." Her amusement faded, replaced with pure horror.

"What's wrong?" Des followed her inside. "Jeez Louise." Upon spying the mess in her living room, his smile died. He nodded toward the open door. "Wait out on the porch while I check it out," he said in a warning tone, bending to pull his weapon out from under his pants leg.

"Please be careful," she whispered.

Avery's frightened words drew his gaze and he noted her pale face and shaking hands, as she stood frozen.

"Don't worry. I know what I'm doing." He flashed an encouraging smile in an effort to wipe the panicked look off her face. "Go sit on the porch. I won't be long...you just stay put."

She nodded and turned, closing the door behind her.

Des stepped cautiously over the bits of broken glass crunching under his leather soles, wondering if the perp was still somewhere inside. After taking the safety off, he cocked his weapon and slowly proceeded through the rest of the room, the gun raised, ready to aim. He nudged the swinging dining room door open and gave the space a thorough inspection. Slowly, he made his way through the bottom level. The disorder ranged from broken glass, tipped-over shelves, and drawers having been emptied, to slashed furniture.

He quickly secured the lower level before carefully starting up the stairs, weapon still drawn. Systematically, he searched each room discovering a similar pattern of disarray, but no sign of the intruder. When he got to Avery's bedroom, he halted, reached into his pocket for his cell phone, and flipped it open.

"Yeah, Sin, it's me, Des," he said, once Sin answered. "We got big problems." He spent a moment detailing what he'd found and ended with, "I think Avery may need you. How fast can you get here?"

Sin assured him he would drop everything and hung up. Des shut the phone with the flick of his wrist and peered into the bedroom. An overwhelming sense of sadness engulfed him as he surveyed the damage. He swallowed regret at not having prevented such ruin, noting very little of the beautifully decorated space that suited Avery had been left intact.

This was his fault. He curled his fist in frustration, wanting to hit something, but not giving in to the desire because he wasn't about to add to the destruction. He hadn't been expecting anyone to slip into her house and do such a heinous act, but he should have. The colonel was responsible. He had no doubt, especially after hearing the man warn Avery against SPC's owners from his hiding spot. The other night wasn't a fluke. Williams clearly thought Avery had something, and given the mess, he clearly meant to find it. His gaze wandered toward the alcove and Des wondered if he already had.

He stole over to her desk spying the computer, now a pile of rubble. Her desk drawers were empty, the contents lying on the floor underneath them. Next to the pile, discarded haphazardly, were several letters.

Des took a moment to read each one. Then sighing, he folded them and stuck them inside his sport coat pocket. Sin might be interested in them, but the perps hadn't been. Otherwise, they'd have never left them for him to find.

He turned away from the destruction and headed back to Avery.

"It's all clear, but your house is pretty trashed. They were obviously searching for something," he said, stepping onto the porch. "I called Sin. He's on his way." Her distracted nod made him wonder if she even heard him. "We'll help you clean up, but you can't stay here."

"This is my home. I'm not leaving." Avery lifted her chin and met his gaze defiantly.

"We'll see," was all he said, turning and heading back inside with her following.

"I called Mary's cell. She took the boys to the movies. Andy's fine. He was already planning on spending the night with Tommy, since they were—" Her words died. She glanced around, before she added in a more subdued tone, "—leaving at six tomorrow morning."

He noticed her tears lurking as she pivoted, taking in the damage.

"Thank God, he had his things packed early. They took them over before I left for lunch." Her focus went to a smashed photo on the floor next to her foot. She bent to pick up the shattered frame, knocking the glass shards out of the way. "This is one of the last pictures I had taken of the three of us." Avery looked at him, her expression pleading, the hopelessness pouring out of her eyes. "Why would someone destroy this?"

Des had no answer. If only one of them had been here the entire time she'd been gone, maybe they could have caught the bastard or bastards who did this. As it was, he'd been hiding on the trail ahead of her and the colonel. Eric, who'd been trailing her, had headed back to the office after she arrived at the parking lot. While she'd been engrossed in files, he'd returned to the house in plenty of time to see her emerge from her backyard gate after parking in her garage. He swallowed the lump in his throat and brushed a hand over his hair.

"Why?" she whispered, shaking her head.

"We'll clean it up. It'll be okay." Des pulled her into his arms, hoping to ease her anguish.

"No. It's not okay. It'll never be okay again." She broke away, as anger replaced some of her hopelessness. "Look at this." She waved a hand to indicate the mess. "Someone invaded my domain. Someone destroyed my things. Someone violated me. And what's worse? I don't even know why." Turning and stepping through the debris, she headed for the front door.

Des watched her go, wishing more than anything Sin was already here. He'd protect her. He had a protective streak a mile wide for those he cared about and took under his wing, and no one could miss the fact that Sin had taken Avery under his protection. He'd help her get through this. Sin's resolve was like a granite boulder...strong...immovable...and impervious to outside elements. Heaven help those who got in his way.

~

Avery's front door opened and closed. She didn't hear Des' footsteps on the porch, but she felt him hovering. She glanced up and noted his guilt-stricken expression. He clearly held himself responsible. Avery patted the spot beside her, offering a semblance of a smile.

"It's not your fault." She worked at keeping her voice steady.

"Yeah, it is." He sighed and shook his head, plopping down next to her, meeting her gaze. "I didn't take the threat at the cemetery as seriously as I should have and look what happened."

Sincere regret spilled out of his expressive eyes. The colonel was wrong. Des hadn't fired the shot at the cemetery. No one was that good of an actor.

"You had no way of knowing this would happen." Her nod indicated the house. Sin's heroic action, covering her and protecting her from the other shots, most likely hadn't been staged either. She felt it in every fiber of her being.

Des rested a hand briefly on her shoulder. "Sin's on his way. In the meantime, we should notify the authorities."

"Do we have to? I'd rather not deal with the police and all their questions right now."

A car drove by and Des' attention was rooted on it until it was out of sight. Then he refocused on her. "No. But it might be safer. This is serious, Avery."

"I know. I can't handle more strangers invading and digging through my personal belongings." She squeezed his hand, now resting on his knee, in reassurance. "Besides, I've read the statistics. They seldom catch people who do these types of things."

"You never know without trying. Calling Keyes and filing a report is worth a shot."

Avery shook her head stubbornly. "No. No police."

"What about Andy? You'll most likely need a police report in order for insurance to pay for the damage."

She stiffened. "Andy will be fine. He's safe with Mary and Steve. After tomorrow, he'll be camping for a week. Right now, insurance is the least of my concerns. I'll take pictures and go into the police station to file a report. If it's not enough, then it's a chance I'm willing to take."

Des expelled another long breath and his expression turned more somber if that was possible. "We'll see. When Sin gets here, we'll do what we can to straighten up." He glanced back at the house before meeting her gaze again. "They were thorough, though. There's not much to straighten in some rooms."

Avery blinked back tears. Her beautiful house, decorated with furniture and fabrics she'd picked out. Her domain was her life, something she had total control over, and now someone had reduced it to broken glass and slashed cushions.

"I need to call Terry." She felt him stiffen. "Sorry, Des." She opened her purse and pulled out her cell phone. She scrolled through to Terry's number, pushed the Send button, and brought the phone to her ear. "I know you two have some kind of history and don't like each other, but I need her."

He nodded. "Do what you have to do. I understand and I'll be nice."

Avery tried to smile at his attempt at humor, but she failed to muster up much of one.

The line rang several times before voice mail picked up.

"She must be in a meeting." She waited until Terry's message ended and the beep sounded. "Ter, it's Av. Something's happened. I don't want to go into it on voice mail, so can you give me a call when you get this? It's important. Thanks."

She glanced at Des after disconnecting. "I guess now we wait for Sin," she said, unwilling to explore the damage without him. She needed his presence too…needed the strength she'd determined was so much a part of his persona, which was odd for her to admit, because for too long she'd pretended to need nothing from anyone, not even her husband.

"Yeah." He looked at his watch. "Shouldn't be too much longer."

They waited.

"You know Sin's not going to like this. He's definitely not going to like the idea of you staying here." Des' voice pierced the quiet. "Maybe you should let me handle him, okay?"

She peered at him, shading her eyes from the sun. "You're good at that, aren't you?"

"Good at what?"

"Handling Sin."

He squinted, eyeing her. "Why do you say that?"

"No reason." When he kept his curious gaze on her, waiting, she offered a wan smile and gave in to his implied request. "I noticed how easily you defused his anger last night."

"An easy task, since he jumped to the wrong conclusions. He merely needed to be set straight, is all."

"Sin says you've been together for a long time." Avery thought back to Sin's revelations and the colonel's dossiers detailing their unruly teen years. Maybe these men did have ulterior motives, but noting Des' smile, she couldn't help feeling the fondness shining from his eyes was genuine. Warmth radiated from them like the sun's rays through glass on an icy cold day. Maybe Des could tell her more about the intriguing man. If anything, learning more about him would keep her mind off what had happened just feet away. "Did Sin's mom really kill herself?"

Des' smile died. His gaze was penetrating, as if weighing her interest along with his response. "How did you learn about that?" he finally asked.

She glanced away, embarrassed to have been caught in her small deception. Did she dare tell him of her earlier mission?

Sandy Loyd

"Avery? Answer the question."

Yes, she thought. He had a right to know. She cleared her throat, stalling for courage. "After lunch, I met with Colonel Williams," she admitted, shrugging. "He gave me a couple of files. I read them."

"Files?" She felt his attention. He waited until she looked up. His intense gaze seared hers. "Just what was in these files?" he asked, after a long moment of staring at each other.

"Background information on SPC's owners." Avery couldn't keep meeting his damning expression and peered down instead. She spent extended seconds examining her fingernails, mentally seeking an explanation. "I went to him with the intention of learning more about you guys. I was curious and concerned." Then she added with more bravado than she felt, "It's not like you didn't get files of your own from the man. He told me as much."

"So Williams provided you with information about us, huh?" Des snorted, shaking his head. "The man's incredible. I'll bet they were real informative."

"I'm sure he was thorough on both counts." She held her chin high. "I wasn't trying to pry. My only purpose was to learn more about Sin. I was hoping you could help me fill in the blanks the file left. Did his mom really commit suicide?"

Des nodded, still searching her face. When he seemed satisfied of her sincerity, his gaze moved to the street.

Avery wasn't sure he would say any more until he sighed. "Yeah, and he found her. I was with him at the time. It was one of the worst experiences of my life and one I'll never forget. Sin spent every second trying to revive her before paramedics got to their apartment. Took an hour and thirty-four minutes and three calls because of the neighborhood. Overdoses were too common and not taken seriously. Hell, they most likely thought good riddance." His voice held scorn as well as sorrow. "They might not have come at all, if not for a guy on the force we knew who happened to be on duty."

Blinking back tears, she cleared her throat, working to stop the lump of sadness forming as his meaning sank in. "I'm so sorry," she said softly, knowing it sounded hollow. His experience brought her reality into a better perspective. A few of her treasures were destroyed, yet they were only material things. She was safe. So was

Andy, thanks to her neighbor, Mary, and an afternoon movie.

"We were kids, you know?" Torment spilled out in Des' voice and pain filled his eyes. "Didn't know shit...certainly didn't know CPR. Who knows if someone arriving any earlier would've saved her and if so, who knows what kind of damage had already been done? According to the note she left, she'd lost her job as a waitress a month before and couldn't find another. She felt she had nothing to live for, not even Sin. She thought he'd be better off without her...they'd barely had enough to cover rent and food as it was. Can you imagine someone being on the brink of despair and thinking a kid would be better off without a mother?"

Avery glanced at her hands, too uncomfortable to keep meeting his pained expression. She couldn't imagine what Sin's life must have been like, what all of theirs must have been like when her life had been so different. To go through their youth, barely getting by, and then to find your mother right after she committed suicide?

"Don't look sad. We survived. Intact and made something of ourselves. Sin made sure of that. He's a good friend and a good man."

She nodded. "He told me about the cops you had as mentors."

Would she have been able to endure such obstacles and come as far? She wasn't sure and the thought made her feel extremely shallow just then. Her husband died tragically, but at least his death held meaning. She'd already suffered his loss—years earlier. If this was the worst to ever happen to her, then she could count herself lucky.

"Yeah, they still ride our butts now and then." Des chuckled. "Both guys made captain a few years ago."

"Which means they no longer have the time to find badass kids to yank on?" she said, moving the topic to anything other than Sin's mother and her suicide.

"Yeah, it does. We weren't the only kids they took on, so in that respect, it was a loss to the streets when they got promoted." He was about to say more, when he glanced up and looked past her.

Avery turned, then stood, and placed a hand over her eyes to block the afternoon sun.

Slowly, she descended the porch steps as Sin walked toward her house at a fast clip. Just seeing his rugged, handsome features made her realize how much she'd come to rely on his quiet strength in a matter of days.

As soon their gazes connected, his pace increased. Seconds later he was right in front of her rendering a comforting smile, the same one that told her he'd take care of everything.

In the next instant, Avery found herself engulfed in his arms, providing a demonstration of his power and force, and making her feel totally safe and secure. She closed her eyes and breathed in his scent, which consisted of a hint of sweat mixed with spicy cologne and deodorant and totally male.

Sin leaned back, holding her shoulders, and peered into her face. "You okay?" His concerned gaze centered on hers, as if searching for the answer in her expression. That heated look made her feel as if he cherished her. A novelty, for sure. She hadn't felt cherished. Ever. Until that night in the cemetery. Until now. His caring whisked away some of her loneliness.

"I am now." Her smile reached her eyes. Sin had arrived. Somehow, she just knew everything would be okay.

He nodded, then looked at Des with raised eyebrows. "Don't worry. We'll take care of everything, won't we?" He let go of her shoulders and started up the stairs.

"Sure." Des stood, chuckling good-naturedly. When Sin reached the top step, Des clapped him on the back and winked at Avery. "See what I mean?"

Avery bit her lip to keep from laughing. Despite feeling so wretched at having her house broken into and trashed, it was hard not to realize how extremely lucky she was to have them with her. She liked them. She felt comfortable with them, mostly because she felt safe with them.

"You should know, Williams gave her some files, not unlike the ones he gave us."

Avery stiffened. Now he was going to hate her because she'd gone behind his back.

"Really?" He slanted a glance at her, then at Des. Yet, instead of anger or irritation, his eyes held curiosity. "Why does that not surprise me."

Sin caught her gaze again with those incredible green eyes and indicated the spot Des vacated with a brief nod. "We'll sort it out later. You want to wait here while we go and survey the damage?"

"I'll go with you." She started up the stairs. "I'd rather not be alone."

Together, they went inside.

"Jeezus," Sin whispered, stopping in the middle of the room. His face registered shock as he pivoted, taking in the mayhem and whistling. "They must've been waiting for you to leave," he said a little louder, focusing on Avery. "Takes quite a while to be this destructive."

Chapter 13

Eager to be back in Baltimore, Esperanza was hampered with the same wall-to-wall mess of cars in front of him that he'd dealt with earlier. D.C. traffic seemed worse than usual. His impatience radiated off him in waves, like the desert heat rising off blacktop in summer, long after the sun had gone down. He sighed, inched along, tapping the brake too often for his liking. Minutes later, after only going several hundred feet, he grabbed a cell phone, not the same phone the colonel had called him on, but another, unknown one. He quickly punched in a preset number.

He now had enough information to determine that this entire operation had derailed. It was time to bow out before his career took a major hit.

"Yeah, it's me. Things are disintegrating around me," he said, remembering his haste in making it to Avery Montgomery's back deck, having parked blocks away with barely enough time for a thorough search. He'd jimmied the lock and was inside the house in seconds. He'd listened for sounds and movement, ready to begin methodically searching. But instead of doing what he'd gone to do, he'd done a quick run-through and left the mess he'd found, letting himself back out and disappearing down the alley to avoid detection. "I've got to get out of the U.S. and fast."

"What's happened?"

"I'm being framed. I don't have time to explain right now, but can I count on your help?"

"You got it. It'll take a day or so to arrange a workable plan."

"I'll be in Baltimore, working on my own plan and setting my own trap. You have my number. Call me when you've made all the arrangements."

Now in Baltimore, Esperanza paced, his eyes going to the video monitors flashing simultaneous pictures of each side of the house. The hidden cameras, installed a week ago in strategic spots around the Montgomery house, provided surveillance assisted with satellites. He wasn't concerned with the current pictures. His main focus was on the recorded footage that he'd rewound. Given the way the person who'd preceded him to Avery's house stayed out of the camera, he had no doubt who was responsible for the destruction he'd noted.

His thoughts went to Colonel Williams and his erratic actions. He had a niggling suspicion the man had turned and was somehow trying to tie him into it. But why? He planned to work his damnedest to solve the riddle before he made it out of the States. If not? He shrugged. It was of no consequence. He would simply file an anonymous report and disappear with no record of his involvement. No one would be able to prove he was ever here once his superior acted. Yet this whole scene galled him. He didn't like being made a fool of.

Mentally, Esperanza reviewed the facts. Someone beat him into the house, most likely to search for the prototypes, not bothering to hide his actions.

The knot in his stomach twisted, the same one he'd felt when he'd first spied the mess. He'd made a swift tour of the house, looking for signs of the intruder, or anything left behind.

In Avery's bedroom, he'd found her smashed computer and drawers—the ones he'd already searched—opened with everything dumped on the floor. On top of the pile were a couple of letters that he'd read and had tossed aside. They'd yielded nothing. Just a dead man's empty promises to his wife and another man's dreams.

Esperanza had already known about the letters' contents, had been present when the two majors had argued over her.

He remembered spending a few more minutes picking through the rubble until he'd heard a car and had glanced at his watch. He should have had plenty of time since the widow was supposed to have been meeting the colonel. Something wasn't right. He damned sure hadn't liked the fact that the whole scene had smelled like a trap.

He felt a noose slipping around his neck now as he watched the replay.

Was the colonel setting him up? The notion chilled him to the bone.

~

"It wasn't as bad as I thought," Des said hours later.

"Yeah." Sin nodded and surveyed their handiwork. When Des had first called, he'd frantically raced over as fast as his car and traffic allowed. His fears had eased a bit after seeing for himself that Avery was okay.

They'd worked as a team, cleaning and sorting and saving what they could, tossing what they couldn't. Like Des said, it could have been much worse.

Avery's admission of meeting with Williams, along with the files the colonel had provided, didn't sit well with him. Sin's earlier reservations about her safety returned full force, especially since she wouldn't agree to call the police, no matter how much he and Des badgered her.

"I don't understand why you won't at least call and have a patrol car stop by," he urged again, trying one more time.

Avery, appearing much more relaxed with her order restored, only shook her head—the same way she had the countless other times, giving the same answer. "This is my home. I don't want any more strangers traipsing through it."

"Someone broke into *your home*." Sin ran a hand through his hair, totally frustrated, his scowl returning. "You're treating it as if it's nothing. What if something else happens?"

"I know it's not nothing," she said through clenched teeth. "But reporting it won't undo the damage." Avery crossed her arms. "I won't be forced out of my home. Besides, what can happen with you two around?"

"Give it up, Sin. I'll call Keyes and make sure a report is filed."

Sin rolled his eyes and heaved a resigned sigh, reaching for patience. "Fine." He threw his hands up in defeat. One thing he was quickly learning about Avery. She could be one stubborn woman when she wanted to be.

"We can protect her," Des murmured from the alcove. He bent to pick up her computer, walking toward them.

Avery presented a weak smile. "The upholstered furniture in the living room seems to be the biggest loss." Only one side of the cushions had been slashed, so they'd situated them so that the damage didn't show. She wiped a hand across her brow, moving her bangs off her forehead. "I guess I'm lucky. My down comforter saved my mattress. It's time for a change of color. I was getting tired of blue."

"Looks like your computer is a total loss, though." Des' nod indicated the mangled debris that had once been her hard drive in his arms.

"Yeah." She shrugged. "I was in the process of acquiring another one. Andy's suggestion. It's a few years old, or antiquated in my son's opinion. He wants a bigger processor and more hard drive space for his favorite games." She sighed. "I just wish I hadn't lost everything on the old one."

"That's too bad," Sin said, meeting Des' gaze. An unspoken communication passed between them, one that said, *Have Scotty take a look*.

Des nodded.

"What?" Avery's attention moved from him to Des, back to him, as her eyebrows drew together. "Why did you give him that look?"

"No reason," Sin replied, without giving away his real thoughts. Whoever did this had a purpose for destroying the computer. He meant to find out why. Scotty was a genius. A little on the eccentric side, but he could take any damaged computer apart and unearth information most people thought lost forever. If not, at least Des had copied information off the drive the night before, so in that respect, they were covered. Sin started for the stairs, saying emphatically over his shoulders, "If you won't call the police, then you need to pack a bag. You and Andy are staying with me."

"Don't be silly," she said, following. "Andy's with a friend, and I'm staying right here."

He stopped at the top of the stairs, pivoted, and took in her stubborn stance.

"No, you're not." Sin's glare dared her to disagree. "I'm not backing down on this."

"You'll have to because this is my home." Avery glared right back. "No one's pushing me out. I'm staying."

"Don't worry, Sin. She should be okay if one of us is with her."

Des' plausible solution rolled around in his brain, making him realize how autocratic he must sound. Still, he had to tamp down a strong urge to protect her. Why couldn't she see the danger? Somehow, he had to make her see his side. He wanted her safe and staying put didn't seem safe.

"Yes. I'll be fine. I told you, I'm not about to be scared out of my house." Avery's chin jutted out in one obstinate lift, highlighting her intention better than any Sharpie. Getting her to budge wasn't an option, not in this lifetime. "Besides, I can't leave. Terry's on her way."

The noise of the front door opening drew their attention.

"Avery? Where is everyone?" Terry yelled.

Avery smiled triumphantly, totally ignoring his fuming expression. "And speaking of Terry." She pushed past him and started down the stairs. "I'll be right down," she shouted.

"She's being stubborn, so you might as well plan on spending the night," Des said, coming up behind him.

Flashing him an annoyed look for throwing in his two cents, Sin trailed after her. "Be reasonable, Avery, you can't stay here."

He halted on the bottom step at the same time Terry closed the front door, then both followed Avery into the living room from opposite directions.

"I am being reasonable," Avery said.

"It doesn't look as bad as I thought." Terry did a three-sixty. "When I spoke with you, I imagined all sorts of crazy things. Are you okay?"

"Of course I'm okay." Avery rolled her eyes. "Will you all quit worrying? This is my house and this incident isn't forcing me to leave."

"Avery, someone went through your things last night." Sin worked to control his rising anger over her single-mindedness. "You said so yourself."

Terry glared at Des and stated sarcastically, "Gee, I wonder who?"

"It wasn't me," Des said at the same time Sin said, "It wasn't Des."

Avery stopped her forward momentum and stared along with Terry, both gazes going from Des to Sin and back again.

"You're sure?" Avery swallowed hard, her escalating fear materializing in the shadows of her eyes. "In all the excitement, I'd all but forgotten."

"It's not something to take lightly," Des said.

"Exactly. Two incidents in less than twenty-four hours is more reason to take this seriously." Sin nodded solemnly. "And if you throw in the incident at the cemetery, it's downright petrifying." He met her gaze, his begging. "Please. At least think about coming home with me."

"If anything, you should stay with me." Terry gripped Avery's hand, her worried expression forming. "I don't trust these men." Her focus moved from Sin to Des and her eyes narrowed suspiciously. "You know nothing about them. What if they're part of what happened the other night?"

"If not for Sin, she might be dead," Des practically growled, sending her a butt-out look. His deep glower spoke more words than the dictionary held, and was usually enough to make anyone take cover and cower.

"Oh, really?" Terry tossed out her own scowl, making herself taller and bearing down on Des, poking his chest with a finger, not the least bit intimidated when his scowl turned darker than an approaching thunderstorm. In fact, Terry seemed to take pleasure in stirring the hornet's nest of Des' temperament. "You have no way of proving that, but one thing you can't disprove. This all started the moment she met the two of you."

Sin glanced at Avery, to judge her reaction to Terry's suspicions. She paid his worried glance no heed. Instead, she got in between Des and her sister.

"Please don't fight, Terry," she said, her expression pleading. "Des has only tried to keep me safe. I trust him." Then, her focus moved to Des and she put her hand on his shoulder. His friend's scowl faded as he intently met her stare, clearly listening. "Terry's only worried about me. She doesn't mean what she said, do you, Ter?" Her placating gaze moved to her sister's. "I'll be fine, really."

"Since it's obvious Avery's not about to follow either of our suggestions, I'll stay here," Sin said, daring both Des and Terry to dispute his claim. Jealousy roared in his soul, seeing Avery defending Des to Terry and seeing how she so easily dealt with Des' irritation with a simple hand on the shoulder, not missing the unspoken affirmation passing between them. "And she's not leaving my sight." He gave each a steady glance, then indicated the door with a nod. "Both of you can leave. She'll be fine with me."

Des looked like he was about to argue, then he nodded. "Fine."

"Scotty's back. I dropped him off a couple of hours ago." He leaned in, so only Des could hear. "Why don't you take the pile of what used to be Avery's computer and see if he can find anything useful on it?" In a louder voice, he said, "Call me later to let me know what's going on."

"Sure thing." Des started for the door.

Avery was about to protest. Sin could see it in the set of her shoulders, and in the way her eyes flashed annoyance brighter than a beacon on a darkened skyline at midnight.

"Mom, Mom," Andy yelled, as the back screen door slammed shut.

Des stopped his retreat and set the computer down.

"The movie was awesome." Seconds later, he appeared in the hallway. He stopped and looked around. "Wow, what happened?" He ran up to Avery and hugged her waist. "Are you okay?"

"Of course I'm okay, sweetheart. We had a small break-in. Nothing for you to worry about." She bent down to return his hug, and kissed the top of his head.

With total absorption, Sin watched Avery's entire body instantly soften. Such obvious love emanated from every one of her pores. A longing deep inside his being burst forth so quickly, he had to squelch the volcano of need flowing too readily from the eruption. He didn't need Avery. He didn't need anyone, especially a woman like her. He was only attracted to her. This cavernous hole in his gut was the result of nothing more than physical attraction. Once he dealt with the attraction, the need would disperse.

"I didn't think I'd see you tonight." Avery laughed, pulling Sin's focus back to her face as she added, "Thought you'd be too busy to say good-bye. Mary said something about going to your favorite restaurant."

"I am. We are. I just wanted to make sure you were okay." Andy grinned. "Hey, Aunt Terry, Mr. Des and Mr. Sinclair." He allowed Terry's kiss on the cheek, before giving Sin and Des nods, then eyeing his mother speculatively. "Since you're fine, I guess I'll go back to Tommy's."

Something in the boy's mannerisms alerted Sin. "Is something wrong? You seem concerned."

"I dunno." He shrugged.

"Something's bugging you. I can tell." When it seemed as if he wasn't going to say any more, Sin prodded, "We can't do anything about it if we don't know what's on your mind."

Andy considered this for a moment. "Me and Tommy were playing spy with our walkie-talkies after we saw Mr. Eric leave. While Tommy was in the front, I was in the backyard, and I saw someone come out the kitchen door."

"What?" Avery's attention was now riveted on Andy. "How? Where? You shouldn't have been here when no one was home."

"We weren't. No one saw us or me. We were up in the trees, keeping guard."

Sin bit back a chuckle at his emphatic answer, delivered in deadpan seriousness. The kid was astute.

"I was climbing down when another guy snuck into the yard and opened the back door."

"You mean there were two men who went in at different times?" Sin met Andy's gaze. "They weren't together?"

"Uh-uh." Andy shook his head. "The last guy didn't stay very long. I think both were in the military. They had real short hair like my dad used to. And like Mr. Des. We waited, to make sure no one was comin' so no one would see us, then we ran to Tommy's house."

"What do you make of it?" Des' question broke into Sin's thoughts.

"Not good." He turned to Avery, reaching for his cell phone. "I'm calling the police. This is serious. Your child was involved."

"Oh my God. I didn't know," Avery murmured, nodding.

~

"I think that'll do it. You'll have to stop by the station to sign the report once I finish," the patrolman said an hour later. "Of course, we'd have a better chance of collecting evidence if you hadn't touched anything."

Des shook his head. "I doubt it. This was a professional job. Whoever did it probably wore gloves and left no trace of his presence. We were lucky to get an eyewitness account of two men leaving, but that may not do us any good, either. I truthfully doubt either are on mug shots, given their descriptions."

The cop sighed. "Yeah, I guess. I've got their statements. Like I said earlier, they can still come in and look at the books when they get a chance. We've already beefed up patrolling, but there will be even more patrolling the area for the next couple of days."

Des shook his hand and thanked him.

Everyone in the room watched him leave.

Sin opened his mouth, but Andy's voice interrupted. "Are you sure you're okay, Mom?"

"Yes, sweetie. I'm fine. Mr. Sinclair will be spending the night, so you don't need to worry." Her eyes flashed Sin a warning. "Isn't that right?"

Sin raked a hand through his hair and sighed as Avery wrapped an arm around Andy's shoulder. Damn, how he wished she'd listen to reason.

"Come on, big guy, I'll walk you back to Tommy's. I'm sure they're waiting to go to dinner. You don't want to miss your favorite."

Andy looked at Sin, his expression still grave. "Remember your promise."

"I will. Don't worry. Have a good campout. I'll keep things here under control. You have my word."

"Make sure you do." Andy nodded, his no-nonsense tone too adult for a nine-year-old.

Though the situation was anything but humorous, Sin stifled the urge to laugh. Smart kid, he thought, as he grabbed his mother's hand and the two walked out the front door.

Des caught his gaze. "While you're protecting Avery, I'll figure out a plan for checking out Esperanza with Scotty."

"Good. I have a weird feeling about him. My guess is he's one of the men who broke in. Maybe the colonel was the other. They're obviously working together." Neither had mentioned either man to the police officer. Seemed futile. Even he had a hard time believing someone sworn to defend and protect his country would go to such drastic measures.

"Definitely worth checking into." Des started for the door, holding up Avery's mangled hard drive, and ignoring Terry's fuming glare. "Scotty's at home, right?"

"Yeah. He was going to take a power nap, but he said he'd be up by six." Sin looked at his watch. "It's seven twenty now. Give him a call."

"Will do." Des nodded. "I also want to check in with our security guard, see if he delivered the goods to the colonel."

"Keep me posted on that too." Sin grinned. Both he and Des had concocted a pretty decent story to offset Williams' obvious interest in the message Scotty sent and one they could capitalize upon. They recreated an e-mail giving Scotty a different motive for returning to the States. Other than checking out Esperanza, this new one focused on using Avery as their quarry. Sin had no intention of letting the colonel know they had joined ranks and every reason to allow him to think they were still adversaries, especially now.

Des headed for the door. "See you tomorrow. If you need me I'm only a phone call away."

Sin waited for the door to shut before turning to face Terry.

Total earsplitting silence filled the air.

"So, what's your angle?" She eyed him intently. Suspicion oozed out of her brown eyes, so similar to Avery's.

Sin smiled. "Angle? I'm afraid I don't follow."

"You may have fooled Avery, but you don't fool me. I'm not as trusting."

"Oh?" Sin continued staring with eyebrows raised.

"I don't know what your game is, but I do know this," she all but snarled, poking him in the chest. "Your intentions better be honorable. You hurt my sister and you'll have me to deal with. You got it?"

"Yeah, I got it." Sin sighed. "I have no intention of hurting your sister." Great! Now he was defending his actions in advance, to her sister no less. "Does Avery know you've decided to become her champion?"

"No, I'm definitely butting in, and I'd advise you not to tell her."

"I'm only here to help."

"I hope so. She's been through enough already. She doesn't deserve you and your partners tearing her apart."

"Of course not," Sin murmured, thinking of her dead husband. Yeah, she probably didn't deserve him and his baggage while she was still grieving for a hero. "Like I said, I'm here to protect her. I'm not sure how, but she's involved in this, and until I find out, no threat you can issue will keep me away."

"Are you planning on sleeping with her?"

"That's a private matter between Avery and me, don't you think?"

"No."

Sin shook his head and smiled. "I've got to hand it to you. You're direct. Don't worry. Avery will be fine. I'll make sure of it."

"That doesn't answer my question."

"You're right, it doesn't." He held her steely gaze, his own clearly saying she wouldn't be getting any better answer than the one he'd already given.

His affair with Avery wasn't her concern, no matter how much she disagreed.

Chapter 14

"You have fun at camp, okay?" Avery said to Andy as she rang Mary's doorbell. "And behave yourself. Make me proud."

"I will." He gave her a big hug, something of a rare occurrence in their relationship, the older he got. Soon he wouldn't allow it at all, so she felt lucky he was so demonstrative now. "I won't worry, either." He spoke with such authority, drawing out an urge to smile. She refrained as he added, "Mr. Sinclair is going to take care of you while I'm gone."

"Oh?" Her eyebrows rose. "He is?"

"Yeah. He promised. I thought maybe Mr. Des or Mr. Eric would be better, since he barks, but he promised not to bark. He says he likes you."

"He said that?"

"Uh-huh." Andy nodded. His solemn expression indicated he'd given the matter much thought. "I like him. How 'bout you, Mom? Do you like him?"

"Yeah, I do," Avery said, unable to hold on to her grin. Imagine! Her son, playing matchmaker. "He's very nice. I think you made the right choice."

"I thought so." He beamed. His animated smile said it all, filling her with a sense of accomplishment. She might not have been a perfect wife or lover, but at least she'd done a decent job of mothering...so far.

She had no time for a reply because Mary appeared, holding the screen door open. "Hey, Av. Is everything okay? I always thought this was a safe neighborhood. I can't believe someone broke into your house and trashed it."

"I'm fine. I appreciate your concern. I'm just glad the boys are okay."

"Thank God Tommy and Andy knew enough to stay up in the trees and out of sight." Mary sighed. "Tommy's excited, even though he didn't see anything. Can't wait to go to the police station when they get back from their camping trip. You're sure that's soon enough?"

"Yes. No sense ruining plans." Avery didn't want to go into too much detail, which would only bring on more questions. Even with Andy's description, it was unlikely they'd find their pictures on any file in the police station, and both Des and Sin agreed. "I have some friends staying with me. Plus, the police officer said he'd make sure the area was patrolled more often."

Mary nodded, accepting her explanations. "Have you thought any more about tomorrow and shopping? I just finalized my appointments for the morning. I should be done around three."

"Sure," Avery said, glad to have another topic to talk about. "I think shopping will be a perfect break from all this."

"I made reservations for six o'clock." When Avery put up a hand to object, she smiled. "They can easily be canceled."

"Okay." Avery's laughter burst forth. Maybe she was on the downward slide of the grieving process because suddenly the idea of shopping and dinner with Mary seemed a perfect way to distance herself from Sin. Oh, she'd allow him to take charge tonight, but she wasn't about to relinquish her control like he apparently was used to others doing. As it was, she cherished her newly hard-won sense of self. For too long in her marriage, she'd simply given her life over to others' needs. It was time to focus on her own.

After concluding plans with Mary, she headed back to her house, humming. The entire way, a sense of urgency pumped through her veins. Sin was spending the night in an effort to protect her. She grinned, wrapping her arms around her middle and hugging herself as another bubble of laughter burst forth. It felt good to know he cared enough to take charge and worry.

"Sin…Terry," she called out after letting herself in the front door and setting the dead bolt.

"We're back here," came Terry's yell. "On the deck."

Avery started for the kitchen and pushed through the screen door a moment later to see both her sister and Sin sitting on deck chairs. Though they looked fine, an underlying bit of tension floated in the air, so different from the usual current of attraction she usually felt around Sin. "Is everything okay?"

"Sure," Terry and Sin said simultaneously. He sighed and raked a hand through his hair. Terry stood, moving toward her.

"Of course, we're fine. I'm just worried about you." She wrapped her in a bear hug. "What're big sisters for, if not for worrying, right?" she teased.

Avery smiled and nodded. "I was about to start dinner. You want to stay?"

Terry laughed. "Hell no, not when I know what you've got cooking." She winked, then turned and headed out the backyard gate. "Just remember, I'm only a phone call away if you need me."

Avery watched her go, slightly puzzled. "Did something happen while I was gone?" Avery looked intently at Sin for some kind of answer in his good-looking features.

"Nothing I couldn't straighten out." He only shook his head and let out another huge puff of air. Then he returned her smile, meeting her eyes, his full of amusement. "Seems your sister is a bit on the protective side."

"Yeah, I guess she is." A relieved sensation slid over her. "Comes from her being two years older. So, what'd she say?"

"She wanted to know if I was going to sleep with you."

Avery's eyes grew wide. Geez, how embarrassing. Unsure of how to respond, she cleared her throat and looked at her hands, examining her fingernails closely. Finally, she felt calm enough to talk. "What did you tell her?"

"I basically told her it was none of her business."

Sin stood and slowly walked toward her, causing her to take a step back when he got too close. His hands on her shoulders prevented further retreat. He looked deep into her eyes and she could see sincerity, along with the humor she noticed earlier, staring back at her in those shimmering green eyes. A woman could lose herself in his earnest gaze.

"This…" he murmured, lowering his head and drawing her closer so his lips were barely an inch above her face, "…is nobody's business but ours."

And then his mouth covered hers. So soft…so warm…so full of promise that Avery moaned, letting the sensation of his lips touching hers overwhelm her. It felt good to feel something besides disappointment and loss. It felt even better to give in to her need for a change and not be responsible for someone else's.

When she allowed him more access to her mouth, he wasted no time in deepening the kiss. He plunged his fingers into her hair at the same time she wrapped hers around his neck in an effort to pull him closer.

Never had a mere kiss consumed her so. Mike's kisses never seemed endless, like this…like time had ceased to exist. How long Sin's mouth lingered, she wasn't certain. An eternity in Avery's mind, when in reality, it probably could be measured in seconds. He tasted heavenly! She could kiss him forever.

When he slowly raised his head and seared her with those liquid pools of hot jade, sending a dagger of need all the way to her core, it was all she could do to keep from bursting into flames from the heat of his gaze. How she wanted to continue kissing him. She wondered what it would be like to make love with him. Maybe she wasn't frigid after all.

Sin kissed her forehead, then leaned his chin on her head, sighing heavily. "I've thought of kissing you again since the moment my lips left yours the other night in the cemetery, if only to find out if it was as good as I remembered."

"Was it?"

"You couldn't tell?" He grinned and wrapped his arms around her, cradling her head against his chest.

How she loved this…just being in someone's arms and hearing the steady thump of a heartbeat, feeling a connection with another human being, something she hadn't felt in far too long, even though she'd been married for a decade. Avery couldn't remember any time Mike held her like she was something precious that he never wanted to let go. If he had, she'd have never sent her letter, she realized just then. More than anything, she wanted to feel desired.

She breathed in the scent of Sin. She never thought about it before, but he had one all his own. Musky. Male. Sweat mixed with deodorant and aftershave. Avery stifled a giggle in the V of his shoulder and arm, remembering Terry's words about pheromones. His scent was intoxicating and exciting. Maybe that's what she found so attractive about him.

"You aren't laughing at me, are you?"

His teasing extracted a full giggle. "No! I'd never laugh at you."

His rich laughter filled the air. "Good. My ego can't take it." He kissed the top of her head. "Damn! I want you in the worst way." He leaned back and nailed her with his gaze. "You know that, don't you?"

Avery nodded. She wanted him, too.

Her face flamed and she had to look down, too embarrassed to keep eye contact. She had no clue what to do next when everything she'd done in her past relationship had been futile and disappointing. Such a sad legacy after ten years.

But she wouldn't think about that now.

What was Terry's advice? To follow her instinct? Her first inclination was to stroke him...touch him all over. Did she dare? Or pull him back for more of his heady kisses. She loved kissing him. Did she dare? She wanted to yank his shirt off and view what had to be a powerful body lurking underneath. Did she dare?

"As much as I want you, it's not a bright idea to get too chummy tonight. You mentioned something about making dinner." Sin took a step back, which added distance, and just like that, his demeanor changed from a teasing possible lover to a total stranger right before her eyes.

He obviously wasn't interested. Guilt and embarrassment filled her. How could she even be thinking of sex?

He cleared his throat and dropped his arms. "I'm trying damn hard to keep this sizzle of attraction from moving too quickly, so we should avoid kissing for the time being."

"I understand," Avery lied, nodding and wondering if he'd suddenly found her as unexciting as she'd sometimes found Mike. The thought made her feel even guiltier. "Dinner shouldn't take too long to fix."

"Need any help?"

Shaking her head, she turned around so Sin wouldn't glimpse the guilt or the disappointment she knew were present in her expression.

"Avery?" The caress of her name, spoken so softly, sounded like a whisper on the wind, and stopped her before she'd taken two steps.

"Yes?" She pivoted, but couldn't risk peering into his eyes, so she kept her glance lowered.

She felt his scrutiny.

He'd silently taken the two steps so that he stood in front of her. Then, gripping her chin between his thumb and forefinger, he raised her head. She had no choice but to meet his curious gaze. "Trust me. This really isn't the best time for what I have in mind."

"Oh?" she asked, her doubts wiped out by the look in his eyes and the sincerity in his voice. "What if I think differently?" What had Terry said about grabbing a chance at happiness and living? Sin made her feel both happy and alive. Something she hadn't felt in years, and she wasn't about to lose this opportunity to experience either. She could feel guilty later.

"It doesn't matter. Too much has happened today. Someone ransacked your house. I'd be a total jerk to take advantage of your vulnerability."

Sin's genuine concern gave Avery all the encouragement she needed to act.

"You mean you're not interested in discovering what comes after kissing?" She boldly closed the small gap existing between them. She'd come this far. She may as well go for broke. She reached out, riding on a wave of instinct, and touched him, let her hands have their fill, sliding down his muscular torso. He flinched under her fingers and his eyebrows rose in a surprised arch as one of her hands moved lower. "What if I am?" She couldn't believe she actually said that, but it felt damned good to do something out of character for her. Tonight she didn't want to be Mike Montgomery's widow. She wanted to be Avery and she wanted to feel wanted. Sin definitely wanted her.

She gave a throaty laugh when he grabbed her wrist, halting her hand in motion. "This tells a different story and doesn't lie."

A sharp intake of air and a hissed, "Shit," was his only response when her fingers continued moving. She grinned. "What if I decided I'd like to explore a little?" she asked, shocking the heck out of herself even more.

"Avery." This time, there was no softness in the one word, more of a warning growl instead. He tugged, pulling her fingers away, and yanked her closer before bending his head. His lips hovered inches from hers. "You are playing a dangerous game."

"Maybe." Sin held her hand awkwardly between them. She wrenched her fingers away so she could touch his face, letting the pad of her thumb slide against his bottom lip. Her chin went up a notch, daring him.

With the swiftness of a striking snake, his lips caught her thumb, sucking it further inside his mouth. His eyes gripped hers while his tongue made love to her thumb. It was the only way to describe the circling torture, doing crazy things to her insides. The few seconds she stared at him, seeing desire burning within his gaze, had to be the most erotic few seconds of her life. Avery felt hot, felt her total being melt, as warmth spread and swamped her with the need to have his mouth doing the same thing…over all of her.

Sin's ringing cell phone cut through the sensual haze, interrupting the moment.

Both froze as the persistent ringing continued. Sin's chuckle permeated the air.

"Saved in the nick of time," he murmured, stepping back. He nodded toward the kitchen, reaching for his cell. "No more games, Avery. Go and fix dinner. After I take this call, I'll check around. Make sure everything is locked up." He then answered with a curt, "Yeah, Des. What's up?"

~

"Just wanted to give you an update," Des said.

"Okay, go ahead." Sin watched Avery's retreat.

"We're finalizing our strategy for tomorrow. Of course you should know Scotty's got some interesting ideas."

"What else is new?" Sin grinned as Des spent a moment detailing their online snooping and plans to take Esperanza by storm the next day. When he was done, Sin added, "Scotty only wants a little action. I'm counting on you to keep him in line and not let anything happen to him. You're up for the task. It's why I earmarked you to go along in the first place."

"Your faith in my abilities is overwhelming."

Sin laughed. "Just humor him. He's okay if you can get past the chip of his high school experiences he wears on his shoulder. If he gets too wacky, you have my permission to tell him to knock it off, but do it nicely and remember we go way back."

"Okay, but you owe me big-time for this," Des threatened.

"I know. And I appreciate it."

Sin punched the Off button, disconnecting. Never had he been so relieved to have Des' interruption.

His gaze went to Avery's back door. He had to forcibly stop himself from going after her, snatching her back into his arms, and showing her exactly what all her teasing was doing to his restraint. "Shit," he muttered to himself. *Some restraint!*

He curled a fist, fighting back lust, and paced, his body still primed…still ready. Jeezus, was he ever ready. So ready, he'd been so close to throwing her on the ground and taking her like an animal. What was it about her that twisted his insides with the desire to give her everything she needed? He'd never been so near the edge of losing it. Never.

He sighed, stuck his hand in his pocket, and jingled a few coins, thinking.

It had to be her vulnerability. He was such a sucker for those big, brown, soul-stealing eyes. That's how he felt right now. Like she was stealing his soul, little by little. Funny, until this very moment, he'd always thought he hadn't much of a soul left to steal.

She'd awakened something inside him that he'd long since determined as dead. Emotion. He'd thought losing Diane and learning of her death, along with his unborn child's, had buried it forever. Avery wasn't Diane. He knew that now, especially after seeing her with Andy.

And Andy? Oh Jeezus. He'd assured the kid he'd take care of his mother. Hell, she had her sister as a champion, too, ready to do battle if he hurt her. That kind of loyalty, even from loved ones, wasn't easily earned.

"Sin?" Avery's voice pulled him out of his thoughts.

He looked up to see she'd appeared at the back door, concern written in bold print across those gorgeous features. He was such a goner, he realized, staring into her dark eyes that drew him in with the promise of everything he'd ever wanted. All he had to do was ask.

"Are you okay?"

He smiled and nodded, still rubbing his neck. It wasn't lost on him. Her question was the same one he'd asked. Countless times in their brief, four-day association. And no, he wasn't fricking okay. He was having a mental breakdown. Why was he even debating taking her to bed? She was obviously ready and willing. Why should he care about her vulnerability?

Sin blew out a sigh as she strolled out the screen door carrying a tray, looking so fresh and clean, like a burst of sunshine after a spring rain.

"I poured a glass of wine. I figured you could use a drink. I'd have brought beer, but I don't keep it on hand since my husband died."

"Thanks," he murmured, taking one of the glasses from the tray Avery set on the table. She picked up the other. Watching her sit, it hit him with a flash of certainty. He knew why. She appeared too fragile for a brief affair, which was all he would ever allow.

Avery Montgomery was the type of woman heroes married and protected for life. Sin knew in his heart of hearts, he was no hero. Somehow, he had to keep his hands and lips off her.

He took a sip, viewing her through a narrowed gaze. "So is Andy all situated and ready for his camping trip?" he asked, in an attempt to move the conversation to safer topics. If he could keep her talking, he could avoid thinking of taking her to bed.

"Andy?" Her sweet laughter filled the air. "You're not using my son as a diversionary tactic, are you?"

"No." Sin shook his head, still eyeing her as a knowing smile flitted across her face.

"Good. Because I should warn you. If you think talking of Andy will dissuade me from my purpose, you'll have to readjust your thinking. I've made up my mind."

"Oh?"

"Yeah. I like kissing you, and I plan on doing more kissing."

"Really?"

"Umm hmm." Her answer accompanied a nod and a playful smile that sent shivers up his spine. She brought her wineglass to her lips and sipped, the entire time holding his gaze. "Come on. I've changed my mind. I've decided you can help me make dinner."

Avery stood with one hand out, beckoning, as one thought ran through Sin's mind.

Why in the hell was he denying himself what she was so obviously willing to give?

Chapter 15

"Jeez Louise! You're nuts." Des' eyes focused on the computer screen Scotty manipulated with fast fingers, typing a mile a minute.

They'd spent the better part of the evening researching, or rather Scotty had.

Des checked his watch, wishing Sin hadn't assigned him to the task of babysitting, which is what this duty amounted to despite all the staggering shit Scotty had unearthed with the click of a mouse. His eyes went back to the monitor when Scotty laughed, the sound sending more alarm through his system. "You really think we'll be able to sneak up on this guy?"

"Yeah. It won't be a problem." He scrolled, zeroing in on the street address in Baltimore he'd typed in only seconds before, using a satellite he'd illegally connected to for the images. Des didn't ask how he did it…any of it…in fact, truly felt he'd be better off not knowing. "This is where we're going."

Both studied the screen.

"I'm looking for the best way inside without announcing our presence." Scotty spent a moment moving the cursor, indicating different sections of the house. "We stay in the shadows of these trees to avoid detection and sneak in this window. It looks inaccessible but with my calculations, we have plenty of space to break in. He won't be expecting a breach from this window because there are so many easier accesses."

Des gaped at the man sitting next to him, noting his intense concentration. Scotty's dark hair was mussed and the thick black frames of his glasses magnified his eyes, now brilliant with excitement. He looked like a Woody Allen clone from one of his earliest movies.

"We're not trained spies, Scotty." He rubbed his face and sighed. Scotty took the covert shit a bit too seriously for his comfort. He had no intention of getting shot at if he could help it. If Esperanza was responsible for Avery's break-in, then he easily could have been the shooter at the cemetery. He was military, so it fit. "Let's just go knock on the door."

"Esperanza is listed as missing. And according to our research, there is no Esperanza. Do you think he's simply going to open the door and let us waltz in to question him?"

"I hate it when you make sense."

Scotty gave him a dirty look. "Just because I wasn't on the force like you, doesn't mean I can't predict human behavior. Despite his cover, he's on the run, and he's looking for the same thing we are. We need to surprise him, then maybe we can learn what he knows."

"And precisely how are we going to surprise him? Even if we somehow luck out and do surprise him, I seriously doubt he'll roll over, once we get inside. I also doubt he'll voluntarily tell us shit." Des shook his head and sighed. The guy surely had ties to Williams, since he was tied to the Xcom2s and the night they disappeared. It had to be the reason both men searched Avery's house—another definite connection. "Given what we've learned and the report you sent Sin, which I read, my guess he's some kind of Special Forces guy we ought not mess with."

"Of course he is." Grinning, Scotty stood and walked over to a cabinet. "But we'll be able to handle him." He pulled out several items, including what looked to be a gizmo with wires attached to a vest. "I've been playing with this stuff, preparing for a mission just like this one. I'm anxious to try it out."

Scotty handed him a large gun with a four-pronged hook sticking out of the barrel and some kind of spinner on top. "What the hell is this?" Des held it up and worked to keep the cynicism out of the question.

"Don't turn your nose up like I'm an idiot." Scotty's nod indicated the gun. "Shoots a five-hundred-pound test line, like what a deep sea fisherman would use, with a hook strong enough to hold two men. It's how we'll access the window. We can't fail."

Des let out a snort. "You're kidding, right? Geez Louise, tell me you're joking."

"I never joke about my inventions. I call this," he said, holding up the other wires and stuff he'd brought out of the cupboard, "the Stun Ring."

"The Stun Ring?" Des rolled his eyes, trying to keep from laughing outright. "Lord, Scotty, what the hell's that going to do?"

"It looks benign, but packs a wallop. I designed it thinking of one of those handshake props clowns use to spurt water from the daisy on the lapel, only this shoots an electric jolt. Fifty thousand volts for three seconds, thanks to my battery pack. You strap it to your back, so it's hidden underneath your clothing. I figured out a way to make it feel natural." He took off his shirt.

"See?" Scotty said, once he had it on and his shirt re-buttoned. "Frisk me. Feels just like muscle if anyone checks."

Des eyed him through a narrow gaze. Scotty had frickin' lost his mind. When Scotty held his hands out, an expectant look peering out of his eyes saying *go ahead, pat me down,* he did. Okay, so the vest felt natural. But did it work?

"Where do you get these ideas?"

"One of my hobbies." Scotty shrugged, taking off the invention and placing it inside a backpack. "I love watching those old spy flicks and recreating some of the tools of the trade Q came up with for 007, if only to see if they're feasible."

"I thought a Trekkie like you would be more into building the Enterprise."

"I have many interests." Scotty sent him another heated look.

"Hmmm. I can see that. So are they?"

"Are they what?"

Des sighed. "Feasible."

"Some are, some aren't. I like experimenting."

"Okay, let's pretend this works." Des nodded at the vest with wires Scotty had shoved into the backpack, thinking the guy was totally certifiable, which only meant he was more so because he was actually buying into it. "How are you going to get close enough to use it?"

"Trust me. I've fully tested everything and I've got it all figured out. I'm five feet six inches tall and weigh a hundred and thirty pounds on my heaviest day. Remember what I said about human behavior. I've met Esperanza…he's textbook. He'll consider you a threat but not me." When Des lifted his eyebrows, not saying anything, just waiting for him to continue, he smiled. "You'll see. They all underestimate me. Always have." Scotty's grin spread and he winked. "But I've gotten even over the years, using my brain. It's much more effective than brawn, especially when it's unanticipated." He nodded at the items in his hands. "This is how we get inside the window he won't be protecting because he won't be expecting an attack from that front, and this is how we stop him."

"Speaking of human behavior," Des said. Oh Lord, Sin was going to kill him if he put Scotty in danger. Letting the gung ho Jason Bourne wannabe standing in front of him loose with Esperanza amounted to as much. "You know, Sin's got your number. He's well aware there's more to this than helping out."

"What do you mean? I *am* helping out."

"Yeah, right. So you mean to tell me you're not planning on playing spy, using Esperanza as a means to get even with all those past bullies in your life?"

"No, of course not. You need me, and my inventions. You'll see."

"So, I get to risk my ass going against some trained warrior with Mini-Me and his inventions as my only protection? Heaven help me. I must be frickin' nuts to be even considering this."

"Come on, Des. It's brilliant." Scotty pushed his glasses higher on his nose, and peered into his eyes, his wide with enthusiasm. "We storm his sanctuary, let him get the drop on us, and when he does, I grab his wrist. He won't be expecting it. He'll be incapacitated for at least a full minute. Plenty of time to tie him up. Then we question him."

"Just like that? I'm not entirely convinced he's part of this. What if he's innocent? We'd be arrested for breaking and entering and battery. Jeez Louise. You can't just go around assaulting military personnel based on hunches."

"Your hesitance surprises me. It's inconsistent with your past behavior." Scotty took his glasses off and rubbed each eye, shaking his head. Then he spent a moment wiping his lenses before placing them back on his face, magnifying his expressive eyes. "I always thought you were the partner who acted first and asked questions later, so quit looking at ways this can fail and find your balls."

"Shit," Des muttered. "You're serious, aren't you?"

"Can't fail." He smiled and nodded. "Besides, we need Esperanza…to find out what he knows. He's the key to why and we're all looking for the same thing. My guess is, if he's Special Forces or CIA like we think, he's above turning traitor, so maybe we can coerce him enough to work with us."

Des nodded, unable to fathom how he'd actually decided to go along with his crazy plan.

"You know how to rappel, right?"

175

"Yeah," Des said, after thinking about the question. "But we'll be going up, not down."

"Don't worry. This wire may look thin, but it's strong enough to lift several hundred pounds. It works like a fishing rod. The torque on the gun will help pull us up. Let's practice."

"I need a drink."

"We can have a beer, but only after we finish practicing."

"Damn," Des muttered under his breath. "Why me, Lord? Scotty was enough to drive anyone to drinking. He needed something stronger than beer, like bourbon on the rocks. And forget just one. He needed the whole bottle.

~

"Go to sleep, Avery," Sin said, sighing and punching the pillows in an effort to get comfortable. His frustration seemed insurmountable.

Another day had gone by and he was no closer to finding his prototypes. To make matters worse, he didn't want to leave Avery alone, but lying next to her on top of the covers on the king-sized bed wasn't the most effective solution. It was pure torture.

"Kissing isn't on the agenda for tonight, but protecting you is. And protecting is all I plan on doing. Understand?"

"Why?"

Avery's question hung in the air. Sin wiped his face and looked at the ceiling, praying for patience…praying for self-control as his was waning…fast.

"What do you mean, why?" He'd spent the evening reminding her that someone invaded her space at the same time trying to gain more information about Williams and their brief visit, but she'd evaded most of his questions, saying tomorrow would be soon enough to discuss problems.

And then after dodging her deliberate attempts at working for another kiss, Sin fully comprehended her game as her main agenda hit him head-on. She had a sweet tooth and he was M&M's. Yet, she had to know if they kissed, he wouldn't be able to stop at kissing.

Soft music and her plying him with wine had been hard enough to ignore. He'd been amused, using alcohol to drown out need…at first. Until Avery found other means to torment him, like brushing into him one too many times to believe the contact accidental, especially when she got bolder in her efforts, all the while flashing her knowing little smiles. Her actions became impossible to ignore.

His body raced with need.

Yet, was she satisfied with tormenting him?

Hell, no. Avery was currently doing everything in her power to incite more lust.

At this rate, he'd never get to sleep. Now he knew how one of those fellows felt who took Viagra or some other pill for ED, or Erectile Dysfunction.

"Don't you want to kiss me?" she asked, throwing out that throaty laugh she'd perfected to drive him more insane. She stroked his arm. "Find out what happens after kissing?"

"Damn," he said under his breath, sighing and turning over. Sin mulled her words over, eyeing her intently. His focus centered on the heart around Avery's neck, one she always wore, hoping the distraction would firm his resolve. When he felt in control enough, he met her provocative expression again, working even harder to appear stern. It was a wasted effort. Lord help him, his willpower was totally decimated. "You know I do," he finally admitted.

"Then I don't understand. Why aren't you taking my proposition seriously?"

Sin laughed, murmuring, "Question of the year."

"You find me and my offer amusing?"

"Yeah, I do. You have no idea how much restraint it takes just to lie still and not touch you. I'd love nothing better than to kiss you right here and right now. But we both know that would lead to making love."

"So, what's the problem?" Avery leaned in and ran a hand over his chest. The move did nothing to still his raging libido. Her husky laughter floated above them. He wasn't sure how much more of this exquisite torture he could take, especially when she reached out and pulled his shirt free. Images of her hands stroking him wouldn't subside. Nor would the idea of discovering her body in the same way.

"Jeezus," he whispered, rubbing his temple in an effort to block the images as well as the pleasure coursing through him when her fingers began a bold exploration of his chest. "You think I'd be such a jerk to take advantage of this situation?" he ground out, clenching his teeth. Sin wanted her with a passion he couldn't remember feeling before. He covered Avery's hand with his, stopping her fingers from sending his temperature off the charts.

Another throaty laugh filled his ears and white-hot heat filled his groin.

"Yeah, I was kind of hoping."

He'd drunk too much wine over the course of the evening, which totally backfired on holding his need in check. He simply couldn't do it any longer. Avery knew it, he could see it in her eyes, as she pulled her hand out of his grasp and her fingers boldly made a downward slide.

Yep! She definitely had her own agenda and just the right touch to inflame him. Jeezus! It felt so good. Sin closed his eyes, fighting the pleasure, but swiftly lost ground. He had to slow her down, or it would be over before it began. He caught her wrist, brought her hand to his mouth, kissed her palm, and then massaged her fingers. Eventually, he began sucking each one thoroughly before moving to the next, keeping his eyes glued to hers.

"You're sure?" he asked, after spending an inordinate amount of time on her right hand.

She visibly swallowed, cast her gaze on his chest, and nodded. His hand moved to her chin, lifting it slowly, not letting her look away.

"Avery? Tell me what you want." He was tired of fighting desire…of fighting her. If she wanted this, then who was he to deny her? He could handle sex, but if he was going through with this, he'd make damn sure she was ahead of him.

Her embarrassment was plain to see in the bit of red streaking up her cheeks. Her hand seemed to speak the loudest about nerves, moving underneath his shirt, playing distractedly with the hair on his chest in the form of figure eights. Though he held her chin with his fingers, she wouldn't keep eye contact—another dead giveaway.

"Avery?" he asked softly. A moment ago, she was a tigress and now a tame kitten. Such an interesting dichotomy in the two demeanors. Had she and her husband been so in sync that she didn't need to communicate what she wanted? Gently, Sin tilted her head so she had to meet his questioning gaze. "What do you like?"

"I…um…I…" She cleared her throat. More red infused her face.

This new shyness was every bit as enticing as her boldness had been.

She tried to pull out of his grip, but Sin held her chin firmly, forcing the issue.

"Well?" he prodded gently.

"I already told you, I like kissing," she finally said after a long silence.

"Okay. Kissing's a start and definitely doable." He chuckled, then bent to take her mouth. He liked kissing too. In fact, he loved kissing, especially kissing her. But he wasn't content with just a kiss. If Avery wasn't inclined to tell him what she liked, then he'd do some trial and error testing, using his mouth and hands to investigate, letting her responses to his touch be his guide.

Her moan sounded, traveling to his ears from the inside through his mouth.

"Do you like this?" Sin whispered, kissing his way along her chin.

"Mmm hmm." The decadent sound drew his gaze for a split second.

Smiling, he let his tongue plunge into her ear, then bit her lobe. "I'll take that as a yes."

"Oh yes. I love it." Avery's voice came out in wispy little puffs of air, as her breathing became labored. "Don't stop."

Stop? Oh no. He couldn't think of stopping now. In fact he doubled his efforts...stroking, caressing, fondling, kissing, biting...sensing her climb higher and higher with the help of his mouth and hands until she cried out, exploding her release, ending his last bit of restraint.

In a deft move, he had her shorts undone, stripping them and her panties off her long, beautiful limbs, so perfect for wrapping around him. Now that she was naked from the waist down, the urge to join her and slide into her warmth swamped him.

Not yet. It was still too soon. He wanted to bring her higher once more.

"No fair," she whispered, her voice full of husky sensuality. "I'm half naked and you're not."

Sin chuckled. "Let's dispense with all the barriers, shall we?" He swiftly shed his clothes, helping her with her top, before grabbing one of the condoms he put in his wallet earlier—just in case—sending up a silent thanks for his insightfulness.

In the next instant, all coherent thought dissipated into a burst of pleasure as Avery's hands possessively stroked his body.

Everywhere she touched he burned, which along with what her mouth was doing to him, only added to his incineration. He quickly sheathed himself, unable to resist sinking into her heat, unable to stop his body from pumping once there, unable to stop himself from giving in to the need she so easily elicited from his soul.

Chapter 16

"Not exactly my idea of a perfect day," Des muttered in the early morning darkness, putting the car in park after pulling into a spot right in front of Scotty's apartment building. Working with Scotty always required patience. Plenty of patience. He sighed, grabbed the cup of coffee he'd taken the extra minutes to buy, and climbed out.

"Hey, guy!" Scotty smiled along with his greeting when he opened the door.

"You look ready for action." Des noted his clothes, complete with black jeans and t-shirt. He snorted, shaking his head. Leave it to Scotty to dress for the part. He grinned. At least the guy wasn't boring. He ignored the fact that he'd dressed similarly for this excursion—matching black jeans and sweater.

"Yeah, I've decided I like the action." He rubbed his arm. "I just don't like getting shot at." He patted his stomach and handed Des his backpack. "Now I'm ready for more!"

They headed silently toward his car.

"Might as well get this show on the road, so I can get it over with." Des stored the pack in the backseat.

In minutes, they were driving north and less than an hour later, Des pulled his four-wheel drive Lexus into a parking spot two blocks from the address he and Scotty were seeking.

"We walk from here." Des glanced around, seeing familiar terrain. Besides practicing, and thanks to Scotty's computer manipulations, the two had spent a good bit of time studying the blocks surrounding their prime target. He turned off the ignition, grabbed the door handle, climbed out of the car, and waited until Scotty stood next to him before hitting the keyless lock. The lights flashed and a honk sounded.

"I can't believe I'm actually doing this." He rolled his eyes heavenward, wondering what lunacy had taken over his mind as he followed Scotty in the direction of Esperanza's house.

They neared their destination. Scotty halted behind a tree and waited for Des to catch up. He nodded toward the two-story red brick house, reaching for his gun with the fishing line and metal hook in his backpack.

Des held his breath as the smaller man dropped the pack, then sidled up to the house, keeping in the cover of trees. Hiding behind a giant oak, he aimed and fired, and damn him, the hook caught. Unbelievable. This plan just might work.

Scotty flashed a triumphant smile and whispered, "Ready? Remember, just like we practiced."

"Yeah, right. Let's go."

Des grabbed the gun while Scotty grasped his shoulders and climbed on, piggy-backing, just as they'd done too many times the night before. The guy was light and his gadget did pull them up, especially since he had the muscle strength in his arms, compliments of workouts at Jerry's Gym three times a week. He also used his quads, almost walking up the wall, reeling in the line as he went. In seconds, they dangled right next to the window. Des planted his feet, gripping the brick with the soles of his shoes to ease some of the pressure on his arms.

"Okay, on three, we swing out then in, toward the window." He prayed the older house didn't have the new double-paned glass. After thorough consideration of the run-down area, they'd decided to take the risk. "Remember, close your eyes and cover your face."

"One...two...three..." Des tightened his thigh muscles, pushed off, and swung out, bracing himself as they hurled forward. Legs up, his feet met the glass with force and it gave.

Definitely single-paned. They crashed through the shattered barrier, their momentum sending them flying into the room.

As practiced, they rolled. Des hit the floor with a thud. He sat up, once he could move. He brushed shards of glass off his shoulder and arms, when his eyes focused on the 9mm Glock shoved under his throat.

"Ah, Scotty?" he whispered. "I think we found Esperanza. Or rather he found us." He flashed his most confident grin, despite his faith in their mission suddenly plummeting to new depths.

The formidable man's angry eyes said it all. They'd be lucky to get out of this alive. So much for Scotty's brilliant plan. Why had he let the quirky geek talk him into what had instantly morphed into an impossible task? If Esperanza didn't kill him, Sin would, for allowing things to veer out of control on his watch.

"Up." Esperanza motioned with his weapon. "Both of you."

Looking a little dazed, Scotty sat up slowly and swept some of the glass off his clothing. "I think I sprained my ankle."

"Help him. Then put your hands above your head so I can frisk you." Esperanza's words were clipped and sounded annoyed, conveying his thoughts loud and clear. He considered them flies, buzzing once too often.

Des helped Scotty rise, shooting him a silent communication with his eyes—don't mess with him—praying the lunatic wouldn't ignore it. Esperanza was no fool. Scotty shouldn't be acting as if he were, which is what their attempting this charade amounted to.

Esperanza indicated for them to move into another room with monitors, one showing a screen split into four sections. He obviously had his own spy toys, Des thought, as the guy patted him up and down and reached under his pants cuff for his .22 caliber gun. Esperanza yanked it out of its holster and thrust it into his waistband at the small of his back, keeping his own weapon pointed on Des.

"Nice to see you again," he said, looking at Scotty. "I take it you're still searching for your prototypes?" When Scotty didn't answer, he smiled. Then, he nodded for him to pick up a pile of ropes at his feet. "Since this isn't a social call, begin tying up your buddy and hurry, because my patience is shot. I'd just as soon put a bullet between your eyes, but somehow I get the idea you're not really my enemy, so I'm cutting you both a bit of slack...this time."

Scotty took a moment, moving in slow motion, and Des had the uncanny feeling he truly meant to play Jason Bourne as Sin had mentioned. He closed his eyes, blanking out the disaster waiting to happen, willing the moron not to do anything rash. Just what he needed to make the night a total bust, explaining to Sin how he'd been stupid enough to let Scotty get his balls shot off.

Des opened his eyes in time to see him trip, falling into Esperanza and grabbing on to his bare forearm, exposed because his sweater sleeves were pushed up. Scotty's ingenuity surprised the hell out of him. He watched in stunned fascination as the powerfully built man shook for a moment before collapsing in a heap right in front of them.

"Told you it would work," Scotty said triumphantly a moment later.

"Yeah? Well, you better pray the shock didn't kill him." He bent down to feel a pulse.

"Don't worry. I've tested it on myself."

"Figures." Des shook his head, heaving a relieved sigh when he felt the steady thump under his finger once he found Esperanza's carotid artery.

"Quit bitching and get tying." He threw half the ropes to Des. "We've only got about three minutes before he gains consciousness and he doesn't strike me as someone who is going to like our getting the drop on him."

Des retrieved his .22 from Esperanza's waistband and reseated it in the ankle holster, also sticking the Glock in between his belt and shirt, in much the same spot Esperanza had used. Then he secured Esperanza's hands behind his back while Scotty worked on his legs.

A moment later, as Scotty had predicted, a thick moan escaped Esperanza and he moved slightly, clearly shaking off the effects of being tased. It took another sixty seconds for him to fully comprehend he was bound. He sat up and leaned his upper body against the wall, smothering another groan. His head slumped forward.

"And here I was going to cut you some slack. I'm trying to understand all this…I have a good idea why you busted into my house," Esperanza finally said in a deep, guttural growl. "But why exactly am I tied up?"

"In due time." Scotty's voice held the same earlier triumph. He strutted back and forth, his eyes alive with excitement behind the lenses.

Des held on to his smile, glancing at Scotty with arched eyebrows, sending a silent command to go ahead. This was his gig. The guy was eating this up like a kid licking the bowl of his favorite dessert. Who was he to spoil his fun? He'd let the geek handle the interrogation for the time being.

"What did you do to me?" Esperanza tilted his head back, eyeing Scotty before moving his focus to Des.

"We'll be asking the questions, if you don't mind." Scotty swaggered when he spoke.

Des chuckled.

Scotty didn't disappoint, working for a perfect ten on the amusement scale, when he added, "You're in no position to be making demands."

"It was a simple question, requiring a simple answer."

"Don't play word games, asshole. You're the one who's tied up, not us."

Des caught the flash of irritation in Esperanza's eyes. "Uh, Scotty. Don't antagonize him."

"We came here for answers," Scotty insisted, turning back to Esperanza, and totally ignoring Des' plea, he kicked his leg. "Did you hear that? Answers."

Des rolled his eyes, quickly deciding it was time to step in before the angry bear they'd tied up somehow got loose. He flashed a contrite smile, going for sincere. "We apologize for this unorthodox method of gaining your attention. However, we felt it necessary."

"Oh?" Esperanza's livid gaze settled on Des. "You come crashing through my window, stun the shit out of me, and then you have the unmitigated gall to say you felt it necessary?" His scowl turned menacing. "No! I demand a better explanation."

"I'll pay for the window."

"Don't make concessions," Scotty said, his tone incensed. "He broke into Avery Montgomery's house and destroyed her things. You told me as much. He should be apologizing for his actions."

Esperanza shook his head. "That wasn't my doing."

"Are you saying you weren't at the widow's house?" If he denied it, Des would know he was lying. His description fit Andy's right down to the navy blue sweater he still wore.

He met Des' stare with one of his own. For countless minutes the stare-off continued, neither backing down, until Esperanza sighed and looked away. Then he glanced back at Des, offering a self-effacing smile. "I was there. But obviously too late because someone beat me to it."

"Someone beat you to it?" Okay, that fit, but he wasn't about to reveal this fact. "Keep going. I'm listening."

Esperanza's shoulders lifted in an unconcerned shrug.

Des waited a moment. When Esperanza didn't say anything, he prodded, "Who do you think it was?"

"I have no idea."

Again, the stare-off, until Des caught Scotty in his peripheral vision.

"Wrong answer, asshole." He moved into position to kick him again, his leg primed, ready to strike until Des' hand on his shoulder restrained him.

"Patience." He gave a slight shake of his head. "You can't kick your answers out of him."

Des turned back to Esperanza. His sigh came out in one large exhale. "Look, I can't hold him off forever. You should understand his motivation. He's itching to make up for all those slights from high school. And me?" He shrugged, then exhibited a grin that didn't quite reach his eyes. "Well, I've got my own issues with guys like you. I don't think you fully realize your precarious position." He crouched, leaned closer, and lowered his voice. "See, we've already broken in and stunned the shit out of you. In my book, a beating will only add a few months in jail, maybe less, if we get probation for extenuating circumstances, so we got nothing to lose if we don't get some answers." He waited a full moment before letting his grin spread and adding, "Soon."

"You think a beating is enough to make me talk? Go for it. But I'd advise giving it your best effort." Esperanza's smile turned feral, sending a shiver of alarm through Des. "Just remember one thing. I always get even."

Des nodded slowly and unbent, standing straight. He tapped Scotty and indicated the other side of the room.

"What? You can't stop now!" Scotty said in his best Mohammad Ali imitation as he followed him. "We're in the driver's seat. He's bluffing."

"I thought you were the brain in this whole fiasco, so use it," Des ground out, curling a fist to keep from hitting him. Damn, he was tempted. More than tempted. "If you think brute force will work on that guy, you're delusional. Look at him. He'll take whatever we throw at him without telling us squat. We need to try another tack."

"Hmmm…" Scotty eyed Esperanza, who only flashed another vicious smile, his entire body language shouting, *Come and get me, assholes.* "You have a point. What do you suggest?"

"Follow my lead and step in when you think you can help. And for God's sake, will you please stop antagonizing him?"

"I'm not."

"Yeah, right. Your very presence antagonizes him."

"You know I can tase you."

"I rest my case. You don't tase allies." Des sighed heavily and stalked back over to Esperanza, who followed his advance with hot, angry eyes. "Let's talk about the night of the ambush over in Afghanistan. I figure it's a safe topic since both you and Scotty were there."

Esperanza remained silent for a long moment, before shrugging. "You've read the report."

"Yeah, I have. Thanks to this genius." He indicated Scotty with a nod. "I've even read the more comprehensive one Williams kept from us."

Surprise flitted over Esperanza's expression for a split second, which was enough for Des to grasp he'd hit a nerve. He grinned inwardly, tsk-tsking and pacing. "We know a lot more than you think we do and we're willing to share information, but we'd also like to gain some." His grin formed on the outside.

Des slanted a glance in Scotty's direction. He did sullen real well. But thank God, he did it leaning against the wall with his legs crossed and his mouth shut, listening for a change.

"Like I said earlier, information-gathering is the only reason for this unorthodox visit. We really do apologize for the inconvenience."

"Yeah, I can see the regret in your eyes. Touching."

Des' hands went up in mock surrender. "Your actions yesterday left us with no other choice, especially if you add in the colonel's questionable behavior. Caused us to do a little digging. And we caught some interesting shit in our shovels." He chuckled when Esperanza's eyebrows lifted. *Ah, so Scotty's right and the guy* has *underestimated us.* "We can't understand why the US military would hire a couple of plants to spy on us, or worse. Steal from us." He paced. "I mean, SPC is merely a company trying to exist and flourish. What's beneficial for SPC is beneficial for America. You'd think the military's job would be to protect that right, not jeopardize it by stealing our secrets."

"That's quite a claim. One I have a hard time believing."

Des nodded. He had Brubaker's last check received for services rendered. Wasn't easy to trace, but Scotty eventually found the link. "How about a special account we came across used by the military, no doubt for spying...and stealing."

Though Esperanza didn't move a muscle, his entire body seemed to stiffen. His eyes glinted something besides anger, something Des figured he'd be better off not knowing.

"The US military doesn't steal from Americans," Esperanza said in a chilling tone.

"Maybe not, but what about one crooked colonel?" The guy still didn't budge, but Des could see his question got him thinking. "Are you familiar with the man?"

"If you've read the file, then you know I am."

"Here's my guess. You're here to take him down. I mean, after all you don't exist. At least, Esperanza doesn't." Des laughed outright at the astonishment that hit his eyes for the briefest second. "Scotty and I did some extensive research. Amazing what you can or can't find on the web these days. So, what are you? CIA?"

"If you think that, then you know I'm not at liberty to say."

"Yeah, and we're working on the same team. I have a feeling our goals are identical."

"Don't pretend you know my goals. They have nothing to do with the colonel."

"So you're not tracking our devices?" Des snorted. "Don't bother denying it. It's our only link. That and a crooked colonel, who's probably behind the theft in the first place. He's not aiding in finding them, that's for damn sure, is he?"

"What do you expect to learn from me? Even if I could talk, what makes you think I'd tell you two shit?"

"We can use each other." Des shrugged. He felt certain Williams had covered his tracks well and was above suspicion. What they'd uncovered was his ace up his sleeve. "You may not think so, but you need us…need the information we have."

Esperanza only chuckled, not a good sign, based on the *not in this lifetime* expression crossing his features accompanying the sound.

Des realized he'd better think of a way to get the warrior on their side, or they'd lose their opportunity for answers, never to have another.

"How about a show of good faith? We untie you and talk."

That got his attention. Esperanza didn't look so amused now. Now he looked curious.

It also got Scotty's.

"What the hell are you doing?" Scotty pushed away from the wall and stormed over to him, getting into his face, or neck, since he stood a good four inches shorter.

"Trust me." He met Scotty's belligerent frown and nodded toward the other side of the room. Both walked in that direction. When they were out of Esperanza's direct earshot, Des said, "I know a little about human nature too. If we don't offer something, we won't gain anything." His nod indicated their prisoner. "He for damn sure isn't going to give us jack shit without it."

"But having him tied up is our only leverage."

"Leverage? What leverage? He isn't talking, so what have we gained?" Des wiped his face, feeling his frustration mount. Nothing was going as planned. "We shouldn't have tied him up to begin with, Scotty. That only antagonized him further. All I'm trying to do is salvage something of our trip up here."

Scotty looked ready to argue with him, but stopped and nodded. "Okay. You're probably right. Go untie him."

"You want me to do it?"

"Yeah, I plan on steering clear of the guy. I kicked him, remember?"

While they were discussing the details of who would do the untying, Esperanza somehow worked his hands free. Out of the corner of Des' eye, he saw him reaching for his legs. "It's a moot point because he's taken care of it."

Scotty stiffened and took a step back when he noticed what Des was referring to. "You're still armed," he hissed. "Don't let him get too close to me."

Des chuckled. "Someday, Scotty, you'll learn how not to piss off those who are bigger than you."

Scotty flashed an irritated scowl. "Oh yeah, like you could give lessons on making friends."

Des strode toward Esperanza, ignoring the comment. "We were just about to untie you." He bent to work on the knots at the man's feet. "Here, let me help you."

When all the ropes were loose, Des pulled the Glock out from behind his back, offered it to him, and hoped the move would give him some of the leverage Scotty referred to. "We're sorry about all this."

Without saying a word, Esperanza nodded and took his weapon, holstering it. Silently, he stalked over to the monitors. For extended minutes, he mutely watched the screens.

Des was beginning to think he wasn't going to say anything, that they'd made the trip for nothing was pretty much a foregone conclusion.

"Tell me everything you can about Williams and your company. I want to know exactly what you do."

"Does that mean you'll answer some of our questions?"

"A show of good faith." Esperanza smiled. "Weren't those your exact words?"

Des couldn't stop the grin from forming. Shit. Caught up with his own words. "Somehow, I doubt I'll get what I came for."

"You'll never know unless you try."

"Yeah, right." Des sighed, and spent a moment considering, then nodded. "No one has figured out what happened the night Montgomery and Crandall died. The Xcom2s simply disappeared, and the last person to see them is dead. There is no trail to follow. It's like they don't exist."

"Tell me something I don't know," Esperanza said.

"Okay, how about this." Des paced. "Williams has comprehensive files on SPC's principals, detailing past incidents which have no bearing on what we're doing now," he said, thinking of Sin's mother's suicide Avery had asked about.

"That's not unusual and certainly expected."

"Maybe. I haven't read them, so I can't be sure. However, I am positive that Williams is behind the sale of two of SPC's stolen products to our competitors. I'm not privy to the way the government operates, but I have to assume there's a bit of impropriety going on."

Des stopped and glanced at Esperanza to gauge his reaction. All he got for his efforts was a mild rise of eyebrows.

"Go on," he murmured. "I'm listening."

"Like I said earlier, Scotty, the boy genius over there—" Des nodded in Scotty's direction "—traced the monetary trail. Once we had the account, it was easy to backtrack to Williams."

"How did you get the account in the first place?"

"I can't reveal how. Just suffice it to know we got it." Des continued pacing. "We think he's the person who trashed Avery Montgomery's house. Now, his actions conjure up many questions, for which I have no answers. Answers I was hoping you could provide." Counting on his fingers, he said, "Why did he trash her house when he tells us she's not involved? Why is he hampering our efforts to find our product? Is he trying to put us out of business? And if he is, why? Why would a colonel in the US Army go to such lengths, unless he's crooked and he's involved? Who's checking up on him?"

"Those are serious allegations. Can you give me verification?"

"I'll give you what we have." Des peered at the man whose face held no expression and went for broke. "We came here seeking information. Williams' actions have put us in a serious bind. We need to find our product or Williams wins, and SPC's headed for bankruptcy. We were hoping you could help us." He then told the man about the two spies on their production line, whose fingerprints showed up on a military file listed as classified, clearly linking them to the colonel as well as a few other withdrawals from the same bank account used to pay Brubaker. "Williams is in this up to his eyeballs."

~

"Don't worry about the window," Esperanza said to the man he knew as one of SPC's partners, Des Phillips. "Let the government pay for the damage." It was the least he could offer in payment for the loss of their prototypes after listening to their story. No wonder they'd taken him by storm. The two had good reason not to trust anyone. Not a good thing, especially in his line of work. From the very beginning of this op, trust had been lacking on all sides. He'd understood that going in. Who to trust, along with who to be wary of, were unknown parts of the puzzle. The selling of America's secrets for profit wasn't a crime he took lightly. It was his job to figure out who was behind the treason. He did have someone he trusted to turn to above all others, thank God. He knew he could count on his mentor, and superior, for support now that this had escalated given the details about the colonel's activities.

"That's quite decent of you," Des said of his offer, grinning. "Considering how we, umm, well, you know. Roughed you up and tased you, and tying you up and shit."

"All in a day's work. I seem to be fine." Esperanza flexed his hands, then bent each leg before stretching out, still feeling the residual effect of being zapped. He'd underestimated McNeil, even wondered why he hadn't retaliated. Esperanza had been sorely tempted to after the pain, not to mention the humiliation, the little guy had inflicted on him. Being tied up hadn't helped his disposition.

Both men were lucky he understood their motivations.

Still, he did question his sanity. Why was he letting them go so easily? Hell if he knew. Maybe it had to do with a guilty conscience. He couldn't prolong their problems and make them suffer more at the hands of the American government that he represented. It didn't seem right, no matter how much they deserved it. He smiled. "See? No lasting effects."

"Thanks, man, and thanks for listening." McNeil held out his hand. "We'd prefer picking your brain, but hey. Guess some things aren't meant to be."

"Yeah." Esperanza shook his hand, as well as Des'. "You understand my position. I'm really not at liberty to divulge information. But you've given me a lot of new intel pertaining to Williams and his actions. Definitely something to reconsider and I thank you for your candor."

"Which doesn't help us any. We aren't letting this go. We have every intention of finding our prototypes, and we damn well think Williams is as guilty as sin," Des said.

Of course they did. His expression said as much.

"I appreciate your position." Esperanza nodded. He sighed and pulled out a card, writing his personal cell number on it and handing it to Des. "You might be in danger. If Williams is behind this, you could become a threat if you get too close. I'll be around for a few more days. I'm a phone call away, just in case you find yourself in a bind." He had a feeling they might need some extra help, given all the fallout transpiring around them.

Esperanza dealt in absolutes. Before listening to what the men had revealed, which coincided with his own suspicions about Williams, he thought for sure he'd have to abort his mission for lack of substantiation. Supposition reinforced with facts made it easier to figure out motive, along with providing him with more reason to shine the spotlight on Williams.

He still had a hard time believing a full-bird colonel in the US Army could be behind all of this, highlighting the very reason why this case was so hard to solve. No one involved, from the testing to the administering, were the usual suspects. All had exemplary records, which in turn made them all suspect.

"Sure, if you'll do the same." Des pulled out a card from his wallet. "Hey, I'm an incurable optimist. It could happen."

Esperanza shook his head, returning the smile. "Drive carefully." He tapped the card Des had just handed him containing a cell number and an address, and watched them walk out into the bright morning sunlight.

He grabbed the cell phone, punched in the preset number, and said, once it was answered, "I have some interesting news to report. Tell me what we have on Williams."

The colonel wouldn't get away with his actions if he was guilty. Oh no! Esperanza had no intention of letting him off. His ride out of Dodge could be delayed another twenty-four hours. And because his trap had only netted minnows, exasperating ones at that, he'd have to think of a way to nail Williams. Since the colonel thought the widow was the key, that's where he intended to focus his attention.

Chapter 17

Sunshine streamed through the opening slits in the blinds, and the narrow splash of bright light landed on Avery's face, easing her out of a deep sleep. The first thing she noticed, after full consciousness set in, was Sin's featherlike breath on her neck, the even rhythm telling her he still slept soundly. Thank God!

Her focus moved to his hands before settling on his mouth. He had the softest touch, not to mention the softest lips.

Heat streaked up her neck as the memory of their lovemaking rushed back in mind-numbing images.

Tell me what you want!

Such a straightforward command but so difficult to articulate, especially given his unrelenting determination to find out what she liked. How could she tell him? Besides being too intimate a topic to discuss, she had no idea what she liked. All she knew was what she didn't like. No way could she tell him that.

Who knew it could be so wonderful? Mike never spent so much time trying to please her. The realization that he'd actually been a selfish lover eased much of her guilt. Terry was right. As her husband, he had a responsibility to share his life with her and chose not to. Even the idea of her letter causing his death began to lessen. All of his hurtful taunts replayed in her mind for a brief instant before she dismissed them as no longer having any relevance. After last night, after the things she'd done and felt, she knew she wasn't frigid.

One bout of lovemaking with Sin was enough to wipe away the misconception forever.

An embarrassed flush rose up, heating her cheeks.

How she'd found the nerve to be so bold, she couldn't fathom. A smile formed, reaching all the way to her toes. Even her hair wanted to smile. She loved making love with Sin. How could she ever think she was abnormal? Still, it was all so new. She needed distance. Now. Waiting until three this afternoon when she planned to go shopping seemed too far off.

Gently, so as not to wake him, Avery slid out from under the sheets, stopping and holding her breath when he grabbed her from behind, pulling her closer and spooning. One hand found a breast, kneading, while the other moved hair off her shoulders.

"Where're you going?" he murmured sleepily into her ear, bestowing warm kisses along her neck.

"The bathroom." She ignored the tingling sensation his lips, hands, and sexy voice were causing and said, "I'll be right back." Sin was obviously ready and willing to go at it again.

He released her. "Okay, but don't be gone long."

Avery heaved a relieved sigh and scooted out of his reach. In the light of day, her courage waned a bit. At the door, she glanced back to see him sprawled out in naked splendor, until he rolled over, pulling the sheet around him, blocking her view. He was gorgeous. She waited a few seconds, shaking the temptation to forget her plans and rejoin him.

No. She shook the thought, thankful he appeared to have gone back to sleep. She tiptoed around the room, quietly grabbing her clothes and other necessary items.

She reached for her cell phone to call Mary on the way to the bathroom to make sure Andy got off safely. Satisfied, she cut the connection and leaned against the bathroom door, intent on taking the few minutes a shower would provide to come to terms with last evening's events.

At the moment, she needed space much more than she needed another orgasm. So much had happened since the night at the cemetery. She needed time to absorb those changes.

Avery hurriedly finished in the bathroom, then snuck downstairs, careful not to step on the stairs with the creaking boards. Seconds later, she was out the front door. As she headed for Starbucks and a cup of coffee, a sense of freedom emerged. Her gurgle of laughter escaped. She felt wonderful. Hugging herself, she looked around at the clear, crisp morning. The memory of the last time she'd walked this way filled her mind. Sin had been next to her.

Her pace quickened the closer she got.

Avery grabbed the handle to pull the coffee shop's door open. Instantly, the same weird apprehension, not unlike the one she'd felt too many times in the past few days, assaulted her. She halted, whipping her upper body around as the hairs at the back of her neck stood on end.

Her furtive glance swept left then right, before checking across the street. Satisfied there was no threat, she headed inside.

"Two large coffees, please." Avery smiled at the perky girl behind the cash register, then pointed to the pastries in the case next to her. "Give me a couple of those, too."

She paid and took a moment to add cream to her coffee with one thought. The feeling hadn't abated, in fact it grew stronger. Slowly, Avery turned her head and eyed every person seated at the tables. No one looked familiar or appeared interested in her.

She capped the coffees and hurried for the exit, wishing she hadn't come out alone.

Outside, she again spent a long minute perusing the street on both sides. Broad daylight with everyday activities—a few pedestrians strolling, others walking faster, cars honking, parking, and speeding off after stopping at the red light once it changed to green—was the scene she spied. Certainly nothing to alert her further.

Avery exhaled the big breath she'd been holding in and started for home, keeping her pace steady, listening carefully as she walked.

Every now and then, she'd stop abruptly and turn around, so sure she'd heard footsteps. But those times she checked, the sidewalk behind her was always empty.

Her pace quickened.

Near her street she was almost running, traveling as fast as she could while also carrying a bag and two coffees in the cardboard holder.

Avery breathed a sigh of relief the moment she stepped onto her porch.

While unlocking her front door, she jumped when it was jerked open.

"Where in the hell have you been?"

She relaxed her shoulders, not expecting Sin's rugged sexiness to greet her. She ignored his livid gaze. "Sin. You're up." She smiled too brightly, working to keep the fear out of her voice.

He was definitely angry, but his anger was nothing to handle compared to the scare she'd had on the way home.

"That doesn't answer my question." He pulled her inside, shut the door, and leaned against it with arms crossed, a stormy expression highlighting his features.

Sin's autocratic stance made it easier to push her fears away. Most likely her imagination was running rampant again, especially after yesterday. She might like sex with the hunky man eyeing her as if she were an errant child, but she wasn't about to let Sin determine what she should and shouldn't do. She'd already put up with one man's influence controlling most aspects of her life. She had no intention of letting history repeat itself.

"Don't be grouchy." Avery lifted her peace offering. "I brought coffee." Smiling, she held up the bag next to the cup. "And breakfast."

"You don't have coffee here to brew?"

"Not the same." She leaned in and kissed his cheek, despite his forbidding scowl.

Sin was all bark and no bite, just as Eric and Des had said. She turned and started for the kitchen, grinning inwardly at his surprised expression, wishing she'd had a camera to capture the moment. It was so Sin-like. "I decided we needed a treat, especially after all the negatives from yesterday. And what better way to celebrate last night?"

"Avery, you just can't leave without at least telling me where you're going."

"Oh?" She placed the bag on the counter along with the coffee. From inside the cupboard she pulled out two small plates, opened the bag, and plopped a pastry on each one. "Would you have let me go, if I'd have told you?"

"No, we'd be making love right now and you damn well know it."

"Exactly. I think I needed coffee more."

"Really?" Sin held her gaze, stalking toward her. "Funny, I got the impression you liked making love with me."

Avery swallowed hard, unable to glance away and unable to refute his claim. She held up the plate with the pastry along with a cup of coffee and used both to put a barrier between them, also stopping his advance.

"Down, boy!" She wouldn't give in to the heat his theatrics generated. He was so damned good at making her pulse race with just a look and the right intonation in his voice. Barefoot, he hadn't bothered to dress other than throwing on a pair of boxer shorts and a t-shirt. At least he wasn't naked. But he *was* sexy, even with bed-head and a light beard, and oh, how she loved looking at him. Too damned much. "Behave yourself and eat your breakfast."

Without releasing her stare, he took the cup and plate, placing both on the counter. Then, he blocked her retreat with a hand on either side of her, stepped forward, and bent, nuzzling her neck. "I'd rather have a kiss."

He spent a moment bestowing wet, sloppy kisses from her neck to her ear and along her jaw, ending at her mouth. Heat flared between them and she closed her eyes, letting a sense of bliss wash over her. His masculine, musky scent rose up, one that still held a hint of their lovemaking from the previous evening.

Heaven help her. How could she think of wanting to make love again? Completely unlike her, yet at the moment, it was all she could think about. Everything about him was enticing.

Sin broke the kiss and leaned back while his hand slowly roamed up her arm, rested on her neck, and took over where his lips left off. He fingered the necklace she wore, sending more sensation shooting through her.

"You are one sexy woman. I shouldn't want you again, but I do." The smile he offered could only be called self-deprecating. Sin sighed, then stepped away, and released her to pick up his plate and coffee. "Maybe breakfast is a good idea."

With her coffee and pastry in hand, Avery followed him through the swinging door. Like the previous day, Sin politely held her chair out and waited until she sat, before seating himself.

He spent a moment lifting the lid off his coffee and blowing on the dark brew. Then, he spoke. "I do wish you hadn't gone out alone, though."

"I was fine," she murmured, totally dismissing the idea of an invisible follower. Her imagination *had* gone into overdrive. She was perfectly safe because Sin was here.

"Yeah?"

Several minutes of silence ensued before Avery looked up to find his gaze on her. She cast her gaze down, uncomfortable with such thorough scrutiny.

Finally, he cleared his throat. "We haven't discussed the events of the last twenty-four hours, specifically your meeting with Williams."

"You don't really think he's part of this?" Avery waved a hand to indicate her house, without glancing at him. Discarding the idea, she shook her head. "You're overreacting." Why would Colonel Williams search her house? Her thoughts went back to what they'd discussed. He'd also mentioned something about Sin believing that Mike had somehow sent his missing prototypes to her.

"Overreacting or not, I want to know exactly what the colonel said."

Sin's no-nonsense tone brought her out of her musings. She met his intent gaze, working to slow the fear creeping up her spine so it wouldn't show in her eyes.

"I'm being cautious." His warm hand covered hers. He squeezed. "Don't worry, Avery. Nothing will happen to you on my watch. I don't believe in coincidences and I don't trust Colonel Williams. And because I plan on looking under each bush, I need to analyze everything, including what you spoke about. I also need to read those files."

"Will you do the same?" she asked, pulling her hand out of his grasp.

His eyebrows rose in an inquisitive slant.

"He told me about the files he furnished." Avery glanced at her hand, now wrapped around the coffee cup, and focused on her fingers. "You know, the ones on Mike and me." Her voice trailed off at the end.

"Okay. I'll have Eric drop them by." Sin sat back, his mind clearly churning. A moment later, his concentrated gaze landed on her face, as if reading her expression once more. He finally sighed. "You seem concerned about something he said. I have this feeling I should be defending myself and I can't figure out what I'm defending myself against."

"The colonel pointed out a few coincidences."

"Go on," he urged.

"Like the shooting in the cemetery. Maybe you set it up to scare me." Avery shrugged, dredging for the courage to ask him outright what had been on her mind since Williams first mentioned the possibility. "Did you? Do you think I have your missing technology and did you use the incident to try and get close to me?"

"It's interesting how he seems to be trying to divide us, using innuendo and manipulation to break us apart," Sin said, not really answering her question. "I know you don't believe your husband would do anything knowingly, but what if he did something unknowingly?"

"Look, let's quit dancing around the issues." Her spine stiffened as anger flared. "Why are you here, if not because you believe I have what you're searching for?" The question came out more heatedly than she'd intended.

"Avery, I—"

"But I don't. Okay? I don't have your missing prototypes." She could tell by his serious expression Sin was going to ask questions she didn't want to answer. "Mike played by the rules. He was the perfect soldier and though he was too smart to be taken in by the colonel, something most likely happened to distract him the night he died. I'm really sorry. I wish to God he had sent them to me, so I could help you." Boy, did she wish that. Then maybe she wouldn't feel even slightly responsible for his distraction. Now, because the prototypes were missing, she had another destination to add to her guilt trip. "But he didn't. He died instead. Can we please talk about something else?"

"Fine. I'll drop it, but I'd still like to see the files."

Feeling his scrutiny again, Avery lifted her head in a defiant tilt and met his gaze. "What?"

"You don't really believe I had anything to do with someone taking those potshots, do you?"

"I don't know what to believe." She offered a nonchalant shrug. "Besides, you never answered my question, which confuses me more."

"Then we're even because I sense you're hiding something."

"I guess we each have our secrets." At that point, she knew Colonel Williams had been right about Sin somehow thinking Mike sent her the missing prototypes.

"I thought you trusted me, especially after last night?"

Avery smiled. His whispered tone held something. The same something she spotted in his earnest expression. Yearning. She closed her eyes and nodded, deciding to place herself fully in his hands for the simple reason, she did trust him. "I do," she said softly, opening her eyes and letting him see the truth in her gaze.

"Thank you." Sin's warm hand clasped hers, gently squeezing. "I'd still like to take a look at those files."

"I'll get them after we eat," she said.

~

"Here you go."

Sin glanced up in time to grab the three files Avery had retrieved once he'd showered. He'd just hung up with Eric, who agreed to drop off the information the colonel supplied to SPC's principals later.

"Thanks." Sin's gaze landed on the heart-shaped locket Avery always wore and he clenched his fist, fighting the urge to yank it off her neck. For some reason, after the night they'd shared, he didn't want to see the memento in such a prominent place, basking on her lovely skin. In his mind, it only denoted one thing. She still pined after her dead hero.

How illogical to worry over a stupid necklace.

His focus dropped to the brown folders and he pushed out the disturbing thoughts. He had too much other shit to worry about than to obsess over something he couldn't control. Of course she pined for him. They'd been married ten years and her hero deserved a bit of pining over. Sin certainly didn't deserve any consideration.

Hell, he'd known Avery for only days, not near enough time to form lasting love. She most likely responded to him out of basic human need. After all, her husband had been overseas a few months before he died. He had to remember, last night was only sex.

Yeah, and if he believed that, then he was the most gullible man on the face of the planet. He could still smell her light scent on his clothes, and God help him, whenever she got too close and he caught a stronger whiff, he responded. He shouldn't even be thinking of sex, not after the multitude of times they'd gone at it last night.

He sighed and opened the first file, the one with his name on it.

Sin read for more than an hour when his cell phone rang. Thankful for an interruption, he pulled it out, recognizing Des' number. "How'd it go in Baltimore?"

"Not well." Des sighed. "We're on our way back from there now. Got us absolutely nowhere. A waste of the best part of the morning."

"What happened?"

"Nothing. We got squat, but Esperanza now knows what we know because we had no choice but to tell him everything we had on Williams. Our show of good faith didn't work and he didn't feel inclined to reciprocate, so we still have no clear idea why the good colonel's bent on destroying SPC."

"It wasn't a total waste," Scotty yelled in the background. "We had an event-filled morning."

"I ought to hit you." The irritation in Des' voice left Sin with little doubt he wanted to pound Scotty into the ground. Nothing new there. Scotty had that effect on people.

"What'd Scotty do?" Sin asked, working to keep from laughing outright, but he failed. Miserably.

"It's not funny," Des all but growled. "If not for him, I'd have spent a peaceful morning. In bed. Sleeping. Esperanza's not working for Williams, at least not on stealing our secrets. So I think we can safely eliminate him from our list of suspects."

"Don't be so sure, Sin. It could be a ploy to mislead us," Scotty interjected loudly.

"Shit, Scotty." Des huffed angrily, then said into the phone, "Do you see what you created? He needs to get a life…preferably one that doesn't include spying. He really sucks at it."

Scotty's voice was muffled as he argued in the background. "I have a life. I don't know why you're bitching. Tell Sin my plan worked. We got into his house, didn't we? Is it my fault he didn't talk?"

"Esperanza's not talking, 'cause that's his frickin' job," Des said heatedly. "He's most likely CIA, for Christ's sake, which means we have no choice but to look elsewhere. You are such a moron. Sin, tell him to stop being such a moron and to use his frickin' brain."

Sin snorted, rolling his eyes. Both men had points. Maybe it had been a mistake pairing the two for this task, but he couldn't do anything about that now.

"So Esperanza's not talking?" Sin asked, to bring their attention back to the problem at hand rather than killing each other.

"No, he's totally closed-mouthed and definitely has his own agenda, but like I said—I don't think he's the one who stole our product." Des' sigh transmitted his frustration loud and clear. "In fact I think he's looking for them just like us."

"So what're your plans?"

"We still have Avery's computer. Might be a lead." He broke off and Sin picked up on his asking Scotty about retrieving the files off her smashed hard drive.

"Of course!" Scotty's indignant voice shot back.

Des grunted in Sin's ear. "Thank God the man is useful for something besides making my life miserable."

"Unless they got corrupted," Scotty amended a moment later, at which point Sin wasn't sure whether or not Des would pull over to the curb and push him out of the car. As he saw it, Scotty's usefulness to Des had plummeted dramatically with those four words.

"I won't be able to do anything with them if they did."

Sin chuckled.

"Figures," Des murmured before saying more loudly, "He's a frickin' lunatic. Do I have to stay with him? Let's switch places. I'll stay with Avery and you can babysit Jason Bourne here."

Sin held his breath for a moment, searching for calm. "You can handle him, Des," he said, pushing out the irritation his partner's comment about switching places brought on. He wasn't jealous. Not of Des. He sighed. "Besides, it won't be for too much longer. Days at most."

"Shit. I guess we should also take a look at those files of Avery's I copied," Des said in a resigned voice. "They may or may not be of interest. Won't know till I open them up."

"See, Sin?" Scotty shouted in the background again. "Easy as one, two, three…we have a plan."

"Yeah, real easy," Des all but snarled.

If only that were true, Sin thought, realizing they were running out of options.

"Anyway, Scotty and I are almost back to D.C. now. I thought you should know the visit to see Esperanza didn't pan out. Sorry to be the bearer of bad news."

"Don't worry. We'll figure it out." Sin tried to sound upbeat. Des' worry was no different from his. The longer they took to find any substantial lead, the closer they got to his deadline and SPC's financial instability. "If he's looking for them, then they must be close and not in Afghanistan like the colonel says."

Des snorted. "Yeah, well I got the impression from his mannerisms he's not a big fan of Williams. Still, he may well think Williams is guilty as sin, but he's a team player. Esperanza doesn't strike me as the type to accuse him without some kind of proof, which we gave him. Little good that does us, though." Des threw out a brittle laugh. "Hell, who knows? Giving Avery's busted computer a look-see just might yield something, since so many people think she's a key player."

"Williams is the key player in this. I just finished reading the files he had on us."

"Oh?" Des hesitated a beat. "What'd they say?"

"They were complete, down to the day you were taken to the emergency room when I hit you over the head with the hood ornament we found. Not one of my best moments or my fondest memory."

"Shit…we were…what? Eight or nine?"

"You were nine, I was ten." The incident was etched into Sin's brain, and one he'd remember forever.

Des chuckled. "A day I'll never forget. A trip to the emergency room, requiring ten stitches, is one of those traumatic events that tends to stick. Your look of horror at what you'd done is what I remember most." Des paused before asking, "How would the bastard get this kind of information and why would he go so far back?"

"I don't know. Maybe he canvassed the old neighborhood and found someone who remembered." Most of the kids he grew up with were either in jail or dead, but their mothers were still around. "The files aren't very complimentary, full of the worst shit we pulled back when we were kids." Sin sighed and rubbed his forehead with forefinger and thumb to ease the building tension. "A very interesting spin on us and our childhood. I don't know what his game is or why he's created files to show us in the worst light, but it doesn't bode well for SPC's security. I have a feeling we were chosen specifically for our background. But that's crazy and doesn't make sense. We created a viable product and sold it to the most logical customer who would benefit from the product."

"I want to take a look at those files," Des said, his voice no longer amused. "I'm with you. I don't have a very good feeling about the whole idea of him keeping track of stupid shit kids pull. I mean, this is the USA for Christ's sake, and we were just kids. Even scarier, those records were supposed to have been expunged. I always thought that meant no one, including Uncle Sam, could view them."

"I forgot about that." Des' statement sent more tension through Sin. The whole idea *was* pretty damned scary. This wasn't nineteen-eighties China or Afghanistan under Taliban rule. Sin didn't know what to think anymore. "Okay," he added on a sigh. "I have nothing else to report on my end. Things are quiet here at Avery's house. I won't turn off my cell. Keep me posted if you find anything."

"Sure thing."

Sin broke the connection with a touch of the screen, wishing their visit with Esperanza had been more promising. He glanced at the files in his hands, his mind full of bleak images of his childhood.

This was going from bad to worse. He felt responsible for his friends who counted on him for their livelihood, which now stood on the brink of peril. He'd give his life for the three men who'd been there for him at different but necessary times in his life. Yet, he didn't see anything short of a miracle helping them find out where the prototypes disappeared to, and even if they did get their miracle, they needed it soon.

The clock ticked, reminding him the chances of discovering the thief grew smaller with each passing hour.

"Bad news?" Avery's question pulled him out of his weighty thoughts.

Sin shrugged. "Esperanza was a dead end." He met her gaze, thinking. "I take it you've read this entire file?" When she nodded, he smiled. "And yet you still made love with me?" He shook his head. "Amazing."

Avery's gaze became more searching. "Why?"

"Isn't it obvious? This information isn't pretty. Paints a very ugly picture of a small group of thugs, as Williams tags us."

"I looked beyond what was written. What I see now is three outstanding men who endured hardship and survived." She sighed. "I hate to admit it, but I probably wouldn't have given you a second glance if we'd met back then. Badass teenagers weren't my thing."

"I know. You went for the hero types like Michael Montgomery." When her eyebrows shot up, he smiled. "I read your file too. Remember?"

"Ah, I forgot." Avery's face brightened with a soft smile. "Can I help it if I'm a sucker for a hero?"

"No. It was your destiny. Besides, cheerleaders and homecoming queens didn't ring my chimes, either. I had no patience for what I considered snobbish, shallow behavior." If that were true, how had he ever picked Diane as a spouse, when she'd been the epitome of shallow, vain creatures? Maybe he'd chosen her on purpose, to show the world he could. Unfortunately, his mistake had almost destroyed him in the end.

"I guess I should count myself lucky you never knew me when, because I'm really glad we spent the night together." She cleared her throat. "It was *nice*."

Nice wasn't exactly the adjective he'd use. *Hot* better described their lovemaking. Or earth shattering.

"They say every woman needs to take a ride on the wild side at least once in her life." Despite the tightness of his problems gripping his nuts like a vice, Sin couldn't stop his grin from appearing when he noticed the slight blush highlighting her cheeks. At least he'd given her a great ride, one he hoped would end her cravings for heroes.

"Okay, so you were a badass teenager and I was a shallow princess. Neither of us is the same person today. Thank God."

"Yeah, I guess you're right." He chewed on the side of his mouth, wondering. Who would she choose if her dead hero were here today? If only he could be anyone else but who he was at that very moment. He couldn't stomach coming in second behind Montgomery. Not with Avery…not after last night.

"Are you okay?" Her hand on his arm drew his attention and he glanced up, seeing concern etched into her solemn expression. "Do you want to talk about your past? About the things in the file?"

Sin chuckled. Such a feminine question and one women always asked. Why in the hell would he want to talk about something he'd spent years trying to forget? He could tell from Avery's expression that she was curious, and he felt he owed her some explanation, but he wasn't about to sugarcoat the truth.

"Poverty is ugly. Not so much the dirt and living conditions." At least that wasn't the worst part for him. No boy really cared about something so trivial. Going without became second nature and the only thing he knew, so why would he care about it? *Ignorance was bliss* worked for him. "What made it ugly was the way others perceived us, as if we were less than human because our moms happened to be single women who tried the best they could."

He glanced at Avery and offered a sad smile. "A vast majority of the poor are women like those I describe, who along with their children, are crippled without male support or education."

Avery placed her hand in his. "That's so sad."

Sin nodded. "It is sad. And what's even sadder, most are destined to live a harsh life. And though society shouts platitudes about how poverty needs to be eradicated, nobody really gives a shit because nothing ever changes…it only gets worse."

Sin broke off a moment to catch his breath and think about his next words.

Avery squeezed his hand reasuringly. The total acceptance he spied in her warm expression spurred him to continue.

"Still, the three of us were tough, but we didn't fit in. You can't have any idea what it's like being white in a neighborhood surrounded by blacks on one side and Hispanics on the other."

He wasn't prejudiced toward either group. In fact, he felt a strange kinship and connection toward those kids who'd merely tried to survive in a brutal world, just like him. He certainly held no animosity toward them. No. He aimed his animosity at the system that created poverty in the first place. One that kept poor people in their place.

"Do you know how Eric and I met Des?"

When Avery shook her head, he offered a wan smile.

"That's because Williams wasn't as thorough as he could've been." Sin sighed, dredging forth the memory of the type of animal poverty created. "A group of kids attacked him. They thought he had money and they were pounding it out of him."

"Why? If he lived in the same neighborhood, wouldn't they assume he was poor like them?"

"Except he wasn't like them. Des' mom wasn't your typical single mom. She worked two jobs. Appearance was important to her, so she scoured the second-hand stores. She always made sure Des was clean and had fairly nice clothes, and he stood out. They assumed he had money. I honest to God thought they were going to kill him. And Des, you know him. He's one mean son of a bitch, was even more so back then. He would've fought to the death before he told them the truth. That he was poorer than them. Shit. How screwed up can the world be? They were beating on this white kid because of perception. When in reality, his mom was actually poorer than the moms of those who were beating him because she wouldn't take public assistance."

"So what happened?"

"Eric and I intervened before a police siren broke up the fight, causing the kids to scatter like bugs running for cover when someone lifts the rock they're hiding under. Got the shit beat out of us for our troubles and a nasty look from Des, who didn't take kindly to our interference." Sin chuckled. "I figured the three of us could use each other for needed protection. Eric eventually convinced Des to give my idea a try. Use my plan to form our own gang, one that worked on the edges. We became the eyes and ears for the other gangs and remained neutral. Both sides respected that. It was not the kind of childhood most kids have, but it was one way of surviving the hood."

"Wow."

Sin shrugged. "You already know how we survived our teens without being thrown into juvie or worse. I guess you could say we worked the system and straddled the line of respectability. When those cops challenged us, we were well on our way to incarceration and hard time. God only knows what would've happened to the three of us without their intervention or if my mom hadn't committed suicide." He stopped for a moment and took a deep breath, reliving her horrible death all over again.

Warmth flooded the spot where Avery's hand gently gripped his arm, drawing his focus.

"You don't have to continue if it's too hard to talk about."

Sin met her gaze and more sympathy and understanding shone in those warm brown eyes. Comforted, he covered her hand and squeezed. For some reason, sharing his past with her did seem to lessen his burden. Her expression encouraged him to continue, so he did.

"When she died, I vowed the cycle would end then and there. I made Des and Eric promise to be somebody other than poor. I wouldn't allow poverty to get them like it did my mother. Her death had to mean something." His friends were all the family he had left and he'd meant his vow. They'd overcome their past or they'd have him to answer to.

He nodded to the files. "You've read what happened. Sometimes all you need is the right motivation. Eric joined the Air Force and earned his degree that way. Des went into the Marines and later into law enforcement. And I went to Stanford, with the help of insurance money." He snorted. "Now I'm respectable, thanks to my dead mother."

"I'm so sorry. It must've been difficult to endure such hardship."

A lump the size of a grapefruit stuck in the back of his throat and he blinked back the tears forming. Sin couldn't meet her eyes. The sincerity pouring out of her soul-searing expression scared the shit out of him. He cleared his throat and looked down at Avery's hand still squeezing his arm.

"She sounds like a courageous woman."

"She fucking killed herself. How courageous is that in the scheme of things?" He all but shouted the question. "I found her. I wanted her to live so much, I'd have given anything to die and take her place." Sin regretted his bitter outburst when she stared at him in stunned silence, outraged horror written so clearly on her face. He closed his eyes and took a deep breath. It was several moments before he heard her soft voice again.

"You don't really believe she wasn't courageous?"

"Maybe...I don't know. I'm certain she died thinking that what she was doing was saving me. And God, sometimes I feel so guilty for buying into it." He broke off to keep from losing it in front of her. When he could talk, he said, "She didn't deserve to have the life pounded out of her little by little with her desperate situation, any more than Des deserved to be beaten. None of us deserve the life we get. Whether good or bad. It's the luck of the draw. Heroes like Montgomery got homecoming queens like you, and I got a mom who killed herself." What's more, he got a woman who betrayed him by running off with another hero, killing his unborn child in the process and destroying his hopes for the future.

"You don't view yourself as a hero?"

The harsh sound of his laughter echoed in his mind. "Hell, no," he said sharply. "Open your eyes, Avery. Don't go putting labels on me, especially that one."

"What have you got against heroes?"

"Not a thing." Another stilted laugh accompanied the assertion. Sin leaned over and pulled her close, meeting her lips with his. It wasn't a gentle kiss. His anger fueled the momentum. At first. Until she moaned and his fury dissipated as need filled the void. Her soft lips melded with his, making him forget all about his past.

When the kiss finally ended, she met his gaze. "What was that for?"

"I simply wanted you to know the difference between a man and a hero. I'm here and he isn't."

Avery glanced away and he reached for her chin.

"No, look at me," he said, forcing the issue. "Don't paint me as someone I'm not. See me for what I am."

Their gazes remained locked. The seconds ticked by...ten...twenty...thirty.

"Okay." She nodded. "You're no *hero*. You're just someone who happened to be passing through when I needed you most." She gave a husky laugh and sidled onto his lap.

Avery leaned closer. "I certainly don't need a hero for what's foremost on my mind." Her eyes gave him a perfect view into her soul, allowed him to see the truthfulness of her words.

Sin grinned, glad to have the gravity of the moment dispelled. Nipping her chin and kissing his way to her ears, he spent long seconds tugging and biting before he whispered, "And just what is foremost on your mind?"

Her throaty chuckle was his answer.

He was dying to be inside her. She was habit-forming. He switched positions, placing her underneath him, and glanced down.

Avery's hand attracted his gaze, as she fingered the heart around her neck. It was a habit he noticed her doing too many times over the past few days. Instantly lust died...replaced with pure, unadulterated jealousy. He hated admitting to such an emotion over something so stupid, but he couldn't stop the acid of uncertainty from rising in his gut, eating away at his soul.

"That's a beautiful necklace." Now was not the time to address the issue, but the comment just slipped out, once it mentally formed. "Intricate."

"Thank you. Mike gave it to me just before he died." Avery fingered it again and her smile turned wistful. "It reminds me of our good times."

"Looks like one of those doohickeys that hold pictures."

"It is. Mike added pictures of the two of us when we were younger."

"Take it off," Sin whispered, bending his head, capturing her chin with his mouth. His lips grazed across her neck, extracting her soft moan.

Her head dropped back giving him more access.

"Why?" she asked breathlessly.

"Isn't it obvious?" Sin kissed his way to her ear, where he spent a moment nibbling. "In case you haven't noticed," he murmured. "We're about to make love, and I'm not into competing with a dead hero for attention."

"What...?" Avery broke away and met his gaze, hers inquisitive. "You're serious, aren't you?"

"As a heart attack. If he were here, who would you choose? Me or him?" The moment the words were out, he realized how much he meant them, no matter that he already knew the answer. He wanted Avery to want him for him. How he wished he could be her hero.

"I'm not sure how to answer that." She eyed him, then laughed nervously. "It's only a necklace."

"Then take it off." He lifted up, gently pulling her into a sitting position. "Here, I'll help."

"Okay." She drew her lustrous hair to the side with one hand and presented her back. "I didn't realize it bothered you."

Neither did I. Sin undid the necklace and set it on the table. In the next moment, he caught her lips again, pushing her back and moving over her body, wanting nothing more than to sink into her warmth and have her wrap those sexy thoroughbred legs around him like she'd done so many times the night before.

Why was he torturing himself with her? Avery Montgomery held him in her grip, like some exotic drug he'd taken too much of and formed an addiction to. Would he ever get enough? The more he was with her, the more he wanted her. And like any junkie, right now, nothing else but the drug mattered. He needed his fix. He needed to be inside her.

Chapter 18

"I wish you'd let me tag along," Sin said, later that afternoon when the doorbell rang.

"Tell me something I don't already know. This is a ladies' night out." Avery laughed and patted his face, then turned to make her way down the hallway. "I'm touched you're worried, but I'll be fine. What can happen in broad daylight with hundreds of shoppers around?"

Avery opened the door and stood aside. "Almost ready," she said to Mary. "Let me grab my purse."

Mary's interested gaze focused on Sin for a drawn-out moment, before moving to hers, with eyebrows raised, definitely asking—*Are you going to introduce me to the hunk?*

"Jeffrey Sinclair, meet Mary Miller." Avery smothered another laugh. "He's a friend I told you about. The one who's staying here for a few days." At Sin's rounded eyes and surprised "What?" she cleared her throat, praying she could keep her embarrassment from showing, and amended, "A good friend."

"Much better," he said, flashing a satisfied grin, taking Mary's outstretched hand. "Any friend of Avery's is a friend of mine."

"My sentiments exactly." Mary laughed. "Friendships are important."

Avery felt a bit of heat rise up her face, but ignored it. "His company designed a product Mike was testing before he died. That's how I know him and his partners."

"Ah, I see." Mary nodded, still grinning. The teasing glint in her eyes told Avery she probably did see…too much. "I don't think I've ever seen you this flustered, Avery."

"Are you sure you don't want my company," Sin chimed in. His gaze snared Avery's, speaking loudly. He was giving it one last shot, using everything at his disposal, even charming Mary as his smile brightened to a thousand watts when he turned back to her. "I have my uses. Besides providing entertaining companionship, I can carry packages with the best of them."

"If he wants to come with us, I don't see a problem," Mary said, at the same time Avery blurted out, "No way. Take a hint. You're not invited." She ignored Mary's shocked expression and indicated the living room with a nod. "Go and make yourself comfortable. I promise to bring you some leftovers from dinner."

"Fine." Sin sighed. He reached out and snaked a hand around her waist, pulling her closer. Totally paying no attention to the fact that they weren't alone, he nuzzled her neck, kissing his way to her ear, where he spent a moment using those wonderful lips to wipe all thoughts of shopping and eating out from her mind. "Think of me and what you're missing while you're shopping," he whispered, before biting her lobe.

He broke away and stepped back. He grazed the side of her face with the back of his hand, tucking a stray lock of hair behind her ear, before lifting her chin to close her mouth. She took a deep breath, shaking the vacant look she knew she presented.

Sin chuckled and steadied her with both hands on her shoulders, turning her gently and pushing her out the door. "Have fun, ladies. I'll be here when you get back."

Mary followed.

"Well, that was interesting." She grabbed Avery's hand as the door shut behind them. "You can fill in the blanks on the drive."

"Blanks?"

"Avery, you don't need to play dumb with me. I saw the way he looked at you."

"The way he looked at me?" She swallowed hard.

"Yes. Like you were an oasis in the desert and he hadn't had water in months." Mary's knowing smile formed. "Then, there was the way you looked at him." She tsk-tsked, shaking her head. "I've never said anything all those times Mike was gone, but I'm glad you found someone who's actually here." She turned to peer at the house before she spun back around, speculation pouring out of her gaze. "I don't know how you survived the loneliness."

"It wasn't so bad," Avery said softly, remembering all Sin had endured.

"Bad or not, it must have been hard."

"I guess it was harder than I let on." Avery had always thought she'd kept up appearances with Mike, but obviously some details you couldn't hide from people who were more than just neighbors. Actions did tend to speak louder than words, which is why Avery decided right after she turned thirty she wanted more than an absentee husband. She craved someone to be there for her…all the time, not just in name or body. Could Sin be that person?

She closed her eyes and sent up a brief prayer. *Let me be more than an interesting distraction.*

Bad childhood or not, he was too good of a lover for her to believe he hadn't had a multitude of women, most likely praying for the same thing. If only he felt the same compelling pull, the same sizzling attraction she felt, then maybe this was *more* for him. It definitely seemed too early to ask outright. She snorted mentally. Like she knew all about relationships and what to do or when? This entire experience was completely new to her. She and Mike had waited years before they made love, mainly because he'd honored her wishes and she was never all that sexually attracted to him. She just figured sex would improve with practice. Boy had she been wrong.

Still, she didn't particularly want to divulge too much information to Mary. Despite being friends, some things were simply better off left unsaid.

"Well, shall we?" Mary nodded toward her car.

Avery waited for her to hit the keyless entry, then climbed inside, content to have a diversion. She needed this outing. Needed a few mindless hours of doing nothing more than discovering what colors were fashionable now and whether or not they'd look good on her.

"Steve called about an hour ago to say the boys were having the time of their lives. He said they were hiking into the back woods and would probably lose reception soon, so not to bother trying." Mary started the car and pulled away from the curb. "Sounds like they're off to a fun week."

"I'm glad." Avery clicked her seatbelt into place. "Andy's been talking about this week for months."

~

Mary took her time in the dressing room as Avery slowly weeded through the scores of racks, searching for something appealing. She already had stuff to try on, but didn't want to undress for only a couple of items.

All of a sudden, the same sixth-sense feeling she'd had that morning tingled along her spine. Someone was watching her.

She was sure of it.

Casually, she turned, eyeing the crowded department store and seeing nothing out of the ordinary. Just a multitude of women, similarly scouring the racks for something they liked.

"Quit being so jumpy," she murmured. She was fine—perfectly safe in broad daylight in the midst of busy shoppers.

Avery went back to the rounder in front of her and pulled out a stunning silk outfit. She walked toward the mirror a few feet away, held it up, and checked out her reflection. No doubt about it. The bold colors brought out her eyes and were perfect for her complexion. She added it to the two other outfits she meant to try on and started for the dressing room.

She had to squeeze through the aisles, hampered by a rush of people who appeared out of nowhere. Suddenly she felt something prick the side of her neck. She turned around swiftly, looking for whoever might have done it.

Her heartbeat quickened as a weird sensation washed over her. Her steps became sluggish, and though her legs felt like cement blocks, she moved with purpose in the direction of the dressing room. Right outside, she spotted a chair and felt woozy, not unlike the world moving in slow motion, with her along for the ride. She sat and placed her head between her legs, hoping the feeling would pass.

"Mrs. Montgomery." The distorted reverberation filled her ears, sounding like whoever owned the voice spoke through a long, distant tunnel. "Come on, I'll help you."

She looked up to see the blurry image of a man pulling her out of the chair.

"No." She resisted as best she could, although the urge to follow was too strong. "Please."

"Avery. What's wrong? Who're you?"

At the same time Avery heard Mary's faraway voice, the man immediately released her and disappeared into the throng of shoppers. She sank back into the chair.

"Avery?" Mary reached for her hand. "Are you okay? Who was that man?"

She shook her head, unable to voice more than an "I don't know." She needed a minute, but she couldn't seem to get other words out. Nor could she formulate her thoughts, to figure out what had just taken place. She took a big breath, but the extra air did no good, in fact made things worse. She leaned her head back and closed her eyes, fighting nausea.

The longer she sat, the more lucid she became. Finally, she was able to open her eyes, and after several more minutes, Avery's vision cleared.

She looked up to see a worried Mary eyeing her intently. She held out a cup of water. "Here, this might help."

"Thanks." She offered a wan smile, unwilling to alert Mary as to how freaked out she truly was. Someone had drugged her. "I'm fine," she lied. "I feel much better now."

"What happened? You've been sitting here for over ten minutes. I didn't know whether to call security or not."

"I felt faint all of a sudden, and had to sit down. I just realized I forgot to eat lunch and it caught up with me."

Unconvinced, Mary stared in the direction *he* disappeared. "Did you know that guy?"

"I didn't recognize him, but he seemed to know me." Avery certainly didn't want to worry Mary, but she understood right then, she'd been too drugged to remember whether she knew him or not. The moment was erased from her mind like it never happened.

Avery rubbed her temples. What had he given her to wipe away her memory like that, and that would work so quickly? The last thing she remembered was looking into the mirror at the outfit she'd planned to try on. She glanced over to see her pile still on the floor close to the mirror where she'd dropped the items. No one seemed to notice them the entire time she sat.

She pointed. "I dropped the clothes I wanted to try on."

Mary grabbed the dress by the hanger and shook out the wrinkles. She held it up and smiled. "I like it." She bent to pick up the other items. "These are nice too. I can wait if you feel like trying them on."

Avery shook her head. "I don't feel like shopping anymore. I'm sorry. I can call Sin. I'm sure he'll come and get me." She wanted to feel safe, and right now the only way she'd feel safe was to have him right next to her. She pulled her cell phone out of her purse and attempted to make the call.

"Put it away. I'll take you home. Makes no sense having him drive all this way."

"No. I don't want you to do that." She *was* beginning to feel normal again, and not wanting to rain on Mary's parade, she glanced at her watch and offered, "Besides, I should eat. I'll just have him meet us for dinner and we can change our reservation for five or five thirty."

Mary smiled. "Good idea. I'll call the restaurant. Here, give me your charge card and I'll have the salesperson who was waiting on me ring these up."

Avery did as she asked, thankful she didn't have to stand just yet. She wasn't sure she could.

Mary walked over to the counter, but her attention only left her for brief periods. While the salesperson ran the register, Mary made her call, the entire time watching Avery with hawk-like efficiency.

"All set." She handed Avery a bag and nodded to her pocket. "Call your friend and see if he needs a ride. We can pick him up on the way. If we leave now, we'll make it in plenty of time."

Avery punched in Sin's number, wondering what he would think of her invitation when she'd been so adamant to escape for these few hours. All thought fled the moment she heard his voice.

"Sin?" A few tears broke free. She turned away so Mary couldn't see them and sniffed.

"Avery? What's wrong?"

How in heaven's name did she tell him she needed him without sounding desperate?

"Nothing," she lied, wiping the tears away and fighting for control. "Mary and I got done early and changed our reservation. And I've changed my mind. I'd love it if you could join us."

"Did something happen?"

"No," she said too quickly. "Why would you think that?"

"Avery? You're upset. I hear it in your voice." Busted. So much for trying to hide her feelings. She smiled into the phone when he said, "I'll meet you. Tell me where."

~

Avery stood on the restaurant's porch while Mary went in to inform the hostess of their arrival, and noticed Sin's car pulling into the lot.

He parked and climbed out.

She started down the steps, almost running by the time they met halfway.

His arms opened, offering a silent invitation. She sank into his warmth, engulfed in his strong embrace, feeling his hands stroke up and down her back, soothing her fears.

At that moment, she knew everything would be okay. Sin had arrived.

His fingers gripped her shoulders. He leaned back. His eyes narrowed, studying her face inch by inch. "You okay?"

There was no mistaking the apprehension laced in the question, his worried features all but shouting the fact. Under his tender scrutiny, her control slipped. The concern in those jade slits was her final undoing.

"I think I was drugged. I think someone tried to kidnap me. But I can't remember." Avery couldn't stop the tears streaming down her face in wet ribbons. She wiped them away, working to keep her emotions from shattering, unused to such attention. She had to admit to a strange kind of relief at being able to dump her problems onto someone else, no matter if only for a brief moment, especially after her very close call.

Someone drugged her and tried to coerce her out of the store.

"Good God. I should never have let you out of my sight." Sin folded her into his warmth once more, his soothing hands rubbing up and down her arms.

Damn if it didn't feel good to just let go and cry, something she hadn't done in years.

"You sure you're okay for dinner?"

Nodding, she brushed at the droplets, now cascading fast and furiously. "Mary was looking forward to it. I didn't tell her about being drugged," she was able to get out through the sobs. "Please don't say anything, otherwise, she'll feel responsible."

"Shush." He wiped away tears with the pad of his thumb. "Don't cry. I'm here now."

Heaven couldn't be this wonderful, Avery thought, feeling his lips on her face as he kissed her tears, making them flow all the faster. His grip tightened, bringing her close enough to hear the steady rhythm of his heartbeat.

For long minutes, Sin did nothing but hold her head against his chest and let her cry, not caring that she must present a sight for the few patrons who'd come and gone in the deserted parking lot. When her tears subsided, he bent to gently take her face between his hands. His thumbs stroked her cheekbones. He kissed the top of her head, before meeting her gaze, his expression solemn.

"You're safe now. I won't let anything happen to you. I promise." The resolve in his voice, as well as the sincerity mirrored in his eyes, told her he meant his vow.

Avery nodded as the weight of her ordeal fully lifted. Now that Sin held her, she did feel safe. She also felt awkward all of a sudden. She wiped her face, giving him a self-conscious smile.

He handed her a handkerchief, which she gladly took, and waited until she composed herself. Then, with his arm around her, he walked her the rest of the short path, ushered her inside the restaurant and up to Mary, who stood talking with the hostess.

The woman quickly crossed off their names. She smiled warmly and grabbed three menus. "Your table's ready. Right this way."

Soon they were seated in the darkened dining room.

A waitress took their drink orders. Sin waited until she was out of earshot to focus directly on Avery. "Tell me exactly what happened with this guy." His imploring eyes met hers, before roaming to Mary's and then back to hers. He clearly expected answers. "And don't leave anything out."

Mary shook her head, offering a quick shrug. "All I know is what I witnessed. I came out of the dressing room and saw Avery sitting. She didn't look so good, and I rushed over to see if I could help. That's when I noticed the weird stranger. At first I thought he was someone who was also trying to help."

"And?" Sin urged impatiently when she stopped talking.

"But I don't think he was…trying to help, I mean. Now that I think about it, he was more likely trying to hurt her because it looked like he was pulling her out of the chair. And then he disappeared when I said something." Her words died.

Noting her stricken expression, Avery placed her hand over Mary's. She squeezed reassuringly. "I'm fine, Mary."

"But you seemed so out of it."

"Must've been low blood sugar or something. I did feel woozy for a few minutes and needed to rest." She flashed Sin a warning plea and gave a slight shake of her head, praying he'd pick up on her cues, despite his demands for answers. She didn't want to get into her being drugged right now.

"That guy didn't do anything to you?" Mary asked.

"No," she lied, eyeing Sin and daring him to refute this.

"Thanks to you. If you hadn't interrupted, God knows what would've happened." She let out the breath she'd been holding on to when he wiped his face and looked away. "I'm sure he was simply some creep taking advantage of my disorientation."

"Well, thank God you're fine now," Sin said, as he reached for Avery's hand and patted it, clearly playing along.

She sent him a relieved smile, but the look he sent her in reply said he still expected his answers. And he'd definitely get them...*later*. Fine! She could deal with him then.

Sin sat up straight and cleared his throat.

Avery glanced up to see their waitress striding up to the table with a full tray. "Are you ready for drinks?" she asked, smiling. "I didn't want to interrupt earlier."

"Sure. Thanks." Sin displayed one of his killer smiles.

Avery's trauma receded, pushed out by the woman's obvious stare taking a trip over Sin like he was a hot fudge sundae and she'd just gotten off a six-week diet. A sliver of jealousy worked its way into Avery's brain. The woman actually gushed when he spoke to her. Unaware of his one-person fan club, he then turned his expectant focus on Avery.

She swallowed the bit of irritation his attractiveness brought on, stilling the urge to kick him under the table, and took her drink from the waitress, murmuring her thanks. After all, he couldn't help others' reactions to his looks. Mike used to elicit gawks too, but unlike Sin, her husband had always been very aware of the glances, at least Avery had thought so. Oh, Mike had been faithful, as far as she knew, but he seemed to appreciate the attention nonetheless.

The waitress handed out Mary's drink, then glanced at Sin adoringly. "Are you ready to order?"

"Give us a few more minutes," Sin said.

Having no more reason to linger, she sent him another megawatt smile. "Sure. I'll be right back."

Avery breathed a sigh of relief when she sashayed away, which was such a wasted effort, considering Avery was the only one at the table who noticed those hips swinging from side to side.

"Okay, back to the guy in Nordstrom," Sin said, pulling her gaze. "What else can you tell me about him? Like a physical description?"

Avery shook her head. "I was too busy feeling woozy to notice him."

He slanted a glance at Mary. "What about you? Did you get a good look?"

"No. He was just some featureless guy. I think he wore a baseball cap, covering most of his face. I'm sorry. I was worried about Avery and really wasn't paying much attention," she offered apologetically. "It all happened so fast."

Sin sighed heavily, flipping open his menu. "We should figure out what we want to eat. Our waitress seems impatient to take our order. This *is* Saturday night, maybe they're fully booked and don't want us to linger because they need our table."

Avery rolled her eyes, knowing perfectly well the waitress lurked so she could keep Sin in her scope. How could the man be so oblivious to such obvious adoration? Despite feeling so wretched, she opened her menu, placing it in front of her face to hide her wide smile. His disinterest pleased her immensely.

After ordering, Sin fired off more questions and Avery answered as best she could. Sin must have realized she could add nothing more to what she'd already relayed, and in fact was becoming quite irritated. After several curt *I don't know's* from her, he finally dropped the questioning.

A few moments later, their food arrived. They ate in silence. The only sounds came from the din of the other patrons as the dining room began filling, along with the noise of forks hitting the plates.

The waitress bore down on their table with the bill after running Sin's charge card.

Avery sent up a silent prayer, thankful the ordeal was almost over.

Sin gripped her shoulder and squeezed. "You okay?"

"Sure." The woeful smile she offered didn't match with her answer, but she was too emotionally drained to care.

"You're coming home with me." He reached for the folder, opened it, and quickly signed the bill. Then he stood and leaned over to kiss her forehead. "No arguing tonight."

Avery stiffened.

He pulled her chair back and gripped her hand to help her rise. She stood and turned to tell him her thoughts about his dictatorial attitude, but his finger went to her lips. "No arguments."

Still holding her hand, he started walking. She had no choice but to let him lead her toward the entrance with Mary following closely behind.

"Are you okay to go home by yourself?" he asked Mary, once they made it to her car. "I'd be happy to follow."

She hit the keyless entry, retrieved Avery's packages, and handed them to Sin. "Don't worry about me. I have a brand new alarm system and I'll be fine. You just take care of Avery." She reached for Avery's arm and squeezed. "Keep me posted if you learn anything."

Avery nodded. Together they stood and watched Mary drive away.

"Come on. Let's get you home."

"Can I stop by my house and get a few things?" she asked, once he had her ensconced inside his car.

"No." He backed out of the space. "Make a list right now. I'll call Des and have him pick up whatever you need."

Chapter 19

Des glanced at the caller ID after the second ring. "Hold that thought. It's Sin, so I want to take this." He pushed the On button and brought the phone to his ear. "Yeah, what's going on?"

"I could ask you the same thing," Sin shot back. He sighed heavily into his ear, and added, "I need you to stop by Avery's house and pick up a few things."

"Sure. No problem." Avery had given him a key the day before. "Tell me what and I'll leave in a few minutes. Scotty and I were just finishing." Des grabbed a pen and paper. "So why is she under protective custody at your house? Did something else happen?" he asked after Sin finished listing Avery's requests.

"Someone went after her while she was shopping." Sin spent a few moments relaying what had gone down in the department store.

"Shit," Des said, once Sin's voice broke off. "You think she was drugged?"

"Yeah, which is why she's not leaving my side. Whoever's behind this is increasing his pressure. He's getting desperate."

"Williams."

"You read my mind," Sin said. "But why would he go after Avery now?"

Glancing back at Scotty's computer screen, Des sighed. The information the geek had unearthed from Avery's broken pile of junk had provided an abundance of food for speculation. Before he came to any conclusions, he wanted to run everything by Sin, and he'd rather do that in person than over the phone. "We'll talk when I get there." Des began pacing. "Scotty's a genius. He's practically solved our problem."

"Call me when you leave her house, so I know you're okay."

"Will do." Des hung up and nodded at the screen. "Can you print off that information?"

Scotty looked at him expectantly. "Not good," he murmured, answering his implied question. "Seems someone drugged Avery in Nordstrom and tried to spirit her out of the mall."

"She's the key. You have to tell Sin. It's right there in the letters."

"Yeah, I'm well aware of what we have." Des opened his phone again. "It's why I want copies to show Sin tonight." He pointed to the printer. "So, get busy and print."

"Who you calling now?" Scotty loaded the paper and pressed a few keys. In seconds, the printer responded.

"Esperanza. He may want to know about the latest developments."

"Do you think he'll help?" Scotty peered up at him as the machine churned. "I mean, he wasn't willing to this morning when we told him about Williams."

"We're not one hundred percent sure it's Williams because Avery couldn't identify him, but I'd bet my life he's involved. If he is, I doubt Esperanza will be happy to know the good colonel is going around drugging and abducting innocent victims." He punched in the number. It rang several times before Esperanza finally answered.

"What?" The one word sounded more like a growl than a greeting.

Des smiled despite the unfriendly tone. "Good evening to you, too. Have you arrested Williams and solved the case of the missing prototypes yet?"

"You're a laugh a minute, Phillips." Esperanza paused. "Well?" he asked when Des didn't say anything. "I don't have all night. Why the call?"

"No patience." Des laughed. He could almost see Esperanza pacing. "You're as bad as Sin." He spent a quick moment informing him of what Sin had relayed about Avery's attack, along with adding the tidbits he'd garnered from the files Scotty had retrieved. If anyone could pound it into something useful, he had no doubt that Esperanza would be that person.

"Give me his phone number."

"Excuse me?" Startled, Des furrowed his brow in confusion. "Whose number?"

"Jeffrey Sinclair's."

"You want Sin's number?"

"Yes. I'm on my way back to D.C., but I want to speak to him before I head out."

"Okay." Des rattled it off, mentally rubbing his hands together because Esperanza sounded like he was planning to help them. Once the connection went dead, he grinned. Maybe accompanying Scotty on his early morning escapade had actually paid off.

"What'd he say? Why is he calling Sin's cell?" Scotty's entire body bristled with eagerness.

Des shrugged, making a face. "Beats me. Esperanza's not one to let me in on his innermost thoughts." He wasn't about to reveal any encouraging news. The geek was already too gung ho for his taste. "Is the printing done yet?" he asked, changing the subject.

"Last page is going now."

"Good. I've got to leave. Sin's expecting me." He fidgeted the twenty seconds it took for the printer to finish before gathering the papers into a pile. He tapped them together and fastened the ends with a paper clip, including the letters he'd found on the floor next to Avery's trashed hard drive.

Minutes later Des sat in his car, driving toward Georgetown and Avery's house.

He started up the stairs after letting himself inside and headed for her bedroom. When he rounded the corner, he almost bumped into Avery's sister.

"What in the hell have you done to her?"

Des' back went ramrod straight, and he cringed at her shrill, accusing tone.

"Terry." Nodding, he stepped around her without answering, unwilling to dignify her allegation.

"I asked you a question." She grabbed his arm, halting his retreat. "Don't you dare ignore me, you bastard."

He frowned, his heated eyes moving to her hand still clutching him. His temper flared hotter than a just-lit barbecue full of briquettes saturated with lighter fluid. "Back off." His hand covered hers, prying her fingers loose. He snared her gaze again, not bothering to bank the hatred he felt for her. "Touch me again, and you'll find out how little patience I have left in dealing with you and your innuendos."

Terry took a reflexive step back, seeming to comprehend she'd pushed him too far. Des offered a sardonic laugh. Good move, he thought, observing her subdued expression. She obviously had a strong sense of self-preservation. "Just stay out of my way."

"I'm sorry," she said, backing down further. "I'm really worried.

She's not answering her cell." She eyed him warily. "Do you happen to know where she is?"

"She's fine." Des retraced his steps, praying she would simply leave. He didn't have time for her shit right now. He strode toward Avery's closet, looking for an overnight bag.

"That doesn't answer my question." Terry followed close behind, obviously overcoming her reluctance to annoy him further. Her tone spoke volumes, shouting loudly and driving home the point. She wasn't leaving…at least, not yet.

"Yeah?" He rolled his eyes. "Well, I've told you all you need to know." He found a suitcase that would work for his purpose and started for the bathroom, ignoring Terry's scowl, which wasn't easy given the daggers her eyes tossed out. He had no doubt she viewed him as the Antichrist who'd come to steal her sister's soul.

Now in the smaller room, Des began stuffing the articles Avery requested inside. The entire time he packed, Terry silently scowled at him as she leaned against the jamb, watching him with the precision of a cat waiting for its prey to make a move so it could pounce.

"You promise me she's safe?" she yelled to his back, when he'd finished and pushed past her into the bedroom at a good clip.

He added those items from her drawers until he found everything on the list. "She's with Sin." He secured the bag over his shoulder and started for the stairs. "He'll keep her safe."

Terry's hand on his arm stopped him and Des spun around, letting the bag drop to the floor. His focus landed on the spot she gripped before rising to her face. His eyebrows shot up giving the silent command. He waited for her to remove her fingers.

Without heeding the implied request, she sneered, "She'd better be or you'll have me to deal with." And instead of backing off, she got into his face, hers distorting with fury and poked him, totally ignoring his earlier warning. "She may trust you but I don't. You got that, buddy?"

On the second poke, he couldn't control his anger from bursting loose. His hand snaked up, grasping her wrist, and twisting her arm deftly behind her back, he pushed her against the wall. He took a step forward, halting an inch from her face.

She hadn't expected the move and was breathing heavily, her features shouting her outrage. There was also something else he spied in those heated eyes—sexual awareness, which brought on his own.

All of a sudden, the atmosphere hummed with an underlying, sizzling current.

Des might still find her body hot enough to tempt St. Peter at heaven's gate, but no way he would act on the sliver of invitation he caught in her eyes, not after their last encounter, when Terry had all but stomped on his heart. Tamping down lust, he said in a threatening whisper, "You've used that finger once too often. I warned you. I don't like it."

She squirmed, fighting to break free from his solid hold, until she froze, clearly encountering what had sprouted between them and he couldn't hide.

Her chin inched up a notch and she met his gaze, her eyes growing bigger in stunned silence.

Well, shit! What'd she expect? She did turn him on like no one else, in some kind of perverted way, much to his disgust.

Des grinned. "Amazing, isn't it?"

"What?" Terry's voice held challenge and her expression goaded him further.

"You deny it?"

"I don't know *what* you're talking about," she said, emphasizing the *what* with a sneer.

He chuckled. "You know, I'd have let this go and apologized for my part, but you had to push it. You don't seem to understand when you've gone too far." He shook his head and sighed. "You've given me no choice but to make my point."

He kept his gaze on her, spying the exact moment his meaning sank in.

Terry's eyes flashed fury. "You wouldn't dare!"

"Well, that's where you're wrong. What's more, you're going to eat your *what*," Des said softly, just before his lips met hers. At first, she fought the kiss and struggled to pull out of his hold. He increased the pressure, using his free hand to grip her neck, stroking the side of her face. He softened his mouth and added his tongue, giving in to the twisted need in his gut to prove she wanted him at that moment as much as he wanted her.

Her moan wafted somewhere above him, the sound pounding in his brain, alerting him better than a neon sign in the dark. He'd achieved his goal. However, he had no intention of stopping...not yet. He spent another long moment kissing and stroking her neck, smiling inwardly over how she'd completely opened herself to his touch. Before he lost total restraint and did something completely stupid—like taking her on the floor after proving it was exactly what they both wanted—he pulled away, then stepped back and waited. Once the sexual haze wore off, he sent her a triumphant smile.

Terry stiffened, glowering at him. If looks could kill, he'd be six feet under with his soul heading south. But he'd die a happy man because he'd finally shut her up.

"I believe this is a first. I've left you speechless."

"Go to hell," she spat out, crossing her arms, still glaring.

"I already caught that message, sweetheart." Chuckling, Des hefted Avery's bag over his shoulders, turned, and sprinted down the stairs.

He reached for the doorknob and looked back. "Oh, and for the record, I'm not a total prick. I'll have Avery give you a call, so you won't worry."

Chapter 20

Avery gazed out the window, her thoughts on the man beside her who shifted the car's gears so efficiently.

Neither had spoken on the drive to Sin's home.

She briefly glanced at his hands and realized that's how Sin did everything. Efficiently.

How he'd risen above his past, after listening to his earlier admissions, filled her with complete awe. This concerned her, as she'd come to fully understand his allure. The longer she remained in his company, the more he seemed to suck her into the vortex of his dynamic personality, leaving her a little hesitant and unsure of how to deal with such strength of will.

Avery could very well imagine his two friends promising him anything and then fulfilling those promises, unwilling to withstand the thought of facing his disappointment. Closing her eyes, she sighed and leaned her head against the rest, remembering the bliss in his arms, both last night and this morning.

"You okay?" Sin lifted his hand off the stick shift and placed it over hers. Warmth immediately enveloped her fingers and spread up her arm.

"I'm fine," she lied, nodding and smiling, without opening her eyes. How could she tell him the truth? The same answer she had the night she met Sin, a lifetime ago, registered. She'd never be entirely okay again.

She'd stumbled, tumbling completely off balance and well on her way to falling head over heels in love with him. In only days, no less! She angled her head and surreptitiously eyed him while he focused on driving. There was so much to love about him. Unfortunately, the emotion left her torn. She refused to hand over her hard-won sense of self to Sin as she had to Mike.

Avery lowered her eyelids and rubbed the bridge of her nose, wishing she could be anyone else at that moment. If she were someone who could easily keep from losing herself in the charisma of strong men, she'd feel like the luckiest woman on the face of the earth. She had no illusions about Sin's remarkable persona. As disconcerting as that was, the feeling she'd had for Mike could be measured in inches as far as depth went. With Sin, it measured in yards.

Eventually, her unseeing gaze went back to the window.

The car slowed and he turned onto an exclusive residential street. Without being obvious, Avery chanced a glimpse at him, her curiosity aroused after noting the well-manicured neighborhood. The colossal brick houses shouted money. Big money.

Sin pushed the garage door opener a second before pulling into the driveway of a beautiful Georgian two-story house.

A smile wormed its way to her face. *The house suits him.*

He came to a stop, switched off the car, and turned to her. The sexy, lopsided smile plastered on his face had the same effect it always did. Her insides performed backflips.

"It's a little messy," he offered apologetically. "I wasn't expecting company."

"Your housekeeping skills are the least of my concerns." Avery snorted. Like a messy house would stop the attraction she felt? Wouldn't that be a welcome change? "We didn't have to come here at all. In fact, we can still go back to my house, you know."

He chuckled. "I want you safe and as weird as it sounds, I like the idea of you here, under my roof."

"Just don't get too used to it." Avery released her seatbelt. "I don't take kindly to being hijacked."

"Okay." Sin sighed and yanked the door open, then climbed out and rushed around to help her, acting as if she were some delicate piece of china that might break unless handled carefully.

His tender actions bothered her—made it much more difficult to ignore him and his force.

"Hey, don't be too angry with me," he whispered, pushing a lock of hair behind her ear before resting both hands on her shoulders, melting all of her resistance. Damn if she wasn't in serious trouble. "I feel responsible for you and until this is over, I'm not letting anything else happen to you. Understand?"

Avery counted to ten, working to stop her racing heart. Finally, she peered into his solemn gaze, a gaze saying everything she wanted to hear and shouting one thing in particular. He meant his words, which only made her feel all the more churlish for her ungrateful thoughts.

It wasn't his fault her baggage from the past left her damaged and abysmally abnormal.

"I'm sorry. I guess I have a lot on my mind." She offered a semblance of a smile, pushing out her concerns as he kissed the top of her head.

"*Very* understandable, given all you've endured today." Sin wrapped an arm around her, gently guiding her toward a door. "Come on, let's get you inside."

His inviting warmth was a flame of danger drawing her closer. She felt like a moth with no choice but to dance about the heated light, hoping not to get burned alive in the process.

Sin's house was what she expected— imposing.

Everything about the sprawling manor impressed her.

The bold colors on the walls, along with the expensive dark wood cabinets and granite countertops in the kitchen, took her breath away. *Just like the man.*

"Des should be here in a little while." Sin led Avery through a long hallway. "I expect him within the hour." The staccato tap of her sandals hitting the hardwood floors echoed as they walked.

Now in a large, open living room, he strode over to a bar and pulled the stopper off a crystal bottle full of amber liquid. "After we're done talking, you can shower if you want. Might make you feel better."

Sin poured two glasses. He offered her one as she sank into the plush, overstuffed sofa. "Here, this will take the edge off while we talk."

Avery took the drink and kept her gaze cast down, wishing she could simply forget the entire incident. She felt safe now that he was near, too comfortable to move or to think.

Sin's cell phone rang.

He glanced first at his cell phone then at her. "Excuse me." He headed for the other room, glancing over his shoulder as the phone's tone blared again. "I need to take this call."

Sin's mumbled replies floated in the air every now and then, but they weren't loud enough for Avery to understand exactly what he was saying. Eventually, he hung up. Seconds later, she glanced up to see him bearing down on her with resolve plastered boldly across his face.

"Okay, now we talk to figure this out."

She sipped. The fiery liquid burned her throat and warmed its way to her insides. She took another sip and nodded. "Okay."

"How in the hell could someone drug you in broad daylight? In a crowded store, no less?" Sin's raised voice cut through the room like a sharp knife, colliding with his granite expression. "I should've been with you."

"You didn't know it would happen," Avery said softly. His tormented features told her he blamed himself, just as Mary had, when in reality Avery had no one to blame but herself. The whole ordeal of how close her call had been came hurling back with mind-numbing speed.

"Avery?"

Her name sounded like a caress, eliciting fresh tears. She blinked them back.

"Are you sure you're okay?"

"I wish I could forget it ever happened." She closed her eyes tightly.

"You can't, nor can we ignore the attack. Before I can assess the situation, I need to know exactly what happened." He gripped her hand and enfolded it into his bigger one. "Let's start at the top."

"I've already told you I have little memory from the moment I quit looking in the mirror to when Mary was asking me if I was all right."

"Then tell me everything you can remember. Maybe we can figure out what you were drugged with."

She spent a moment detailing the nightmare, or as much of it as she could.

"Let me see the spot." Sin swept the hair off her nape, searching the area she pointed to. "Hmm."

Avery noted his slow nod, but she couldn't read anything into his now blank expression. "What're you thinking?"

"You say it was fast-acting?"

"Yeah. I remember feeling the prick and within seconds, I could barely walk. I vaguely remember an urge to do so when he told me to go with him. It was like I felt compelled to move, which seemed weird, given how hard it was to do so." Avery shrugged. "I kind of felt like one of those marionette puppets. You know?"

"It obviously wore off quickly, so maybe that was intentional, which probably means he had a plan. Maybe drug you further, once you were under his complete control."

Sin stared at her through narrowed slits at length without speaking. When she could stand his silent treatment no longer, she jutted out her chin. "What? Do I have something on my face? Why are you eyeing me like I've done something wrong?"

"Sorry. I was thinking." He shook his head and smiled.

"And?" she asked after more silence.

"Are you sure you can't remember anything about the guy who grabbed you? Any little thing would help."

Avery squeezed her eyes shut, struggling to remember, but nothing rushed forward.

She glanced at him and lifted her shoulders. "No. I can't even remember if I recognized him or not. I wish I could."

"Williams most likely orchestrated the attack and either he or someone under him executed it." He pulled his cell phone out of his pocket, flipped it open, and punched up Scotty's preset number. He answered on the first ring. "Scotty, I need you to research something. Swift-acting drug, that leaves the bloodstream quickly and causes amnesia." He spent the next few seconds relaying the symptoms.

"He's fast." Sin flashed Avery a satisfied smile and placed his hand over the microphone. "I hear the click of the computer in the background." His attention went back to his phone, listening. Finally, he nodded. "No problem. Let me know when you have something. Thanks." He ended the call, then stuck the phone in his pocket and paced.

"Why would Williams go to so much trouble?" she asked minutes later, verbalizing the question foremost on her mind while watching him pace restlessly on the thick Persian rug. "I mean, I met with him yesterday. He could've grabbed me then."

"I don't know." Sin stopped and wiped his face in obvious frustration. "Maybe your presence gave him the opportunity to have your house searched and when he didn't find what he was looking for, he panicked and tried to have you kidnapped. I'm reaching, I realize, but nothing else makes sense."

"Do we have to analyze this now?" Avery didn't want to think about it any longer. In five short days, her life had turned into a nightmare. She sighed, rubbing her temples in a circular motion to keep her headache from spreading.

Sin nodded, eyeing her. "You're right." Concern highlighted his features. "You're dead on your feet and look exhausted. This can wait till morning." He strode toward her, holding her gaze. Sitting down next to her, he grabbed one of the sofa pillows, and stuck it on his lap. Then patting the pillow, he offered her a warm smile. "In a bit, I'll show you to the guest room. For right now, just relax a few minutes and let me hold you."

Avery wasted no time curling into position, possessing little energy to do anything else. Total exhaustion had long taken over her body, as thoughts of hitting the pillow and simply sleeping her worries away filled her. Plus, the bourbon had totally calmed her. She smiled, feeling safe and secure with the knowledge that Sin would protect her. In moments she drifted to sleep, lulled by his fingers stroking her hair.

~

At the house outside Baltimore, Esperanza focused on the monitor of the camera facing the backyard. Had he imagined the shadow stealing across the screen or was it real?

His smile broke free. His patience might be coming to fruition. The US government owned the house, and according to Esperanza's false military personnel file, it was listed as belonging to his next of kin. Hopefully someone had taken his carefully-orchestrated bait and followed him.

After watching for five minutes, he relaxed and dug out his cell phone.

A noise stopped him. Esperanza disconnected the call to Jeffrey Sinclair, set the phone aside, and reached for his 9mm Glock. With gun arm raised, he stole to the door. He waited. Listened. When nothing happened, he snuck a peek around the doorframe. Splintered wood exploded inches from his face as the familiar *pop pop pop* of muzzled gunshots shattered the silence. An instant later, he felt a sting on his arm.

"God damn it all." He returned fire before hurling himself back, trying to avoid being a bigger target. He fired a few more rounds, ignoring the burning in his upper arm. Footfalls heading toward the back of the house gave him an indication of where his quarry went. A coppery smell reached his nostrils. He looked down and examined his arm as the stickiness of clotting blood spread.

The bullet just grazed—nothing serious.

Esperanza grabbed his shoulder in an effort to put pressure on the wound to stop the bleeding, then took off after him, moving swiftly along the wall to remain out of the line of fire.

In the kitchen, movement near the door caught his attention. He aimed and shot in rapid succession. The outside kitchen door was already swinging open as he ran closer. Using the frame as cover, he searched the twilight.

Shit! I lost him.

An engine roared to life nearby before a car peeled away.

Esperanza muttered another expletive. Eventually, a barking dog was the only sound he made out—that and the invisible evening insects chirping in the semidarkness. Whoever had shot him was long gone. He turned, strode back inside, and closed the door.

At the sink, he snatched a towel, pushing against the outside of his arm an inch below his shoulder, creating more pressure. He then headed for his bags for a first aid kit he always carried. He cleaned and checked the wound carefully. It wasn't serious. When the bleeding slowed to a small trickle, he dressed it as best he could, complete with antibiotic cream, gauze, and white medical tape.

Esperanza quickly washed the blood away, changed shirts, and then set about the task of searching for the intruder's spent shell casings. He dug two bullets out of the woodwork and picked up the casings off the floor. A trickle of unease inched up his back as he examined them. Both were from the standard Army-issue sidearm. The Beretta M9—9mm and unquestionably military.

He hadn't counted on Williams being so foolhardy as to attack him. Why? Unless the good colonel, as Des had called him, thought Esperanza had uncovered something about the prototypes. Williams obviously didn't trust him any more than he trusted Williams.

Back at his monitors, he studied them intently and thought about his next step.

It was time to drive south for a chat with SPC's owner.

Just then, he caught a flash of movement on the monitor covering the front door. He pushed a button to bring his visitor into focus and enlarge the picture.

He sat up straight and watched in stunned fascination as the man rang the bell a minute later.

Esperanza hurried toward the summons with one burning question. *What the hell was that asshole's game?* The guy definitely gave the word bold a new meaning.

"Colonel?" He kept all emotion from his expression. His nod indicated for his guest to come inside. "I know this is cliché, but you're the last person I expected to see."

"It shouldn't be a surprise. I'm here for the same reason you are. We're working on the same team, trying to uncover the continuing thefts of military technology. Remember?" Colonel Williams walked over to the sofa. "You don't mind if I sit?" he asked, doing so and making himself comfortable.

Esperanza eyed him while his mind spun.

True, Williams was in charge of this bizarre mission. Bizarre because the enemy they were trying to knock out was one of their own—a traitor. Everything pointed to it. What was even scarier, everything now pointed to the man sitting in front of him, holding his hands up in mock surrender. The one in charge. Made perfect sense as to why he'd gotten away with it for so long.

"I understand your concern." Williams offered an affable smile. Esperanza might interpret his expression as friendly, except the affability didn't quite extend to his eyes when he added, "I don't trust you either, but Emerson vouched for you, so here I am."

"Emerson vouched for me?" His gaze narrowed. Was the colonel telling the truth? He'd given his contact and commanding officer a full accounting of Williams' actions, informing him of his suspicions. Yet, why would he lie about something he could substantiate? "Then, you don't mind if I make a call, confirming this?"

He couldn't afford not to verify the claim. Williams spearheaded the investigation, a perfect position to keep others from finding out about his involvement. Anyone connected with the missing prototypes was suspect and in his mind, this guy, crossing his legs while smiling so smugly, had morphed into public enemy number one.

Esperanza pulled out his cell phone, brought his superior's information up on the small screen, and made the connection.

"It's me, Esperanza," he said, once his call was answered. "I have an interesting visitor."

"Humor him," Emerson shot back, seeming to understand he referred to Williams.

"Excuse me? I'm not sure I understand?" Esperanza presented

his back and moved out of earshot. When he was positive the colonel couldn't hear him, he hissed into the phone, "Has nothing I reported been noted?"

"This goes higher than you. My hands are tied. I've been informed your orders haven't changed. You're to work with him and give him any assistance he asks for. Are we clear?"

"Why? He's involved. The guy is corrupt...misusing his power."

"You have your orders." A second later the line went dead.

Esperanza stared at his phone with no clue as to what was going on, but there was no way he was about to follow orders to the letter and trust Williams. He turned back to him, and using the same technique he used on scumbag terrorists when undercover, he kept all thoughts hidden behind his good-natured smile, giving a much better attempt at it than the colonel had.

"Seems I'm wrong in doubting you. I'm to assist you further."

"That's always been your role. I don't appreciate your going behind my back."

Shaking his head, Esperanza's smile turned self-deprecating. "And I'm not in the habit of having to clean up messes." So much for trusting Emerson with the news about Williams. The guy was good...covered his back. He'd give him that.

"Messes?" Williams eyebrows rose an inch.

"Trashing Avery Montgomery's house and later trying to abduct her?"

"I don't know what you're talking about."

"That wasn't you?" Williams was also very convincing. If Esperanza hadn't had his early-morning visitors, he'd most likely believe him. "Try again. Had your scent all over it. Then you can explain why you're abusing American citizens and misusing your power."

"You'll have to be more specific."

"So you haven't been spying on SPC?" Esperanza hit a nerve, but the only indication was a small reflexive tic on Williams' face. No other sign showed as the stare-off continued. "Well? You either have or you haven't. Should be easy to trace."

"Four words. Need to know basis." The colonel enunciated every syllable.

Esperanza snorted. "Convenient, wouldn't you say?"

"No. I'd say you're searching for answers in the wrong

direction. It's why I'm here."

"Oh?"

"Yes. Consider this a friendly warning. I'd hate to see your career in jeopardy."

"Thank you, sir," Esperanza nodded. He'd play the colonel's game, even though nothing the guy had said in the last few minutes changed his opinion. No way in hell he'd trust him. Williams sat on the living room sofa for one reason and one reason only—to rattle him.

He was pretty damn sure his trigger-happy intruder was the same man offering his friendly warning. "Consider your warning heeded. Now you'll have to excuse me. I was on my way out. I have plans this evening."

"Of course. I expect a full report on your findings no later than 0800 hours, though." He stood. "I'd leave out the speculations and only present facts, if I were you."

They walked together in the direction of the front door. He waited until Williams reached for the handle. He left him with his hand on the knob, to leap up the stairs two at a time, sprinting for his monitors. He focused on the one picturing the colonel leaving the house. On the porch, Williams stopped to pull out a cell phone and made a call.

Esperanza turned on the sound. In the next second, the colonel's firm voice burst through the speakers.

"What do you have?" He was silent a moment, clearly listening. "Good." Again silence. "Got it. Yeah, he's made contact...I believe he's headed south." A smile lit his face. "Keep me posted and I'll do the same."

The colonel stuck his phone into his pocket, his Cheshire grin spreading.

He turned and headed toward the street.

Esperanza kept his attention glued to the screen. The guy reeked of corruption. When Williams was out of sight, he ran downstairs and out the door all the way to the curb. He searched the quiet street, both north and south, and started around back to make sure the colonel was long gone.

It's time to meet with Jeffrey Sinclair. He strode into the house. The man, along with the widow, held the answers. Like the colonel said, he had every intention of appeasing his curiosity with a drive south.

Chapter 21

Sin leaned against the sofa with his eyes closed, and Avery's head resting on the pillow in his lap. He absently stroked her lustrous brown hair until her contented exhale interrupted his silent reflections.

He reached for the glass of bourbon sitting on the table next to him and took a sip. As he returned the glass to the table, his focus landed on Avery's features, so perfect in sleep. Her worry lines had all but disappeared, no longer distorting her beauty. Her even breaths let him relax for the first time since he'd received her distressed call.

He was heading into deep emotional shit. Watching her, he understood exactly how deep. He bent, kissed her forehead, and heaved a weary sigh. The idea of taking her somewhere and forgetting all about his prototypes was more than a passing thought. It became a driving need. Yet, he couldn't forget his duty to his friends or his company. Too many people depended on SPC for their livelihood.

Sin held the woman he loved wishing with his whole heart things could be different. Without moving a muscle he sat, having no idea how much time had passed until a knock sounded at the door.

A moment later, Des entered, halting his progress into the room when he saw Sin. He dropped Avery's bag, nodded toward the kitchen, and held up some papers. "Scotty's been busy. I think you should read these."

"Oh?" Sin's eyebrows shot up. "Is something wrong? You don't sound too pleased."

He carefully slid out from under Avery's head, gently placing it on the pillow. She sighed, mumbled something unintelligible, and settled back into the sofa.

"Shush. She's sleeping," he whispered.

They moved further away from the sofa.

"I'm not sure you're going to like what we uncovered," Des said in a low voice. "I want you to get the full picture, but the first pages are somewhat damning."

Sin glanced over at Avery, who appeared to have gone back to sleep. "Can't be that bad, especially if it points us to our goal."

"Yeah, well...do you promise to read everything...completely...before jumping to conclusions?"

The cautious tone caught his attention. He looked closer at Des' face and the vice in his gut tightened a turn.

"I promise." Sin looked to the heavens, praying he could handle his friend's news. He followed him out of the room, but not before grabbing his almost-full glass along with the decanter of bourbon. Judging from Des' somber expression, he had a feeling he was going to need more than one stiff drink.

Des was already seated at the island in the kitchen when he rounded the corner. He pulled out a card and threw it on the granite counter. "Esperanza's. I called him earlier and told him about the attack on Avery. Said he'd give you a call, but after our conversation, you might not want to wait."

"Okay." Sin set his drink and the decanter down and picked up the card, pocketing it. Then he started for the cupboard and took out another glass. He added ice from the fridge, along with a shot of bourbon.

"You look like you need a stiff one." He placed Des' drink in front of him and plopped on the bar stool next to him. "So, what's up?"

Sin brought his glass to his lips and gulped nearly half of the amber liquid in one swallow. The warmth sliding down his throat did little to ease the chill now running through his veins.

"Read through these." Des handed him the clipped stack of papers. "All of them, before forming an opinion."

He undid the paper clip and set it aside. "Let's just take a look-see at what's put that pained expression on your face." Then, he started reading.

"The first few pages are e-mails sent back and forth between Avery and her husband in the weeks before he died. The real meat is further on."

The knot of tension constricted as Des' explanation filtered past his brain, but he didn't comprehend it. All he could grasp at the moment was what the e-mails meant. Avery had intended to leave her hero. He had a hard time believing it. But there it was in black and white, on the pages in her own words. Des said to read further before forming an opinion, but he couldn't stop one from mushrooming inside his brain.

Did he really know her at all?

Obviously not. Not when she could be so callous as to send her husband such horrible news while on the battlefront, and in e-mails, no less! "Avery was leaving him?"

He hadn't realized he'd spoken the question out loud until Des said, "Yeah. But keep reading."

Sin nodded and flipped to the next page, a letter sent before the e-mails began, and he gave a small sigh of relief. Still, a letter seemed a cold and distant way to end ten years of marriage, but it *was* better than an e-mail. His relief was short-lived, however as he flipped the page.

"There are several from Crandall, too." Des' voice sounded like it was coming from a long tunnel and he could barely understand him due to the roaring in his ears. "The last pages are two letters written to Avery. One from Montgomery and one from Crandall, postmarked days before they died, no doubt in response to her last letter. Remember, you promised. In order to get the full picture, you have to read through everything."

"How could she?" Sin quickly forgot all about his promise. "Was she having an affair?"

"*Read* the other letters, first. It's not what you—"

"What're you reading?" Des' voice was cut off when Avery's angry question filled the room.

"Avery," Sin acknowledged, not meeting her eyes and keeping his tone even. "Have you been standing there long?"

"Long enough." She jutted out her chin, her expression combatant.

"Sin, if I were you, I wouldn't jump to conclusions before knowing all the facts," Des warned softly. "Hey, Avery," he added cheerfully, nodding her way as if no tension existed in the room, when in reality the air crackled with it. "You should give Terry a call so she knows you're okay."

"I thought you were sleeping." Sin eyed her thoughtfully. She really seemed put out.

"Obviously." Without responding to Des or his comment, she stormed over to the island, her gaze accusing. "And in case you didn't hear my question, I'll ask again. What are you reading?"

"You mean *this*?" Sin held up the pages he'd just gone through, ignoring Des' warning about jumping to conclusions. He laughed, but there was nothing pleasant in the brittle sound. Damn, what a talented actress. Outrage poured out of every cell of her body. Almost as good as Diane's had been. But he knew better than to be taken in by another woman who could be so treacherous. He had the proof right in his hands, and could only thank God he found out in time, before he did something stupid like tell her he loved her. He'd stopped himself from falling over that precipice with barely a second to spare. As far as he was concerned, there was no other conclusion to jump to. In fact, it jumped at him.

Everything he'd thought about Avery had been an illusion. Not real and so similar to his experience with Diane. "I have my own questions. Oh, you're good, lady. I'll give you that. You had me going." Sin gave a disgusted snort and let his gaze rake over her stiff posture, working to still the urge to wring her neck. "Were you going to leave your husband?" He shoved the pile of papers at her, unable to stop the condemnation he felt from escaping through his eyes.

"Yes, but that's none of your business." Avery took the pages and scanned, flipping through them. "These are *my* private e-mails," she said, her voice furious and condemning. "You printed copies of my personal e-mails?" She broke off. Her gaze narrowed, meeting his. "How did you get these? I remember deleting them. You've been through my stuff, haven't you?" She eyed him with an anguished expression, not unlike the pain he felt right then, one of his heart ripping apart. "It's the only way you could've gotten these. Did you break into my house and trash it?"

"No," he growled. How dare she turn this around and make him out to be the villain. He averted his eyes, unwilling to let her manipulations sway him.

"Sin?" She paused until he met her gaze again. She brushed at the tears now streaking down her face. "Did you make love with me just to calm my fears and suspicions?"

"I...I...um..." Her question, along with the torment accompanying her words, stunned him and he glanced away again before the guilt he felt rising showed in his eyes.

He swallowed hard. "Avery, I—"

"Did you destroy my things?" she asked, cutting him off. "Was it you, getting revenge for what you think my husband stole?"

"No. Of course not." Shit! This wasn't going so well, he realized, especially after turning to Des with a pleading glance and getting his I-told-you-so look.

In an instant, his entire value system disintegrated. Sin didn't know what to believe. He only knew he'd gotten too close and the horrible pain weighing on his chest was too similar to what he'd felt after Diane's death. He raked a hand through his hair. "You don't really think I'd do something so heinous?"

"I don't know what to think anymore. My whole life has turned upside down and you're making accusations."

"And mine isn't?" Oh, she was good. Had self-righteous indignation down pat and he wasn't about to let it influence him. He wasn't on trial. Her actions needed an explanation, not his. "I want to know what these letters mean."

"You've read my private business. You tell me."

"You were leaving your husband? For Crandall?"

"What?" Avery looked at him as if he'd lost his mind.

"So, you weren't having an affair with Crandall?"

Anger flared in those bright brown eyes just before she threw the papers at him and slapped his face, knocking him back a step with the vehemence of her momentum.

"You bastard." She turned to grab her purse.

It took a moment before he recovered. By then, Avery had stormed off, leaving him with huge doubts. Oh Jeezus. Why hadn't he listened to Des?

"Avery, wait…" His cell phone rang. He let it ring and followed her through the hallway.

Des was right behind, saying, "I told you not to jump to conclusions, good buddy," at the same time Avery shouted, "Screw you. I'd rather be dead than stay here and listen to your accusations."

"You're not helping any." Sin shot Des a withering look. He'd messed up royally. He grasped that real quick, having peered into her livid face while she slapped him. No one was that good a liar to manufacture such a reaction. "Avery, get back here," he yelled, slowing to shut off his ringing cell. "You're not leaving. It's unsafe."

"Spare me your concern," she yelled back. "You can't tell me what to do. I'm in charge of me. You got that? Me. I only listen to myself."

"Yeah? Well, someone tried to kidnap you."

Avery stopped and turned around. "That was probably you, too."

"Why would you think that?" Totally shocked, he stalked up to her. "All I've ever done is try to protect you."

"Terry's right. I didn't need protecting until I met you."

"I can't believe you're saying such shit." Had she lost her mind?

"Oh?" She crossed her arms and eyed him, letting her seething gaze rake up and down his body. "Can you look me in the eye and tell me this whole setup wasn't to get closer to me?"

Sin swallowed hard, knowing in all honesty he couldn't do what she asked. He was so screwed.

"You got what you wanted." She shook her head, her lips curling into a snarl. "You men are all alike. We don't matter to you. Not really. All that matters is the prize."

"Prize?"

"Yeah, prize. That's all I am. That's all I've ever been. You want me for much the same reason Mike did."

"That's not true." What was she getting at now?

"Isn't it? You even had the audacity to ask me who I'd choose if Mike were alive today." She snorted, then waved her hand to indicate everything around them. "That's all this is to you guys, just one-upping each other, jockeying for position. You're no different than my husband was. I'm only a conquest. Something to win. Well, congratulations on your win."

"What the hell are you talking about?"

"You know damn well. You seduced me so you could get closer to me…go through my things." When he started to object, she cut him off. "Don't try to deny it now." Avery hesitated a moment, then added, meeting his gaze with an intent expression, "Admit it, Sin. You only used me to find your precious product. You certainly don't care about me…or my feelings." She pivoted and ran out the front door.

His dazed glance flew to Des.

"Don't look at me. I frickin' told you what not to do." Des rolled his eyes. "Why is it you never listen to me?"

Sin ignored him, going after her. "Wait, Avery. I can explain."

But Des' hand on his arm stopped him. He spun around, flashing an annoyed grimace. "What?"

Unperturbed, Des nodded toward the kitchen. "I'll see if I can smooth things over with her. You go and finish reading like you were supposed to in the first place." He turned, following Avery, saying in a loud, obnoxious voice, "Don't listen to him. He's being an ass. He can't help it, given his past."

Swearing under his breath, Sin strode up to the counter and bent to pick up the fallen pages she'd thrown at him right before her hasty departure. He poured himself another drink and sat, taking a long sip. Then his attention went back to the papers in front of him and he scoured them, doing what Des had told him to do in the first place. Still, he kept focusing on one sentence in an e-mail. He'd asked about her feelings for Chandler. Why would Montgomery ask if he didn't sense some connection?

~

Avery sat on the porch steps with the wind completely deflated from her grand exit. Talk about feeling stupid. She looked around, totally lost without a clue as to where Sin lived. She hadn't been paying attention on the drive. She stomped her foot, trying to hold back tears. But they had a mind of their own, overwhelming her, and not stopping, flowing even faster when she thought of the way Sin obviously regarded her. It was bad enough to be considered some prize, but his opinion went beyond. Like she was some vicious piranha who preyed on trusting spouses. It hurt to have him think the worst of her without even knowing her side. What was worse, he was so right. She had no excuses for her actions. She'd done the unthinkable. She'd not only killed her husband with her selfish demands. She'd killed a good friend.

Like the day before, she felt Des' presence rather than heard his quiet approach.

"I'm sorry."

Avery brushed back tears and looked up, eyeing him with a slanted brow. "Why are you apologizing?"

"I'm the one who went through your files. And you're right about us getting close to you on purpose. It was my idea. Yet in the process, I'd like to think we've come to trust each other."

The sad smile Des sent her made her feel a little churlish because he was right. She did trust him.

"Still, this whole misunderstanding is my fault."

"No, it's not." When he didn't say anything, just stared off into the horizon, she added, "But I'm curious. Why do you feel so responsible?" Heck, she bore most of the responsibility with her letters in the first place. If she'd waited until Mike came home to ask for a divorce, his attention would have remained focused on staying alive, and this whole fiasco would never have happened. Oh heavens, would her guilt ever go away? Des had to view her as a piranha too.

"I knew he'd jump to the wrong conclusions before he read through everything."

"What else could he conclude?" Avery's head moved slowly from side to side. "You've read everything. It's pretty damning. The cruel wife sends her husband a Dear John letter while he's on the battlefront protecting the homeland, and e-mails fly back and forth. I don't see how you can stand there and console me, and still want to be my friend after I've done the unthinkable."

"That's not how I view the situation. I count myself lucky to have you as a friend. And I *am* sorry. I did know how Sin would react." Des shrugged and met her gaze. "Who knows, maybe I did it on purpose to cause a rift." She let the question form in her eyes. "Wishful thinking on my part. I'd give anything to be more than a friend. Sick, isn't it?" he asked.

When his meaning sank in, a knot formed at the back of her throat. "Oh, Des." What else could she say?

He placed his hand on her shoulder and gave a reassuring squeeze. "I understand. We're friends. Okay?"

Avery nodded. "Now I'm the one who's sorry. What a mess. Even if I weren't half in love with Sin, I'd probably always view you as a friend."

He laughed, but she heard little humor in the sound. "I figured that out already." He wiped his face, offering a wan smile. "But you shouldn't take Sin's actions and comments personally. This isn't about you."

"Isn't it?" The look of disgust Sin gave her felt pretty damned personal.

"No." Des sighed and sat down next to her. "And in my defense I will say, I did try to warn him ahead of time, knowing he'd be a little sensitive to the news in the e-mails. Still, I should've been more diligent in my efforts. He's a little gun-shy where women like you are concerned."

"Women like me?" She muffled a laugh. "I'm not sure if I was just insulted or not."

"I meant it as a compliment. Guys like us don't usually attract women like you."

"Oh?" Avery's eyebrows slanted up another inch. Even though Des did nothing for her physically, he was an attractive man few women would turn down. In fact, all three men from SPC were hot and she couldn't see how they'd ever worry about attracting anyone.

"Yeah, you're out of our reach, given our background. A little untouchable."

"Untouchable?" She snorted, not buying his explanation. "Let's be honest." After last night, she was positive, Sin didn't view her as untouchable. No. Sin was the one who was out of reach and untouchable now. "I saw the look he gave me. I'm the lowest form of vermin on the planet. It was written in every fiber of his being from his expression to his voice, and I picked up on it loud and clear."

Des looked straight at her and mulled his next words carefully, before heaving a heavy sigh. "He doesn't really think that."

"No?" She eyed him, holding his gaze until he grinned and glanced away, shrugging sheepishly.

"Well, maybe a little," he admitted. "But like I said, he has motivation." He remained silent for a moment. "Has he mentioned his wife?"

"Ah, yes, the wife." Avery had forgotten about her.

She brought forth the memory of what she'd read. Williams' file briefly touched on a wife who had died in an automobile accident, but it happened over five years ago. Sin had been married for less than a year. Because he never mentioned it and all the other information had overwhelmed her, she'd skimmed it, not really absorbing what it meant.

Of course, in all honesty, she'd have to confess to skimming over that bit of his past, mainly because she didn't want to think of him involved with another woman. Was she totally insensitive or what? Why hadn't she asked him about her? She groaned inwardly. Because she didn't want to have to swap stories and spotlight her own miserable marriage, that's why. Damn! Just more reason to feel guilt. Why had she ever gotten involved with Sin? She should have known it would be painful in the end, once he learned her dreadful secret.

"We never discussed his wife," Avery said softly, shaking her head no, when he seemed to be waiting for her answer. "The subject never came up."

"I thought not, despite how tight you two have gotten. It's something he rarely talks about."

"Was it worse than his mother dying?" In her mind, not many horrible experiences could top that one.

"Yeah. I think so." Des sighed and looked away.

When he remained silent, she prodded, "Well? Tell me about her."

"I met Diane Blake at their wedding." Des glanced back at her. "I don't like to speak ill of the dead, but she and I never connected. From the moment I spied her cold, calculating expression when we first shook hands, I sensed Diane was bad news. Nothing but a social-climbing viper who sank her fangs into Sin, knowing he would go far. Seems her fiancé had jilted her. The guy skipped, so Sin was a rebound. Had to be, because it was obvious that she didn't love him…was just using him. Of course in his own way, Sin used her, for her socially prominent family. They had strong connections in the San Jose area, and in my opinion, marrying her validated him."

Tears trickled down Avery's face as the truth hit her. Sin didn't love her. Not in the same way she loved him. Even if he forgave her, it wouldn't matter. He regarded her as a conquest, someone to legitimize him, much as his first wife had. She could see things so clearly now, as if a gauzy film had lifted. The relationship she shared with Sin was no better than what she'd had with Mike. Her husband had used her as an adornment and Sin would use her for validation. She needed more. She brushed the tears away and listened to Des drone on about Diane and Sin, and the entire time her heart ripped, little by little, with each word.

"But he did care for her. She got pregnant right away, something she'd never planned. By that point, I think she realized her mistake in marrying someone like Sin. She wanted an abortion and a divorce, and had been very vocal about it. But Sin put his foot down…notified her family about her pregnancy, who told her she would be cut off without a cent if she created a scandal, which only enraged Diane. Her actions didn't bother Sin. The prospect of a child to love excited him too much and he wasn't about to let her manipulate him. His child would be born and would have a father."

Des offered Avery a sad smile. "We both know how it feels to be fatherless, so I have no doubt that fact drove him and kept him focused. Especially when she did such horrible things, like cheating on him and berating him. Then, the guy who left Diane rebounding for Sin in the first place comes back and wants to take over from where he left off. He was another spoiled, wealthy individual with unending resources, and Diane's leaving with him presented no great sacrifice, even if her parents cut her off."

He broke off a moment and took a deep breath before adding, "The story ends with Sin identifying her body, two weeks before their baby's due date. I don't think he's ever gotten over that particular incident." Des wiped his face and sighed. "So maybe now you can see why he's a tad sensitive."

"Of course." Though she nodded and offered Des a semblance of a smile, Avery's heart ached more. There was no way Sin loved her, especially after hearing the story about his deceased wife. He'd protect his heart from pain. He obviously had his own reasons to avoid involvement, just like her. He'd also read her dreaded secrets in those e-mails. She had her reasons for wanting out of her marriage, but she wasn't blameless in the process that brought her to that point.

"Let's go back inside and see if he's finished reading."

Avery's head bobbed up and down in agreement, but she didn't move to rise when Des stood. "You go ahead. I need a few minutes."

"Okay," he murmured. "I'll be in the kitchen with Sin. We all need to talk, so come join us when you're ready."

Ready? She'd never be ready. How could she face him now? It was all she could do to sit calmly on the steps and not run screaming down the street. Why oh why had she fallen in love with him? The urge to flee and never look back overwhelmed her.

Des must have sensed her turmoil. He squeezed her shoulder. "Don't worry, Avery. We'll figure it out. Give Sin a chance. He's a good guy and he won't disappoint you."

Avery nodded, not believing him. Des' placating encouragement gave her little solace. Both men knew too much. How could Sin ever forgive her horrible deeds when she couldn't forgive herself?

Chapter 22

Sin's phone vibrated and was enough to drag his attention away from the letters.

He tugged the device out of his pocket and noticed an unfamiliar number. "Yeah?"

"Jeffrey Sinclair?" a voice he didn't recognize shot back. "I spoke with your friend, Des Phillips, and told him I'd be calling."

"Esperanza?"

"That's what I go by," he answered. "I'd like to meet with you. I'm on the interstate about five miles outside of D.C. I should be there in less than fifteen minutes."

"Here?" His request stunned him, even though Des *had* mentioned something about a call. Did this mean he was going to help him and his friends with Williams? "Why?" Sin asked cautiously, unwilling to be too optimistic. With so much shit going on, he had no time to spend on the guy if he couldn't be helpful.

"It's time to join forces. I have information you'd be interested in knowing."

"Oh?"

"Yes," Esperanza replied. "And I believe you have information I'd be interested in."

"Okay. But are you sure it's safe? Williams seems to be getting desperate."

"I agree. His strategy has definitely changed. He might be joining us at some point, so we have to prepare for that possibility."

"I'm not sure I like this development."

"My strategy has changed, too. It's much easier to keep an eye on him if I go along…let him think I trust him. In my opinion, he's underestimated you and your partners. I'm not sure what his game is, but he most likely believes his tactic today worked to separate you and the widow."

"How did you hear about that?" Sin asked, still cautious.

"Your partner. I'm glad he had the foresight to make the call."

"You think Williams was involved?" He thought so too, but Esperanza's opinion added more weight. Made him think he had a chance at winning if he chose to fight.

"Or someone working under his orders. You and the widow are a link to the answers I'm after."

"Hmmm." Sin took a moment to absorb this news. Could he trust Esperanza? Did he dare? "We're all here," he finally said. "So come on by. We'll have a party. I take it you know where the house is?"

"Of course. I'll be there soon."

The line went dead. Sin sighed, cut the connection, and went back to his reading. Minutes later, a tap on his back door drew his attention.

He glanced up to see Scotty's grinning mug through the glass, before he opened the French patio door and stuck his head inside. "Hey, Sin."

"Scotty. You're a little out of your neighborhood." He rubbed his face in frustration. Dealing with him and his quirks was all he needed to make his night a total bust.

"Yeah, but I thought I might drop off the information I found concerning your question about drugs." Scotty pushed through the door and strode up to him.

"There is such a thing as a telephone, you know," Des said, coming into the room from the other direction.

"Of course." Scotty sent Des an annoyed look. "I decided my news warranted a personal visit." He turned back to Sin and held up a bunch of wires attached to what looked like some kind of vest. "You need to put this on."

Sin ignored Scotty and looked at Des expectantly. "Where's Avery? Did you talk to her? Is she okay?"

"She's fine. She'll join us in a minute. Finish reading?"

"Sin, did you hear what I said?" Scotty's voice kept him from answering Des' question about reading. "I want you to wear this."

Sin eyed the wires suspiciously and struggled to keep the skepticism out of his tone. "What the hell is this?"

"See what you've created," Des said at the same time Scotty said, "Don't ask. Just do it."

Sin fired Des a be-nice message with his eyes, and then turned to Scotty. "Why?"

"I have a feeling about tonight," Scotty said. "I want to make sure you're prepared."

"Prepared?" Sin bit his cheek to hold on to his smile after noting his serious expression. He chanced a glance at Des, who only rolled his eyes. "Just what are we preparing for?"

"Contingencies." Scotty straightened and used a forefinger to push his glasses higher.

One thing about Scotty, Sin decided, unable to stop the grin from forming. The guy could always make him laugh even when the situation looked absolutely bleak. "Contingencies?" he repeated, taking the stuff from him, glancing from his full hands to Des and then to Scotty, hoping for more clarification.

Scotty nodded slowly. "After you called, I got to thinking about quick-acting drugs. There are too many to count, most not easily obtainable unless you're a physician doing colonoscopies, and usually those drugs are administered via the IV, or intravenously. Avery's symptoms and the method of delivery say whatever he used was advanced—meaning high-tech. I say it has CIA written all over it."

"CIA?" Des groaned. "Scotty, you've got spies on the brain." He turned to Sin and his impatient look said, *See what you've done.*

Scotty stiffened, then fingered his glasses, glaring at Des. "Who else would use SPC's product? Maybe the government didn't want to pay for our technology?"

Sin looked up at the ceiling, searching for patience, as Des laughed and goaded, "Is that the only hypothesis you can come up with?"

"No. I did stumble upon some interesting shit on experiments some groups are doing with insect venom, specifically black widow spiders and scorpions. Then you have poisonous frogs and all the research being done on them. One website I visited detailed how they've isolated different elements in the venoms and poisons, trying to duplicate them for use, mainly the paralyzing qualities, which surprisingly enough can affect memory in humans. I can't vouch for the validity, given my research wasn't thorough."

Des snorted. "Avery's attack wasn't perpetrated by some radical group using insect venom."

"You underestimate those groups and you underestimate the Internet," Scotty said, his eyes burning with indignation.

"You need to get a life. You spend too much time on the computer."

"Des has a point." Sin shook his head, sighing. He didn't have the energy to play referee with all the shit flying around right now.

"It could happen." Scotty's chin jutted out.

"Why?" Des voice rose. "You need motivation. Who would be interested in us besides the colonel?"

"Several companies use spider, snake, and scorpion venom in manufacturing antivenin in the US. They're also researching ways to produce the antivenin without having to *milk* the donors. It's both costly and time-consuming. All I'm saying is, think of the possibilities."

When Des looked at him as if he'd lost all his marbles, Scotty's chin inched higher. "If someone's figured out a way to duplicate nature, maybe it can go through the body quickly, and depending on the dose, leave the body just as quickly unless more is administered."

"Aren't those venoms painful?" Des asked, his voice now derisive. "And again, I ask why? Why would such a group be interested in us?"

"Well, there are a few holes in my theory." He took his glasses off, systematically cleaning each lens.

"Your holes are as big as the sun." Des rolled his eyes, visibly gathering patience.

"You have to admit he's right, Scotty." Sin tried to defuse the situation when Scotty's hand fisted and he looked ready to take a swing at Des. "Those are some pretty big holes. You seem to have gotten off on another tangent."

"Ya think?" Des yelled, throwing his hands up in the air. "He's always going off on tangents."

"Fine, mock me if you must. See if I care." Scotty turned to Sin with a pleading look. "The least you can do is put on my stun ring."

Sin hesitated and raked a hand through his hair, resting it on the back of his neck, rubbing in indecision. The last thing he wanted to do was hurt Scotty's feelings, but there was no way he was going to follow through on his request. "I'm not wearing that."

"Go ahead, Sin. I know for a fact it works." Des smiled, clearly enjoying his discomfort.

"Please. It's important to me. My gut tells me you'll need it."

Sin sighed. Sometimes it was easier to humor Scotty than try to argue with him. And occasionally his weird hunches were dead-on.

"Fine." He stood and began unbuttoning his shirt.

When he had it on and his shirt tucked in, he said, "Tell me how it works."

Scotty spent a moment going over the instructions. When done, he flashed a satisfied smile. "There. Now I can breathe easier. You know they have scorpions and black widow spiders in Afghanistan."

"You're weird," Des said.

Sin chuckled, wondering if the world had tilted off its axis. His company was on the brink of peril, his love life in shambles, and he was wearing Scotty's contraption, listening to him spout off about spiders and scorpions while Des called him weird.

"Trust me." Scotty pushed his glasses higher on his head, his smile becoming smugger. "Better to be safe than sorry."

"I feel like a goddamned fool."

"That's 'cause you are a fool." Des chuckled. Then he sobered. Straightening while clearing his throat, he stared past his shoulder.

Sin turned, following his gaze. Avery stood in the doorway, only she wouldn't meet his searching look.

"Did you finish the letters?" Des asked, yanking his attention to their pressing problems.

"Yeah."

"Good." He pulled out a stool and patted it, before grabbing another one and plopping onto it. "Come on, Avery. We need to discuss these." Des held up the letters and printed e-mails.

Scotty walked toward the French doors. "I'm taking off." Grinning, he reached for the handle. "Call me if you need me."

"Sin and I have a few questions," Des added once Scotty left, patting the empty stool again.

Sin watched her nod and walk further into the room, relieved he didn't have to speak. Whatever he said at this point would be a mistake.

Des turned over one of the sheets, took a pen out of his pocket, and drew a line on the page. "Let's do a timeline and see how it flows."

"A timeline sounds like a decent plan," Sin agreed.

"From what I can tell by postmarks, Montgomery got the first letter three weeks before he died. The beginning of March? Correct?"

"Yes." Avery nodded, still averting her gaze from Sin's, so he had no idea what she was thinking. The hint of color on her face could mean anything from annoyance to embarrassment. Sin prayed for the latter, but somehow, he wasn't quite sure if Des had helped or had hindered his case. Given her demeanor, it didn't appear they'd resolved any issues.

"Then we have a bunch of e-mails going back and forth for a couple of weeks. When was this letter sent, do you know?"

But resolving their differences didn't really matter. Sin sighed, wishing he'd never laid eyes on any of this; especially Montgomery's last letter, asking for a second chance, basically wanting to work things out when faced with divorce papers.

Even though he'd already read it twice, he went over the missive one more time.

Your letter requesting separation, along with a divorce in six months, stunned me, providing a chance for reflection. Avery, you aren't thinking this through. You're being selfish in your demands. You need to give me an opportunity to rectify my mistakes, if indeed they are mine. Marriage takes two, as I've always said.

I'm not good at showing my feelings. You and Andy mean everything to me. It's why I fought so hard in trying to make the world safer. In all my soul-searching, I've come to realize one thing. What's the use in fighting for something, if the reason you're fighting so hard disappears right in front of your eyes?

Give me the chance to make things right. I refuse to believe you won't after ten years. If you need answers, look behind us for them. They're there, as surely as my love is there. And think of Andy. A boy needs his father. I've enclosed my heart for safekeeping. Wear it always and think of me. We'll survive this and when I get back to explain in person, we'll sort it out. Don't deny me my chance to rectify my errors. And remember. Keep my heart safe.

Sin picked up the letter, wondering what would have happened if Montgomery hadn't died. Would Avery do what her husband asked? What would her answer be today? Would she look to the past only to realize what she and her husband had together was more than one night spent in pure bliss in Sin's arms? He shouldn't be torturing himself with such stupid questions, yet they wouldn't leave his brain and the answers tore at his heart. Why had he fallen in love with another unsuitable woman who loved another man?

Though Avery wasn't like Diane, the situation held similarities. He craved the unattainable. He yearned to take Avery's hero's place, to love her, to protect her, to provide her son with a father, and to have their love in return. Things he had no business desiring.

"Where is this locket?" Des' question pounded in Sin's brain, drawing him out of his miserable musings. "Scotty and I think he sent it for a purpose."

His focus flew to Avery's neck, where she absently reached for the heart, but her hand hit only skin because he'd told her to take it off.

The doorbell pealed, interrupting what she was about to say.

"That's probably Esperanza," Sin replied, answering Des' raised eyebrows and standing, only too happy for the disruption so he wouldn't have to think about the memento. It was tangible proof Montgomery still held Avery's heart.

He started for the front door as Avery's voice filled the air.

"It's in my purse. I put it there earlier."

"The locket accompanied the last letter, correct?"

Sin didn't catch her reply, but he came back into the room with Esperanza following, just in time to hear Avery say, "He was reminding me of better days." She offered Des a wan smile. "The sad part is, they were more his better days than mine."

Des glanced at Sin, his gaze shifting to Esperanza, and indicated the piece of paper in his hand. "Since you were in Kandahar in the weeks preceding Montgomery and Crandall's deaths, you can help. We're recreating a timeline of events."

Esperanza nodded. "Good idea. Let me take a look at what you've got so far." He moved to stand next to Des, who handed him the piece of paper. He remained silent, eyeing the page carefully. "I remember when he got this first letter. I was on CQ."

"Explain CQ to them," Sin said, when he looked up and noticed their blank stares.

"CQ means charge of quarters...like guard duty," Esperanza clarified. "I was brought in for added protection, but I wasn't told who they suspected. I made sure I had the duty more times than not, because it gave me the opportunity to keep a better eye on things. Anyway, Montgomery and Crandall were arguing in his office, a common occurrence in those last weeks, I might add. I also remember their last big argument." He exhaled, then took a deep breath. "My diligence didn't pay off. A few nights later, they were killed and the prototypes were stolen out from under our noses. Just as before."

"Before? You mean there have been more thefts?"

"Yes. Which is why Colonel Williams planned this operation. We were working together to flush out an obvious traitor."

"Shit," Des said, snorting. "Kind of like having a fox watch the henhouse, wouldn't you say?"

"Appears that way. According to Williams, the technology for the Xcom2s wasn't viable, a big part of the plan, if we couldn't stop another theft from taking place. The perfect setup."

"It's viable," Sin interjected. "The technology works. I'm glad Scotty's not around to hear you say the military had such little faith in his brainchild."

"But what if Williams wanted us to think that? I'm sure Montgomery realized the viability, and in my opinion, something spooked him...something he discovered," Esperanza said. "According to records, the major sent a package to his wife three days before he died, the same night I heard him and Crandall arguing over his wife. Again. It's that package I was looking for."

"They discussed me?"

"Yes. You seemed to be in the middle of every argument I overheard."

"Can you tell me what they said?" Avery searched Esperanza's expression, hers imploring.

He eyed her for an extended moment. "Crandall chastised Montgomery for using you so callously. It was something he was always doing, but this night his words were much stronger...angrier. Montgomery told him to mind his own business. You were his problem and he would deal with you when he got home. Crandall called him a selfish bastard. Montgomery only laughed and goaded Crandall, saying he was upset over circumstances. He had you, Crandall didn't, and you'd never love him." Esperanza gave her an apologetic glance. "I hope you understand. Your marital problems weren't my concern, but I couldn't totally ignore their conversations because I had my duty. It took me a while to figure out they were discussing the prototypes."

"I should never have sent my letter," Avery said softly. "It distracted him from doing his job and he died."

"No, I disagree." Esperanza shook his head. "He wasn't distracted. Just the opposite, in fact. Judging from his argument with Crandall, he may have been lacking as a husband, but he was a damned fine soldier and quick to use what was at his disposal. Your letter gave him the perfect cover to protect the technology from being stolen. I should've trusted you enough to ask about it earlier and saved us all weeks of conjecture."

"That would mean the prototypes disappeared days before he died," Sin said.

"I believe so." Esperanza met his gaze. "How he was able to hide the fact that the Xcom2s were missing from the time he sent the package to when he was killed only shows how truly good he was at his role. No one suspected they were missing until Captain Marring and I found the empty CD case the night of the ambush after the shooting ended."

"Oh my God." Avery dug her locket out of her purse and held it out like it was contagious. "I *have* had them all along."

"Is that what Major Montgomery sent in his last letter?" Esperanza asked, taking the necklace from her and examining it.

"Yes." Avery nodded slowly, blinking back tears. "I should've known he wasn't being sentimental. It was so unlike him."

"Unbelievable." Des grunted. "All this time and they were so close."

"That's what he meant when he said look behind us for the answers." Avery glanced at Sin, her expression woeful. "I thought he was talking about the past...about wanting to be with me. But in reality, he knew someone was going to steal them and was protecting them. It makes perfect sense now." A few tears trickled down the sides of her face. "His duty always came first. Always. I wonder if he really cared at all for Andy and me."

"I'm sorry, Avery." Sin held her gaze, without a clue as to what else he could say to console her. Montgomery's actions painted him as one cold son of a bitch. Not her hero, that's for damn sure. "Can I see the locket?"

When she handed it over, he opened the catch. "I need tweezers. And a magnifying glass." He nodded to the cabinet across from the bar. "Top drawer. There are some jeweler's screwdrivers in there too."

Des hurried to do his bidding, rooting through it and pulling out a pair of tweezers, along with a set of tiny screwdrivers. After another few seconds of searching, he found the magnifier and passed the items to him.

Elation filled Sin as he gently tugged Avery's picture loose and then Montgomery's, seeing what he hoped for and ending his month-long search. Yet his joy fizzled when he glimpsed briefly into Avery's eyes and spied such raw pain. At this point, he wished for any other outcome for her.

Why do those we love have to let us down by doing such disappointing deeds?

"Here. I brought this along." Esperanza supplied the special CD case used to house them. "Had a feeling I might need it."

Sin took the case and pulled out his cell phone to call Scotty. Since the project was his baby, he needed his expertise. He walked out of earshot, giving and getting instructions.

"Done." His satisfied grin in place, Sin hit the disconnect button and pocketed his phone, along with Avery's heart. "The fail-safe is disabled, stopping the self-destruction."

"Congratulations. You've solved the puzzle. Now hand them over."

Sin, along with everyone else in the room, turned toward the voice coming from the hallway.

Colonel Williams stood, holding out one hand and pointing a gun with the other.

Chapter 23

"I'll take the CD case."

"The prototypes belong to SPC." Sin stiffened as Colonel Williams walked further into the room, his weapon trained on them. "Why should I turn them over to you when you've never been interested in finding them?"

"You have your facts wrong. They belong to the military until the testing is complete." He smiled, but the smile didn't quite reach his cold eyes. "Plus, I've been very interested in finding them. Now that I have, hand them over." Williams turned to Des, who stood next to Esperanza. Both men tried to reach for their guns. He shook his head. "Uh-uh. Hands up and keep them where I can see them. And no sudden movements."

Avery slipped behind Des, as he put up both hands and said, "I'm cool."

Esperanza slowly did the same.

Williams nodded and met Esperanza's steady gaze. "As of now, you're relieved of your duty."

Esperanza didn't respond, but his expression spoke loudly. Lesser men might cower after receiving such a glare.

"Consider it payback." The colonel's smile broadened. "Such a pity we couldn't work together. This has always been my operation. Unfortunately, you don't quite grasp chain of command."

The stare-off continued.

"We seem to be at an impasse." A sliver of irritation ran down Sin's spine over the confident expression Williams wore.

"No impasse. You're interfering in a military investigation. And I won't allow it." Williams waved his weapon. "Give me the CD case. Now."

Sin eyed the gun, which gave the man a slight edge, but there was no way he would let him win. Suddenly, he remembered Scotty's contraption. He caught Des' gaze and could see that their thoughts traveled along the same path. His subtle nod told him all he needed to know. Sin walked toward Williams, offering the case.

"Much better." The colonel nodded. The second his fingers

made contact, Sin pretended to trip and grasped the man's arm in an apparent attempt to steady himself. He let go as Williams' body shook and contracted, then collapsed in front of him.

"Well, I'll be damned. It actually worked."

Des chuckled and grabbed the gun out of Williams' hand. "Yeah, imagine that."

Sin glanced at the man on the ground, still trying to grasp what had happened. "Okay, we've got a crazy, conniving colonel who's turned traitor passed out in my kitchen, one I might add I've just electrocuted the hell out of. So what do we do now?"

"You give me the case."

Sin looked toward the voice. In all the commotion, the guy had obviously snuck into the kitchen using the same route as Williams.

"Marring," Esperanza said, eyeing him warily.

Marring pointed a Beretta 9mm at him. "Your weapon. Put it on the floor in front of you and kick it toward me. No heroics, or I start shooting. All I want is the prototypes."

"I'm surprised to see you." Esperanza slowly took his gun out of his holster. "Thought you'd be in Afghanistan for at least another week."

Marring ignored his comment and indicated Des with the gun. "You too. Drop your weapon and kick it over. I have no intention of hurting anyone, as long as I get what I want."

Esperanza began to hand over his weapon, but aimed at the last second.

Marring didn't hesitate to shoot him.

Swearing, Esperanza dropped the gun to grab his arm as blood seeped from between his fingers.

"Now kick it over here like I asked in the first place." Marring's voice turned menacing. "And keep those hands where I can see them so I don't get trigger-happy. Next bullet will be in the heart. As you've discovered, I will shoot if I have to."

Esperanza's foot pushed the gun across the floor. Des dropped his and copied his movements.

No one else moved a muscle.

"That's more like it." Marring stepped further into the room, halted to pick up each gun, and placed both in his back. The entire time he'd kept his weapon trained on all of them, now grouped around the colonel.

When Esperanza glared at Marring, Sin realized he didn't want the man for an enemy. His cold expression shouted one message. Marring had better run fast and far because there wouldn't be enough space on the face of the earth to hide once he got away.

Marring ignored his look. "I extended my agreement with Uncle Sam. In return, I got immediate leave to come home. Convenient, don't you think?" An amused smile spread across his face. "I have enough time to tie up loose ends and disappear with plenty of money to live in luxury for the rest of my life. Regrettably, I can't start my journey until I finish my last contract." He scrunched his nose and whispered conspiratorially, "My business associates don't appreciate being stiffed, especially when they've already paid half. It's nothing personal. You understand?"

The colonel stirred, groaning.

Marring looked at Sin and his smile deepened. "I'll take the CD case now."

When Sin started toward him, he shook his head and offered another chuckle. "I saw your brilliant performance, but you don't get an encore. Place it there and step back."

"I applaud your cunning," Esperanza said. "Especially since you were there when the majors died. I caught your stunned look when we opened the case, so I ruled you out as a suspect. A costly mistake."

"You led me on quite a chase." Marring clucked. "Wasn't sure who had them, but I knew it was either you or one of the majors. No one else outside McGeek was interested." Marring looked pointedly at Williams. "He was positive the geek had done it, and his misdirection kept the heat off me."

Sin wanted to understand more about a man who would sell out his fellow soldiers. "So the ambush was really your planned attack?" He placed the CD on the counter and walked slowly backward, holding his hands high.

"More or less." Marring pocketed the case and met Sin's gaze. "No one was supposed to die. Montgomery and Crandall caught me talking with my buyer. Unfortunately for them, my buyer saw them, and he couldn't let them live for fear of being found out. In the pandemonium, I was to grab the case. Then I could disappear when my time was up."

"It doesn't bother you that people died?" Williams asked, having regained consciousness enough to realize what was taking place. "That in selling America's secrets, you're killing more men."

"Shit, you're naïve." He laughed. "In five years, I've watched more men die in my arms than I can count on my hands and I've seen friends maimed. I've given twenty years of sweat and blood to my country. And for what?" Marring snorted. "For a few lousy bucks, while others get rich? I'm only emulating the greedy bastards of major corporations who sell to the highest bidder. Every soldier on the front knows American technology is coming at them from her enemies and we don't have the means of protecting ourselves because we're ill equipped, so don't preach to me about killing American soldiers."

His face distorted in disgust. "It's every man for himself. I'm only trying to survive, which became more difficult when I found the case empty. I had a damn hard time convincing my Arab backer to give me another chance." He flashed a sardonic grin. "Enough idle chitchat. It's time to take your cell phones out of your pockets and toss them on the floor." No one moved. He raised his weapon and aimed. "Now."

One by one they did as he asked.

With the task completed, Marring waved the Beretta toward Sin's vaulted walk-in wine cooler next to his pantry. "In there. All of you." When no one budged, he barked, "Move." He pointed the weapon at Des. "You—help him," indicating the colonel who was stretching and rubbing his arms. "Don't try my patience. Just do as I ask and no one else will get hurt."

"Do as he says." Colonel Williams rose unsteadily with Des' help, and limped toward the cooler. "He won't get far."

The others fell in behind, following single file through the door Marring now held open.

"If you're thinking your backup will cover your ass, I'd rethink. They won't be any help for at least forty-five minutes. They got a healthier dose than I gave Montgomery's widow." He shrugged. "My information on dosage was incorrect, otherwise this entire scene could've been avoided. I'd have gotten the prototypes and Avery would've woken up in the ladies' room with no memory. I certainly didn't expect such worthy adversaries. I had to improvise and become creative in dealing with you." He turned to the colonel. "Seems your information on them is a little skewed. They're not your average thugs."

Marring displayed a satisfied smile once they were all in the tiny, cold room. "Hopefully you'll have enough air to last till help comes. If not? Well, suffocation is a much cleaner way to go than gunshot wounds. I hate seeing all that blood." He turned to Esperanza and his grin twisted into a scornful sneer. "But yours I don't mind seeing so much."

Sin watched him shut the door with a final click, extinguishing the light at the same time.

In the dark, he searched for the switch and flipped it on, before moving to the door and jiggling the knob.

"He's jimmied it from the outside." Sin sighed. "He's right about our air supply. We need to sit calmly and conserve it. With five of us, we won't last long if we don't. The cooler's sealed, kept at fifty-seven degrees for my wine collection." Unfortunately, there also wasn't much room. Five adults took up most of the space standing, and as they all sank to the floor, it became even more crowded.

"Sitting's good. I feel light-headed." Esperanza leaned his head back against one of the empty shelves and slid down, almost crumpling. "I'm still bleeding."

"Let me see how bad it is," Des said.

Sin took off the t-shirt he wore underneath his polo, and using his teeth, ripped a hole before tearing it into strips.

Esperanza shook out of the jacket and shirt he wore, swearing. "I'm getting tired of being shot. It hurts."

Grinning, Des searched the wound carefully. "Looks like the bullet only grazed you. You're lucky it's not worse, but it's bleeding like a son of a gun."

Though his expression appeared anything but happy, Esperanza allowed Des to treat the wound with pressure. "I'll survive," he said a moment later. "My pride may not. That's twice today someone's gotten the drop on me." He directed his gaze at the colonel. His expression hardened. "You didn't follow procedure. You kept me in the dark about Marring. Why?"

"I could ask you the same question. You also withheld vital information. Why?" The colonel scowled. "You had a job to do and you let civilians get in the way."

"You abused your authority." Anger radiated off Esperanza.

"I did what I had to do to protect America's secrets and I'd do it again. A hundred times over if I thought I was right." Williams looked at him with disgust. "But you. You were warned, yet you let thugs influence you, and look what happened," he spewed, almost spitting. "He got away. I had everything in place, and you fucking had to impede my efforts and mess this up."

Esperanza's eyes grew the size of quarters. "You're blaming me for your ineptness?"

"Gentlemen," Sin said, drawing their attention. "Can we focus on the problem and assign blame later? You're wasting precious air, arguing."

"And you." The colonel sneered, ignoring his warning and pointing at him. "Why don't you admit the truth?"

"What truth?" Sin's eyebrows shot up.

"They don't work."

His jaw dropped. "You actually believe that, don't you?"

"Yes. You may have fooled a few in business, but you can't fool me. I've had you and your company investigated. Thoroughly. My sources delved much deeper into your backgrounds than the usual secret security checks. We spoke with anyone and everyone—neighbors and friends who knew you when. Funny how open people are to another's past."

Sin stiffened. "We have nothing to hide. We're simply a company, trying to make a living, just like millions of other Americans."

"No." Williams vehemently shook his head. "SPC is full of con artists. You and your partners tried to scam Uncle Sam, only I caught on and stopped it. Never in a billion years could a bunch of streetwise punks like you come up with such a product. But you were perfect for our plans." He pointed a finger at Esperanza. "And you? You'll be reprimanded for going behind my back."

"I don't understand." Sin's gaze narrowed. "SPC had an agreement."

"Yes. We did. All you need to understand is our agreement still holds. No confirmation, no money."

"Then give us the chance to prove it works. We created the product in good faith."

"Of course you say that now. Marring saved you from further embarrassment. And if he hadn't, it wouldn't matter. I'll not waste the taxpayers' money on more testing." He gave a derisive snort. "Top brass agrees with me. We used you for one reason only, to flush out the ring of traitors selling on the black market within the military."

"Why are you so sure our product doesn't work?"

"Why?" Williams laughed outright. "Why would I believe otherwise? What else can I expect from men who have your pasts. Thankfully, I've kept my eye on you and your company. When you told me about the fail-safe, I began to think you and your partners were in on the theft to keep from being found out." His lips curled in a snarl. "No possible way SPC could be legitimate."

"What have we ever done to cause such a biased opinion?"

"One based on research." The colonel crossed his arms, his expression turning smug.

"Our company is legitimate." Sin realized it did no good to defend himself after staring into Williams' eyes and seeing only contempt. Instead, he went on the offensive. "So, the military's answer is to destroy us? You're the one who has done some questionable deeds, not us."

"You wouldn't stop with your incessant probing, which interfered with our initial investigation. If not for that, we might have caught on to Marring much sooner. Everyone connected at that point was suspect, including SPC's owners. Marring discovered we suspected Montgomery's letter to his wife before he died. We weren't able to intercept it—and had her watched. Others also watched, which is what alerted us. We couldn't let the principals of SPC mess up our carefully laid plans, so I planted diversions, allowed other thefts, to redirect your attention." He paused and glared at Avery. "Unfortunately, even those plans backfired when you visited the cemetery every night Sinclair and his partner were watching. I had to do something to scare you away."

Avery stared back at him as a look of horror crossed her face.

"I've done nothing wrong." Sin shook his head. Disgust filled him, despite already possessing the knowledge of Williams' involvement of his other thefts and those shots fired. "This is America. The last time I checked, a man is innocent until proven guilty and you overstepped your bounds."

"I won't apologize for my actions. America is fighting the most important war since her inception with terrorism. I'm a soldier in that war, also fighting greed within her military. I have no qualms about using underhanded means, if it nets results. So people can live free. Nothing in your file made me think I could deal with you any differently."

Sin gaped. The guy couldn't be for real. Yet his heated manner and fervent gleam told him everything. Williams actually believed his drivel. Self-righteousness oozed out of his every pore.

He sighed as doubts overwhelmed him. Would he ever live down his childhood? When people viewed him, if they knew what he'd endured, would they only see a thug from the hood and judge him lacking because he'd been a fatherless boy who'd struggled in his youth?

No matter how far he'd come, he couldn't outrun his past.

He glanced at Des to gauge his reaction.

Des rolled his eyes, his shrug saying, *We are what we are.*

So like him. Sin wished he could emulate him. Des never apologized to anyone for anything. His gaze narrowed as a thought struck. So why couldn't he? He was president and CEO of a profitable company. He completed what he had set out to do after his mother died, and she would be proud of him. Like Des, Sin decided right then and there that he was done apologizing for something out of his control. He was what he was. He refocused on the colonel and for the first time saw him through Des' eyes. He was a narrow-minded little man.

He felt Avery's hand on his arm. "Don't listen to him, Sin. That's not how people view you. It's certainly not how I see you." She squeezed reassuringly, drawing his gaze. "I know you and you aren't that seventeen-year-old, any more than I'm the same person who let a selfish man use me for ten years. It's only a part that helped shape us. Think! Without the experience, would you be as strong as you are now?" Honesty poured out of her eyes. She believed in him and she loved him. He saw those facts as clearly as he saw the tears now streaming down her face. "Whether you accept it or not. You *are* my hero."

"You're a fucking fool, Colonel Williams," Esperanza whispered. "And I'm a bigger fool for allowing you to distort my judgment." He sighed, leaned his head back, and closed his eyes. "America no longer has the ability to stand for truth and justice when the people who are in charge act worse than those who are her enemies."

"War doesn't allow for such sentiments."

Esperanza chuckled. "Tell that to those who fought so valiantly in World War II. Thankfully, they're part of a dying breed and most will never see what their sacrifices have generated. You've made a mockery of all of us now fighting so hard, including those who died so we could live free."

"You have no idea how bad it's gotten," Colonel Williams said. "Our boys are dying on the battlefront because our secrets are sold to the highest bidder. Too many top-secret designs have made their way into enemy hands. I had no choice but to take matters into my own hands, to investigate. I see my duty as ultimately saving lives as well as protecting the military from undue embarrassment."

Esperanza shook his head. "The end doesn't justify the means if those means aren't honorable."

"Not so," the colonel scoffed, brushing Esperanza's comment aside with a wave of his hand.

Esperanza only smiled. "Then what differentiates you from those you're fighting?"

"Americans want to feel safe. Safety has its price. My actions may seem contemptible, but my motives are pure, I assure you."

"Spare me your excuses." Esperanza glared. "There is no excuse for misuse of power."

"I misused nothing," Williams spit out. "I have the full support of my superiors. My actions became expedient when we discovered captured insurgents using technology barely out of testing. I determined then and there I wouldn't stop my quest until I rooted out the traitors. I focused on those with access—those doing the testing. I was given the go-ahead to do whatever needed doing in my investigation. I couldn't watch young boys die any longer with full realization one of their fellow soldiers most likely sold them out."

"Time out." Sin smiled and gave the hand signal. "I don't need to hear any more."

"What are you talking about?"

Sin reached into his pocket and pulled out Avery's locket. "The prototypes?" He couldn't contain his smile from spreading, as he held on to the high of discovering Avery's belief in him, and nodded at the locket. "I never put them in the CD case, so Marring left with an empty container."

He glanced at Esperanza. "I didn't trust you and wasn't willing to put my company's future in the hands of someone I didn't trust."

Esperanza cracked a smile. "No offense taken, but I don't think Marring's going to be happy when he finds out."

"You'd think he'd be more thorough, given his earlier experience." Sin chuckled. "I wonder if he'll check it before he hands it over. Hopefully, for our sakes, he won't." His focus landed on the colonel until he had his full attention. "Let me assure you, the recording device *is* working. Now, the way I see it, you have two choices."

"Oh?" The colonel didn't look pleased.

"You either agree to my terms or disagree." Sin grinned. "Consider this a renegotiation." His grin died. Without flinching, he held the colonel's gaze, letting the man see the seriousness that had replaced humor in his eyes. "You'll agree to the contract being fulfilled and the testing complete, which means you owe us our bonus as promised, since we met the agreed-upon deadline. In return, we'll keep from going public with your…um…how do I put it?" He broke off for a moment. "Indiscretions? Yeah, that's a good description. Oh…and we'll toss in a product that works." He let out a contented sigh. "This way everyone comes out with something." His smile reappeared. "Don't you agree?"

The colonel's gaze narrowed. "I don't believe you."

"Then call my bluff." He shrugged. "Either way, I'll be paid, but you'll go down." Sin choked back his laughter at his pained look.

"I see." Williams nodded. "I have no choice then, do I?"

"Not in my opinion." He had to admit, it felt pretty good to hold his future in his hands. He pocketed the locket and squeezed Avery's knee. "Don't worry, sweetie. Scotty should be here soon. Then I'll get you that bath I promised."

Sin glanced at Esperanza. "I feel I owe you another apology. I told him to return to the house, but to do so cautiously." His shoulders lifted in another shrug. "What can I say? My self-protective instincts were on overdrive."

"Sin…? Where are you?"

As if his words had conjured Scotty's voice, the sound penetrated into the small room.

Chaos reigned when everyone jumped up at once. They pounded on the door, yelling, "In here."

Seconds later Scotty opened the door and fresh air rushed in.

Sin grinned and met the colonel's surprised gaze. "Proof positive. The Xcom2s work. I transmitted everything that happened from the moment I programmed in the code." He knew he was gloating, but could barely contain his enjoyment over the colonel's expression. "I'm not sure the signal made it through the cooler's wall, but it doesn't matter. Our conversation was still recorded."

Nothing could diminish the happiness he felt. Avery loved him and his company remained solvent.

His elation didn't last.

Almost immediately, men like Williams overran his home, asking questions, occupying Sin's attention. During this time, Avery grew distant, lurking in a corner next to Des and Scotty, and making him wonder if he'd misread her earlier actions.

"Colonel," one of the officers said, coming up to Sin and Williams. The ambulance with Esperanza had just left, taking him to the emergency room due to his wounds. "We found Captain Marring, sir."

"Good. We're finished here and ready to interrogate him."

"I'm afraid that won't be possible. A highway patrolman found him at a rest area off Interstate 95 south of D.C. with a bullet in his skull. Guess he didn't check the case before he handed it over."

"How sad." Williams heaved a heavy sigh. "Captain Marring was a decorated soldier. Had a spotless record. And he ends his life a traitor, killed execution style by the very people he turned traitor to. We would've been much more lenient." The colonel shook his head and his shoulders slumped. He met Sin's gaze, his full of misery. "For what it's worth, I am sorry I misjudged you and your partners. I did what I thought I had to do, and I failed. Esperanza's right. Despite my lofty motives, my actions make me no better than Marring, and only add to the problem." When Sin didn't respond, he added, his voice sounding wearier, "The world is changing. No longer black and white. The men we expect to be heroes aren't so heroic anymore. And the ones you think have no heroics in them surprise the hell out of you. We'll consider the testing complete. You'll have your check for the negotiated amount including bonus in less than two weeks. You've certainly earned it."

He started down the hallway behind the trail of the Army CID investigators. Sin followed. At the door Williams turned back. "This is where I bow out. The US Army will honor the rest of your contract. You'll be contacted by the proper department head and given instructions as to fulfilling our earlier agreement. Make sure Mr. McNeil is available for training once you start shipping the product."

The next instant his hall stood empty.

Sin closed the door as Des entered his line of vision. "So that's that, I guess."

"Finally, we can relax and reap the rewards of our hard work." Des clapped him on the back. "Don't let others spoil this moment, Sin. You deserve a bit of gloating. Don't apologize for your past. We are what we are." He chuckled and winked. "Great men."

Sin nodded slowly, not so sure about the great, but happy with the knowledge that he was okay.

"I thought they'd never leave," Scotty said, coming up behind them. "Man, I could never do their job. Too anal."

Des snorted, then laughed outright. "Have you glanced in the mirror lately?" He turned in his direction. "I hate to break this to you, Scotty, but if you look up anal in the dictionary, your picture is next to the definition."

Sin chuckled. It felt good to finally have something to laugh about.

"I'm gone. I don't need to stay here and be insulted by the likes of you." Scotty waved to Sin. "See ya Monday. We can work on figuring out a way to meet our new deadline with the military. I don't want anything to interfere with production."

Sin nodded. SPC had three months to deliver the first shipment of a hundred Xcom2s.

"I'm taking off, too. It's been a long day. I'll give Eric a call and tell him the good news." Des followed Scotty out.

Sin watched as both walked, laughing and joking, to their cars. Once they drove off, he shut the door, blocking all noise and creating a deafening silence.

Avery's voice broke into the quiet. "So everything worked out for you. I'm glad."

Sin turned to see her standing a few feet away, and noted her forlorn expression.

"Is something wrong?" He stepped away from the door and strode up to her. Looking into her sad eyes, he pushed a lock of hair behind her ears, brushing the side of her face with the back of his hand. He lifted her chin and stared directly into the same gaze that never failed to yank a reaction from his gut.

"Wrong?" She exhaled a long, arduous sigh. "What could be wrong?" She held his gaze, then caved as tears filled her eyes. "I'm such a fool."

"Shush." He smiled and pulled her into his arms, hugging her fiercely. "You're no such thing."

"I am. A total fool. I actually felt guilty for thinking I killed him, more concerned over whether or not he forgave me…and…and…he used me. That's all I was to him. Something to use." She leaned back. Torment as well as tears spilled out of her eyes, when their gazes met. "'*He had you, Crandall didn't, and you'd never love him.*' Esperanza's exact words. Can you imagine anyone gloating so horridly to his best friend?" She glanced away, shaking her head. "What did I ever see in him? He was my husband and he was such a bastard."

"It's okay, Avery. People we love aren't always what they seem or what we need. Sometimes you find out right away, other times it takes years."

"I kept making excuses for him. To Andy, Terry, my mother…even the neighbors. It was easy. He was never around and when he was, I pretended." She placed her head in his shoulder and sobbed. "He never loved me."

"I love you." He kissed the side of her face, and whispered the words again. "I love you, Avery. If you give me the chance, I'll make you happy. I swear. I'll make you forget him. Just give me the chance."

She pulled away. "I can't think right now." She dropped her hands to her side and took a step back. "I'd like to take that hot bath you promised, if you don't mind."

Sin nodded, working to keep his disappointment from showing. She needed time and space. He meant to give her both.

"Come on." He grabbed her hand and led her toward the spiral staircase, picking up her suitcase along the way. "I'll show you the guest room and bath."

~

In the gigantic room, a room as elegant as the rest of the house, Sin pulled out towels and washcloths, and pointed. "Bath is right

273

through there. Everything you need should be there. If not, holler and I'll get it."

Through her tears, Avery watched him leave and close the door with a final click. She'd hurt him. The pain she spotted in his eyes registered, making her feel like a monster for putting it there. More guilt. Would she ever feel normal? She didn't want to add to his hurt, but she was simply too numb to think at the moment. In five days' time her life had completely unraveled, tearing her down to nothing.

Everything she thought of her life with Michael Montgomery had been bogus.

She consumed herself with the task of preparing a bath, pushing Mike out of her mind. She didn't want to think about her miserable marriage. It was over. Finally over. All the years of loneliness…all the years of feeling that something was missing from her life. Over.

Glancing around, she spied an array of products, including a bottle of fragrant bubble bath, thankful Sin had an indulgent streak, yet wondering at the reason he kept something so feminine on hand. She turned on the taps, letting the hot outpace the cold.

In moments, steam filled the room. She sank into the hot water with a soft sigh, trying not to think of the women who'd been here before. She laid her head back and closed her eyes, allowing the surrounding heat to restore her energy.

Little by little, memories of Sin infiltrated her brain. Her mind refocused, switching to the events of the past week. Reality, as well as warmth from the water, swamped her. She had a choice. She could wallow in Mike's selfish actions, or she could stop letting him destroy her happiness from the grave. As for Mike? She'd made up her mind about him long before she mailed her letter. He belonged in her past. Did Sin belong in her future?

Sin said he loved her. He had a strong persona…his power pulled people with him. So much like Mike. Yet he was nothing like Mike. He understood what love meant. He gave as much as he expected from others. She felt it in every fiber of her being and she felt his love with every glance since they made love.

Did she dare take the chance and love him back?

YES!

Avery jumped out of the tub and hurriedly dried off, rushing because she didn't want to waste another moment.

She found a plush bathrobe Sin had laid out on the bed. She shrugged into it and started out of the room. Barefoot, she padded along the thick carpet, following the light and using it as a beacon in the darkened house.

She slowed, halting outside his room.

Through the space between the door and the jamb, she spied him lying on the king-sized bed, one hand behind his head, the other holding the locket he examined.

She spent a moment observing.

"He *was* a hero, you know."

She jumped at Sin's voice. He obviously knew she stood watching him. She pushed her way into the room and nodded. "I know."

"His quick thinking saved my company and I'll always be thankful for his actions. I *am* sorry he had to use you to do it, though."

"He loved his job. Loved the danger and loved being where the action was." Avery slowly walked toward him. "We weren't meant for each other. I wasn't sure how we lasted so long, until his mother and I talked after his father died. Seems their relationship wasn't much different, so it's all he had as a guideline. We both settled. I was his prize. A homecoming queen. And he was the football star with a promising future. What more could I want?"

She stopped at the bed and smiled, letting all the love she felt for him show in her eyes. "But I do want more…so much more."

"I'm no hero, Avery—"

"Don't say that." She knelt next to him. "You're my hero. You saved me." She put a finger to his lips when he meant to disagree. "I won't allow you to deny it."

Sin's gaze met hers, locked in a silent battle.

Finally he sighed and looked away.

"Would you like to know why I sent him a request for a divorce in a letter?" she asked.

This question caught his interest and he glanced at her with raised eyebrows.

She smiled. "Because we never talked, really talked. I didn't know him and he didn't know me. I woke up one day and looked at my life. My twenties zoomed by before I finally understood I wasn't part of it. I was living in a shell, going through the motions of life, no longer feeling. Part of me was dead and I couldn't live the rest of my life being half dead. And then you came along and saved me. With one kiss, you brought me back to life and made me feel again."

"Damn," he whispered, tucking a stray lock of hair behind her ears. "You make me feel like a hero."

His sincere eyes focused on her as he stroked her face, and she couldn't stop the burst of love from exploding inside her.

"I'm only a man. One likely to make mistakes and I can be every bit a bastard as your dead husband."

"Which I'm sure will make for some interesting fights. You should know, I won't roll over and lose myself again. If we do this, we do it hand in hand. As equals."

"I wouldn't have it any other way."

"And another thing—"

"Avery?" he said, cutting her off. "I realize you need to talk, but we can talk later. Right now all I want to do is this," he whispered, just before his lips met hers.

Sin's mouth was soft and warm and so enticing. But before she lost herself in his kisses, she pulled back. "I love you, Jeffrey Sinclair. And not because you're my hero, but because you are who you are. Someone who loves me."

"My sentiments exactly."

Sin reached for her, pushing the robe off her shoulders. Seconds later, all Avery felt was hands and lips moving over her body. She grinned. *Thank God I'm alive* was her last coherent thought before he slid inside her, wiping everything from her brain but the feel of him.

~~The End~~

Thank you for reading *The Sin Factor.* If you enjoyed this story, please help others find it by posting a review where you purchased it—share a link, tweet about it, Facebook it… Everything helps in this new internet world.

About the Author

Sandy Loyd is a Western girl through and through. Born and raised in Salt Lake City, she's worked and lived in some fabulous places in the US, including Arizona, Northern California and South Florida. She now resides in Kentucky and writes full time. As much as she loves her current hometown, she misses the mountains and has to go back to her roots to get her mountain fix at least once a year.

She spent her single years in San Francisco and considers that city one of America's treasures, comparable to no other city in the world. Another city she loves is Washington D.C. With all the museums and history, our nation's capital is like no other. Her D.C. Badboys Series, beginning with The Sin Factor, are all set in the D.C. area. The mystery/suspense stories are full of twists that keep the reader guessing, along with a few harrowing scenes and of course, a heartwarming love story. The characters are fun, normal people who are trying to get by, just like people everywhere.

Check out her website at www.sandyloyd.com for release dates of Des and Terry's story. Email her at sandyloyd@sandyloyd.com

Like her on Facebook www.facebook.com/sloydwrites and she'll keep you updated as to releases or follow her on Twitter www.twitter.com/sloydwrites

Made in United States
North Haven, CT
14 March 2023

34032018R00168